SALVAGED

Jay Crownover is the *New York Times* and *USA Today* bestselling author of the *Marked Men* and *Welcome to the Point* series. Like her characters, she is a big fan of tattoos. She loves music and wishes she could be a rock star, but since she has no aptitude for singing or instrument playing, she'll settle for writing stories with interesting characters and make the reader feel something. She lives in Colorado with her three dogs.

ALSO BY JAY CROWNOVER

JAY CROWNOVER

SALVAGED

A Saints of Denver novel

HarperCollins*Publishers*

HarperCollins*Publishers*
1 London Bridge Street
London SE1 9GF

www.harpercollins.co.uk

A Paperback Original 2017
1

Copyright © Jennifer M Voorhees 2017

Jennifer M Voorhees asserts the moral right to
be identified as the author of this work

A catalogue record for this book
is available from the British Library

ISBN: 978-0-00-811630-9

Set in Dante MT Std

Printed and bound in Great Britain

This one is for the survivors. The fierce and the fighters, the ones who refused to break. This book is for anyone who needs to know it can and will get better . . . Those who need some reassurance that there are good guys out there. Believe that there are hot, sweet, special nice guys who don't mind finishing last. *wink wink

I saved the best hearts for last ♥

INTRODUCTION

When I introduced Poppy in Rowdy and Salem's book, I had no idea she was going to become the character who readers asked me about the most. Every day someone asked me if she was going to get a book, asked when her story was coming, but more than that, they really really wanted her to get a happy-ever-after. They demanded that she love and be loved better than any of my other characters. She'd been through hell and back, and without a doubt, my readers felt she deserved someone who would treat her right and be good to her.

I think that speaks to why we all love to read romance so much. It's the idea that the heart can heal from anything and that there really, truly is someone out there who can make all the bad things that may have happened to harden a heart disappear. That there is someone who can find us and guide us to a better place no matter how lost and alone we might feel. Readers didn't want her to be afraid anymore. They wanted her to be romanced and won over.

Make no mistake, I can give some good romance;) . . . but it's not the norm for me. I have never considered myself a romantic at heart. I love love, and I adore all the sexy, sweaty things that go with it. But hearts and flowers, wooing and soft persuasion . . . yeah . . . I ain't got no time for that. I like my romance a little ugly, a little dangerous, and a whole lot messy. So that made getting into the groove for this book—the one that was about hearts healing and real romance—challenging. It required soft and I am much more comfortable with hard.

It's not very often I sit down and put two people with pure hearts together. It's a rare case when I'm writing two people who are genuinely kind and caring, who are simply looking for something better out of each other and out of themselves. I tend to drift toward making at least one of my main characters all kinds of twisted and torn, but that isn't the case here. Yes, they both have demons to slay and mountains to climb, but Poppy and Wheeler are simply good people who have had more than their fair share of bad thrown their way . . . they are so much more than what they have experienced. More than any other characters I have ever written, when they stumble they get right back up and keep going. I'm going to be honest, I had a rough end of 2016. Things with family, my dog, things changing professionally . . . it made the task of writing about perseverance and unwavering optimism, writing about hope and courage, a bit of a challenge. But that's why I write, why I tell the stories I do. It's an escape, a way to live in a place that has all the things reality might be missing at the moment.

In order to do these two justice, it took some digging deep, some honest self-evaluation and self-examination, on my part to get to the soft center of myself that I usually keep hidden from the world. Really, I like to pretend it doesn't exist at all. I desperately wanted to get it right—for Poppy and Wheeler, but more for the readers who were rooting for the girl who had been ruined to be Salvaged and returned to her former glory. For the tenderhearted who wanted the nice guy to finally catch some kind of break.

I think I ended up exactly where I was supposed to with all of it . . . I mean at the end of it all I was emotionally spent and exhausted in the best way. I think I took a hundred naps! It's been a journey, the best adventure I could have ever asked for, one shared with my readers through these eleven books set in my favorite place. I couldn't be any happier with where we (and all of our friends caught between the pages) ended up.

This is where we belong ☺

~Love & Ink

Jay

When you go in search of honey you
must expect to be stung by bees.

—Joseph Joubert

Prologue

I was the kind of guy that thought I had it all figured out. It came from having spent my entire childhood caught up in chaos and upheaval. When I was old enough to call my own shots and make my own way, I did it with a single-minded determination and unwavering dedication. I knew what I wanted. Every move I made, every step I took, moved me toward that perfectly planned future I had been dreaming of from the minute I realized I was all on my own. A realization that came far too early and was brutally reinforced every single time I was forced to bounce from one temporary home to the next.

I clung to the idea that I would do everything differently. I would make decisions which would lead to a life that was easy, smooth, and as steady as a car with a new alignment and high-end shocks. I found the girl that was meant to be mine and clutched her in a death grip. I went out of my way to be whoever she needed me to be, to never give her any kind of reason to go. I made her the center of my entire world, not realizing she might feel trapped there as time went on. I was holding on so tight I never felt her trying to wiggle her way free.

I started a business, bought a house, and made plans . . . so many plans. Plans that would be considered simple and boring to some, but they covered everything I wanted since the time I was four years old. They were the plans that would give me the life I'd been longing for since the minute I was left on my own.

I had my eyes on the prize, the promise of what could be if I worked hard, took care of my woman, and did everything that the person who was supposed to love me and care for me didn't do. I would have held on until the bitter, burning end, but there was nothing I could do when the rope was cut.

At that point all I could do was fall.

I felt my grip on everything I was trying so hard to hold on to slip the day she walked into my garage, hiding behind one of my friends. Rowdy St. James worked at the tattoo shop where I got the majority of my ink done. He called and asked me to empty out my shop of employees and other customers one Saturday afternoon so that he could bring his girlfriend's sister in to look at a car. He didn't need to explain why the garage needed to be cleared out, not that I would have asked. The girl had been all over the news months before. You couldn't get away from her terrified face and shaking body as her horrifying ordeal was splashed all over the news. Her husband had abducted her at gunpoint. Salem, her sister and Rowdy's lady, had been a victim of the attack as well. Poppy Cruz only went with the lunatic she was married to, in order to keep her sibling safe. It had resulted in a nightmare that I couldn't imagine anyone coming back from. Without question I cleared out the shop so she wouldn't have to worry about being surrounded by a bunch of dirty, boisterous men that wouldn't know how to behave around someone as fragile and delicate as she appeared to be.

I didn't want her to be scared of anything ever again. It made no sense, but it resonated inside of me.

Things at home had been rocky, rougher than class-five rapids in spring, but I was paddling for my life and prepared to ride it out. I couldn't let go. I wouldn't let go. I saw Poppy the day she walked through my shop and I started to feel how sore my hands and my heart were from holding on.

Her head was down, eyes focused on the tips of her shoes. Her shoulders were hunched over and her long hair hid her face. She was skinny, so skinny, nothing but skin and bones. She was nothing that I should have noticed, not because she was clearly doing everything in her power to be invisible, but because I was supposed to have my eyes locked on my future and doing whatever I could to salvage it. But I did notice her and I couldn't look away once I did.

She was obviously terrified, clearly out of her element and uncomfortable, but it wasn't her unease that called to me . . . it was her loneliness. I could feel it filling up the space that separated us. Stretching, growing, expanding until it was all I was breathing in and exhaling back out. It was bitter on my tongue and heavy across my skin because I knew the feeling well. I lived with it pressing me down and pushing me forward every minute of every day. The reason I was so set on the way things had to be, the reason I was singlemindedly set on settling down and building a life with the girl that was slipping through my fingers was because I never again wanted to be as alone as this girl was. I didn't want to be left and forgotten. I'd barely survived it the first time.

I did my best to sell her a car that was as beautiful as she was . . . a classic with clean lines and a flawless finish. She picked something practical and boring but that was ultimately safe and reliable. I understood her choice but her reasons behind it grated and annoyed me long after she left the shop. When she wasn't standing in front of me, she should have been easy to forget; after all, everything in front of me, everything I had been working for and toward, was falling down in front of my eyes. My world was collapsing in on itself and everything I thought I was so goddamn sure of turned out to be nothing more than lies and illusions. In the middle of all of it, I couldn't forget her sad eyes and shivering, shaking form. Her loneliness clung to me, unshakable and unforgettable. I didn't think I would see her again and against my better judgment I often found myself wondering how she was doing and if she had gotten a handle on all the things that seemed to be crushing her under their inescapable weight.

I was wrong about seeing her again, just like I was wrong about doing everything in my life differently from how my mother had lived hers would ensure my happiness. I was wrong about hard work and sacrifice being enough. I was wrong about holding on when what I was holding on to desperately wanted me to let go. I was left with bleeding palms, rope burns around my heart, and scars on my soul.

The next time I saw Poppy Cruz it was *my* loneliness that was filling up the space, suffocating me, choking me, making me forget to handle her with care. I was nothing more than a searing, open wound. One that was raw, aching, throbbing, and leaking my broken heart and shattered emotions out everywhere. I felt like I'd lost everything, like my entire life had been nothing but a waste of time, nothing more than building blocks knocked over with the swipe of a careless hand. The girl I loved didn't love me back, my future was ultimately nothing more than a fuzzy, fractured blur. I couldn't see anything clearly other than the waste and ruin of all my best laid plans.

But I saw her. And I saw that I scared her.

It was the last thing I wanted to do but my loneliness was just as big and just and consuming as hers was. It spread out, hungry and angry, looking to consume anyone that might try and challenge its reign.

I tried to pull myself together, apologized because I knew our paths would cross again now that she lived next door to my best friend. I didn't want to be another man that she was terrified of. I locked the loneliness down, wrestled it into submission, and tried to quiet down the wild inside of me that was howling, screaming at the loss of its mate. I wanted to be nothing more than gnashing teeth and tearing claws but I swallowed those instincts and allowed myself to act like a kicked puppy that just wanted to whimper and cry.

Poppy had been through more than I could imagine. She was the one I couldn't look away from, but even then, she managed to slip past me and disappear. She looked like honey but she moved like a ghost. I memorized everything about her even though she hardly let me see her face.

I wasn't supposed to be looking at anything other than how to salvage the mess my life was in, but she was all I could see.

Chapter 1

Poppy

I couldn't believe I was doing this.

I was pretty sure sometime over the last week my body and brain had been taken over by an alien life force that was making me act the opposite of how I normally acted.

Even before I was scared of my own shadow, I wasn't the type that went out of my way to seek attention from the opposite sex. Making boys drool and collecting broken hearts was more up my older sister's alley. I tended to be the girl that only spoke when spoken to. I was always shy and hesitant, especially when I was around someone I found attractive. I'd had more than one man tell me that it was endearing . . . little did I know my obvious uncertainty about my own appeal and allure clearly marked me as prey to those same men. I was an easy target. Something I swore to myself I would never be again. Which was why there was no logical explanation for why I found myself currently parked in front of a very industrial-looking building as I tried to work up the courage to go inside.

The garage was on the outskirts of downtown Denver. Tucked

away among factories and buildings that were now gentrified and redeveloped into upscale apartments and trendy eateries near Coors Field. The garage looked like it had escaped every dime of big money sunk into making LoDo prime real estate. It was a throwback to when this part of the city was still rough and unsafe for people to be out walking their little dogs on designer leashes after dark. The bricks on the outside had faded paint from when the garage was some kind of shipping warehouse. The old paint blended in with newer graffiti that the owner hadn't bothered to power-wash away. There was also a mural, a beautiful depiction of the Rocky Mountains, that stood off in the distance; it covered all three of the massive metal doors that allowed the cars access in and out of the building. It was a statement piece. One that was impossible to miss. It softened the entire feel of the building and the tall metal fence with its wide gate that surrounded it.

I knew that one of the guys who owned the tattoo shop where both my sister and her boyfriend worked had painted the mural in trade. Wheeler, the guy I was here to see, if I ever got up the nerve, worked on Nash Donovan's muscle car and in turn Nash had turned the garage doors into something that even the most dedicated taggers and graffiti artists appreciated too much to deface. Salem, my sister, mentioned that Wheeler was never opposed to a solid trade. Which explained why the majority of the mechanic's skin was inked in colorful images courtesy of Nash and the rest of the artists who worked at the Saints of Denver.

I was used to being surrounded by heavily tattooed individuals—heck, my sister started marking her flawless golden skin before she was legally old enough to get a tattoo in order to annoy my father. However, Hudson Wheeler was by far the most decorated human I had ever come across. The designs swirled up each side of his neck and across his throat. They dropped down over his wrists and splayed wide across the back of his hands. He had artwork across his chest and it crawled from the base of his hairline all the way to the top of his jeans across his back and abdomen. He was a walking art installation. And while all that ink and color might have been overwhelming on someone else, with the graceful, thoughtful way he moved and the quiet, measured way he spoke, all the color and noise that covered his body worked for the man that was known as Wheeler. I figured out after the first time I met him that his skin was telling the world his story because he didn't want to be bothered with repeating it over and over again.

My father would be appalled by the way Hudson Wheeler looked. He would hate everything about him. That meant I allowed the trickle of attraction that had worked its way through the fear and doubt that suffocated me on a daily basis to take root and grow. Anything that my dad disapproved of was something that I was more than willing to embrace with open arms. I was late to defiance, but did it ever feel good.

Taking a deep breath and tapping my fingers on the steering wheel, I looked over at the little box that was on the seat next to me. A small grin tugged at my mouth when my eyes landed on the contents. I had no idea if Wheeler was in the market for this particular kind of gift but I figured if he didn't want it I would take it home until I figured something else out. It was a bold move, bringing a man I hardly knew this kind of gift, but as soon as I saw it I knew Wheeler had to have it.

I scolded myself for being foolish and impulsive, silently telling myself that I was setting myself up for the kind of embarrassment and ridicule that would cripple me. It had taken me endless hours of therapy and unwavering amounts of tough love from my family and friends to get to the point where I could leave the house without having a full-on panic attack. Taking a step so far out of my comfort zone felt like I was jumping off a cliff without knowing if there was anything down below to cushion my fall. If Wheeler rejected the gift, if he made me feel stupid for trying to do something nice, it very well might undo all the hard work I'd put into getting back some semblance of a normal life. Trying to cheer up a man that I had no ties to or no investment in seemed like a foolish risk to take, but I still packed up the box and drove down here. I tried to talk myself out of going inside, my mind screaming that this was a mistake. It didn't work. Even though I was a nervous wreck I still ended up grabbing the box, muttering under my breath at the contents like they could reassure me this wasn't going to blow up in my face. I was shaking from head to toe as I exited the car.

The box shifted in my hold, making me gasp and mutter a few choice words. My father would hate that I was swearing, so I made it a point to do so at least once a day. I had to shut the car door with my hip and I jumped when it slammed shut. I watched wide-eyed as one of the painted metal doors started to roll up. I squinted behind the dark lenses of my sunglasses as a lone figure walked to the edge of a bay and deftly jumped down, ignoring the ramp that led up into the building. I gulped a little bit because there was no mistaking the tall, lean figure that was making his way toward me. The late-afternoon sun made his already burnished hair glow like autumn fire, and highlighted the dips and valleys in his arms and across his broad chest as he wiped his hands on a red rag that he pulled from his back pocket. He had the top half of his coveralls unfastened and hanging around his waist, leaving him and all that artwork that covered him on display in nothing more than a black tank top that had a hole on the side. He looked dirty and a little rough. Both things totally worked for him . . . and for me. I'd almost forgotten what lust felt like. I was attracted to him and that terrified me because in my world attraction led to nothing but heartache and hurt. Still, here I was, standing in front of him even though everything inside of me was screaming to run as far away from him as possible.

I moved as the box shifted again and stopped as he lifted his chin up in the direction where I had parked my very nondescript sedan. "Something wrong with the Camry?" Wheeler's voice was warm and smooth, like expensive liquor sipped on summer nights, but his eyes were cold. They were the palest blue I had ever seen, a blue so washed out and light that they had a silvery shimmer to them. They were also sharp and intent, not missing much, including the box I was having a hard time keeping a hold on as he got closer.

"Um . . . no. The Camry is fine, thank you." Rowdy, my sister's boyfriend and the father of my soon-to-make-an-appearance niece or nephew, had strong-armed me into buying a car from Wheeler when I finally decided I was emotionally well enough to live on my own after I fell apart at the hands of the last man that was supposed to love me. Wheeler tried to sell me a 1957 Bonneville that was hands down the coolest car I had ever seen, but I balked at the idea of riding around in something that was guaranteed to attract unwanted attention. Especially attention of the male variety. Rowdy cringed when I handed over the cash for the Camry but Wheeler just smiled like he understood why I made the choice even if he didn't think it was the right one.

I nervously shifted my feet and watched as that icy gaze of his landed on the box clutched to my side. Right on time the contents let out a little half bark, half yelp that had Wheeler's rust colored eyebrows lifting up almost to his hairline and made his tattooed hands pause where they were still wringing the red rag tightly between them.

"Is that a puppy?" He sounded curious and slightly amused, which I took as a good sign. Most of the men I'd dealt with in the past would have been furious that I had not only showed up unannounced but did so with a tiny, wiggling puppy in tow.

"It is a puppy . . . I . . . uh . . . well, someone dropped them off at the vet's office where I work and I thought that since Dixie is leaving and taking Dolly with her, and you seemed so fond of her that maybe you wanted one of your own . . . well . . ." I was rambling and talking too fast but I couldn't stop the words from rushing out one after the other. Dolly was my neighbor's pit bull, my neighbor who just happened to be Wheeler's best friend. "Plus, you own a house, so you can have a pit bull or maybe you need him as a guard dog for the garage. With some training he could be perfect. You can take him to work with you, which is great since most puppies have to live in a crate while they're being trained." I shifted my feet again and looked down at the dog, who was whining up at me like he felt sorry for me because even a nonhuman could tell I was making a mess of this. "Pit bulls are illegal in the city limits so we have to adopt them out because shelters will euthanize them if we can't find them homes, and no animal deserves that."

He didn't answer me but he did reach out and take the box from me. The brindle-and-white puppy immediately jumped to the edge of the box and started yipping at and sniffing the new person that was within licking distance. Wheeler put the box on the ground and picked up the solid little body and held the adorable animal up in front of his face while the puppy barked excitedly and wagged his stubby little tail. "He's cute."

Oh lordy, was he ever . . . and I wasn't talking about the dog.

"Um . . . I know it's kind of presumptuous but I thought maybe you two could help each other out." I cringed as I unwittingly stumbled into personal territory where I absolutely didn't belong. It had been nothing more than bad timing and admitted curiosity that landed me right in the middle of Wheeler's personal life imploding. I shouldn't know that his now-former fiancée had cheated on him, prompting him to cancel the wedding only a few weeks before they were set to walk down the aisle, and I also shouldn't know that this wasn't the first time his woman had stepped out on him. But I did know and it had me feeling all kinds of ways about what he had been through. I knew that Wheeler was a nice guy, one that deserved a bit of happiness while he healed from that kind of devastating heartbreak. And really, who couldn't be happy when they were holding a puppy, especially when that puppy was already clearly in love with him.

"I'm going to miss Dixie more than I'm going to miss Dolly." He gave me a crooked grin as he mentioned my neighbor.

The fact that I lived next door to Dixie was the reason I knew all the gory details of his recent breakup. She was his ex-fiancée's sister as well as his best friend. The walls were thin and Dixie was one stranger that I trusted enough to get close to, so I spent a lot of time at her place. It sucked that she was getting ready to move to Mississippi right when Wheeler needed her the most. But her boyfriend was there and she missed him. It was obvious she wasn't happy being in Denver when Church wasn't.

I cleared my throat and lifted fingers that had a visible tremor in them to my hair. I pushed some of it behind my ears and winced when the motion knocked my sunglasses sideways. I didn't know if I could handle this conversation eye to eye but it was move the sunglasses or look like more of a spaz than I already did. With a sigh I pushed them to the top of my head and froze as his frosty eyes locked on mine. They were so cold, they could freeze me from the inside out . . . instead I suddenly felt warm all over and heated in way that was foreign and strange. I'd never been so physically drawn to anyone and it made me anxious and agitated. I didn't know what to do with it. I wasn't in any kind of place emotionally to be crushing on a guy with the kind of complicated history and tangled future Wheeler had. I was only recently able to take care of myself in the most basic of ways. There was no way I had it in me to take care of him as well . . . and that's what he needed . . . a woman that would step up to the plate and fix all the things that woman he wanted had broken. A woman who was selfish and thoughtless. A woman he very well might still be in love with.

"If you don't want him I'm going to ask Dixie to take him. Dolly can always use a friend. One of my coworkers took home his sister and the doc I work for found homes out of state for the other two boys in the litter. This little guy was the last one that needed a home. I couldn't stand seeing him left alone while the rest of his family found forever homes. Like I said . . ." I shrugged a little and looked away from that piercing stare. "I immediately thought of you." Wheeler was looking for his forever home too, I just knew it.

He bent down and put the puppy on the ground. The stout little animal started to jump on his lower legs and nipped at the

worn leather of his sturdy and stained boots. Wheeler put his
hands on his hips as he watched the puppy. I was almost a hundred percent certain that bringing the abandoned ball of slobber
and love had been the right call when those arctic-colored eyes
lifted back up to me. His expression was hard to read but it was
clear something was stopping him from embracing my gift with
open arms.

"I don't know that I have the time to take on a puppy right
now, Poppy." He lifted a hand and rubbed it across the back of
his neck. His mahogany-colored eyebrows pulled into a vee over
the top of his nose and the corners of his mouth pulled down
in a frown that was too harsh for his pretty face. I liked it much
better when he smiled and his twin dimples cut deeply into his
cheeks.

I bit my bottom lip to keep the distressed noise that I could feel
climbing up the back of my throat at bay. I knew he might say
no but I couldn't hide the fact that I was disappointed by his decision. I honestly felt like he and the puppy would be good for one
another, that they could bring a little joy into each other's lives. It
stung that Wheeler wasn't ready to open his heart up again, even
when it was to something that was so obviously eager to love him
unconditionally and irrevocably, unlike his ex.

"It's okay. Like I said, I'll take him home until I can find a
place for him." I crouched down and wiggled my fingers to get
the dog's attention, and grinned when he bounded over, tripping
over his front legs as he scrambled in my direction. "I can take
him to work with me and hold on to him until I figure something
out. One of the boys at the shop will step up if Dixie doesn't want
another dog."

I heard him sigh and looked up to see him watching me intently. He opened his mouth like he was going to say something, then snapped it shut, his teeth audibly clicking together. I didn't know much about Wheeler, but what I did know I liked. He was nice. He was polite. He was thoughtful and he was kind. But more than any of those things, he went out of his way to hold himself in a way that wasn't threatening or intimidating because he was aware without me saying a word how jumpy I was around people, men in particular. I hated that they were bigger than me. I hated that I knew firsthand how badly they could hurt me if they had a mind to. I hated that I wilted and cowered under their attention, even if it was innocent and friendly. The fact that he took care not to spook me spoke volumes and made me feel awful for putting him in such an awkward position.

"Poppy . . ." He sounded regretful and I had no interest in dragging the torture out any longer for either of us. I scooped up the dog and buried my nose in the top of his head.

"Seriously it's no big deal. I love him and I'm happy to hold onto him until I can find him a proper home. It was stupid of me not to consider how busy you are with everything you have going on in your life right now. A puppy is a big commitment and that's not something you can put on someone else without discussing it with them first." The dog swiped his tongue across my face, no doubt feeling my distress and rising panic. I wanted to tuck his warm little body to my chest and run away like I was trying to score a touchdown in the other team's end zone. "I should have known better." That was a common refrain, one that chased me in my nightmares and blasted through my head every single second I struggled to survive the torturous hands of my abusive husband. I found myself repeating dangerous, harmful patterns where the men in my life were concerned, and through it all I told myself over and over again that I should have known better. My therapist would tell me I was being too hard on myself, that I was shouldering the blame for the actions of men that I had no control over. But blame was hard to let go when it was what you lived and breathed.

Wheeler made a noise that sounded like he was choking and then bent over at the waist so that his hands were resting on his knees as his breath wheezed in and out. His wide shoulders shuddered and then tensed like he had taken a blow that knocked the wind out of him.

I didn't touch anyone, not even the people that had grown up hugging me and loving me. But I was compelled to reach out a shaky hand and put it on his colorful shoulder. The puppy gave a yip of approval and I tried not to fall to my knees as the warmth from his tattooed skin blazed through my fingers and shot up my arm. It had been a long time since I'd let myself have any kind of human contact, and even longer since that kind of contact didn't leave bruises and welts on my skin and tattered lesions across every surface of my soul. He felt so vital. So necessary.

"Are you okay?" The shoulder I was lightly touching tensed even tighter and I let go as if his skin burned me when he righted himself and I ended up frozen in that frigid stare of his.

"No. I'm about as far from okay as I have ever been." He let out a brittle-sounding laugh and narrowed his eyes at me. "When a pretty girl shows up trying to make the shit show that has become your life better, it should be okay, but it's not."

He sighed and rubbed a hand over his face like he was tired. "I can count on one hand the times in my life someone bothered to ask if I was okay, Poppy." His mouth twisted into a wry grin that would look harsh on anyone else but with those dimples of his still managed to look downright adorable. "Most of those times have been Dixie asking. It wasn't even the right sister."

I was horrified and didn't bother to hide it as I huddled the wiggling puppy to my chest like his warm little body could protect me from the images his awful words brought to mind. "That's terrible, Wheeler." My voice shook and the words sounded squeaky. I already knew too much about him and this was more information that I didn't feel like I had earned the right to have.

"It is pretty terrible but not nearly as bad as my ex telling me that she's knocked up with my kid." I gasped and took a step backward as his words landed like blows. "A kid we definitely didn't plan on. A kid I am in no way ready to raise with a woman I can't stand to be around. A kid that is going to have to bounce between houses and be shuffled from one place to another always trying to figure out exactly where home is."

He sounded shattered and he looked the same. Those eyes of his were colder than anything I'd ever seen, his skin was pale and taut over the sharp angles of his face, making the smattering of freckles that dotted his nose and cheeks stand out even more than they normally did.

A baby.

Those words always hit something delicate and unprotected deep inside of me. When my sister first told me that she was expecting a baby, I wanted to be happy for her but that happiness had to fight its way through remorse and sorrow so thick it felt like it was crushing me. The same thing was happening right now as Wheeler watched me. Everything inside of me wanted to unravel but I was holding it together, barely. He should be happy that he had a precious little life on the way, even if he was less than thrilled with the circumstances surrounding the arrival.

I took another step backward and almost fell over. Wheeler
reached out a hand like he was going to catch me or stop my fall,
but I flinched away and tightened my hold on the dog so much so
that he yelped in protest. Frantically I pulled my sunglasses from
the top of my head and shoved them back over my eyes. I could
feel moisture building, and if I started crying I needed something to hide behind. He wouldn't understand why his words
stripped me bare and I didn't have it in me to explain the reasons
why they cut so deeply. I'd used up all my limited courage and
nerve getting myself out of the car and offering up the puppy.

"Well, congratulations on the baby." I didn't sound like I meant
it even though I honestly did. "I'm gonna take this little guy and
head home and make some calls about who might be in the market for a puppy."

I scrambled back some more and watched wide-eyed behind
my sunglasses as Wheeler advanced on me. He followed me until
my back was flat against the side of the car and he was looming in
front of me with only the puppy to separate his chest from mine. It
was the closest I had been to a man in a very long time. Even with
him being irritated and riled up, I couldn't say that I was worried
about him taking out his feelings on me. He didn't scare me. The
way he made me feel did.

"I'm sorry, Poppy. If I was in a different place in my life I would
be pretty fucking excited that a girl like you had me on her mind
and went out of her way to do something really sweet for me. If
I wasn't already struggling to get my head around being a new
father, I would happily take on the task of being a puppy parent."
God, he was nice. Even when he was looming over me looking not
very nice at all. "There's something about you, something about
those eyes and the soft way that you speak, that makes me want to

tell you all my secrets. Secrets that sting. I want to tell you that the last time my life was this fucked up was when my junkie mother was dropping me off at a fire station in some rinky-dink mountain town in the middle of a snowstorm. Our car broke down, because it always did. She didn't take care of it and she sure as shit didn't take care of me." I felt my mouth drop open in shock but couldn't move as his voice dipped lower and his eyes got even colder. His words sent shivers up and down my spine.

"I was lucky that it was a manned station and not one of the volunteer houses that sits empty until a fire is called in. There was a very nice fire captain there that took me in for the night. The next day I was dumped with child services and I spent my entire childhood jumping from one foster house to another. She didn't even have a coat for me. She dropped me off in jeans that were too small, a T-shirt that was stained and torn, and in tennis shoes that were shit for the snow because they were mostly duct-taped together." He blinked at me as I gasped in horror and that harsh scowl that cut into the pretty lines of his aristocratic bone structure was back. "I was fucking four years old."

I wanted to hug him. I wanted to comfort the little boy he was and the man that was clearly struggling in front of me. Knowing that I would freak out if we actually made that kind of contact while both of us were so raw, I scooted to the side, careful not to brush up against him, and pulled open the door so I could put my panting, slobbering bundle down in the passenger seat. I kept the door between us as a barrier while all I wanted to do was get away from his desperation and pain. I needed to take a minute to process the fact he had a baby on the way with a woman that had destroyed him and ruined the idyllic life they could have had together. That hurt in ways I didn't want to pick apart while he was standing so close looking at me like he could see right into the center of my every thought and feeling. I had too much of my own hurt; I couldn't believe that I was feeling his as well.

"I'm so sorry you had to suffer like that. Good luck with everything, Wheeler." I couldn't bring myself to tell him I would be around if he needed me, even though the words were tickling the tip of my tongue. I slipped into the car and wrapped my fingers around the steering wheel like it was some kind of lifeline. I reached for the door to pull it shut but it wouldn't budge because his hand was wrapped around the top of the frame. He bent his head to look down at me and I could see a riot of emotions blowing through his cool gaze. He was pissed. He was frustrated. He was sad. He was irritated and he was maybe, just maybe, a little bit excited.

"Gonna need more than luck. But seriously, thank you for thinking of me. I can't recall the last time someone did that." If I was someone else, someone stronger, braver, someone fearless instead of fearful, I would have climbed out of the car and given him that goddamn hug. He looked like he desperately needed one.

But I wasn't someone different.

I was the girl that had almost died trying to make her father happy and win his approval.

I was the girl that let her sister leave without begging her to take me with her when that was all I really wanted.

I was the girl that fell in love with the wrong boy and paid a price so heavy for it that I lost everything.

I was the girl that married a monster, and even though the demon was physically dead and buried, he still lived inside of me, where he haunted me, hounded me, hurt me.

As always, I was afraid, so I didn't do anything other than shut the car door when he let go and drive away. I really couldn't fix all the things that were wrong with Wheeler's life and I wasn't about to let him close enough to see exactly how broken my own existence was because I'd yet to be able to fix myself.

The puppy whimpered like he knew what I was thinking and disagreed with me. Luckily, he was a lot easier to ignore than the taunting voice in the back of my head that kept up the steady refrain of *You should have known better.*

Love will find a way through paths
where wolves fear to prey.

—Lord Byron

Chapter 2

Wheeler

W hat you're looking for isn't between the blonde's legs, Speedy."

I shifted my gaze away from the blonde that was very obviously eye-fucking me and turned my attention to the bartender that offered up those unwanted words of wisdom. As always they were spoken with a distinct southern drawl. I lifted an eyebrow at him and was treated to one lifted right back.

"You didn't find it between the brunette's legs last week or between the redhead's the week before that." He put another drink in front of me even though I'd had more than enough. I watched as he leaned on the bar across from me so that I had no choice but to look up at him as I slid the mixed Southern Comfort and ginger ale closer to me. "The fact of the matter is, no matter how hard you try, you can't fuck away a broken heart. You aren't going to find a magical cure for heartache spending an hour inside a pretty girl or one spent at the bottom of a bottle."

I knew Asa was right but I had no intention of telling him that. Instead I took a healthy swing of the drink and flashed a smile that was fake and forced in the direction of the blonde. When I turned back toward the bartender he was shaking his head at me. I didn't know Asa Cross very well even though I'd sold him a sweet Nova that needed some work a while back. We shared common friends and his boss at the bar was a silent investor in my garage. Something I tried to keep in mind so that I didn't make an ass out of myself while trying to drink myself numb.

For reasons known only to the overly observant southerner, he'd taken it upon himself to be my voice of reason every single time I stepped into the bar. Admittedly each time I did so I was looking for dangerous distractions. I didn't want to go home to an empty house with nothing but regret and dread for company. I appreciated that he didn't want me to chase after my own ruin, but I'd handled my love life so carefully for so long that I was beyond ready to dirty it up a little. Being thoughtful and considerate got me nothing but being abandoned and betrayed. It was time to see what I got when I was careless and reckless.

"I've told you before, I've been with the same girl since I was sixteen. Nothing wrong with seeing what else is out there now that the shackles are shaken off." I wanted to sound more excited about the prospect of sleeping my way through the entirety of eligible women in Denver than I actually was. The reality was that women liked me, they always had, but I'd been saying no for so long that saying yes felt weird. Misplaced guilt took the fun out of being a player. That was something I couldn't even convince myself I was until the third or fourth drink.

"Anybody that takes a little bit here and a little bit there is going to end up hungry at the end of the day, Speedy. You're a man that's used to having a full plate, these snacks aren't going to do anything for you. You're going to starve." Asa nodded and pushed off the bar, leaving his convoluted words hanging heavily in the air. He made his way over to a customer at the other end of the bar top, giving the blonde the opening she'd been waiting for to make her move. I tried not to wince when she slid onto the empty stool next to me. Her perfume was strong and sickeningly floral. It was inescapable as she leaned an arm on the bar top and turned her body toward mine.

She was pretty in a very made-up kind of way. I didn't particularly have a type. I'd been with Kallie for so long that I'd forgotten what my preferences had been before her. Watching this woman's very painted lips turn up at the edges and her alarmingly long eyelashes flutter flirtatiously at me, I realized that high maintenance and overly done was not high on the list of things that made my dick hard.

Unwanted, an image of Poppy Cruz holding that adorable puppy and looking at me like she was ready to bolt at any second flashed through my mind. Now, her easy and untouched kind of beauty made my dick hard without question. In fact, I could feel it tighten and twitch against my zipper at nothing more than the thought of her.

She was the most beautiful woman I had ever seen and she didn't have to do a single thing for me, or anyone else to notice it. She didn't wear makeup, not a stitch of it. Even without it, her lips were a rosy pink and her eyelashes were long and a flawless fan of inky black. They did a great job of keeping her stunning but sad amber gaze hidden from prying eyes. Her skin had an enviable golden hue that could only be achieved through heritage and blessed genetics. Her hair was an unusual mix of browns that ranged from dark chocolate strands to rich caramel-tinted highlights that I doubted came from a salon. The girl didn't do anything to enhance her stunning looks, which included hiding her slim frame in clothes that were several sizes too big. I'd only ever seen her wearing the most boring, neutral shades that did their best to wash her out and make her look ordinary when she was anything but. She was born to be a hot rod but for reasons that were hard to think about she was living her life like she was meant to be a minivan. Even camouflaged and covered up, the way Poppy Cruz looked totally worked for me in a way this very practiced blonde did not.

"Hi." The blonde breathed the word out and put the straw sticking out of her drink to her lips in a move that had clearly gotten her what she wanted more times than not.

I took another swig of my drink, turned my head, and inclined my chin in a greeting that was far less seductive than hers. "Hey."

"You've been sitting over here by yourself all night. I thought I would come and see if you wanted some company. It's never very much fun to drink alone." She was right. Drinking alone sucked, so did sleeping alone and living alone and doing pretty much everything alone when you were used to having someone by your side.

"I'm Tessa." She stuck out a hand and I noticed that her fingernails matched the ruby red of her lips. That seemed like a lot of effort to put into catching company for the evening. The most I'd done was put on a clean T-shirt.

I took her fingers in mine and watched as her gaze drifted over the dark spots of grease and oil that seemed to be a permanent part of my skin at this point. It didn't matter how many times I scrubbed them, parts of the garage were always marking me as a man that got dirty and worked with his hands. She didn't curl her lip or pull her hand away and wipe it on her very tight jeans. I always considered that a win. "Wheeler."

Both her eyebrows lifted and a playful smile tugged at the corners of her mouth. "Is that your real name?"

I grinned back because that was a question I got a lot. I heard her suck in a breath as she watched my face when I smiled. My dirty hands might turn some women off but I'd never encountered one that was immune to my smile. God bless dimples. I'd never understood what the big deal was, but they were the reason Kallie noticed me when she first walked into the wrong class when we were in high school together, so I was always glad I had them. They made the work of going home with a willing woman far easier.

I slammed back the rest of my drink and set the empty glass on the bar in front of me. "It's my last name." My auto-shop teacher in high school had started calling me by my last name because there was another Hudson in the class. After a while he'd told me he'd never had a student that was so naturally skilled and adept with cars as I was, so the name became a badge of honor. You couldn't be a guy named Wheeler and not know your way around all kinds of things that went fast and sounded loud and mean. I'd never had anyone invested in me enough to give me a nickname before. Never had anyone care enough to praise me or compliment me. After high school the name stuck because Wheeler was who I decided I wanted to be. He was someone worth something.

"I like it." I bet she did. But I bet she liked the way my tattooed biceps flexed under the plain black cotton of my T-shirt even more. I'd started getting tattooed when I was really young. I had more skin that was marked than not. Now that I was single I was finding that women liked the ink and the body it covered almost as much as they liked my dimples. In fact, they liked the way I looked so much I didn't have to put very much effort into trying to be charming or interesting if I wanted to get them into bed. It made me feel a little queasy when I thought about how superficial and unimportant it all was. I forced another smile to distract us both, which made her sigh.

"Thanks, it gets the job done." I watched as she sucked on the straw some more, clearly waiting for me to give her some kind of sign that I was good to go. I wanted to be good to go, but the longer she stared at me, the more I silently compared her to the woman that stood in front of me earlier, obviously scared but forcing herself to do something nice for a stranger anyways. There was no question that there was something about the terrified and nervous Poppy that I found charming and endearing. This girl had none of that and it was making everything inside of me slam on the brakes instead of pushing the pedal down to move things along faster.

The empty glass in front of me disappeared and a full one reappeared. "Last one, Speedy." The southern drawl lost its smooth edge as his gaze shifted between me and the blonde. "You want another one, doll?"

The girl paused like someone had hit a button on a remote that controlled her movements. Her huge fake eyelashes fluttered and dropped in reflex at the sound of Asa's voice. She'd been so focused on me up until that point she didn't realize there was other attractive and available dick hanging around. Objectively speaking, Asa was far better looking than I was. There was nothing about him that was difficult or complicated to look at. He hadn't spent a lifetime covering up his skin in order to keep from being overlooked. There was also none of the edge that

I had from being unwanted and left behind that sharpened his gaze. Hell, if I had to pick between the two of us, I would go with the southern bartender myself. He had an easy, effortless way about him that I most definitely did not have. I couldn't remember the last time anything in my life had felt easy. Plus, he was charming as hell, something I most definitely was not.

"Uh . . . no. I'm good." Her painted lips turned up at him the exact same way they had turned up at me and a shiver of unease shot down my spine.

I was tired of being second best and underappreciated. When the blonde turned back to me after Asa moved on to finish his last call, I pushed my untouched drink in her direction and hauled myself off of the barstool. "Last drink is on me. Have a good rest of the night." She blinked at me in confusion and opened her mouth to say something but I shook my head and walked away from her before she could say anything else.

I really was good at saying no, much better than I was at saying yes. Even after the girl made me feel like a piece of meat, like nothing more than a dick that could be interchanged with any other dick for the night, I still didn't have it in me to be a total asshole. I didn't want my rejection or disinterest to hurt her because I was still in the throes of how badly Kallie's desertion had hurt me. I wasn't the type that lashed out, which made the fact I'd spilled my guts and dropped all my baggage at Poppy's feet yesterday super unexpected. There was just something about that beautiful girl with her wounded eyes that made me want to assure her she wasn't the only one feeling shredded and alone.

It was late fall in Denver, well past the time of year that you could be outside in the dark of night without a coat on. The chill in the air cleared up some of the fog in my head and cooled some of the still-simmering anger in my blood at being disregarded as I walked over to my perfectly restored and lovingly maintained '67 Eldorado Cadillac. The car was my baby. She was the reason I took shop when I was a teenager and she was the thing that gave me purpose and directed me on the path that would lead to my own business and a way to provide for myself. My Caddy was my passion, the first thing that I'd ever owned that was mine outright, and she was a culmination of everything I'd ever been taught and had learned to apply to something real. There was no way in hell I was getting behind the wheel after a night of drinking. She had a million memories tied to her and I doubted I would be able to recover if anything took them away. I felt like my life hadn't really had the chance to start until I walked into that tiny, undersupplied garage at Brookside High School and laid eyes on the mangled, dismantled beauty that was the former husk of my baby.

I ordered an Uber and propped a hip on the hood as the cold started to filter through my drunken melancholy. It and the idea of going home to an endlessly empty house made me shiver. I turned my head as the noise from the inside of the bar followed Asa out when he opened the door and did a quick scan of the parking lot. His gaze landed where I was leaning against the Caddy and I saw him let out a breath of relief. He shouted over his shoulder for someone to watch the bar for a second and then he let the heavy door shut behind him. He made his way over to where I was shivering and trying to keep my teeth from chattering.

"I was worried you were going to let the blonde take you home. Didn't think I had to worry about you taking yourself home when you aren't in any state to drive." His breath left little puffs of vapor in the air and he didn't bother to stop his teeth from clicking together as he rubbed his hands up and down his arms. "I like you, Speedy. Don't make me take you to the ground for your keys."

I held up my phone and showed him the map with the indicator that my Uber was only a few minutes away. "Called for a ride. I wouldn't risk my car by driving drunk."

He shook his head at me and rocked back on his heels. "You're worried about your car and not yourself. You need someone to set you straight, Wheeler. I've been trying the last few weeks but I'm not getting through."

I lifted an eyebrow and shrugged at him. "I come by for a drink and the company. I don't remember signing up for a therapy session."

He snorted at me and rolled his eyes. "You might not want to hear it, but you should listen anyway. When a man that's made more than his fair share of mistakes sees another man driving off into the ditch, he isn't much of a man unless he tries to get all those wheels back on the road. Sometimes it takes a tow truck, sometimes it only requires a little push from some helping hands. I understand your old lady did you wrong, but you aren't going to make it right by drinking yourself into the kind of man you wouldn't waste your time on if you ran across him." He pointed a finger at me just as the Uber pulled into the lot and the driver flashed his lights. "Get yourself out of the ditch, Wheeler. There's nothing good down there and all you'll end up doing is spinning your wheels."

I wobbled a little as I pushed myself off the car and put my phone in my back pocket. "I'm good at fixing things that are left behind and broken down, Asa. Don't worry about me." I had booze-fueled confidence to make the words sound more certain than they were.

He sighed again and looked down at the toes of his boots. "It's never fun to see a good man get knocked down." When he lifted his head back up there was concern stamped clearly across his face. "It's even worse when that man doesn't seem interested in getting himself back up. I'm cheaper than a shrink, Wheeler, and my office is a lot more fun."

The man was going to be spreading himself thin if he was trying to save every lonely heart that sat down at his bar. He was weeks away from opening his own speakeasy-style bar in the heart of LoDo and that meant double the amount of advice to dole out to people that probably weren't going to listen anyway.

"I'll keep that in mind, Asa. Take care of that beauty." Most would think I was talking about his pretty cop girlfriend, but anyone who knew me or knew anything about how a real gear-head operated would know I was talking about the Nova. He was doing the bulk of the restorations himself but occasionally he would bring it by the shop for a mechanical issue his limited knowledge couldn't handle. It was a sweet ride and I was glad it found a good home. Besides, it wasn't like anyone needed to tell Asa to take care of his girl; he treated the redheaded cop like she was his entire reason for existing . . . kind of the way I'd treated Kallie until it all went south.

I gave the Uber driver the address to my place in Curtis Park and tried to tamp down the now familiar hollow and vacant feeling that came with heading home to an empty house. I'd bought the place a hot second after I slid my ring on Kallie's finger thinking that she was finally ready to settle down and grow up. We'd been together since we were nothing more than kids; however, while I'd gotten more ambitious and more focused on building something impossible to take away from me over the years, she seemed stuck in place. She was always a handful, a bit of a princess with an annoying tendency toward drama and hysterics, but she loved me and she never left me. So I put up with it all. Now that she was gone, hindsight was startlingly clear and I could see all the ways that we had been moving in different directions long before her first indiscretion. I wanted stability and a solid foundation. She wanted to party and be free all while letting me take care of her and support her. Being needed was nice, but not when it turned into being needed for the things I could provide instead of being needed for the man that I was. I'd turned into an ATM machine instead of a boyfriend and a lover. The worst part was I let it happen by not being able to tell Kallie no. I was too worried that if I denied her she would go. In the end it didn't matter how much I gave, or how hard I'd loved: she went anyway.

"Whoa, what happened to that house?" The Uber driver's voice pulled me out of my morose thoughts. He was motioning toward the blackened and burned shell of the house that was across the street from mine. It was the house where Brighton Walker and his daughter, Avett, had lived until trouble came calling in a pretty dramatic way.

My buddy Zeb had bought the ruined dwelling and was slowly working to restore it, but the progress was slow and the building looked like it had seen much better days, because it had.

"Fire, but nobody was hurt." The driver muttered something I didn't hear and pulled into my driveway. I tripped over my own feet as I climbed out of the back of the car and I hated that my hands shook as it took several tries to get the key in the keyhole on the front door. I'd never been much of a drinker. When your mom was an addict and clinically unhinged, that tended to make indulging in anything that had the ability to lead to a habit leave a bad taste. The last few months I'd been drinking to forget and to stop the memories, but leaving my car behind and being hungover in the morning was starting to wear thin.

I needed to find a better way to cope with all the things that were eating at my insides. Unbidden, an image of wide, golden eyes looking at me like I'd kicked the puppy she was holding when I told her Kallie was pregnant with my baby and I had no clue what I was doing and no time for another innocent soul in my life rolled through my hazy mind. It also baffled and confused me why that news made her look like she was going to fall over. I wasn't exactly thrilled that Kallie was having my kid, but I couldn't see a reason why that would affect Poppy, especially as drastically as it had.

Once I was inside my house I tossed my keys on the fancy table that Kallie had insisted on buying for the hallway. The dumb thing cost a bundle and all I used it for was a key holder and a place to toss the mail when I remembered to check it. It was another reminder that I should have put my foot down, should have found a better balance, not that any of that mattered now.

Sighing, I kicked off my boots, pulled off my T-shirt with one hand, and plopped myself down on the couch. When Kallie still lived here I would have had to completely strip and shower before I was allowed to sit on the ridiculously expensive, pale gray piece of furniture. It was not a couch that was man-friendly . . . especially when that man was rolling around under cars and was shoulders deep in engines all day. I'd been horrified when the delivery guys dropped it off, but Kallie cried and told me I didn't understand her decorating vision, so I relented. Now I didn't give two shits if the dumb thing ended up with grease stains and dirt all over it. I was going shopping for a new one as soon as I had a day off and was sober enough to remember I needed a new couch.

I put my feet up on the coffee table, turned on the TV, not bothering to turn it down when screaming, bitching housewives from some county came on the screen. With any luck the SoCo would do its job and I would drift away before the loneliness suffocated me.

The last thought I had before I let my eyes shut was that if I'd taken the puppy from Poppy there would have been something waiting for me to get back home . . . hell, I would have had a reason not to go out in the first place.

Maybe a puppy was just the kind of practice I needed before my actual baby made its appearance. And if pretty Poppy Cruz wanted to give me a hand figuring out how to be a good puppy parent, I definitely wouldn't complain. For the first time in months I went to sleep with an almost smile on my face instead of the frown that felt like it was as much a part of my skin as my tattoos.

Chapter 3

Poppy

Trying to get the rambunctious puppy to walk on a leash was turning out to be more of a challenge than I thought it would be. He was tiny, but his little body was strong and he was determined not to cooperate. I was sure we made quite a sight as I struggled in vain to get him to walk next to me. Instead, he danced and leaped around at the end of the lead like a balloon with the air rushing out of it as he bounded from one smell to the next.

I was freezing because I hadn't bothered to change out of my scrubs after work and the weather was fast turning toward winter temperatures. My heart might be firmly located in Colorado but my blood was still used to the Texas sun and sweltering heat. It didn't help matters that I could probably stand to add a few pounds on my naturally thin frame. I'd never been built with the kind of curves that could stop traffic like Salem was, and after my husband abducted me at gunpoint and ran with me across state lines, all while doing the most horrible things imaginable to my body and my mind, I'd lost what little appetite I had to

begin with. I could go several days without eating because way-
ward thoughts and memories of being violated and tortured had
a sneaky way of creeping into my mind when I least expected
them. They always made my stomach turn. I knew I should do
a better job taking care of myself, but it was easy to forget that
I deserved better, so I was constantly reminding myself to take
each little victory as a sign that I was on the right path. There
were days I ate three square meals and managed to keep it all
down, but there had yet to be a night that I didn't wake up in a
cold sweat with a scream locked in my throat and my heart racing so fast it felt like it was going to explode.

I rounded the corner at the end of my block and came to a halt.
The puppy took that as a sign that we were done playing and
started jumping all over my lower legs and pawing at my shins.
He whined at me until I picked him up, and as soon as he could
reach my face, his little tongue started darting all over my chin
and cheeks. I wondered if he could feel the tension that made my
limbs stiff and the anxiety that tightened all my muscles. I felt my
breath catch in the back of my throat and there was no stopping
my eyes from rapidly blinking to make sure what I was seeing was
real and not a figment of my imagination.

He looked like one of those black-and-white art prints that
hung in every diner and restaurant I'd ever eaten in. The one
that was a throwback to another era when cool was something
you had to cultivate and couldn't buy on Amazon. He was leaning against a black-and-silver car that looked like it should be on
the cover of a hot-rod magazine and not parked on a busy and
crowded Capitol Hill street. He had on dark jeans and a dark
canvas jacket that had the logo of his garage embroidered on the
front. His ankles were crossed on the curb in front of him and

one booted foot bounced up and down, giving the impression that he'd been waiting for me for a while. His arms were crossed over his chest and his eyes were locked on mine as I stood still, unsure what to do. He had an effortless kind of charisma that radiated off of him. It was equal parts intimidating and irresistible. I couldn't decide if I wanted to rush toward him or run as far from him as possible.

The puppy made the decision for me. Seeing another human, and thus another opportunity for pats and rubs, he threw his wiggling little body out of my arms before I could react. He hit the ground with a sharp yelp and then bolted right for Wheeler. I let out a gasp and took off after him thinking I could catch the end of the leash that was trailing behind him. I didn't want him to run into the street or veer off into a yard where he didn't belong. I was light-years away from being able to handle a confrontation with a hostile stranger that didn't want the puppy in their yard.

I didn't need to worry because Wheeler pushed his long, lean frame off the polished side of the car and reached the scrambling animal within a few strides. He crouched down as the puppy hurled himself into his arms and scooped the excited bundle up in one fluid motion. Then he was rising to his full height, which meant he was towering over me when I reached where he was standing. I was embarrassed at how out of breath I was. I was supposed to be stronger than I was before, but I could hardly handle a little jog up the block or the way my heart raced at the sight of him.

I shook my head and put my hands on my hips as I looked up into those arctic eyes. He was scratching the puppy under the chin and looking at me from under lashes that had the barest hint of red in them. "Why don't you have a coat on?"

It wasn't what I was expecting but his question reminded me that I was cold and that the lightweight hoodie that had the Saints of Denver logo on it wasn't doing much to keep the bitter chill in the air off my skin. The shirt was probably the most exciting garment I had in my closet. It was the only thing I owned that was bright and colorful. I rubbed my arms up and down and fired my own question right back at him. "What are you doing here?"

The puppy barked like he was telling me not to be rude but I was unsettled by Wheeler's unexpected appearance. It wasn't the typical unsettled that I struggled with because he was a man that I didn't know. It was the kind of unsettled that made parts of my body I forget could react to an attractive man feel warm and tingly. The kind of unsettled that had me involuntarily leaning closer to him as he started to shift so that he could pull his heavy jacket off one arm without letting go of the dog.

"I wanted to talk to you about the dog. Did you find someone to take him yet?" He shifted the puppy to his now bare arm and I watched the endless amounts of ink that covered his skin move and flex as he shook his other arm free of the coat.

"Uh . . . not really." The truth was I hadn't put that much effort into finding someone because I didn't want to let the puppy go. In just a few days I'd grown attached even though I knew I wasn't allowed to keep him in my apartment. I'd already asked since Dixie was allowed to keep Dolly, but the landlord informed me they were grandfathered in before the laws surrounding pit bulls in Denver changed. My little guy wasn't that lucky.

My response made Wheeler chuckle. He stared at me silently as he held out the coat he'd taken off in his free hand.

"Put this on." I stared at him like he'd suddenly started speaking Russian until he shook the coat again and frowned at me. His voice was serious and left no room for argument when he repeated the command. "Put this on, Poppy. I want to talk to you and I know you aren't comfortable inviting me up to your apartment."

I winced at the reminder of how spazzy and skittish I acted when I'd had to knock on Dixie's door while he was house-sitting for her. He'd invited me into the apartment and it took every single ounce of courage I had to step over the threshold. Once inside with him, I'd been so jumpy and twitchy that both Wheeler and Dolly had given me a wide berth and plenty of space to freak out. Wheeler went to find what I needed for Dolly and didn't even try to hand it off to me. He set it on the floor a few feet away from where I was quaking and shivering and then took himself all the way back across the room to the kitchen so I could gather everything up and make my escape without having to get too close to him. I'd wanted to cry tears of gratitude and sob with remorse at the same time. I hated that I couldn't fight through the fear and just act normal.

I took the jacket he was holding out for me with shaking hands and fought the urge to bury my nose in it to see if it smelled like him. I liked the way that he always kind of smelled like he'd had his hands in something mechanical and messy. There was no expensive cologne for Wheeler, just the clean smell of soap, the lemony scent of whatever he used in that thick head of reddish-brown hair, and the persistent trace of how he made his living. It was honest and it was real. The way it surrounded me was intoxicating as I slid my arms into the sleeves of his jacket. The material went down well past my fingertips and the bottom hit me at midthigh. I was instantly warm, wrapped up in his scent and his lingering body heat. In fact, I couldn't recall ever being this cozy.

I took a deep breath and moved my hands so I could push the hair that had escaped my messy topknot out of my face. "It's cold, you can come up. I can't promise that I'm going to be a great hostess or anything but I think I can handle a quick conversation without passing out at your feet." He'd never asked on any of the occasions when we were together why I acted like such a basketcase around him. I figured somewhere along the line someone had given him the CliffsNotes version of what had happened to me. He could fill in the blanks with a quick Google search from there. My nightmare had a million links.

It was his turn to rub his arms up and down to keep warm as he considered me for a second. Apparently deciding he was going to take me up on my less than hospitable offer, he put the puppy down on the sidewalk, wrapped the end of the leash around his tattooed wrist, and nodded toward the front of the building. I scowled as the little troublemaker immediately fell into trotting steps right next to those booted feet like a good boy.

I followed Wheeler up the cement steps and almost bumped into his back as the big, glass security doors swung open. He shifted to the side with the dog but I was still right in the line of fire as four men who appeared to be college aged came out of the building. It was an affordable complex right in the heart of Capitol Hill, so there were a lot of young professionals and students that occupied the apartments around mine. Typically, I was sequestered, safe and sound, in my apartment with the locks thrown by this time. I rarely encountered anyone coming and going, and when I did, I kept my head down and stuck strictly to my side of the hallway. This random run-in was a first and it was going to end horribly as I stood stuck, like a deer caught in headlights. I was going to throw up. I was going to make myself a liar because there was a very real chance that I might end up passing out at Wheeler's feet the closer the men got to me.

The laughter coming from the young men rasped across my skin and had my breath wheezing out of me in short, shallow pants. I needed to move. I needed to get out of the way. I needed to get safe. I put up a shaking hand as if I could ward off the oncoming collision and closed my eyes, mentally taking myself someplace far far away as I braced for the impact.

It never came.

My breath rushed out and my knees almost buckled as I heard Wheeler's deep and unfailingly steady voice tell the other men, "Hey, fellas, how about you let the lady slide past you real quick?" There was nothing in his tone but friendly inquiry and maybe a hint of gentle warning that they didn't want to ignore his request. Since I had my eyes closed I didn't see, but rather heard, the guys offer up an easy agreement. I couldn't tell how close they were to me, but in the span of a heartbeat I could tell they had stepped aside and my path to the doorway was clear.

A fuzzy handful was shoved into my unsteady grasp and I could feel Wheeler's body heat as he stepped next to me, close and reassuring, but not touching. "Come on, honey, let's get you and the pup out of the cold."

I forced my eyes open and gave a jerky nod as I buried my face in the puppy's warm neck. One foot in front of the other, I forced myself through the security door Wheeler was holding open.

"Thanks, fellas." He flicked his fingers out from his forehead as I kept my gaze locked firmly on him instead of the men that had to be wondering what on earth was wrong with me. I heard the other men mutter back a bunch of "no problems" and "any-times" but I couldn't bring myself to look in their direction.

Thankfully my apartment was located on the ground floor. Moving out of Rowdy's sister's house and into a place of my own had been a huge step forward in my healing process, but I knew that there was no way I could ever chance being stuck in an elevator alone with a man I didn't know. That would send me into a full-on breakdown. Fortunately, I found a place on the ground floor that luckily happened to be located right next to Dixie Carmichael's apartment. I knew Dixie from the bar that Rowdy liked to hang out at, so it wasn't like there was a stranger sharing the wall with mine. Eventually Dixie and her bubbly, sunny disposition wore me down to the point that I could go over to her place and didn't freak out if she came into mine. I was going to miss her when she was gone. And I really didn't want to think about the prospect of having a new person living that close to me.

"Give me your keys, Poppy." Wheeler's voice was still even and calm as could be even when he had to repeat himself for the third time because I was just standing in front of my door staring at it like it would magically open for me.

"What?" I looked at him dumbly as I continued to cuddle the dog trapped uncomfortably in my too tight grip.

He held out his hand, palm up, and lifted one of his mahogany-colored eyebrows at me. "Keys, unless you want to hang out in the hallway the rest of the night. I can do that but I think the puppy needs something to chew on because he's about to make his way through the cuff of my jacket." He nodded at my arms and I gasped when I noticed that the dog had indeed chewed his way through the too long material that was hanging over my hands.

"Oh no! I'm so sorry. I didn't notice." I scrambled to pull my keys out of the wide pocket that ran across the bottom of my hoodie. My fingers were still shaking so badly that I immediately dropped the keys on the ground by my feet. Before I could bend to pick them up, Wheeler moved and not only had them in his hand but had the door open and me moving forward with nothing more than a shift of his body behind mine.

Once we were inside, he took the dog from me so I could strip his coat off and get control of my violently shaking body. Effortlessly, he found the spot in the tiny kitchen where I had been keeping the Puppy Chow and settled the tiny terror in with some food and water. He was far too comfortable in my space but at the moment I was so grateful for his presence I didn't care.

I put my hands to my cheeks and held my face. I could feel heat under the surface and I could hear the rush of blood between my ears.

"Are you going to be okay? Do you need me to get you something? Should I grab Dixie?" He sounded genuinely concerned about me and that only made me shake even harder.

"No, I'm fine." I wasn't fine and hadn't been in a very long time. "Dixie is in Mississippi. She took Dolly down because Church moved into the house he rented for them and she wanted the dog to get used to their new home and so she could see what it was like to have a yard." I was babbling but I couldn't stop the words from pouring out. "How do you move me without laying a hand on me?"

He looked up from where he was watching the puppy dig into his chow. Those blue eyes were like lasers as they cut into me from across the room. He put his hands on the counter and leaned forward. "What are you talking about?" His voice still held that same even tone but there was something in it, some deeper note, that let me know he knew exactly what I was talking about.

I wrapped my arms around myself in a protective hug and met his look with a pointed one of my own. "I get stuck, frozen with fear. I end up caught between memories and reality. Most people grab my arm or touch me somewhere to get me moving again. Either that or they go around me like I'm in the way. You made me move without doing anything."

His eyebrows shot up and the corners of his mouth pulled down in a frown. "People shouldn't touch you unless you tell them it's okay, even if you are in the way."

His words had me shivering in a completely different way than I had been before and I was the opposite of cold. "I didn't use to mind it." The words cracked and sounded almost as broken as I felt on the inside. "I mean being touched. It wasn't until . . . after."

He lowered his gaze and I saw his chest rise and fall as he sucked in a deep breath. "The reason doesn't matter. If you don't like it, people should respect that. No one has a right to put their hands on you unless you want them there."

Right there in that moment I thought I wouldn't mind it too terribly much if he walked across the room and replaced the frail and thin arms that were currently holding me together with his thick, strong, tattooed ones. It was probably the only touch I would ever crave but I would never be brave enough to ask for it, so I cleared my throat and awkwardly made my way closer to where he was standing. I lifted myself up into one of the barstools that was across the counter from him and put my hands on the cool surface separating us and prayed they would stop shaking.

"So what did you want to talk to me about? I'm assuming you

reconsidered my offer and want to take the furry little terror off my hands." The puppy looked up from where his entire face was buried in his water dish and gave me a look of doggie disdain. I couldn't help but grin at him. "I'm kind of attached to him now, Wheeler. I don't think I'm going to give him up." It felt like months ago that I'd stood in front of him, knees knocking together, offering him the puppy. In reality it had only been a few days but that was time enough for my heart to attach itself to the rambunctious and destructive puppy. I would have to move, buy a house or something, but I would do it save the dog. I could be a hero and not a victim for a change.

His lips twitched and I almost fell out of my seat when those twin dimples flashed at me. The boy was a heartbreaker without even trying. Now that I was close enough to him to actually study him, I was pretty sure the light smattering of freckles across the bridge of his nose was going to be my undoing. The dimples were too much, and the freckles were overkill. It wasn't fair. A man shouldn't be allowed to look both badass and adorable. Hearts weren't meant to withstand that kind of onslaught and there was no way a vagina stood a chance against that kind of appeal. Speaking of which, I felt something deep inside of me start to get warm and my thighs clenched in response. I hadn't been aware of my body and its reactions to the opposite sex in a long time.

"Have you given him a name yet." The dimples cut deeper when I scowled at him in response.

"No, but that's because I want the right name. He's going to be stuck with it forever." I pouted a little as he laughed and shook his burnished head.

"He's a dog. Call him Good Boy and he'll be happy." He looked down at the dog and then back up at me with a barely noticeable wince. "I shouldn't have let you leave the other day. I wanted to take him. I should've taken him, but my head's all over the place right now and I can't even tell which way is up half the time." He lifted a hand and rubbed it across the back of his neck, which lifted the bottom of the black thermal he was wearing up and revealed the tight cut of his abs over the line of his jeans. I wasn't surprised that he was tattooed there as well, but I was a little shocked that he seemed to be sporting a clearly defined six-pack. He wasn't built bulky and thick like a lot of the other guys that were now a regular part of my life thanks to Salem and Rowdy and the tattoo shop. I should have guessed that hauling motors in and out of cars and throwing tires around all day led to having the kind of body that would have a lot of women pinning him to hot guy boards on Pinterest left and right.

"I'm terrified about the prospect of becoming a dad. I let that fear take over most of my life and I dismissed the idea of taking on more responsibility out of hand. The truth is, my house is lonely right now. I'm lonely." He looked at me like I should have something to say to that but I couldn't figure out what my response was supposed to be. There was a time when I was young and naive to all the ways a man could hurt a woman and I knew that girl would know what to say to him, but she was long gone. I was here biting my tongue to keep from saying what I was sure was the wrong thing. "I think the puppy might help me settle into the idea of being a new dad."

I made a face. "You want to practice your parenting skills on a puppy?" It wasn't a horrible idea but it wasn't the best one I'd ever heard either. If I was in his shoes I would be hitting up all those buddies of his that were well on their way to populating Denver with the next generation of marked men and women. Hell, his best friend from childhood had recently become a father to an adorable five-year-old, the results of an ill-thought-out one-night stand. Zeb Fuller wasn't any more prepared for fatherhood than Wheeler seemed to be and yet he'd landed on his feet and found himself a perfect little family with only a few mishaps along the way.

"No . . . well, kind of . . . I don't know. In my head it sounded more reasonable and less crazy than that. What I do know is that I need something in my life to focus on besides the panic and resentment that's been eating me alive lately. I can give him a good home."

I looked down at the dog, who was now happily chewing on the dangling end of one of Wheeler's shoelaces, and sighed. I didn't want to give him up but the only reason he was here now was because of the man standing in front of me.

I'd spent my entire life trying to make men happy, trying to get them to love me by giving them everything I had. Apparently it was a hard habit to break because even though I didn't want to, I heard myself begrudgingly tell Wheeler, "Fine. You can have him, but if you get tired of him, or if you think he's too much to handle and want me to take him back, you have to know that I'll never forgive you for that. I'll never forgive myself for trusting you. You can't do that to him." Or me, I told him silently. The puppy plopped himself on his butt and looked up at both of us. His head swiveled between the two of us as his tongue lolled out the side of his mouth. I felt my heart squeeze in my chest and tears burned at the back of my eyes. This sucked but I knew it was the right thing to do. I knew all about needing to find something that tethered you to reality. Without it, the past and the possibility of a shattered present could fling you into a really ugly place that was hard to escape from. At the moment I only had one hand out of that particular pit of despair and I was doing my best to pull the rest of my body out with an uncertain grip.

He cocked his head to the side and considered me thoughtfully for a second. Those dimples flashed again and this time I couldn't contain a sigh. He must have heard it because his lips lifted up and some of that ice that chilled his gaze seemed to thaw.

"I'm not going to get tired of him and you're not going to miss him because we're going to share custody of him. I don't know what to do with a puppy any more than I know what to do with a baby. You're an expert on the subject seeing as how you work with animals all day long. I figure you can help me train him." He pointed to where the dog had abandoned his shoelace and was now in the living room sniffing along the edge of the couch like he was looking for a place to go to the bathroom. I gasped and flew out of my chair so I could stop the impending couch ru-inage. "Let's be honest, there is no way I'll be able to juggle a dog and a newborn. Once Kallie and I figure out some kind of custody arrangement, you can have the dog when I have the baby."

I put the dog back on the floor in the kitchen just in case he decided he really did have to go. I looked up at Wheeler like he'd lost his mind, because the way he was talking right now I kind of figured he had.

The dimples were back as he shifted position so he was leaning against the counter with his legs stretched out in front of him. "It all makes sense. I knew you weren't going to want to give the puppy up after I fucked up and I know I'm not ready for all that responsibility on my own. It's the perfect solution."

I shook my head at him and threw my hands up in the air. "I think you're insane."

He continued to grin at me and I realized belatedly that when I'd moved into the kitchen it put me close enough to him that I could feel the heat his body generated and could see the way his muscles flexed and moved each time he laughed.

"Well, I think you're pretty but that doesn't have anything to do with anything. Take me up on my offer, Poppy, please."

It was the second time he's brought up the fact that he found me attractive. I used to be, but I'd gone out of my way to be anything except that ever since I was released from the hospital after Oliver died and the police pulled me away from the horrific scene that was our last moments together. How attractive Wheeler found me wasn't what I should be focused on, and yet I couldn't stop his words from spinning around in my head or the way they made my heart dip and my breath shudder.

"Fine. I'll help you with the dog, but once he's older and you and the baby are settled into a pattern, you have to keep him full-time. Kids need a pet." Or at least in my experience, they wanted one and were never allowed to have one because their tyrannical father thought they were dirty and unnecessary. I cringed at the memory.

"I can do that." He stuck out his hand, and before I could think twice about it or recoil at the thought of touching my palm to his, I put my much smaller one in his firm grasp. I let out a little whimper when his fingers closed over mine, too stunned that I was touching another person on purpose to move. "It's a deal, honey." His words were quiet and soft. He let go far earlier than I wanted him to but I was still in shock, so I just stood there with my mouth hanging open and my eyes wide as he told me, "He needs a name before I go."

I took a step back and lifted a hand to my throat. I wanted to get it right, which is why I hadn't given him a name yet. I didn't like the pressure of trying to come up with something fitting while Wheeler had those chilly baby blues locked on me. "You pick."

Slowly his head shook back and forth in the negative. "Nope. You've known him longer and spent more time with him. You should get to pick what we call him."

I looked down at the dog, who was now on his back, all four feet in the air as he wiggled around the floor fueled by nothing more than excitement and joy. I cleared my throat and looked down at my feet. "Happy. We should call him Happy." I winced as my voice did that thing where it broke in the middle of my words again.

"Happy? Like the guy on *Sons of Anarchy*? You didn't strike me as a biker babe, Poppy."

It was my turn to cock my head in confusion. "What's a Son of Anarchy?" I didn't watch much TV. It was all too violent and I'd made the mistake of stumbling onto a *Law & Order: SVU* marathon on cable a few months ago and ended up curled up in a ball on the couch crying my eyes out because the content hit too close to home. Even something as simple as watching television Oliver had tainted and destroyed.

His eyebrows shot up again and his whole body vibrated as he started to laugh. "Never mind. Why Happy?"

I shrugged, worried that he hated the name and was just being nice. To avoid those prying eyes I crouched down so I could rub the puppy's pink little belly. "Because he was left at our office, left like he was nothing more than forgotten baggage. He was dropped off by someone that knows how difficult it is to find homes for pits in Denver and that didn't care that his actions might result in the entire litter having to be put down. None of that matters to Happy. He still wags his tail. He still chases the ball. He gives kisses and isn't afraid of anyone. He still manages to be happy." I couldn't even slightly remember what that felt like but I desperately wanted to.

Wheeler cleared his throat and pushed off the counter. He carefully stepped around me and made his way over to where his thoroughly chewed coat was resting on the back of the couch. At first I thought he hated the name, that he was going to tell me to pick something else. Instead, in that firm tone that never seemed to waver, he told me, "Happy it is. I'll touch base with you tomorrow so we can set up some kind of schedule. Make yourself dinner and have a good night." At first I recoiled, thinking he was making a subtle dig about the fact I was noticeably too skinny, but somewhere, some sense of rationality rose up and reminded me sternly that only moments ago he told me he thought I was pretty. I wondered if maybe that girl that hadn't been broken was somewhere deep down inside of me still.

He flipped the lock on my door before he left and I knew without looking that he was waiting on the other side until he heard that I slid the chain in place and threw the dead bolt before he left. I leaned back against the door and let my head hit the wood with a heavy thud. The newly named Happy trotted over and plopped his fuzzy butt right on my feet as he looked up at me.

I hadn't had a good night in ages. That being said, this one was as close as I'd gotten in longer than I could remember.

Sighing, I picked up the dog and made my way into the kitchen so I could make myself something to eat.

Chapter 4

Wheeler

"Thank you for agreeing to meet with me. I honestly didn't think you would."

She used to be my everything; I would have done anything for her and tried my best to hand her the world. Now she was surprised I agreed to have coffee with her before I had to be at the shop. It was crazy how quickly things could change, including Kallie.

She'd always been the prettiest girl I had ever seen (until Poppy Cruz came wandering into my garage all golden-eyed and heart-broken). Kallie had the kind of easy and effortless all-American good looks that appealed instantly to a kid that always felt like he was on the outside of normal looking in. Her long blond hair was shiny and thick. Her baby-blue eyes were wide and guile-less looking. Her skin was the perfect peaches and cream with a touch of freckles that was the only thing about her that matched her to her redheaded older sister. Dixie was short and curvy, Kallie was tall and thin with legs that went on for day and days. She turned heads then and she made men weak in the knees . . . not that it was male attention she was interested in attracting.

But there were subtle changes that only someone that had spent years loving her and memorizing every line of her body and every nuance of her expressions would pick up on. For instance, that creamy, carefully made-up face had a hint of ashy green to it. The way she was picking at the muffin in front of her, and clutching the herbal tea I'd ordered for her, made me think she'd entered the phase of her pregnancy where nausea was her constant companion. Her painstakingly maintained mane of blond locks was also looking a little rougher than usual. Kallie wasn't the type to throw her hair up in a ponytail and head out, but today her silky waves were piled up in a topknot that looked like it hadn't been brushed or styled. She was also wearing sneakers. In the nearly nine years that we'd known each other, I'd never seen the woman in anything other than designer footwear that cost almost as much as some of the used cars I moved through the shop.

They weren't huge differences but they were enough that it made the woman I had thought I was going to spend the rest of my life with feel like a stranger. She seemed unsure of herself and nervous, which was also a huge change in the dynamic between us. For the majority of our relationship Kallie had me wound tighter than a string around her little finger. I was so scared of losing her, of losing her family and the only sense of security and normalcy I'd ever known, that I'd let her lead me around by my dick and dictate the entirety of the way we were together. I never argued with her, never pushed back, and that meant she always had the upper hand. It wasn't a smart move on my part. She was already spoiled as the baby in the Carmichael household and she had some serious princess tendencies that I'd always secretly hoped she would grow out of. As it turned out, having me at her beck and call only intensified her sense of entitlement. I'd literally created a monster, one that had no problem tearing my world apart and feasting on my heart.

I sighed and rubbed a hand over my tired face. I'd slept restlessly last night, caught between satisfaction and guilt at the artful way I'd maneuvered Poppy into agreeing to spend time with me. I wanted to feel bad for manipulating her into a situation she'd obviously wanted to say no to, but I couldn't. I wanted to be around her and I wanted her to get used to being around me. I knew it was selfish and that I was walking over very dangerous ground, but I couldn't stay away. She was hiding and I was seeking.

"I told you I was going to be here for you and the baby, Kallie." I picked up my coffee and took a healthy swig. "I didn't say I was going to be happy about it."

She made a noise low in her throat and her fingers tightened on the mug until they were almost white. "I hate how awkward things are between us." She looked up at me under her long lashes. "I've apologized a million times, Wheeler. Are you ever going to forgive me?"

I blew out an aggravated breath. "Have you told your parents why I called the wedding off yet?"

She flinched and as her gaze shifted away I caught a glimpse of guilt in her eyes. She didn't need to answer my question when her actions answered for her.

I snorted and leaned back in my seat so that I could put as much physical distance between the two of us as possible. "So your mom and dad still think I dropped you for nothing, that I kicked you out of the house that I bought for you, for no reason?" I wanted to scream at her, to tell her to grow the hell up, to shake some sense into her. Instead, all I did was shake my head in disappointment. "They think I left you out in the cold even though you're having my kid?" It was so disappointing. They were the only real parents I'd ever known. They took me in no questions asked the minute Kallie brought me home. I fell in love with her family almost as quickly as I fell in love with her. The way they'd had no problem believing the worst about me when Kallie and I split hurt almost as much as letting her go. Dixie had offered no less than a hundred times to intervene. She hated the way her parents had turned on me and wanted desperately to set them straight, but I refused to let her get involved. I was used to being let down by the people that were supposed to love me, so if they wanted to think the worst, I was inclined to let them. Plus, it was practically impossible to come clean about why I'd finally walked away without laying all the secrets Kallie wasn't ready to share out on the table. Too many years being the one that protected her meant I couldn't sell her out just to gain her parents' favor.

She exhaled slowly and lifted her sky colored eyes up to mine. "I'm going to tell them. I just haven't found the right time. Everything has been crazy with Dixie getting hurt and then deciding to move to Mississippi. I don't want to put any more on them at the moment."

It was an excuse. She didn't want to pull the curtain back on the real reason for our split. She wasn't protecting anyone but herself. "What does Roni think about all of this?"

Roni was the woman that Kallie had been having an affair with, while she was still involved with me. She was the woman that Kallie realized she wanted to be with more than the man she had spent the majority of her youth with. Kallie loved me, but she was supposed to be with Roni more.

At least that's what she told me when I confronted her after her older sister let the cat out of the bag by accident. Dixie would never have shared such a personal secret but I'd ambushed her one night after Kallie told me about the baby. I needed to vent and there ended up being a whole lot of yelling and confusion, most of it on my part. Somewhere along the line Dixie thought the reason I was upset was because of Roni when she thought I was talking about Kallie's affair instead of the baby. Dixie felt horrible for spilling her sister's deepest secrets but I wasn't sure Kallie would have ever come clean to me if she hadn't.

Her gaze shifted away again and she chomped down on her lower lip. "She isn't happy. Since I've been staying with my parents, there hasn't been much time to see her or to talk to her. She wants me to tell them the truth too, but neither one of you knows how hard it is for me." She shifted in her seat. "I'm already a runaway bride and an unwed mother. I feel like that's plenty of disappointment for them to deal with right now."

I sighed and leaned forward in my seat. "They are not going to be disappointed in you because you fell in love with a woman, Kallie. They are going to be disappointed you lied and hurt people that love you and care about you while trying to hide who you really are and who you really love." I shook my head at her. "That's why they're so mad at me right now. They think I hurt you."

"My parents love you, Wheeler. You're part of the family and always will be." She tentatively lowered a hand to her stomach and gave me a surprisingly steady look. "We are in this together, but you have no idea how hard it is realizing your life is never going to be the same. It's scary enough coming to terms with that on your own . . . thinking about how my parents might react . . ." She sighed and shrugged helplessly.

I nodded at her. "We *are* in this together, but you have someone else that's in it too, Kallie. If you plan on keeping Roni around, then you need to be honest with everyone, including yourself, about the role she's playing and will play in our baby's life." I wasn't going to reassure her that her parents were going to be reasonable and understanding again. I'd said the words a million times in a million different ways but it hadn't done any good. She was going to have to have that conversation with them and find out for herself that they would love her no matter what. She lowered her gaze and her teeth bit even harder into her lip. Knowing well and good those were signs that she was done with the conversation, I changed the subject. "What did you want to talk to me about that couldn't be handled over the phone?" She'd begged me to meet her this morning, and like a sap, I caved and agreed. "I have to get going soon." I didn't really since I made my own hours and I was the boss, but I could only handle so much time around her. It still hurt, being with her but not (with) her.

She shifted nervously in her seat and let go of her tea. She started tapping her fingertips on the table in front of her and I wanted to reach out and put my hand over hers to keep them still. I didn't want to make her anxious but until we found our way to some kind of new normal with each other, this was how it was going to be. I felt cut open and raw, she was fidgety and unsettled. I'd never realized how deeply we'd relied on each other to keep our worst traits at bay from the rest of the know-ing world. She held me together and kept all my jagged edges smoothed out and less dangerous, I kept her calm and quieted all the restlessness in her that made her so volatile and needy.

"I have a doctor's appointment next week. I wanted to see if you would come with me." She was heading into the second trimester, so the baby was starting to seem very real. Soon she would be showing and we would be to the point where we would know if we were having a boy or a girl. I'd gone with her to one doctor's visit but her mother had been there as well and it was a terrible afternoon for all of us. She'd asked me to go a couple more times and I'd refused thinking it would be easier for all involved. Seeing the nervousness on her pretty face right now, I understood that wasn't the case.

"Did you ask your mom to go this time?" My tone was flat because she could make this all better if she just stepped up to the plate for once in her life. If she took care of someone else instead of expecting everyone to take care of her.

"No." The word squeaked out and she jolted. "Uh . . . I talked to Dixie and she sort of mentioned that it's our baby and that we're the ones who are going to raise it, not Mom and Dad, so we needed to figure out how to coparent without them in the middle of us. I don't want to go alone because it's scary, but Dixie is right. It should be you and me."

Dixie was a fixer. It's what she did. She also had the annoying habit of seeing straight to the heart of a situation and knowing the best way to get everyone involved on the right path. Even more, she was the only person in the world that could make Kallie see beyond her own selfishness.

I groaned a little as I nodded in sullen agreement. "I'll go with you. Just text me the date and time."

Her lips quivered into a tiny grin. "Thanks."

I finished my coffee and pushed back from the table. I stopped and went still as stone when her fingers touched the back of my hand. I expected it to burn or for a familiar tingle to shoot along my skin. There was nothing. There was no jolt like the one that had almost taken me to my knees when Poppy's shaking fingers lightly grasped mine yesterday.

"Um . . . I know it's none of my business and I have no right to pry, but Dixie mentioned you've been dating a lot recently." A tight expression pinched her face and her eyes narrowed. "I . . . ugh . . . I just want to tell you to be careful. You're a really nice guy, Wheeler. There are a lot of women out there that will take advantage of that." She should know. She was one of them.

I shook her hand off. "I'm fucking . . . not dating." She recoiled, which made me soften my tone when I told her, "You're right, it's none of your business."

"Rebounds never work out." There was some of the old Kallie shining through.

I rolled my eyes at her. "I gotta go." I turned my back on her and headed toward the door only to be brought up short when she called my name. One of these days all those years of conditioning to heel at her command would break. I couldn't fucking wait. I looked at her over my shoulder, impatience clear in every line of my body.

"I was the wrong one, but the right one is still out there." Maybe she really did want me to be happy, or maybe she simply wanted me to find someone so that I was less likely to screw up trying to raise our kid on my own. Either way her words weren't ones I wanted to hear.

"When you figure out where you want to live, you can have all the furniture in the house. I'll put it in a storage unit and cover the cost. If you plan on staying with your parents for the long haul, or get to the point where you're playing house with Roni, you can sell it all and use it for whatever we need for the baby. I'll see you at the appointment, Kallie."

I heard her quiet gasp as I pushed out the door into the bright Denver sunshine. That meeting had gone as well as could be expected and I was surprised that spending time with her wasn't as awful as it had been the first few months after we'd split up. She still wasn't my favorite person to be around, but seeing her and sharing the same air as her didn't make me feel like I was suffocating and bleeding to death from a broken heart anymore. Things between us had been rocky before the split, so I think the reason everything felt so exposed and sensitive after the breakup was more the loss of what I'd *thought* I had, rather than the loss of what I'd *actually* had. She took my stability with her when she walked away and left me with something totally shakey and unsure. She ripped the foundation I'd steadfastly built out from under me, and that left me in the wind . . . exactly how my mother had. Exactly how the child welfare people had left me each and every time they had to place me in a new home with a temporary family.

Feeling restless and uneasy about just unsteady everything in my existence currently was, I pulled my phone out and pressed a finger to the name of the single thing that put a stop to all the questions and uncertainty. All I had to do was picture Poppy's wide, timid eyes and everything that was screaming and thrashing around inside of me went quiet. It was so much easier to focus on overcoming her aversion to closeness than it was to think about straightening out my own mess. I was convinced I could prove to her that there were men in the world she didn't need to be afraid of, that there were men who would do right by her even if that rightness came with a little bit of maneuvering. She said I moved her without using my hands and she was correct. Everything I did around her was me trying to get her to move closer to me. I pushed her to take steps that she needed to take in order for her to be comfortable around me. I wanted to see if there was any way she would be open to something more than our current tense friendship.

I wanted her, but I wanted her to want me back even more. Partly because I knew I was a safe bet for her once she was ready to jump back into the dating pool. I wouldn't take advantage of her and had every intention of handling her like I did one of my classics that was on the verge of falling apart. I would tread lightly and deliberately until all the parts were in working order and then I would prime her and make her purr the way she was always meant to. I wasn't scared of the work and I had every confidence that the end result would be a thing of pure beauty and something that was priceless.

The phone rang for a long time, and just when I was about to hang up and send a text, the call connected and her breathless voice rushed out a quick "hey."

I frowned at my reflection in the side of my car and trapped the phone between my ear and my shoulder as I unlocked and opened the door. "Are you okay?"

She gave a brittle-sounding laugh. "Uh . . . I'm fine. I ended up alone in an exam room with a male patient for a little longer than I was comfortable with because the doc had an emergency in another room. The guy's dog could sense my anxiety and had a little meltdown. You actually called at the perfect time." She exhaled and I could practically hear her entire body shaking in the way her voice quivered. "You gave me an excuse to get out of the room. I don't usually freak out so badly at work. I guess that near miss with the guys from the apartment yesterday has me a little on edge. My therapist is going to have a field day with me during our next session. I always think I'm getting better, but then the universe decides to show me that I'm not."

I heard a dog bark and she called to someone that she needed five minutes. I hated that she was so hard on herself when her reactions were totally normal considering everything she had been through. "You let me into your apartment last night even after those guys scared the piss out of you. You voluntarily stood in the kitchen with me and you shook my hand. You wouldn't have done any of those things a couple months ago when we met." She was moving in the right direction even if she couldn't see it because she was still looking over her shoulder.

She breathed out again and her voice was very soft when she told me, "I think that has more to do with you than it does with me."

Her words made my heart stutter and skip a beat. I wanted her to trust me but her handing that information over so quickly was unexpected. I didn't think I'd done a thing to earn her trust yet. I had to clear my throat before I could reply. "I was hoping we could meet up after I get off work tonight and start to work on some kind of schedule with Happy." I couldn't hold back the grin when I said the puppy's name. "I'll order pizza and make sure you eat dinner." She went quiet on the other end of the phone and I wanted to kick myself for pushing too hard too fast with her. "I can always come to your place if you're more comfortable with that."

She sighed. "It's not that."

I scowled at myself in the rearview mirror and reminded myself that this was all about the long game with her. She was a good distraction at the moment but I wanted her to be around long after the dust of my currently imploding life settled. "What is it then?"

I could picture her tugging on her lip and shuffling her feet nervously because her nervous habits were becoming as familiar to me as my own. So hurriedly that the words smooshed together and were barely discernible, she admitted, "I don't like pizza."

Stunned that she was worried about telling me something as simple as that, I found it was my turn to sigh. "Is that all? I'll order Mexican or Chinese food. Hell, I can even whip up some sandwiches or some mac and cheese."

She gave another one of those laughs that sounded shrill and slightly hysterical. "I don't eat tomatoes. I hate them."

I nodded even though she couldn't see me. "Okay, so pizza sauce is out, but they make white pizza, we can always do that instead." Getting to know this woman was like walking across a minefield. Every step I took toward her felt like the ground below me might detonate and throw me a thousand steps backward, injured and unable to keep fighting my way toward her.

She whimpered a little bit and I felt it like a kick in my stomach. I hated how hard something as simple as telling someone else what she did and didn't like was for her. If her shitbag husband wasn't already six feet under I would have gladly helped put him there.

"Oliver loved pizza. He told me it was unnatural and ridiculous that I wouldn't eat it. He'd demand that we order it for dinner once or twice a week and I'd have to sit and watch him eat while I sat there starving. He always told me if I didn't want to eat what he provided then I could go hungry."

I swore and curled the hand that wasn't holding my phone around the steering wheel so tightly that my knuckles turned white. My voice was gruff and uneven when I told her, "I'll feed you whatever you want to eat, Poppy."

She made a strangled noise and then cleared her throat. "I have to get back to work. I have a group meeting after work tonight, so I won't be by your place until after seven or so." She hesitated for a second and then quietly handed over, "My favorite is cheeseburgers. I could eat them every day of the week."

She didn't look like she'd had a cheeseburger in years but if that's what she wanted I would make sure she had the best one Denver had to offer. "Cheeseburgers it is. I'll text you my address and see you later tonight."

She mumbled a hasty good-bye and I hung up, anger at everything she'd had to suffer through coursing thick and heated through my blood. She deserved so much better and I was becoming increasingly aware of the fact that I really wanted to be the one to give it to her.

Thoughts firmly on Poppy and what other kinds of horrors she'd had to endure through the course of her marriage, I drove through downtown Denver and made my way to my garage.

Back when I was younger and Zeb and I had too much time and too much youthful curiosity on our hands, we'd spent many a night at illegal parties held in this very same building. The place had history, both personal and collective, so it meant the world to me that I'd been able to save it. The ancient brick had been slated for demolition so that some developer could come in and build more trendy condos and shops to cater to the LoDo sprawl. I'd scraped together enough money from the sale of my first full rebuild outside of school. It was a 1970 Barracuda that was still winning medals at car shows across the country, to lease the space for a year. I continued that pattern for five years—build, sell, pay for the lease on the building, barely getting by until I got hooked up with Nash Donovan and Rowdy

St. James. It started out as a mutual admiration for muscle cars and ink and turned into something that allowed me to get my hands around a major part of my dream. Those two introduced me to Rome Archer, who came at me with a business offer I would have been a fool to turn down. Rome wanted to be a silent partner in the garage. He helped me buy the building outright and set me up so that instead of bleeding money back into the business, I could actually start earning a real living. Rome was the only reason I was able to finally afford a down payment on a house. I owed those Marked Men more than they would ever know.

I parked in the spot that was designated for my Caddy. There was a small office attached to the garage where customers could wait and where the gal that handled all the paperwork and scheduling of projects worked. I'd tried to set Kallie up in that position, thinking the garage could be ours, that we could make our dreams come true together, but she barely lasted a week before I'd had more than one of my guys threaten to quit if she wasn't gone. She hated how dirty the garage was and she didn't give two shits about the classics we worked our asses off to breathe new life into. The girl drove a freaking Audi, for God's sake, even when I offered to find her and build her whatever she wanted. I should have known then it wasn't meant to be. It was a beautiful car but it had no soul and no story.

Snorting at the thought, I stopped short when a baby-blue Hudson Hornet came pulling in through the open gates. It was a '53 if my guess was right, and I was pretty sure that it was. It was an incredibly rare year, so rare that this was the only one I'd seen outside of a hot-rod magazine or a car show. I watched the car roll to a stop next to the Eldorado and took a minute to admire it. I was named after this car, at least that was what my mom told me in one of her few lucid moments when the drugs and demons I couldn't see loosened their hold on her.

A man stepped out, tall, with salt-and-pepper hair, silver side-burns, and expensive mirrored sunglasses covering his eyes. He was dressed in jeans and a dark canvas coat much like the one Happy had ruined last night over the unofficial almost-winter uniform of all Coloradans, a button up flannel over a thermal. I thought he looked vaguely familiar but so many people came in and out of the garage, a lot of them just wanting to look, that I couldn't be sure we'd ever met before.

I lifted my chin in greeting. "Nice ride."

He repeated the gesture. "If that's yours then I return the sen-timent." He indicated the Eldorado with the flick of his fingers.

I shrugged. "It's mine. She was the first rebuild I ever did. My high school shop teacher felt sorry for me and let me buy her for a song right before graduation. He helped me finish her up and to this day he stops by once a month to see how we're both holding up."

The man made a face that I couldn't read and shifted his weight on his feet. He seemed nervous but I didn't have time to stand around chatting about my Caddy. I had a Wayfarer that I was trying to restore and finding parts for the old girl had proven to be a real bitch.

"If you need something specific, go in and talk to Molly, my receptionist. She can point you in the right direction. I can tell you now I don't have any original parts for a Hudson on hand but I know a guy that is a wizard when it comes to tracking down the unfindable."

The older guy took a step back and leaned on the side of his car like the wind had been knocked out of him. He had really cherry taste in cars and looked pretty cool for an old guy, but damn, the dude was weird. Everything about him seemed tense and a little bit off.

"The garage is yours?" The question seemed like it was ripped out of him.

I shrugged again. "Yep. All mine." I motioned toward the door that had the "Open" sign on it and inclined my head, eager to get to work. "Like I said, Molly can give you a hand with whatever you need. I'd be happy to get my hands on that Hudson if you need someone to work on it."

The guy cleared his throat and shook his head like he was trying to clear it. "Uh, yeah. I might be back. I just rolled into town for a quick visit and your garage came up when I started poking around asking about who might be able to handle a rare classic. I was looking for something specific. I didn't think I'd find it so quickly."

I nodded because I knew how hard it could be to come across the original parts you needed to do a whole rebuild. "You can find anything if you look hard enough. I guess I'll see you around."

The guy nodded again and this time he grinned. "Didn't catch your name, kid."

I lifted an eyebrow at him. This whole exchange was getting stranger and stranger by the minute. "Wheeler, Hudson Wheeler. I'm actually named after your car."

The guy flinched and the grin on his face died. "It's nice to meet you, Wheeler. I'll be back."

Without offering up his name in return, he disappeared back into his badass car and pulled out of the parking lot in front of the garage like the cops were after him. I waved a hand in front of my face as the hot rod kicked up dust, and wondered what in the hell had just happened.

Today was a day full of loaded conversations and I'd never considered myself much of a conversationalist.

Chapter 5

Poppy

I feel guilty, you know?"

The girl that was speaking couldn't be any older than sixteen. She was fairly new to the group meetings, but every time she spoke we all went quiet and listened intently. She seemed so strong, so much tougher than I was. Her father had hurt her in unimaginable ways, and when she tried to tell her mother, the woman had accused her of lying and trying to break up the family. As a result the girl had run away from home and had spent the last several years living on the streets. The things she did to survive, the way people took advantage of such an innocent soul, made me so angry. Someone should have been there to keep her safe, just like someone should have been there to keep me and Salem safe from my father's tyrannical rule. Just like someone should have kept me safe from Oliver and his ruin. That was the entire purpose of these group meetings: to help us all realize that we weren't alone, that our stories were shared by women across all walks of life. We were there to keep each other safe. The thing that tied us all together was that we were still here, we survived, and that made us bigger and better than the people that had done their very best to destroy us.

I was watching her so closely and she must have felt my stare because her eyes landed on mine and held as she kept talking. "I feel like I don't deserve a nice house and nice clothes for school. I feel like having all these friends and being popular is all just a scam that I'm pulling on everyone. I feel like I'm in the wrong life." She gave a bitter laugh and lifted a hand to wipe away a lone tear that trailed down her cheek. "Why should I still be here planning on going to prom with a really nice guy that treats me like I'm something special when so many of the girls I met while I was on the run don't get a shot at the same thing? What makes me special? Why did I get a chance and not one of them?"

It was a common theme that she described. Guilt about moving on and finding peace after living a nightmare for so long. Apparently her aunt had gotten suspicious when her mother wasn't able to offer up an explanation as to where her daughter had gone. The girl's extended family had launched an all-out manhunt to find her, and when they did they were appalled by what they found. They knew all along her father was abusive and dangerous. They'd been trying to get her out of the house for years until her mother and father had gone on the run to protect their dirty little secret. She'd had people in her corner that loved her, but wasn't allowed access to them, kind of like the way my parents did their best to keep me and Salem apart after Salem left home. Under my dad's thumb and surrounded by my mother's passive agreement, I never had a chance to let the idea of rebellion take root. I only wished I could have been as brave as this young woman.

"Eventually that guilt will lessen and you'll appreciate the fact that you get to have a chance at all the things you deserved

from the beginning. It's part of the conditioning you were sub-
jected to for so long for you to think you aren't worthy of the
good things that are going to come your way, but you are, all of
you are." The woman that ran the group was a survivor herself.
She always spoke to us in a calm, even tone and it was apparent
to all of us that she took our healing and progress very personally. This wasn't a job for her: helping women that had been
abused live beyond the damage done by their abusers was her
life's calling, her passion. I admired her so much for turning her
pain and experience into something that was beneficial for others to learn from. "Good things will find you if you are open to
them."

Without thinking I blurted out, "How do you know that something or someone is actually good? I think it's safe to say we've all
been fooled by something that seemed to be good but turned out
to be really, really bad."

When Oliver first started courting me after I moved home
after my disastrous first year at college, he seemed nice enough.
He was really into me and treated me like a total gentleman.
He courted me like the preacher's daughter that I was and never
pushed for anything I wasn't ready to give. He handled me like
I was something delicate and he never, not one time, brought
up the supposedly shameful reason I'd had to run back to my
less than understanding family with my tail tucked between my
legs. That had been reason enough for me to give him a shot
after I told myself I was swearing off men forever. I felt broken
but he assured me over and over again that what had happened
wasn't my fault.

I should have known . . . like always . . . that it was a front. Any
man my father practically handpicked for me, a man that was

active in my father's church, and believed the fire and brimstone my dad spouted nonstop, couldn't be okay with what had happened to me and the choices I'd made.

On our wedding night Oliver called me a whore and yelled at me for an hour about not being a virgin and saving myself for him . . . even though he *knew* the nightmare behind why I wasn't untouched and inexperienced. From there the abuse spiraled and worsened until I was having to hide bruises and marks all over my body. Sometimes the words hurt worse than his fists did and all I could do was question how I let myself end up in a situation that was a thousand times more horrible than the one I'd run from.

Both the teen and the counselor turned their attention to me and I realized that everyone in the small group was watching me. Typically I didn't say much, I listened and learned. It helped me feel not so alone and less like a fool to know I wasn't the only one that should have known better. This was probably the first time I'd ever actually spoken up when it wasn't my turn to add something to the conversation.

The group didn't use names, to protect anonymity, so the counselor motioned to me with a soft smile. "Well, you can't ever be absolutely certain something or someone is good because things can change on a dime. Even the happiest and healthiest of relationships can collapse over time and even the best of circumstances are prone to experiencing a rainy day. All you can do is listen to your gut, pay attention to any warning signs and any red flags that are presented. It's up to you to determine if the good outweighs the bad in whatever you face from here on out. You have the tools. You have earned them by surviving everything life has thrown at you."

I bit my lip and cocked my head to look at her questioningly.

"But my judgment has led to the worst experiences in my life. What if I can't tell if the good outweighs the bad?" Unwittingly my thoughts turned to Wheeler. He was the first person I had let slip past the iron guards I had put in place since enduring Oliver's torture. I refused to let anyone close, emotionally or physically, because if I had enough room to run, then there was no possible way I could be hurt again. I kept a wall up between me and the rest of the world, and so far, it had served its purpose, but now I was wondering if it was keeping all the good out as well as the bad.

There was a lot of good in Wheeler. A person would have to be blind not to see it. He seemed like a nice guy, he respected my personal-space issue, he was ridiculously good-looking, and my libido that I thought was long gone lit up like Christmas lights around him. I genuinely didn't mind being alone with him or being close to him, which felt like a mini-miracle at this point. I liked the way he looked at me and I liked the way I felt compelled to look at him. I didn't want to hide around him.

The flip side of all of that was that I was smart enough now to not ignore the negative that was also circling around the attractive mechanic. He had a baby on the way that he clearly wasn't ready for. Soon fatherhood was going to have to be his first priority, not calming a skittish girl that had an obvious crush on him. He had a tumultuous relationship with his ex and I wasn't sure he was anywhere close to being over her, which had the potential to lead to a whole lot of heartache if I let him get any closer than he already was. Plus, there was the big unknown, the big what-ifs that kept me awake at night and made me wonder if I could ever actually let anyone get as close as they would need to be if I ever wanted to have a real relationship.

Oliver had hurt me in the worst ways a man could hurt a

woman and it wasn't the first time. Sex with him had never been particularly pleasant, it always felt like some kind of punishment for him not being my first. Before Oliver, my only sexual experience had been with the man that I convinced myself was my true love. Sex with him had been exciting, something new and forbidden, since I grew up in such a conservative household. I honestly couldn't get enough of it. It made me feel free and far more in charge of my life than I had ever been . . . at least it had until I got pregnant at barely eighteen. At first, I thought it was meant to be. I was foolishly in love and had no problem spinning unrealistic fairy tales around the college football-star that told me whatever I needed to hear in order to get into my pants. I was picturing a life together, a happy little family, but all of that was painfully unrealistic and woefully naive. I told my knight who came clad in cleats and a jersey about the baby, expecting him to be as excited as I was, and was heartbroken and destroyed when he told me to get rid of it.

It was like a slap in the face. I thought college and this perfect boy were my way out, the escape I'd longed for from my father and his long-reaching influence, but in a heartbeat all those dreams were shattered. He told me I was nothing, just another stupid freshman girl that was willing to spread her legs for the campus golden boy. He laughed at me when I cried and scoffed at me when I told him I thought we were going to be together forever. He walked away still laughing but came back months later when I refused to terminate my pregnancy.

Even without him I was planning on keeping the baby. I was going to face my father's wrath, stand up to his scorn, and suffer through his disownment if it meant I could be the best mom ever. I was convinced this baby was meant to be, that it was a sign that I had a bigger purpose in life than being the perfect daughter and proper little wife he'd trained me to be.

The baby's dad convinced me to come over to his place with promises of reconciliation. He told me he was done sleeping around, that he only wanted me. He promised that he loved me. I was stupid. I was so desperate for it to be real that I forgot about his ugly, twisted reaction when I told him we were going to be parents. As soon as I knocked on the door, I knew I'd made the world's biggest mistake.

He yanked me into his apartment and proceeded to beat me within an inch of my life. My dad was a dictator and a tyrant, but he used his words and withheld his love to secure obedience and submission. I'd never had anyone lay their hands on me before. It was terrible. To this day, I could still taste my own blood, blood I choked on as he hit me over and over again, making sure that his blows were focused on and around my still-flat stomach. He wanted to punish me for defying his wishes, but more than that he wanted to make sure there was no way I left that apartment still pregnant.

He got his wish. After fifteen minutes I passed out, and when I woke up I was back in my own dorm room and I knew something was seriously wrong. There was blood everywhere and I felt like my entire body was being turned inside out. I crawled to the tiny bathroom and it was there that my body did what it had no choice to after the football player was done with me. I lost the baby as I sat on the bathroom floor, bleeding, alone, and torn apart in too many ways to name.

Luckily, my childhood friend and the boy that had lived next door to me my entire life was at the same college. At the time I had no clue he'd followed me there, but when he found me hovering on the brink of death in my dorm room, I was so grateful that he did. That boy was Rowdy, who was now desperately in love with my sister and building the kind of family I'd always wanted. He took care of me and then he went and took care of his teammate who was responsible for my condition. The school had a mess on their hands with the three of us, but I was so heart-broken and mortified that I packed myself up and headed back to the only thing I knew without a backward glance. I didn't stick around to press charges like I should have and I didn't stick around to vouch for Rowdy like I should have. Because of me he lost his scholarship, got kicked out of school, and disappeared. It was a lucky twist of fate that his path had crossed with Salem's after so many years.

So sex, even good sex, wasn't something that I'd had a lot of success with and there were a lot of unanswered questions that were constantly floating around in my head now that I realized I might actually want to have it again. Every time I caught sight of that ink that scrawled across Wheeler's stomach and across the back of his neck, I wondered where it all went. I wanted to know if it dropped below the tops of his jeans and I was curious if those freckles of his stopped at the bridge of his nose. I'd never been so physically aware of the way I reacted to a man before him but I wasn't sure I could do anything with the way he made me feel.

The counselor's light voice jerked me away from the mental scale, where I was weighing all the things that were swirling around in my head. "You have to stop blaming yourself for what happened to you. Those choices were not yours. Your judgment is not in question. All you could do was react to the situation the best you could have, given the circumstances. You were a victim, not an accomplice." That was a common refrain, both here and during my private sessions with my therapist. I didn't make the choice to go with Oliver willingly when he abducted me. He'd pulled a gun on my sister and threatened to shoot her if I didn't go with him. I did what I had to do in order to keep her safe. At the time it seemed like the only option, but now I always wondered if there was another way. If I should have been smarter, stronger . . . better.

I felt like I couldn't trust myself to know if what I was doing was right, when it seemed like everything I'd done prior had been wrong. Maybe I didn't feel like I deserved the kind of normalcy and goodness that was in my life now. Maybe, just like the teenager who was watching me closely, I was also stuck in place where I would wonder what I'd done right to deserve this new life. I didn't feel like I'd done a single thing to earn it.

The group broke up shortly after that and my feet couldn't move fast enough as I made my way to the little coffee shop that was on the corner down the street from the building where we met. Happy yipped at the end of his leash and danced up on his tiny hind legs as he saw me coming. My heart felt heavy and my mind was foggy with too many things to wade through, but the sight of the excited puppy and the welcoming smile from the stunning blonde who was puppy sitting did wonders towards lightening my heavy mood.

Sayer Cole was Rowdy's older sister. I considered her something of a guardian angel and she was most definitely my mentor. The woman had been raised by a man that gave my father a run for his money when it came to emotional manipulation and cruelty, but she was now happily settled with a great man and helping him raise his son. She just happened to be Wheeler's best friend from childhood's woman, so I hadn't mentioned to her that I was going by to see Wheeler after the meeting. She would tell Zeb and then everyone in our tight little circle of friends and family would know something was up and I didn't have it in me to explain to them that they shouldn't get their hopes up or give Wheeler shit. I had no clue what I was doing and there was a good chance I was about to crash and burn, taking Wheeler down with me.

I slid into the seat across from her, noticing her nose was a little pink from the cold. Like a lot of coffee shops in Denver this one was dog-friendly, so there was no reason for Sayer to be sitting outside.

"Why aren't you inside? Was the puppy acting up?" As soon as I was sitting, the dog scrambled his little body against my legs demanding to be picked up. I lifted the warm, wiggling bundle into my lap and laughed when his tongue immediately attacked my chin. "Thanks for agreeing to watch him for me for the hour."

She waved a hand and smiled at me. "I had to make a couple calls. I have a client in the middle of an ugly custody case and she needed to be talked off the ledge. I came out here to take the call. The puppy was fine. I think I should talk to Zeb about getting a dog for Hyde. Little boys should have a dog to play with." She shivered a little and I knew it wasn't from the cold when she muttered, "My father refused to let me have a pet. I wanted one so bad after my mom died. I was so alone in that house with him. I think a pet would have saved my sanity."

I made a noise in my throat and buried my face in the puppy's scruff. "Same. My dad said they were dirty and that we didn't do a good enough job cleaning the house as it was. It was bullshit. My mom scrubbed that place on her hands and knees every single day. He just didn't want us to have something that we wanted." I sighed. "It's probably a good thing we didn't have a pet. He would have used it against us to get his way."

Sayer nodded solemnly. "Same." She smiled at me and changed the subject. "I'm picking up dinner for my boys on the way home, do you want to join us? Hyde would love a chance to get his hands on that little guy." She pointed at the dog I was cuddling.

I shifted my gaze away from her and let out a little groan. So much for keeping the fact that I was planning on seeing Wheeler secret. If I told her I had plans she would think I was regressing and avoiding spending time with other people, and I didn't want that. She'd offered me shelter when I needed it and her gentle giant of a man was one of the main reasons I'd convinced myself to go back to work and forced myself back into society. I saw the way he was with Sayer, watched him break down her walls and build her back up. I realized I couldn't hide myself away forever, because when someone that came along that really wanted in, nothing would keep them out.

"I have plans tonight. Maybe another night this week I can come over with the puppy." I couldn't meet her gaze as she froze and blinked at me like an owl.

"You have plans?" She sounded stunned and I couldn't blame her. I'd hidden myself away for so long that I understood her surprise.

"Yeah. I uh . . . actually got the puppy for Wheeler to help him through his breakup. He was house-sitting for Dixie when all of that started to go down, so I inadvertently ended up with a front-row seat to all the carnage. I told him I would help him train Happy until he was ready to be left on his own. I'm taking the puppy over to his place and having dinner with him." The words sounded weird as I said them. It'd been such a long time since I'd planned a normal evening like that. I didn't really know what to do with it, and clearly neither did Sayer. She kept staring at me like I had sprouted horns.

"You're having dinner with . . . Wheeler? Just the two of you?" She blinked slowly and tilted her head to the side. "Well . . . that's surprising. I didn't even know you knew him."

I cleared my throat and shifted on my chair uneasily. I hated being put on the spot. "He sold me the Camry a while ago and then he was next door a lot when Dixie was in Mississippi. Our paths kept crossing." I shrugged a shoulder. "I guess I got used to him somewhere along the way."

Her lips twitched slightly and her blue eyes sparkled with humor. "You got used to him?"

I nodded a little and lifted my eyebrows at her. "Yeah. Why?"

She laughed and shook her head. "Nothing, you just might not want to mention that to Rowdy. You know the guy you grew up with. The one who would die for you, the one who will move heaven and earth for you. The guy who you also still flinch around, the guy who you still struggle to hug back, the guy who you can't look in the eye half the time, the guy you cancel on at least once a month when the two of you made plans. I think it might hurt his feelings if he knows you're making plans with another man when you still have a difficult time being alone with him." Rowdy was her little brother; of course she would immediately think about how hard it was for me to be around him and how deeply that hurt him.

I peeked at her over the top of Happy's head. "Wheeler hasn't seen me at the lowest points in my life. Rowdy has." He was there to pick me up after the college jock destroyed me and when Oliver nearly killed me. "I love him, but that can be hard." Especially when I was trying to be anyone but that girl.

Her smile faltered and all her teasing stopped. A serious look took over the mirth in her eyes and sympathetic understanding colored her tone when she told me, "I get that. I'm glad you found someone you're comfortable spending time with outside of family. Zeb has known Wheeler since they were kids. He went out of his way to give Zeb something to focus on when he got out of prison and he looked after his mom and his sister while he was locked up. By all accounts Hudson is a good guy and you couldn't have picked anyone better to get involved with."

"Whoa . . ." I held up a hand and leaned back in the chair. "Don't get ahead of yourself, Say. We aren't involved. He just broke off his engagement and that's not even the start of how complicated it is. He's nice to me and doesn't treat me like I'm going to shatter, even though it's obvious I might. I wanted to do something nice for him, and he needs my help. That's all."

She hummed a little and pushed a strand of platinum-blond hair off of her forehead. "I would agree that it was something simple if I didn't know you, Poppy. You got him a dog and you agreed to have dinner alone with him. Those aren't baby steps, love, those are leaps and bounds."

I groaned again and squeezed my eyes shut. "Did you know his ex is pregnant?"

Sayer was one of the few people in Denver that knew about my baby, and the only reason she did was because she had been there when Salem and Rowdy shared their happy news about my impending niece or nephew with us. She held me together when I felt like I was going to fall apart. I was happy for my sister but I couldn't deny the burn in my heart when I thought of everything

I had lost. I should have a six-year-old at home, a child that was the love of my life. Instead, all I had was a dead husband, a cargo hold full of baggage, and the kind of nightmares that followed me into my waking hours.

She gave a sharp nod. "He told Zeb one night over drinks. Zeb said that Wheeler was pretty shocked by the news but he's sure that he'll settle into it. He didn't have it easy growing up, so I'm sure he'll do everything in his power to make sure his child has everything he didn't."

He seemed more than shocked when he revealed the news about the baby to me. He seemed upset, almost angry, and that made me incredibly uneasy. I liked Wheeler but I knew I couldn't spend time with someone that resented and regreted a life that they were half responsible for creating. It wasn't fair to the baby, and it wasn't fair to those of us that would do anything, give anything, to have a chance to love what we'd lost.

"It's a lot. My past is so complicated and ugly and his future is so uncertain. Right now all I'm trying to do is be his friend." The kind of friend that was constantly picturing him naked and wondering what it would be like to have those tattooed hands all over me. So, like his best friend ever, really.

"Honestly, I'm thrilled you want to be his anything, so I'll take it." She reached out a hand and put her chilly fingers over mine. "One day at a time, Poppy. That's what you focus on. Not what was or what will be, but what *is*. You get through this dinner with him and then you get through whatever the next day brings with or without him because you will be all right no matter what happens. Okay?"

I nodded in agreement and forced a shaky smile. "Okay."

I could do one day at a time because I was finally in a place where I realized how very lucky I was to still be here making my way through the days, be they good or bad. I might not implicitly trust myself to do the right thing, but I did know if I stepped wrong and stumbled, there were plenty of people around me waiting to pick me up. For the first time in my life, I had a safe place to fail, which made me strong enough to want to try and live again.

Chapter 6

Wheeler

I couldn't stop watching her.

It wasn't anything new. When Rowdy first brought her by the shop in search of a car for her, I found myself unable to look away. I felt guilty as hell about it at the time because I was supposed to be a happily engaged man well on my way to planning a forever with Kallie, but there was something about Poppy that I found compelling. Initially it had been her mixture of beauty and sadness that caught my eye. In a perfect world she would never know the kind of ugliness that could make those golden eyes so haunted and afraid. The more our paths crossed and the more she let her rigid guard down around me, the more I realized the reason I couldn't look away was because she was a constant surprise. Just when I thought I knew how she was going to react or behave, she did something completely unexpected. Like show up at my garage out of the blue with a rambunctious puppy because she knew I was having a rough time in my personal life and could use a distraction.

Or like now, when I was entranced watching her do something as simple as eat dinner. I thought when I handed off the cheeseburger, minus tomato, she would nibble and pick at the messy meal delicately and carefully. She was so slight, seemed so fragile and breakable, that I was shocked when she dug into the burger with gusto and wolfed down the accompanying fries. At first she was nervous because she kept looking around my open living space like someone was going to jump out from behind the furniture and snatch her up. But eventually she asked me if I was going to eat all of my onion rings and I realized she simply had a healthy appetite when it came to food she liked. Once again, I imagined doing all kinds of really graphic and horrible things to her former husband. I figured the only reason she managed to get so thin and waif-like was because she had spent so long being denied the things she actually enjoyed eating. Her life had only recently become her own and it was obvious she hadn't quite settled into being able to indulge herself and give herself permission to cater to her own wants and needs.

I handed over the onion rings silently and tried to get my mind off of what those wants and needs might be and how many might apply to me.

"This place is really nice. I like how it's decorated." Her gaze was still darting around like she was searching out unseen enemies and she was fidgeting on her end of the couch, where we had set up in front of the TV. I told her she could be in charge of the remote and wasn't at all surprised when she told me she didn't really watch TV. I didn't know a single female of any age that didn't know what *Sons of Anarchy* was thanks to the prolific screen time given to Charlie Hunnam's ass. Even if they weren't into the violence and the Harleys, there was no denying they tuned in for Jax Teller. Since she insisted she was indifferent to whatever was on the screen, I turned on *Fast N' Loud* on the Discovery Channel. I sucked in a breath when I realized that it was the first time I'd actually gotten to pick what was on the TV in my own house. I'd always let Kallie have control of the remote, even during football season, which meant I hadn't seen the Broncos play since we'd moved in together.

Scowling a little over my wandering thoughts, I told Poppy, "Thanks, but it's all going soon. Kallie picked all the furniture out and did all the decorating. I told her today that she could have it all."

Her lips twitched and I noticed she had a little bit of ketchup on the side of her mouth. If she was any other girl hanging out on my couch, eating a burger I brought her, I would reach out and swipe it away, but I didn't want to spook her or alarm her by touching her without her permission, so I pointed to the spot on my own face and lifted my eyebrows at her.

She blushed prettily and gestured to the stupid, pale-colored couch. "I kind of figured. You don't strike me as a dove-gray kind of guy."

I snorted. "What kind of guy do I strike you as?" I was honestly curious about her answer.

She lifted a shoulder and let it fall. She was still dressed in her work clothes and her hair was pulled up in a high ponytail on the top of her head. She didn't have any makeup on and she hadn't managed to get all the ketchup off her face, and yet that simple gesture, done with an unpracticed and effortless grace, managed to be more provocative and alluring than the striptease I'd been given by the last girl I brought home in an effort to fuck my problems away. I balled up the wrapper to my burger, picked up the bottle of Laughing Lab that was in front of me, and reminded myself Poppy Cruz was all kinds of look-but-don't-touch until she asked to have my hands on her.

"I would guess black leather because that seems to be the standard for any guy who lives alone, but your car is so nice and you obviously aren't afraid of a little color." Her brandy-colored eyes swept across the tattoos that circled my throat and dropped below the collar of my T-shirt, and skimmed over the ones on the back of my hands. "So maybe something blue or red with white piping."

I hadn't really thought about what I was going to replace Kallie's awful choice in couches with but now that she mentioned it I kind of liked the idea of something red. I could try and find something that looked vintage but was still comfortable enough that I could sit my happy ass on it in front of the tv and watch some goddamn football whenever I wanted to. It would be reclaiming my space.

"I bought this house and pretty much handed the task of making it a home off to Kallie." I ran a hand over my face and nudged the puppy that was asleep on the toe of my boot. Happy lifted sleepy eyes to mine and begrudgingly got to his feet so I could stand up and take the trash to the kitchen. "I wanted her to love it here. I wanted her to make it her own." I blew out a breath and shook my head when Poppy's knowing eyes hit mine. "I didn't realize that when she was putting the house together she was leaving me out in the cold. None of this is for me." It never had been and I could see it all so clearly now. "When I was growing up I never lived anywhere long enough to have my own space. I guess I got used to trying to fit myself into whatever nook and cranny was left." I'd blindly allowed Kallie to push me out of the first home that was actually mine because I was so depressingly accustomed to not belonging anywhere.

I heard Poppy exhale a breath and then her fingers were lightly touching my arm. If I hadn't been so twisted up inside my own memories, I would have let out a victory whoop. I understood the significance of her voluntarily putting her hands on me two days in a row and I could only pray that she did as well.

"This place is all yours now, Wheeler. You worked hard for it and you deserve to make it a place where you want to be." She tilted her chin down a little and let go of her hold on my arm. "You should make it a place that both you and your child will think of as safe and warm, a place you both can grow into . . . together."

Her words made me physically jerk, so I took a step away from her and turned to make my way to the kitchen. I hadn't stopped to think about the fact that I was going to be responsible for creating a home not only for myself, but also for my kid. I'd never settled anywhere, the closest being the spot on Zeb's bedroom floor when we were teenagers because his mom never told him no when he asked if I could stay over. I didn't know if I had the tools required to turn a house into a loving home for someone else, especially considering I'd failed at doing it for myself up until this point in my life. It wasn't like anyone had set an example for me when I was growing up. I'd been shuffled from place to place so often that to this day I still had stuff in boxes from when I'd moved out of my apartment and into this house with Kallie. That same stuff had stayed in boxes regardless of what foster home I'd been in. They were never unpacked and they sat gathering dust waiting for the next time I was uprooted and displaced.

I heard Poppy follow me into the kitchen and wasn't surprised when I heard the puppy as well. The little dog wanted to be right in the thick of things and wasn't keen on letting his humans out of his sight.

I tossed the trash and leaned back against the counter where the sink was. "I'm going to need a nursery. Fuck. What do I know about putting together a nursery?" I was clueless.

Poppy stood on the opposite side of the kitchen where a big butcher-block island divided the space that Kallie told me she designed to be something called shabby chic. To me it looked like she had taken her grandmother shopping and let her pick out whatever struck her fancy. The more I was noticing my ex's mark on my house, the more aggravated and restless I started to feel. That unease was intensified by the woman looking at me with sympathy and understanding shining out of her eyes.

"You know home isn't really about what color your couch is or what you hang on the wall." Her voice was quiet like always but there was a firm thread woven throughout it that refused to be ignored. It was like she knew the words she was saying were going to matter to me long after she was no longer standing in front of me, so she had to make them unforgettable. "Home is about knowing you are in the right place with the right people." She gave me a lopsided grin. "Plus, once you know what you're having, you can get on Pinterest and learn all about how to decorate a nursery."

That startled a laugh out of me. "Do I look like I know how to use Pinterest?"

She cocked her head to the side and lowered her lashes shyly. "I'll show you how."

I pushed off the counter and took the steps required to move me across the space separating us. I needed to change the subject before I came up with any excuse I could find to keep her close. I copied her pose on the opposite side of the island and hid a grin when her gaze went immediately to where my T-shirt pulled tight across my chest and tugged against the bulge of my biceps. "Is that why you came here when you got out of the hospital? Denver was the right place and your sister found the right people?"

I watched her shutters close and her walls go up. The brightness in her eyes dimmed as her lush mouth pulled into a frown. Right in front of my eyes the woman that had devoured her cheeseburger and enjoyed a simple night in front of the TV, like any other twentysomething typically did on a weeknight, turned into the woman that had escaped near death at the hands of her deranged lover. She shrank in on herself, almost as if she was trying to disappear inside her skin. It was the first time I'd ever directly addressed what she had been through and I regretted bringing it up, but the elephant in the room couldn't be ignored forever, not if we were going to be spending as much time together as I wanted.

"I'm sorry, Poppy. Not my story, not my business."

She shook her head and wrapped her arms around herself in a gesture that I was starting to recognize as one she used when she was extra anxious. She wouldn't let anyone else touch her, so she had resorted to wrapping her own arms around herself when she needed a hug.

"No, it's okay. I mean, I know you know. Everyone knows. I was on CNN for goodness' sake." She shifted on her feet and bit down on her lower lip. "No place felt safe after I got out of the hospital. My head was so caught up in everything Oliver had done. My body was broken just as badly as my mind, but Rowdy and Salem refused to let me disappear. They brought me here because they knew I wasn't up to fighting my parents if they showed up to take me back to Texas. I was ready to give up on everything. Everything felt so pointless and hopeless. I always seemed to end up back where I started." She tugged on the end of her ponytail and lifted her eyes to mine. The pain and the force of her bad memories sucked the air out of my lungs. I'd been let down and disappointed a lot in my life, but I'd never been destroyed like she had. It was gut-wrenching to see. Watching Poppy struggle to pull herself back from the edge of horror made me question if I would be strong enough to rebuild myself the way this young woman had. She'd been devastated but here she was, still fighting and forging on. "They chose me and as I got better I chose them back. So yes, I'm here because of Salem and Rowdy. I was lucky I got Sayer as well. They are my right people."

I exhaled and ran a hand through my hair. She was right. She had made national news with headlines that screamed Kidnapping, Rape, Suicide. I remembered vague images of a frail body covered in blood and other too-horrible-to-imagine things being wheeled into an ambulance. I never stopped to process that the image on my television was this beautiful woman standing in front of me now. The knowledge turned my stomach and left a bitter taste in my mouth. "I'm going to ask you a question but you don't have to answer, okay?"

She considered me for a long moment and then nodded as she whispered, "Okay."

I tapped my fingers on the wood between us, my expression knitting into one of genuine curiosity. "Why didn't you want to go with your parents? Believe me, I know all about being seriously disappointed by the people that are supposed to love you unconditionally, but you went through so much, why wouldn't you want as much support around you as possible?"

If it was possible she shrank into herself even more. She went pale, her normally rich and exotic skin tone dulling out. She leaned forward and rested her elbows on the butcher block and then cradled her forehead in her hands. For a minute, I thought she was going to pass out. I moved over to where she was propped up and stood close to her. I almost put my hand on the center of her back until I realized that was probably the worst thing I could do at the moment. I desperately needed her to give me permission to touch her. Keeping my hands off her, especially when everything inside of me was dying to comfort her, was taking a near Herculean effort.

"Forget I asked. Clearly, it's a good thing your sister swooped in and brought you here before your parents showed up." Her reaction had me thinking they were in the running for the shittiest-parents-in-the-universe award right next to my mom.

She shook her head where she held it and peeked at me through a narrow slit between her spread fingers. "The stuff that wasn't on the news is almost worse than the stuff that was."

I barked out a startled laugh. "How is that possible?" Her husband had stalked and tortured her. If that wasn't enough she'd had no choice but to watch the man eat a bullet because he was too much of a coward to take responsibility for his actions when the cops caught up to them. I couldn't imagine anything being more horrific than that.

I heard her mutter something that wasn't clear and after a drawn-out moment where I thought she was going to shut down on me, she pushed off the counter and reached up to pull her hair out of the elastic holding it so she could rake her fingers through the long honey-tinted locks over and over again.

"My father is a difficult man. When he came across the border as a child, it was a terrible experience for him. His mother died when they were making their way through the desert in Texas and my grandfather convinced my dad that it was his fault. He told him she died so he could live. He insisted the only reason they were making their way into America was because my grandmother wanted a better life for my father than he would have in Juárez." She huffed out a breath and lifted her eyes to the ceiling. "The truth was my grandfather had gotten in business with one of the cartels and there was a price on his head. The whole family was in danger, but instead of taking responsibility for his actions, he blamed my dad and used his guilt to ensure his obedience and compliance. They were lessons my father learned well and had no problem passing on to his own children. Behave or bad things happen. I honestly believe he still holds himself responsible for his mother's death."

I blinked at her and opened my mouth to say something but shut it just as quickly when I realized I had no words. My upbringing was no picnic but it was a breeze compared to what she was revealing about hers.

"Salem used to push and push him. I think she was trying to force him to break. She wanted him to do something, to leave some kind of mark so she could prove that what was going on inside our house wasn't right." She let out a strangled-sounding laugh and put a hand to her throat like she was trying to capture the tragic sound. "But he never hit us, not once. He simply let us know every single minute, of every single day, that he deserved better, that God had let him down by saddling him with a worthless, ungrateful family, daughters that were sinful and unworthy. I did my best to please him. I followed in my mother's footsteps. I walked on eggshells and didn't speak unless spoken to. I brought home straight A's and only allowed people he approved of in my life. I tried to be perfect."

She lowered her head so that our gazes locked, and once again the memories and recollections shining out of her eyes battered against me. Her experiences hurt and I wasn't the one that had to live through them.

"Occasionally, he would act like I'd finally done something right, like I'd earned his approval. I would soak those moments up like a sponge, until I realized the only reason he lowered himself to giving me any kind of praise was to hurt either my mom or Salem. We weren't his loved ones or his family. We were toys he played with and tormented for his amusement."

She closed her eyes briefly and let out a sigh that had so much emotion in it I thought it was going to knock her off her feet. When her eyelids fluttered back open I knew I needed to stay braced for the rest of her story.

"It wasn't until I moved home after my freshman year of college that I realized what a truly awful man he was. Without me and Salem in the house the only person around to take the brunt of his blame and brimstone was my mom. He never loved her. He married her because she served a purpose and had standing in the community. She was good for his image and legitimized him as something more than a struggling immigrant. The only reason he stayed with her was because a wife and kids were part of the required packaging if you wanted to sell yourself to others as a man of God and as an upstanding citizen. He couldn't preach about relationships and family if he didn't have his own."

"Poppy . . ." I breathed out her name not sure if I was urging her to stop or to keep going. My mom left me but ultimately that abandonment saved me from a life of being dragged from flophouse to flophouse as she chased after her next fix. I always felt like I was missing out not having a real family consisting of both a mom and a dad, but Poppy's revelations were making me feel like maybe I had lucked out by getting left behind. Things had never been great, but they hadn't ever been as bad as she was describing. Who wanted four walls to call your own when you were trapped inside them with a nightmare that never ended? Unending days of belittling and breaking down sounded unbearable.

"When I came home from college, he told me over and over that I was a disgrace. He didn't bother to hide the fact that he was disgusted by the mere sight of me. Salem was long gone by then and my mom was so emotionally stripped and physically worn down that I was his only available target. I spent so much of my life trying to earn his love, killing myself for his approval, that I let him convince me I was nothing. I believed him when he told me I couldn't be trusted to make decisions for myself. I'd made a mess of things the first time I struck out on my own and there were no second chances."

I wanted to ask what went wrong when she left for college but I didn't get a chance to put a word in edgewise. She placed her hands flat on the counter and leaned toward me a little, her long hair slithering over her shoulders and down around her face. If I pressed forward I could get my hands in it and stop her from hiding, but something told me she needed that layer of protection between us as she continued giving me words that wounded.

"My father is the one that brought Oliver around." When she said his name her entire body convulsed. "He was a deacon in Dad's church and had all the things my father thought would make an acceptable son-in-law." She frowned, her eyebrows snapping sharply above her nose. "Meaning he was a carbon copy of my dad: controlling, abusive, angry. He hid it well up until he had a ring on my finger, but not even an hour after our vows, he let his true colors shine through."

"Why didn't someone help you? Where was your sister? Your mom?" The words came out far angrier than I intended them to but I was furious she'd had to face all of that on her own.

She gave another one of those high-pitched, hysterical laughs and shook her head slowly from side to side. "Salem didn't know until after the fact. She would have stopped it. She would have driven to Texas from wherever she was and kidnapped me to keep me from making such a big mistake, and my mom . . ." Again her head rocked back and forth. "She wouldn't ever cross my father. If he hadn't spent a lifetime ruining her maybe she would have tried to keep me from making the same mistake she did, but there was nothing left in her. I found that out the hard way when I told her that Oliver was hitting me and she told me to try harder to make him happy."

"The fuck!" My hands tightened into fists and I couldn't stop myself from rounding the counter and walking right up to her. We were so close that I could feel the way she was vibrating and I knew she could feel the heat of my anger coming off my skin. "That's not okay, Poppy."

She turned her head to look at me and I instinctively reached out a hand to stop her from moving away from me when she took a step back. I stopped myself before my hand landed on her arm and her eyes locked on my palm hovering awkwardly in the air. She faced me, and reached up and grabbed my dangling appendage and carefully laced her fingers through mine. I was stunned at the undeniable strength I could feel running through the thin and delicate digits.

"It wasn't right, which is why, when Salem got the whole story, she stepped in. She put herself between me and everyone that has ever hurt me. She went to Texas and blackmailed my father in order to keep him away. She doesn't know that I know, but I overheard Sayer telling Zeb the story one night. She protected me and fought for me when I could barely stand being around her. She forced her way in after I did my best to shut her out because I was so ashamed that I'd ended up just like our mom." Her voice dropped and she squeezed my fingers. "She did all of that because she loves me and she wants to defend me when I can't defend myself. That's how she made Denver home for me."

We stared at each other for a moment that seemed to stretch on infinitely. She held my hand but it felt more like she had those shaking fingers curled around my heart.

"Poppy." I whispered her name and she tilted her head back and blinked up at me.

"Wheeler." I was astounded that there was a hint of amusement in her voice. How she could find anything to laugh about after what she just told me was unfathomable. Her father had handed her off to a monster like it was nothing. She made her way out of hell with one of the purest hearts I had ever seen.

"I really want to give you a hug, probably more for me than for you, but I told you not to let anyone touch you without permission." I knew I sounded a little desperate but I didn't care. "So, can you put me out of my misery and give me permission to hold you, just for a second, please?"

Her eyes widened and then her obscenely long lashes dropped as she nodded timidly. "Okay, since you asked so nicely." The humor was now thick around every word and she was laughing for real as I carefully wrapped my arms around her.

I sighed into the top of her head as I pulled her to my chest. Her hair smelled like flowers and felt like silk as I rested my cheek against the soft strands. We stood like that for a long time, me with my arms curled around her as she stood stock-still. I could feel her heart beat and I wanted to think it was racing like it was because she was affected by my touch rather than because she was terrified of being so close to a man she didn't know all that well.

I told myself not to breathe, not to move a single muscle, as her hands slowly lifted and gently touched my sides above the tops of my jeans. It felt like her palms were burning their imprint into my skin as they slowly, achingly started to inch their way around my back so that she was lightly holding me in return. I heard her make a sound that may have been one of pleasure, but just in case it was one of fear, I leaned away from her so I could see her face.

Her gaze was centered on the tattooed candle that was burning bright and surrounded by light and smoke right on the center of my throat. She watched the movement as I swallowed hard and her gaze drifted up to mine.

"No one has ever asked me for permission for anything before. No one has ever cared what I wanted before." The murmur of her words brushed across the base of my throat and my cock went instantly hard. I knew she felt it because her eyes popped wide and her breath hitched as she looked up at me and ordered quietly, "Ask me what I want right now, Wheeler."

I was equal parts terrified and intrigued by what her answer was going to be, so I tightened my hold on her and lowered my head so that my lips were hovering right by the tantalizing curve of her ear. "What do you want right now, Poppy?" I would give it to her no matter what it might cost me. I'd never had much but it seemed like everything compared to what she had. I wanted to take the entire world and wrap a giant bow around it and hand it to her. I'd tried to do that for Kallie, but she'd never appreciated it. Something told me Poppy would never dismiss anything that she was given because the only thing she was used to taking from people was their bullshit and abuse. Anything gifted from the heart and with kindness would be cherished and treasured.

I could see some kind of internal battle waging behind the glow in her fantastic eyes. She was balanced on the precipice of something, trying to decide which way she wanted to fall; lucky me she picked the option that landed her in my arms.

"I want you to kiss me."

Like I said, I couldn't look away, not for a minute, because the girl was full of surprises. It was my turn to chuckle lightly. "Well, because you asked so nicely." I tossed her words back at her right before I bent and touched my lips to hers.

Chapter 7

Poppy

It was too soon . . . probably for me and most definitely for him, considering he was all set to marry someone else up until very recently, but that didn't stop me from blurting out what I really wanted from him.

I didn't know what it was about this guy that made me do things that were totally outside of my comfort zone. I'd never made the first move in my life. I'd never had to because the few men that had been in and out of my life had targeted me and hunted me like I was easy prey . . . I was. Too young and naive, too broken and scared, both physically and emotionally. Like the predators they were, they could see my weakness from miles away, so they came to me. They never gave me a chance to decide if they were what I really wanted or not because they moved in for the kill so fast that I was consumed by them. They took me down and left me bleeding before I understood what was happening. There was no time to decide if I wanted those angry kisses and those hard hands on me. There was no room to move if I felt threatened or afraid.

Wheeler was different.

There was no question that I wanted to know what his lips felt like when they landed on mine. I'd never been touched by tattooed, work-roughened hands, and more and more I found myself drifting off wondering what that would feel like. He tore apart things that were battered and beaten down and put them back together so that they were shiny and new. He took something that was worthless and made it priceless. I couldn't deny that there was a part of me that wanted to know if he could do the same thing with me.

Plus, I wanted a kiss . . . just one. A single kiss that I wouldn't regret later on down the road. One I'd asked for. One that was mine. One that wouldn't make me kick myself and say "I should have known better" because I did know better but I was asking him to kiss me anyways. I wanted a kiss that was given, not taken.

He didn't touch me even though I'd given him permission to do so.

He let his hands fall from my back, where they had been resting when he hugged me. I got the sense that he didn't want me to feel trapped, that he wanted me to be able to pull away at any moment if I changed my mind. His silent consideration and unwavering thoughtfulness made me even more certain that I wanted him to close the few inches that separated us. I wouldn't have asked him to let me go but I realized as he leaned down from his far superior height that I was glad he did. I was the one moving closer. It wasn't him pulling me. I couldn't see anything beyond the burning blue of his eyes.

When his lips touched mine I stopped breathing. I barely felt them but I felt the heat they generated all throughout my body. It was a featherlight hint of pressure but the impact almost took me to the ground as my knees started to quiver and shake. I had to put one hand on the center of his chest and the other on the countertop to keep myself from folding and falling to the ground.

He tasted like beer and something else that was infinitely male. He tasted like excitement and fantasy. He tasted forbidden and destined all in the same sweep of my tongue across the barely opened part in his lips. If this was kissing, then I'd been doing it wrong since day one. This felt like being kissed by someone that knew how important it was for a girl to get kissed right. He erased the greedy and selfish lips of the college train wreck and he obliterated the painful, punishing lips of the man that had married me and then done his best to end me.

Wheeler took a step closer, our chests pressed against one another, and instead of feeling crowded or controlled, I wanted to press myself more fully into him. It was the freedom he gave me to get away that kept me moving closer in. I moved the hand that was capturing each beat of his heart up the solid wall of his chest and curled it around the side of his neck. He had a bluebird tattooed there, and with each pulse of his heart it felt like the wings were fluttering delicately under the tips of my fingers as I traced the vein that ran under the inked skin. This was by far the closest I'd willingly been to a man in ages and I didn't stop to process the fact that I wanted to get even closer.

I leaned all the way into him, forcing him to catch himself on the counter, because even with my mouth hungrily licking and nipping at him, and even with my breasts flattened against the clearly defined muscles of his chest, he didn't lay a hand on me. He wouldn't, when I opened my mouth to give his gently seeking tongue access or when I lifted up on my tippy toes so that I could have a better angle to get my hand around the back of his neck so that I could pull him down more fully into the kiss. I wanted to make this moment last forever.

It was sweet. It was hot. It made me forget, for just a second, that I was afraid.

His teeth grazed my bottom lip and I shivered but not because I was scared that he was going to bite. I shivered because that little nip made my heart race and had all the parts of my body that had sworn off men reconsider their vow. My nipples pulled tight and rubbed against the lace of my bra. That spot between my legs that I told myself I was going to pretend didn't exist after Oliver, reminded me that it was still there and in perfect working order by pulsing quick and hard. The quiet ache made me shift uncomfortably and there was no refuting the fact that being this close to him, having his tongue dance across mine, was making me wet with want.

It was such a foreign feeling. So much stronger and bigger than the innocent desire fostered from believing empty promises and perfect lies that fell out of a pretty and practiced mouth. This was the kind of yearning that had teeth. The kind that sank into your bones and worked its way deep under your skin. This was the kind of longing that could and would push out everything else until it was the only thing left. There was no room for fear or regret because craving and hunger took up all the available space. Instead of being empty, I was full of all the amazing things this man made me feel. My starving soul and hungry heart wanted to be greedy and gluttonous. They wanted to eat him up and go back for more.

He turned his head, slanted his mouth a little, and then moved in deeper and with more determination. His hands stayed firmly at his sides but I still felt like he was touching all over. His breath whispered across my lips, the very tip of his tongue slicked across the seam, and I opened without a second thought.

He didn't touch me with his hands but his tongue left no damp, slick surface unexplored. He tasted. He teased. He taunted when I asked for more without words. He was gentle but there was no mistaking the fact that he was kissing me in a way that would be remembered. The imprint of his lips on mine, the flavor that was all Wheeler, was going to linger forever on the tip of my tongue. He was everywhere and yet the only places where we were touching were the places where I was clinging to him.

Tongues twisted, teeth clashed, breath mingled, and I was pretty sure his name escaped on a whisper but I was so busy trying to inhale every single second of this moment that I swallowed it and kissed him back like I was ravenous . . . because I was. This kiss fed something deep inside of me that had never been fed. I didn't know what it was like to get what I wanted. I didn't know what it was like to be treated like . . . to be kissed like . . . I was something precious and prized. It was all enough to go to my head and make any common sense I had fizzle and wave. It might be too soon but this kiss had me ready to remember what it was like to dream and hope for something and someone special.

I let go of the counter and was lifting up my other hand to touch the side of his face when a loud crash had us both breaking apart. I gasped, he swore, and we both blinked at each other like someone had suddenly turned on the lights in a very dark room. He took a step back as I steadied myself and we both jumped as another crash sounded from the living room. His dark eyebrows shot up as I suddenly bolted into action, barking out, "The dog!"

as I ran toward the other room. I heard his heavy footsteps behind me as we raced to see what kind of destruction our lack of
attention had caused.

Happy had the entire coffee table knocked over on its side and
was eagerly licking up the spilled contents of Wheeler's abandoned beer. The puppy's little tail was wagging furiously as he
stopped lapping up the mess to look at us, so proud of himself
and looking for accolades.

Wheeler groaned and stepped around me to pick up the sturdy
little dog. He held the wiggling animal up in front of his face,
much like he did the day I first brought him to the garage. "Not
cool." The puppy yipped excitedly and fought to lick Wheeler's
face. "Is the beer bad for him? Do we need to worry about him
getting sick or anything?" He bit the words out and his face shifted
from post-kiss bliss to something much harder and angrier. His
adorable dimples were long gone and that scowl that seemed to
have staked claim between his brows was back.

I bent to straighten the coffee table. "How much was left in
the bottle?"

Wheeler looked at the now empty bottle on the floor and
shifted his gaze back to mine. "Less than half." He seemed far
more upset than a little spilled beer called for as he shifted the
puppy in his arms and started to pace back and forth in front of
me as he waited for me to answer.

"It should be fine. A little bit of beer isn't bad for dogs. Just
keep an eye on him throughout the night and see if he gets sick
or seems to act funny. If he does, text me and I'll come back over
and look at him."

Wheeler rounded on me, eyes wide and a heated flush working its way up underneath the ink that covered his throat. His

sharp cheekbones turned a furious shade of pink as he ground out between gritted teeth, "You can't leave him here with me. You have to take him."

The puppy looked up at the man holding on to him like he could sense his mood and the happy, tongue lolling stopped, replaced with a whimper and a full-body shake. I had a similar reaction. I crossed my arms over my chest and told myself not to freak out as the butterflies he woke up in my stomach turned into stone. I'd had my share of men that seemed good only to end up as something beyond bad in my life. I watched them change right before my eyes. I hated to think that Wheeler could be one of them, that I had been so wrong again, but the chill coming from those arctic eyes of his and the way he was looking at me like all he wanted was for me to take the puppy and go had me seriously second-guessing everything I thought I knew about this man.

"No, not tonight. Tonight he's supposed to stay with you. That's why I brought him over." I wasn't used to saying no, so the words came out far weaker than I intended them to. I knew how important it was to stand my ground now, to make my boundaries clear. So, even though it was hard, I didn't back down even when he growled at me in frustration.

Wheeler gave his dark head a shake and continued pacing back and forth in front of me. "You can't leave me alone with this puppy, Poppy." He stopped in front of me and I realized that the frost coming from his big body wasn't anger at the mess or the dog but fear. Anger, I had no space for, no tolerance or time for, but fear . . . that was an old friend and I understood how powerful and consuming it could be. Fear could exclude all else if you let it and I didn't want that for him. He was wild-eyed and barely containing his panic as his voice shook. "I obviously have no clue what I'm do-ing. The dog isn't even here for a few hours and I'm already drop-ping the ball. What if I get so distracted by my dick that I forget that I'm supposed to be taking care of a baby? Jesus." He shoved his free hand through his hair. "I'm not ready for this . . . for any of it."

The last of his words sliced through my already tender heart like a double-edged knife. I knew he wasn't ready, that his heart-ache was still too fresh and new, but having that knowledge vali-dated still hurt.

"Well, I hate to be the bad guy, but you don't have much of a choice. The puppy needs you and your baby sure as hell is going to need you regardless if you're ready or not." I kind of needed him too but I wasn't sure I was anywhere close to admitting that. "Shoving the responsibility off on someone else isn't go-ing to help you prepare for everything that's coming your way, Wheeler." I tucked some hair behind my ear and reached out to pat the puppy on the head. He whimpered at me and I looked up at Wheeler as he gave me a worried look similar to the one on the puppy's face. "You can do this, Hudson. I know you can."

Maybe it was because I used his first name or because I moved my hand from the dog's head to the center of his chest, but the harsh lines on his face softened and some of the stark terror leaked out of his eyes. He took a shuddering breath and slowly lowered his head so that he was looking at the tips of his boots.

"Sorry for the freak-out. I usually have a better handle on my-self than that. Lately, I feel like I'm drowning, and instead of try-ing to swim for shore, I just keep getting pulled out deeper and deeper." He did look like a man that was very much adrift, one who was looking for anything that seemed familiar and solid.

Taking a calming breath, I stepped into him and wrapped

both him and the now calm puppy in my arms. I hadn't accepted a hug in forever and it had been twice as long as that since I'd offered one. But this hug felt right. It felt necessary. It felt right. I squeezed him quickly and let him go.

"You might feel like you are flailing but you're keeping your head above water and that's all that really matters. I promise I won't let you sink, even when you want to." That was a lesson I'd had to learn the hard way. It was difficult to appreciate everyone that was trying to help you when all you wanted to do was wallow in your own misery. I told him the very thing that made me go through with not only showing up at his house tonight but also asking for that kiss. "You will figure all of this out, one step at a time." I didn't tell him some days were going to seem impossible because those days always passed. I cleared my throat and made my way over to where my coat was thrown on the back of the couch that was most definitely not meant for a guy like Wheeler. "Thanks for dinner. Next time we get together, we'll actually work on improving the dog's behavior instead of ours."

He didn't say anything but he did make a strangled noise that might have been a laugh had the circumstances been different. I was at the door ready to let myself back into the real world when he stopped me by saying my name softly. I looked at him over my shoulder and felt my heart turn itself inside out.

The man and the dog, both looking lost and a little bit scared, made me want to take my coat off, put my purse down, and agree to stay so I could hold both of them. They needed to figure this out on their own and Wheeler really needed the time to see that there was no perfect way to be a puppy parent or a people parent. He was going to have to find the way that worked best for him.

He lifted his hand and rubbed the pad of his thumb across

the curve of his bottom lip. I watched in mute fascination as his tongue shot out and followed the same trail, almost like he was trying to find any part of our kiss that might be lingering there. The motion made my thighs quiver and had all the air in my lungs whooshing out.

"When I said I wasn't ready, I didn't mean I wasn't ready for you, honey." Inadvertently my gaze slid across the front of him and landed on the very obvious bulge in the front of his jeans. He chuckled and shook his head at me, his voice deep and rough when he told me, "That's not what I meant. Any straight guy with working equipment would be ready for you at the drop of a hat if it was only about sex. I'm ready for more than that."

The butterflies woke back up and they didn't just flutter, they did the damn electric slide across one side of my belly to the other. He sounded so sure, but with everything else he was dealing with, I didn't know how he could be. I refused to be one of the weights that was tied around his waist dragging him down under the surface of that dark and murky water he was treading. Besides, I didn't know that I had more to give to anyone, even myself. Most of the time I felt like I was hollowed out and empty. Half the time I was getting by on the bare minimum. I couldn't afford to give what I had left to someone else, even if that someone made me act like a girl who had never been broken, a girl that didn't have anything to fear.

"You only recently got out of a long-term relationship that had a very complicated ending. The last thing you need is to start another one that has a nearly impossible beginning."

I was out the door and headed toward my car when he called my name once again. I told myself to keep going but my feet stopped moving of their own accord and once again I was look-

ing over my shoulder at him. He was standing in the doorway,
shoulder braced against the side, arm above his head with the
puppy still in his grasp. I needed to memorize every single thing
about that image because it was one that communicated very
clearly that while my mind might not be ready for whatever it
was he was offering, my body sure as hell was. My heart was
caught somewhere in the middle of the two. Never had a game
of tug-of-war been so complicated.

"I saw you, Poppy. When I had no right and no reason to be
looking, I saw you." The words hung between us as I paused
by the car and stared up at him. "I saw how sad you were, how
afraid you were. I saw how angry and alone you were. I saw how
desperate you were to hide." I shivered and opened my mouth to
respond but no words came out. It didn't matter because he kept
going. "All those things that you think make this something that
is impossible to start, I saw them long before you saw me and I
still couldn't look away." He tilted his chin up in that badass way
guys had and pushed off the doorframe. "Shoot me a text when
you get home so I know that you're safe. I'll call you if Happy
needs you." Not if he needed me, but if the dog did.

He was gone from sight by the time I got myself into the car
and buckled in. I couldn't breathe. I couldn't see straight. I sure
as hell couldn't drive, so I sat there in front of his house for a solid
twenty minutes while I struggled to get myself under control.

There was no seeking approval and begging for forgiveness
because there was no hiding the faults in the dark. He had already seen them all and he kissed me anyways. Because I wanted
him to and he wanted me to have what I wanted.

With shaking hands, I started the car and managed to make
my way home. I even managed to send the ordered text message

to let him know I was safe and sound. He sent back a simple *k* that I stared at for far longer than I'd like to admit. Rowdy often texted to check up on me and to make sure I hadn't retreated back into the void, but I'd never had a man whose lips had touched mine, who told me he saw me and was ready for me, bother to keep tabs on me. In fact, it was usually the men I was intimate with that I needed protecting from. Everything with Wheeler was so new, and that made it all the more confusing.

Still holding my phone, I called my sister before I realized my finger touched her name. She picked up on the first ring and I wasn't surprised that she sounded overjoyed to hear from me. I'd put Salem through the wringer over the last few years, but each day I got closer to closing that gap I'd allowed the men in my life to wedge between us. At the time I didn't realize isolating me from the person that loved me the most was a way for them to maintain control but I saw it so clearly now.

After returning her greeting, I blurted out, "I asked Wheeler to kiss me tonight" with no preamble or warning.

She gasped and I heard something clatter. I realized it was the phone a second later as she screamed, "Oh my God," but the sound was muffled and sounded like it was coming from miles away.

"You kissed, Wheeler, as in the guy who just canceled his wedding to a raging she-beast?"

Her voice was shrill, so I had to hold the phone away from my ear. "Um . . . yeah."

She let out a breath and I could picture her chewing on her lip and pacing in circles as she continued to fire off questions. "When did you start seeing him? How long has this been going on? Are you ready to date? You know he has a baby on the way with his ex, right?" She took a breath and let it out slowly. "Are you okay?"

I shook my arms free from my jacket and let it fall in the center of the floor. Tonight was the kind of night that made me wish I drank. I didn't touch anything that had the ability to lower my defenses or inhibitions. I'd done a good job of being an easy target most of my life, and I learned early on to avoid anything that made going in for the kill easier. I threw myself on my couch and stared unseeingly at my ugly popcorn ceiling.

"I'm fine, or I will be." That was the mantra that kept me going when giving up felt a million times easier.

She sighed and her voice was breathless with something I hadn't heard her direct toward me in a very long time . . . hope. "You wanted him to kiss you?"

Grouchily I snapped, "Yes. That's why I feel like I'm losing my mind. I haven't wanted anything to do with anyone in months and months and the first guy I find myself attracted to is in the middle of a horrible breakup and impending fatherhood. When am I going to learn?" She laughed a little, which made me even more annoyed. "I don't see what's funny about this situation, Salem."

She paused and when she spoke her voice was thick with emotion. "I'm laughing so I don't cry." She exhaled heavily and I was the one fighting back tears when she told me, "You've never let me in before when you were tangled up with a guy. I always felt like you didn't trust me to know what was going on in your love life because I left. I let you down and you couldn't let me in. I'm sorry that you're freaking out right now, but honestly I've been waiting for this phone call since I was eighteen and put Texas in my rearview mirror. I missed so much, Poppy. You have no idea what it means to me that you are giving this to me now."

No amount of laughter could hide the fact that she was crying uncontrollably. She was pregnant but her words made me doubt hormones were the sole reason behind her outburst.

I sniffled a little and used the tips of my fingers to brush away the few stray tears that managed to escape the prison of my tightly closed lashes. "He's nothing like anyone I've ever known."

She made a considering noise and there was a smile in her voice when she asked, "Is that so?"

I sighed. "It scares me because my heart has been wrong before."

She snorted and her tone was sharp when she told me, "No, your heart was listening to what someone else was telling it to do. This is the first time it's been able to speak for itself. Listen to it, little sister."

"I'm afraid of what it might have to say, Salem." My voice shook and so did my hands.

"That's how you know the message is important, Poppy."

There wasn't much to say after that, so I told her good-bye, promised to set aside a weekend afternoon for her so we could get together, and hung up.

She was right that the message might be important, I just wasn't sure I was in the right place to hear it.

Chapter 8

Wheeler

Istayed up with Happy all through the night. I didn't take my eyes off him for a second, a task that was much easier to do without the silent, unassuming temptation that was Poppy Cruz hovering so close yet just out of reach. I was pissed at myself that I got so distracted by her pillowy lips and intoxicating flavor that I forgot about Happy and his penchant for getting into things. I wanted to be the guy that could do it all, juggle all the balls: run a business, romance the girl, train the dog, be a good dad and a supportive coparent, but every time I took my eyes off one ball, they all seemed to fall. It was frustrating and infuriating because there wasn't a single ball that I was ready to let go of. I needed to learn how to be a better juggler . . . like one that was good enough to work at a circus or entertain kids at birthday parties.

After spending the night with Happy curled up at my side, dreaming his puppy dreams, which made his tiny paws kick, I knew that he was worth every headache he was inevitably going to cause and every hour of lost sleep that was going to make my workday miserable. He was so fucking cute and cuddly that

I didn't mind the other side of the bed being empty for once. There were honestly no words to describe how relieved I was that he didn't seem to have any issues from getting into the things he wasn't supposed to the night before.

I felt the same way about the girl who tasted like honey and moved just as thickly and slowly through my blood.

Everything I did with Poppy was slow and careful. It was thoughtful steps moving toward each other until we met somewhere in the middle. There was no rush. Everything was deliberate and done in a way that meant we could get it exactly right.

I never considered how much of a turn-on it could be to kiss someone while not laying a single finger on them. It had been shy. It had been hesitant. It had been tentative . . . and then it changed. It got demanding. It got needy. It became desperate and frantic in the best way. Without the use of my hands I had to lure her closer with nothing more than my mouth. I couldn't feel her, so I had to taste every single bit of her I could. I couldn't hold her, so I had to keep her in place with passion and the allure of what else was waiting.

I almost lost it when she wrapped her arm around the back of my neck. Everything inside of me was screaming that I should pin her to the counter, that I should put my hands on her pretty honey-colored skin, that I should grind the throbbing flesh behind my zipper into the sweet apex of her thighs, but I didn't. I kept my hands to myself and gave her the kiss she asked for, the one that I hoped let her know that I was dead serious about being ready for whatever was waiting for us. She was the only thing I really felt like I had a handle on anymore . . . and I'd barely touched her.

I texted Poppy to let her know both the puppy and I escaped

the night unscathed and asked if she wanted me to drop him off at her place or her work. Happy was still too little to come to the garage during the day. I didn't want to kennel him in the office and I couldn't have him running around the shop because of all the chemicals he would be able to get into. Poppy agreed that he needed to be a little bit older and definitely better trained before he could spend his days wandering around the garage and the fenced-in lot around the warehouse. She replied that she was home, so I stopped and grabbed some doughnuts on the way over.

She looked as tired as I felt when she opened the door. Some of the sleepiness faded as she took Happy from me, cooing at the puppy while simultaneously looking at the brightly colored box in my hand. I hefted it up. "I brought you breakfast." I wiggled my eyebrows at her. "Tomato-free."

A tiny grin tugged at her mouth and I felt like I was seeing the sunshine for the first time. It was beautiful and that itty-bitty hint of happiness from her, that sliver of light that glowed from inside of her, reinforced the fact that she was worth every effort caring for her was going to take.

"I think you're trying to fatten me up. You're always telling me to eat and bringing me food."

I wasn't trying to fatten her up. I was trying to get her to take care of herself. I had no clue what she looked like before Rowdy and her sister brought her back to Denver to heal, but I doubted she was built like a strong wind could blow her over. The smaller she was, the easier it was for her to disappear, and I didn't want that for her. I wanted her healthy and strong enough to withstand whatever life was going to throw at her. I wanted her to fight, not fade away.

She put Happy down and took the box as I held it out to her.

She looked at it, then up at me. She nibbled nervously on the inside of her lip before asking softly, "Do you want to come in and share these before you have to go to work?"

Hell yes I did. I wanted that more than anything because she was inviting me in without question or hesitation, but I couldn't. I had an appointment with a buyer for one of my higher-end builds and I couldn't afford to blow him off or keep him waiting. He was a repeat customer, one that liked to spend money on the especially hard-to-find classics.

"Can't. Gotta see a man about a car. I'll give you a call after work, and if you're up to it I'll swing by and we can work on getting Happy some much-needed manners." I chuckled. "He snores and takes up more of the bed than something that small should be able to."

Again, that barely-there smile danced around her mouth. "Okay. I guess I'll see you later."

I was going to be dead on my feet, a walking zombie, but I would play through the pain if it meant I got to spend time with her. I tilted my chin down at her and turned to go but stopped short when her fingers wrapped around my elbow. She was reaching out to touch me more and more. I wondered if she even realized that she no longer hesitated to lay her fingers lightly on me when she wanted my attention. I felt that gentle touch all the way through my body. My dick took instant notice and I bit back a groan as her eyes heated and got soft and warm. She balanced the box in one hand and reached in and pulled out a decadent-looking chocolate doughnut with the other. I brought her a full dozen because I had no clue what kind she preferred, so I covered all the bases.

"Take one with you. You can't go to work without some kind

of boost since you were up all night." I took the sugary confection from her hand and my gaze landed on her fingers, where some of the chocolate frosting still clung.

The simple gesture of offering me something because she wanted to take care of me in return meant more to me than Poppy would ever know.

Keeping my eyes on hers, I took a step closer to her, and slowly, so slowly, so that she would have plenty of time to move her hand away, I lowered my head to where it was still hanging in the air in front of mine. I heard her suck in a breath, watched the way it made her breasts rise and fall under the too-big thermal she was wearing, but she didn't tell me to stop and she didn't pull away as I carefully and deliberately slicked my tongue over and around her finger. The frosting was a burst of sweetness in my mouth, but her creamy, velvety skin was even sweeter. She exhaled slowly as I ran the tip of my tongue across her knuckle and down into the sensitive vee between her fingers. I flicked it back and forth and gave the innocent space a very dirty kind of kiss. The frosting was long gone but I wanted the image of what I could do to her, do *for* her when she was ready for it, to linger in her mind for the rest of the day. If I could make her pant and sway on her feet by simply playing her fingers, she had to know that kind of pleasure I could bring her when I got my fingers on the good stuff would be well worth the risk she was going to have to take by letting me in.

When I was done, I brushed a kiss across the back of her hand like some kind of cheeseball. It might have been ridiculous and antiquated but the gesture made her sigh and had her looking at me like she might drop the bakery box and pull me inside the apartment so she could have her way with me.

As awesome as that daydream was, I really did have to get to work, so pushing Poppy and letting her figure out how far she was willing to go with me was going to have to wait. "Have a good day, honey."

She stared at me silently for a drawn-out moment, then she shook her head quickly like she was trying to shake off whatever sexual haze I had wrapped her up in and blinked those stunning eyes at me. "You too, Wheeler."

I would, because it started out with her.

I got stuck in traffic, so I ended up being late for my meeting but it didn't matter. The car collector still picked up the '67 Ford Fairlane and made a ridiculous offer on the Wayfarer even though it wasn't close to being done. I was on my way to the office to mainline a gallon of coffee when I got waylaid by another visitor who was obviously from out of town but knew his shit when it came to classic muscle cars. He mentioned he was in town visiting a friend that had recently relocated and that one of the guys at the tattoo shop where I went for my work gave him my name and told him if he was a car guy he needed to see my setup. The dude was big, looked like a felon, but talked engines and horsepower as well as I did. He was driving a shitty rental but his pretty red-headed girlfriend wasted no time in telling me that she inherited a '69 Super Bee when she and the bruiser got together. When I asked what kind of ride he rolled around in, they both cringed and he grumbled something about a bad accident totaling his car but didn't elaborate. I was smart enough not to pry.

The guy might have secretly scared the piss out of me but the hour and a half I spent showing him all my pride-and-joy projects was really enjoyable. It wasn't often I met someone that was as committed to bringing the old beasts back to life the same way I was. I felt like he was a kindred spirit and his girlfriend was sweet. She didn't say much but when she did the monster of a man smiled and answered her questions thoughtfully and patiently. It was pretty clear he loved two things with equal passion, muscle cars and the girl standing by his side. He was careful with her in the same way I was careful with Poppy.

After they left I once again went in search of coffee, the sugar rush from my doughnut starting to wear off, but was interrupted in my quest by another unexpected visitor. I spotted the Hudson long before it pulled into the lot. I paused in front of one of the bays and waited while the beautiful machine coasted to a smooth stop in front of me. Whoever took care of making the motor run was good . . . really good. There wasn't a single knock or whine, which was rare for a car that still had so many of its original parts.

I lifted my chin as the guy from before climbed out and made his way over to where I was waiting. "You're back."

Once again he had mirrored aviators on, so I couldn't read his expression but he did give a little nod. "I am. I actually have a lead on a car that I thought you might be interested in."

I crossed my arms over my chest and narrowed my eyes. I didn't take on special projects for profit. I wanted to sink my time and my money into cars that I felt really needed me. I didn't want to build any kind of flashy hot rod for a weekend warrior, not that this guy gave off the entitled vibes those wannabe gearheads had.

"I usually track down my own builds. I'm picky about what I want to take on. I usually have to work on them on the side because it's the regular maintenance and customer cars that pay the bills. I tend to only invest my time and money into one car at a time. I've been babying that Wayfarer for six months."

No matter how hard I tried, I couldn't put my finger on why I was so sure I knew him from somewhere. I figured it had to be my imagination because this was the second time he'd sought me out and he hadn't indicated that our paths might have crossed before. I could see my own puzzled expression in the reflection of the mirrored sunglasses he didn't bother to take off.

"I understand that, but this is an opportunity I doubt you'll want to pass up. I know someone that's getting rid of a '52 Hudson convertible. The original body and chassis are intact but the motor is all tore to hell and patchworked together from different years and different makes and models. It's scrap. I don't have the space or the time to take it on since I'm sort of in limbo at the moment, but I thought you might." His dark eyebrows lifted and his teeth flashed as he gave me a knowing grin. "I mean a guy named Hudson should own one . . . it only seems right."

I blew out a whistle and rocked back on my heels. That was an offer that was practically impossible to say no to. "That's quite a score. Why would you want to pass it on to a guy you don't know?"

He lifted a silver-and-black eyebrow as he told me, "I have eyes and I know my shit, kid. You take care of your cars regardless if they are a classic or a daily driver. You're putting out beautiful work, and honestly, I'm dying to see what you could do with the '52. I know the seller really well, so I can probably get a few grand knocked off the asking price."

I watched him, still trying to place where I could know him from, when it occurred to me I didn't even know his name. He'd taken off after I told him I was named after his car the last time he visited.

"I didn't catch your name the last time you stopped by. Seems like I should know it if you're offering me a score and a deal." I cocked my head to the side and considered him through narrowed eyes. "Are you famous or something? I can't shake this feeling that I've seen you somewhere before. You look very familiar."

The man let out a rusty-sounding laugh and shook his head. He offered a hand and his grip when we shook was firm and confident. I wasn't sure if it was my overly tired mind playing tricks on me or not but I could have sworn the guy gave my hand an extra squeeze there at the end before letting go.

"Name's Zak Brady." He waited a second to see if I would have any reaction to the name and when I didn't he sighed and shifted his weight uneasily on his booted feet. "I'm not famous but I've made a decent name for myself in certain circles where horsepower is king. I'm not sure anyone would be familiar with it outside of California, but if you ever head out to the West Coast, people will point you in the direction of my garage the same way they pointed me toward yours." He grinned at me and I found myself staring stupidly because I *knew* that face was one that I was familiar with. It was making me bonkers that I couldn't place him. "I must have one of those faces, the kind that reminds someone of someone they think they know."

He pulled his wallet out of his back pocket and handed over a business card that had a bunch of shiny silver car parts embossed on it. His name was stamped in black and there was contact information as well as the address for a garage in Orange County. "You can reach me at the number on there and the website is up-to-date if you want to check it out so you know I'm not trying to scam you. Figure out what your bottom line on the Hudson is and if it's reasonable I'll see what I can work out. If you decide to pass, no hard feelings. We both know that kind of car will find a buyer in a hot second. I'd like to see it go to a guy who appreciates what he's got and what it could be, but I learned early on in my career that I can't save every beauty that comes my way."

He looked away and I had the distinct feeling we weren't talking about cars anymore. Every time this guy showed up at my shop it got weird and I wasn't really sure what to do with that. I tucked the card in my pocket and told him, "Let me look at some things. I'm not going to tell you that I'm not tempted but I also have my first kid on the way so anything that's going to cost a mint has to be carefully considered. I'll give you a call in a few days after I crunch some numbers." Before Kallie had dropped the bomb that we were going to be parents I would have snapped up the Hudson without a second thought, but now I had someone else I was responsible for making good choices for, even if that someone wasn't quite here yet.

The older guy made a noise that sounded a little like he was choking and rubbed his hand over his mouth.

"You're going to be a dad?" The words wheezed out and he loudly cleared his throat to cover the obvious strain in his words. "Congratulations, kid. That's great."

His reaction was so bizarre that I decided I'd enough of the conversation. There was something about this dude that was a little too intense for me. "Well, it wasn't exactly planned and the circumstances could be better but I'm gonna do my best by the kid." I snorted a little bit and looked down at the worn toes of my boots. "I had a shit example set for me by my own parents, so if anything, I know what *not* to do." The guy made that choking noise again and I hooked a thumb over my shoulder at one of the open bays. "Thanks for stopping by and for having faith in my ability to handle the Hudson but I gotta go pay the bills. The minivans and SUVs are what keeps the lights on, and the guys who work for me paid. There's no shortage of them waiting to be fixed." I patted the pocket where I stashed his card and assured him, "I'll let you know which way I'm gonna go in a few days."

The guy seemed to shake himself out of a stupor and flashed me that friendly and familiar grin. "Sounds good, kid." He ambled back to his car.

I roughly scraped a hand down my face and tilted my head back so I was looking up at the clear Denver sky. "I'm too tired for this. All I wanted was a cup of coffee." The sky didn't offer any kind of sympathy but Molly had a fresh pot of coffee in the office when I finally made my way inside. If I wasn't so wrapped up in pretty Poppy and wasn't too smart to court a sexual harassment lawsuit, I could have kissed the girl in gratitude.

The rest of the day dragged on much as I expected it to. I was chugging Red Bull at two in a desperate bid to keep going, with lackluster results. I wanted to cry when I called it a day for the rest of the crew at the end of regular working hours but knew I still had to stay to make up for my wasted hours during the morning. All I wanted was a beer and a soft bed . . . well, a softer woman wouldn't hurt anything, but I didn't want to be greedy.

I was shoulders-deep in the engine of a Jeep Cherokee when my phone started ringing. I knew it was Poppy by the bright, cheery ring tone I'd assigned to her. I was always the one that reached out to her, so the fact she was calling me, especially when I told her I would be in touch after work, had everything inside of me going on alert.

"Poppy?" I couldn't hear what she was saying because she was crying and her voice was so shrill and high I was pretty sure only dogs could understand her. She was incoherent and I could practically feel the way she was sobbing through the phone line. "Honey, I need you to slow down and tell me what's wrong. I can't understand you."

She wailed again but I heard her take a calming breath, and even though her voice cracked, she managed to get out, "I dropped Happy's leash when we were out walking. He's gone! He's going to get hit by a car or attacked by a bigger dog! I can't find him anywhere!" She started sobbing again and I pictured her collapsing in on herself in the middle of the sidewalk, falling apart with no one there to hold her together. I wiped my dirty hands on the legs of my coveralls and started shutting down the garage before I was really aware of the fact I was moving. The task usually took an hour but I didn't bother to sweep the floors or shut off the lights. I made sure all the machines were shut off and that there was nothing left on that could burn the place down as I raced out to my car.

"Give me twenty minutes and I'll come find him." I kept my voice calm but on the inside I was just as scared as she was. Happy might be a pit but he was still a baby and he had no idea what was out there in the big bad world. He was so small that I didn't want to start thinking about all the bad things that could befall him if I couldn't find him.

"It's too late. I ruin everything." She sounded heartbroken . . . no strike that . . . she sounded broken period. It made everything inside of me tie itself in knots and had my heart kicking double time with worry and in fear.

I almost dropped my keys getting into the Eldorado and swore loudly, which made her cry even harder. "Poppy where are you?"

She didn't reply for so long that I strongly considered hanging up and calling 911. She sounded like she needed help and I was still too far away to offer it to her. I was terrified of what I was going to find when I finally made it to her.

"Poppy?" I barked her name with more force and that seemed to get through.

She wheezed through the line and told me she was walking up and down the blocks near her apartment complex off Downing. She was looking in the decorative bushes that lined the walkways leading up to most of the converted Victorians in that part of Capitol Hill. She said she was also checking under cars and in the alleys that passed between buildings, which led me to scolding her to be careful. I was worried about her wandering the streets in her obviously hysterical state. She was as much at risk as the puppy was.

I found a spot on the street to leave the Caddy and bolted up and down the side streets calling both the dog's name and the woman's. I was out of breath by the time I found Poppy. She was walking up the opposite side of the street from where I was jogging, looking lost. She still had on the lightweight sleepwear she was wearing this morning with no coat and nothing but a pair of flip-flops on her feet. Obviously, she hadn't been planning on keeping the dog out long and whatever had distracted her into letting go of that leash must have been pretty serious. I hoped like hell it wasn't something as simple as someone crossing her path on the sidewalk, because if that was the case, she had much further to go on her path to recovering from her trauma than I thought.

I rushed across the street and wrapped my arms around her as she immediately threw herself into my chest. She tucked her head under my chin and against the front of my T-shirt where my coveralls were opened, and the shirt immediately got soaked through from her tears. I palmed the back of her head as her lithe frame shuddered uncontrollably against mine, and whispered that everything would be okay in her ear. I needed to get her somewhere safe and then I needed to find our dog.

"Let's get you inside so you can warm up. I'll look for Happy until the sun comes up if I have to. He's tiny, he couldn't have made it very far."

She shook her head back and forth, her entire body moving as sobs ripped from her chest. "I can't believe I let him go. Everything that loves me, I let go."

I didn't understand what that meant but I didn't think she was in the right frame of mind to have a heart-to-heart about it. "Honey, you're freezing. You have to go inside."

She pulled her head back from where it was burrowed into me and blinked up at me. "I have to find Happy."

"You will, but you won't do him any good if you freeze to death." We stood there staring at each other for a long time and I realized she wasn't going to move. She was stuck on the spot, lost in her own grief and trapped by whatever had started this mess in the first place. I didn't have a coat since I was still wearing my coveralls from the garage, so I decided the next best thing I could do to warm her up and get her to move was to hold her close and cradle her in my arms like she was a baby. I knew if she hadn't been lost in the throes of her meltdown, she would protest because there was no part of her that wasn't touching me, but since she was numb and practically catatonic, I swung her thin legs up into my arms and marched with her back to her apartment like she was my bride and I was carrying her across the threshold on our wedding night. She was so light, barely any kind of burden in my grasp. I vowed to bring her doughnuts every single morning until the day I died if it would give her the sustenance she obviously needed.

When I rounded the corner of the block where her apartment building was located, I almost dropped her when I saw a furry little blur dart around the side of her building. There was no mistaking that brindled coat or the excited way the puppy moved. Even though he was just a baby, he obviously knew where home was. He'd found his way back to love and shelter. Smart dog.

I put Poppy on her feet by the front door and told her I would be right back. I hated to leave her in the state she was in but I figured the best way to snap her out of it was to get the puppy back in her arms, whole and healthy.

Happy thought we were playing a game. Every time I got close enough to grab him he darted the opposite way. He barked and yipped, having a grand old time. Finally, I figured out if I crouched down on my haunches and just stayed still, the goofy little guy would come over to me looking for his head pats and tummy rubs. When I scooped him up I couldn't believe the wave of relief that washed over me. I had to take a second to pull myself together because I didn't want Poppy to see how upset I had been. She was already a mess, I wasn't going to add any more to it.

When I got back to the front of the building she predictably lost her mind when she saw I had the dog safely in my grasp. She started crying in earnest again and couldn't seem to make her words work. I handed the dog over without a fight, waved her off as she babbled her thanks over and over again, and felt my heart squeeze as Happy tried to burrow into her chest the way she had burrowed into mine.

Now more than dead on my feet, I decided I was done for the day. I needed a few hours of shut-eye and I needed to know both my dog and my girl were safe. The only way to accomplish all of that was to pile all of us into the same bed. I didn't know if Poppy was ready for that yet, but I was too tired to ask. I picked her up, Happy delighted to be in her arms again, snuggled close. I made my way down the hallway into her apartment, and trudged along until I found her bedroom with no help or protest from her.

I set her on the bed, pulled off her flip-flops, and bent to tug off my boots. I didn't want to crawl into her bed with my dirty coveralls but I didn't have the mental fortitude to deal with another emotional breakdown once she realized she was in bed with a half-naked man.

I pulled her to me so that her back was plastered to my chest. I rested my arm around her thin waist as she continued to cuddle against me and coo at the dog. My eyes drifted shut as I felt her press more fully into me. I tightened my hold on her and inhaled the floral scent that clung to her hair. It had been a long day but I would do it all over a hundred more times without a single complaint if it ended me up exactly where I was right now.

Chapter 9

Poppy

Most nights I woke up shaking and frozen all the way down to my bones. I couldn't remember the last time I woke up feeling warm and safe, not to mention rested and refreshed. I blinked my eyes and waited for them to adjust to the thick darkness that was coating everything in my room. Happy was standing in front of my face, paws on my pillow, little tail wagging. I wrinkled my nose as his tongue shot out to lick the tip, waking me the rest of the way up. I had no recollection of getting into bed and I definitely didn't remember falling asleep with the weight of a heavily tattooed arm locked firmly around my waist.

I waited for the panic. I anticipated the terror and the anxiety that would typically rise up and choke me when I fully realized I wasn't, that there was a man behind me, breathing deep and even. I expected my skin to crawl, my eyes to tear up, and my heart to stop beating. I predicted the fear that would paralyze me and render me helpless . . . but none of it came. I was still rattled and unsettled from the phone call that had blindsided me and caused me to drop Happy's leash, but all the icky, awful things I thought I would feel when I ended up in bed with a man again were nowhere to be found and I was pretty sure it was because it was *this* man I was cuddled up to. I might not know if I could trust my own judgment, but when my defenses were down, and when my mind was all tangled up in memories and mistakes from the past, everything inside of me decided it could trust Hudson Wheeler. All my barricades tumbled down and crumbled the instant he showed up to take care of me. I couldn't let him hold me and comfort me fast enough when the past showed up with its gnashing teeth and inescapable grasp. I didn't keep the pain from him . . . I welcomed him inside of it with open arms and let him take the brunt of some of it.

I'd spent every second since Oliver had pulled that trigger making sure no one ever got close enough to hurt me physically or emotionally. I was determined to make myself unbreakable and unmovable. I wanted to be strong and definite like Salem was. I wanted to be untouchable and unattainable like Sayer was. But I wasn't. I was still too soft, too easily wounded. My armor was made of feathers and fluff and all it took was that voice on the other end of the phone to pierce right through it. If Wheeler hadn't shown up when he did, I would still be wandering up and down the streets calling Happy's name, and he was right: I would have been frozen and of no use to anyone because I couldn't think. That phone call had launched me right back to a place I never wanted to be again, and instead of facing it head-on and confronting my fear, I let it overwhelm me and cripple me . . . just like I always did. Fear was familiar and it was far too easy to let it take over all the other things I'd allowed myself to feel as I moved on from my abduction and attack.

Happy started to playfully growl and jump around in front

of my face, pawing at my hair and butting his soft head against my chin. I had no clue how long we had been curled up in bed but I bet it was long enough that the puppy needed another trip outside. He was ready to play but it was well past both of our bedtimes. I didn't want to wake Wheeler up but he had me pinned tightly to his front. I could feel his chest rising and falling steadily behind me and there was no give in the iron band of his arm where it rested firmly across my middle. I was also lying on one of the sleeves of his coveralls, I could feel the snaps digging into my legs, which, now that I was awake, was totally uncomfortable.

I shifted my hips and moved my legs, the initial warmth I'd felt when I woke up now spreading to other, more intimate parts of my anatomy. I was sure the flush on my face was visible even in the pitch-blackness and the silence surrounding us made the sounds of my breaths rushing in and out between my parted lips obscenely loud. Wheeler made a noise behind me and his hold around my waist tightened and then immediately loosened. I was going to roll away from him so I could get Happy off the bed before he made any more noise, but before I could Wheeler's tattooed hands reached around me and plucked the little dog off the pillow, where he was now chasing shadows across the fabric.

"I'll take him outside and then set him up in the kitchen for the night. You go back to sleep." His voice was rough and groggy and there was no room in it for argument. I had to sit up and scoot over to free the part of his coveralls I was lying on and he grunted a little when he was finally free to stand up. "Sorry for crawling into bed with you still in my work clothes. If I got anything dirty let me know and I'll replace it."

He scratched Happy behind the ears and set him on the floor

so he could pull his discarded boots back onto his feet. I stared at his back, eyes tracking the way his plain T-shirt stretched across the span of his wide shoulders. I pulled my knees up, wrapped my arms around them, and rested my cheek on the bony surface as I continued to watch him. When he lifted his arms up over his head to work the kinks out of those long and lean muscles, I couldn't hold back a sigh. He turned his head to look at me over his shoulder and I told him truthfully, "You can ruin every single set of sheets I have. You showed up and cleaned up a mess I made that was way more difficult to deal with than a few grease spots. If you can clean up after me, I have no problem cleaning up after you."

He turned back to the bed, hands on his hips, and I noticed that the collar of his T-shirt was ripped and that fabric was hanging down over his collarbone, revealing what looked like part of a mountain range and some kind of animal inked on the center of his chest. I had a feeling I could see his skin a thousand times and each time I would find something new to look at.

"Everyone ends up a little bit out of place every now and then. I'll put you back where you're supposed to be, Poppy." He grinned, and even in the dark I could see those twin dimples digging enticingly into his cheeks. It made my toes curl into the covers and had my breath moving faster and my skin tingling in a way that was impossible to ignore. "That's what I do, ya know. I put things back the way they were supposed to be. I make things the way they were before someone didn't treat them right."

I scrunched up my nose at him and squinted as he turned on the small bedside light. "I'm not a car, Wheeler. You can't find replacement parts for all the things inside of me that don't work right anymore."

He bent at the waist, put his fisted hands on the bed, and leaned over so that his lips could lightly touch the top of my head. It was a kiss that I felt all the way through my entire body. His care reached places inside of me no one had ever touched before, places that lit up and exploded like fireworks every time he did something nice. They were places that were growing and expanding, pushing out the other areas inside of me that had long been dark and scarred.

"Nothing about you needs replaced. What you got runs just fine, it just needs a tune-up and some proper maintenance." His tone indicated he was the guy more than up for the job of getting me back in working order. I should tell him I'd never been a hot rod. "I'm taking Happy out and getting him settled; then I'll get out of your hair so you can go back to bed."

He started for the door, the puppy happily nipping at the heels of his boots. I called his name and waited for him to turn around before I asked him, "Aren't you going to ask me what made me let go of the leash? Don't you want to know why I was in such a sorry state when you found me?" Honestly, I didn't know what to do with the fact he wasn't blaming me, questioning me, accusing me. There was zero censure or condemnation from him and I had no clue how to navigate that. I had platitudes and apologies itching to crawl off my tongue but he didn't ask for any of them.

"No. I don't care what happened, I just care that it *did* happen. I hate that something upset you to that point and I hate that you feel like you owe anyone an explanation for feeling however you feel. Everyone made it inside safe and sound, so whatever bad shit happened, it didn't win tonight and that's what I think we should focus on." He always made it sound so easy. His acceptance and reassurance settled around me like a velvety blanket.

I closed my eyes and rubbed my cheek against my knee. "My

mom called. I haven't spoken to her or my father since Oliver took me. She'll occasionally send an e-mail to make sure I'm alive and to tell me that Salem and Rowdy need to stop living in sin, but I haven't heard her voice in months and months." I let out a shaky sigh, and when I pried my eyes back open I saw that he looked angry enough to spit nails. He understood that my safe space had been breached, that hearing from my mom brought back memories of more than just Oliver. The tenuous hold I had on my sense of safety was ripped away by that voice with its soft Texas drawl and thinly veiled accusations.

"I erased all my social media after everything that happened when Oliver took me. I couldn't handle strangers trying to pry into my life. But Salem must still have hers up because Mom knows she's pregnant. That's why she called." I let out a sharp laugh. "She was crying. Can you believe that?" I didn't expect him to answer, so I kept the words coming. "She was crying. She was sobbing because she didn't know that she was going to be a grandmother because Salem hasn't spoken to her since she was eighteen other than to threaten her to stay the hell away from me." I sighed and hugged my folded-up legs more tightly to my chest and started to rock back and forth a little. "She called me because she knew I would listen. She called me because she knew I was the one that would hear her out." I blinked back tears and dug the sharp points of my fingernails into my skin. "She called me because she knew I understand what it's like to be trapped in a marriage that might very well end up killing you."

I choked a little on the emotion that was clogging my throat, so it took me a minute before I could finish telling him everything that was crowding my mind and punishing my heart. "She told me she missed me. She's alone in that house with my father, suffering through the gossip of everything that happened with me and Oliver, and you know what? . . . I feel bad for her." Like the sap that I was. My stupid heart couldn't stop caring about the wrong people. "I worry about her bearing the brunt of my father's wrath, about her having to shoulder the blame he no doubt levels on her for both my and Salem's failures. That's enough to crush anyone." I sighed again. "Somewhere in all of that, I went numb and let go of the leash. I was so caught up in feeling bad because I was hurting for someone that previously hurt me that I let go of the one thing in my life that actually needs my constant love and attention. I got swept up in what was and forgot all about what is. That's a dangerous place for anyone to be." I could get lost in the dark and lose all the ground forward I'd gained.

Wheeler stayed by the door but the intensity shining out of his baby blues was strong enough that I felt it like a touch as he stared at me from across the room. His voice vibrated with unidentified emotion as he told me, "Like I said, it's easy to get a little bit misplaced, honey. It didn't take you very long to get back to where you were supposed to be. Cut yourself some slack. I told you what happened to me when I was little." He'd been left, callously dropped like he was lost luggage when he was too little to understand what was happening to him. That hurt to think about as much as imagining my mother living alone under my father's rule. "We all need someone to bring us in from the cold." He would have died if someone hadn't been there to take him in, and chances were I would have been in a similar situation if all the people that had been there, holding the door open for me to places that were warm and safe, hadn't pulled me in out of the cold when I was ready to freeze.

Wheeler disappeared out the door. Watching him go, I realized he'd been at work all day, with very little sleep, and had dropped everything to come to me the second I called. He brought me inside and we collapsed. All of it was a little hazy and a lot fuzzy but I knew that in all of it there had been no time for food. He was always feeding me, making sure I had fuel to keep going, so I figured the least I could do was return the favor.

I climbed off the bed, took a few seconds to pull my hair up in a shifty topknot, and detoured to the bathroom to splash some cold water on my face so that I looked a little less like a train wreck. I wasn't any kind of gourmet chef, and since my appetite was iffy at best I didn't keep a stocked pantry. I had the basics and the staples, so I decided breakfast for dinner was going to have to do. It was creeping up on midnight according to the clock on the microwave but my suddenly growling tummy didn't seem to care.

I was scrambling eggs in the pan and jumping around by the stove to avoid popping bacon grease when Wheeler came in through the front door. He paused for a second, eyes locked on me as I moved around the kitchen as if the sight of me doing something as normal as cooking was some kind of modern marvel.

"I figured you didn't get a chance to eat dinner." I waved a hand around the mess I was in the middle of like it was self-explanatory. "You're always feeding me. Now it's my turn."

He blinked and those bright eyes of his got heavy-lidded and dangerous looking. "You didn't have to do that."

I shrugged and started shoveling hot food onto plates. "I didn't have to, but I wanted to."

He made a noise low in his throat as he took the plate from me and sat down on the opposite side of the counter. We ate in companionable silence and I didn't bother to argue when he offered to do the dishes when we were done. I took my time setting up Happy's bed and blankets in the kitchen after Wheeler put his doggie gate up across the opening and I realized I was stalling because I didn't want him to go.

My mom's call had resurrected a lot of bad memories and old ghosts, and I knew once I was alone with them they were going to do more than haunt me. When I woke up with Wheeler wrapped around my back, with him holding me so tightly that there wasn't any room for anything to get between his skin and mine, I felt protected. It felt like all the sharp and pointy things that pricked at my vulnerable places were going to have to get through him before they could lodge into me. He wouldn't let them draw blood. I wanted to be the kind of woman that could face all the things in the dark that scared her, face them alone, but I wasn't, at least I wasn't yet, but I was slowly getting there.

Wheeler was wiping his hands on a dish towel and watching Happy turn circles on his bed. There was a grin on his face and those dangerous dimples were flashing, and I knew I was about to say something I would immediately want to take back. It was one thing to be in bed with him when I was practically catatonic and unaware of my surroundings. It was another to ask him to be there when I was wide-awake and in full control of my actions.

"It's late. You can just stay the night here if you want."

His head turned toward me so fast I was sure he gave himself mild whiplash. His dark eyebrows shot up and his hands curled around the edge of the sink. "Thanks for the offer but I don't think that's a good idea."

I was surprised how disappointed I was by his answer. Teeth sinking into my bottom lip, I was petulant when I asked him, "Why not?"

His eyebrows danced up even higher, if that was possible, and his dimples cut even deeper into his cheeks when his grin turned into a full, blinding smile. Holy hell, was he pretty.

"Because I'm wearing what I wore to work all day. I'm covered in grease and grime. I was exhausted when I showed up, so nothing could have kept me on my feet. I'm not going to crawl into bed with you and get you all gross and nasty."

I looked him over and didn't find a single thing that I would consider either gross or nasty. "Take a shower and stay." I hated that I sounded desperate and needy but they were honest emotions. Ones that seemed to be stronger than the fear that was always hovering right behind them. "Please, Wheeler. Stay." He was wavering, I could see it in his eyes.

After a minute of silence, he caved. He gave his mahogany-topped head a shake and turned his gaze up to the ceiling. "All right, I'll crash for tonight, but if it gets to be too much for you I'm moving to the couch." He lifted up the dangling arm of his coveralls and let it fall. "I'm ditching these if I stay, Poppy. You sure you really want that?"

I felt my eyes widen and my heart kick hard at the uninvited image of him sprawled out across my bed wearing nothing but all of that ink and a smile. I swallowed hard and gave him a jerky nod. "I think it'll be fine. I'm tired and it's been a rough day. I'll probably be asleep by the time you get out of the bathroom." Lies. All of it lies. I'd never felt more awake and energized in my life.

He knew I was lying. I could tell by the smirk on his face and the way his shoulders shook with silent laughter. "Okay. I'll be in shortly, then."

I gulped and practically ran toward the bedroom. I had no idea what I thought I was going to do in there but it felt like I needed to get ready for some kind of momentous occasion. I remade the bed and noticed he had indeed gotten smudges of black on the light green fabric, but I really couldn't have cared less. I liked seeing the smudges there. It was like he had left a mark, a sign that he was the first man I had let willingly into my bed, a reminder that he was the only one I woke up next to unafraid. I picked up a few stray articles of clothing that were tossed around, moved some of Happy's toys out of sight, and generally made the place as presentable as I could now that he wasn't dead on his feet and would notice that I tended to be kind of a slob when left to my own devices.

When there was no busy work left to be done, I dug through my purse for any kind of minty breath enhancer. I didn't want to breathe bacon and eggs all over Wheeler, not that I assumed I would be close enough to share air with him. Still, I thought it was better to be safe than sorry.

Once that was done, I had no option left but to crawl under the freshly tucked covers and wait. I could hear my heartbeat thudding between my ears and couldn't keep my limbs still. My arms moved over and under the comforter a hundred times while my legs thrashed and kicked like I was trying to swim to the side of a pool. I wanted to turn the lights off, to hide and pretend like I hadn't been the one to set this all in motion, but then I would be in the dark, alone with my ghosts and demons, and that was exactly why I'd asked him to stay in the first place. He kept the monsters at bay.

I was silently calling myself all kinds of names and telling myself to grow up and act like an adult. I'd been married, for goodness' sake, I'd been pregnant. Surely I could handle one night sharing a bed with a guy I was attracted to without falling apart.

That theory went up in smoke when the opposite side of the mattress suddenly dipped down and the scent of my shampoo and freshly washed man invaded every sense I had. I turned my head just as Wheeler was reaching over to click out the light that was on the nightstand and couldn't stop the gasp that ripped from me at the sight of all that taut, colorful skin spread out before me.

He hadn't just ditched the coveralls; the torn T-shirt was also gone, leaving him in nothing more than a pair of yellow boxer briefs. No boring white or black for Hudson Wheeler, he was full of color from head to toe. Even the red in his still-wet hair seemed brighter and more vibrant against the plain white pillowcase behind him. Looking at him was enough to cause a sensory overload, and when he asked me if I was okay all I could do was nod. He reached for the light again and the word "stop" rushed out from my lips before I could think about why I wanted him to leave the lights on.

The tattoo on the center of his chest was mountains; I would bet good money they were the Rockies. People born and bred in Colorado took an inordinate amount of pride in being local and native to the state. In the center of those intricately detailed peaks that matched the ones painted on his garage was a massive, angry, snarling wolf head. The ears were cocked; teeth were bared and blood dripped artfully and meaningfully in scarlet ink all the way down his torso. He had the word "Cadillac" and the famous logo that went with the car company tattooed across his stomach. Across his side, the one closest to me, he was inked in a manner that looked like all his skin was peeled and ripping away, only to reveal a complex network of gears and wires. It was meant to look like his insides were mechanical, like he was part machine, and it did. I noticed that one of his arms, the entire sleeve, all the way down to the tips of his fingers, matched that biomechanical design. Peeking out from either side at the top waistband of his boxer briefs were heavy, black designs that didn't seem to have any rhyme or reason. They matched each other perfectly and crawled up over his sharply defined abs like they were some kind of map to the promised land. There wasn't a single part of him that didn't have some kind of design or marking on it. It was all beautiful and my hands were reaching out to touch it before I stopped to consider that he was practically naked, in my bed, by my invitation, and that putting my hands on him might be construed as something more than utter fascination.

My fingers skimmed over the wolf and his entire body shifted and coiled tightly next to mine. I traced the line of dripping blood all the way down his sternum, stopping only when it turned into the petal of a realistic rose that hung below a scary-looking skull. I saw his body move, watched as the fabric of his underwear stretched and tightened, but I couldn't stop touching. I wanted to memorize it all and learn the story behind every drop of ink.

"Why a wolf?" The eyes of the animal stared at me, angry and hostile. That was no house pet. Wheeler's spirit animal was wild and feral.

His fingers lifted and circled my wrist. I flattened my hand so that it was pressed against his stomach. He held it there, still, even after I wiggled my fingers, letting him know I wasn't done touching.

"A lone wolf. One that does whatever it takes to survive until it finds a pack that will accept him." His words snaked around my heart. Loneliness and sadness were ringing loud and clear in every syllable.

I watched him thoughtfully and didn't put up much of a fight when he used the hold he had on my wrist to pull me across his body so that I was straddling his thinly covered lap while he reclined with his back against the headboard. It had been forever since I had something hard and throbbing between my legs. And I was sure I'd never had anything there that was as impressive and as hot as what Wheeler was working with. I put both of my hands on the wolf and met the guarded look in his burning blue eyes with one of my own.

"Wolves mate for life."

"Yes, they do."

I shivered against him as his rough hand slid underneath the loose fabric of the thermal I'd been in all day. It was far from sexy bedroom wear, but if the erection I was starting to slowly grind on was any indication, it didn't matter what I was wearing, because whatever it was worked for the man below me.

His breath hitched as I started a slow rocking back and forth on the ridged flesh that was rubbing right against my cleft. My thin cotton pants did little to keep the heat we were generating hidden and I could feel arousal, both mine and his, starting to make the fabric between us damp.

I curled a hand around the side of his neck, capturing that bird that lived there in my palm, and leaned forward so I could lightly touch my lips to his. All along I knew this was the kind of distraction I needed to keep the ugly things that wanted to destroy me far, far away. In the light, with this man and his colorful skin and kind eyes, I was a million miles away from anything that could hurt me. I was lost, always turning in circles, but with Wheeler, everywhere I ended up he was there waiting for me, setting me back on the right path. The path that involved his hands coasting up my ribs, tracing fine lines between all the bones. The route that had his hands gently cupping my breasts and his lips letting out a guttural sound when he found them bare and the tips stiff and hard in anticipation of his touch.

He swallowed my gasp as his rough fingers scraped across velvety-smooth skin. My nipples pulled into points so tight that they hurt until he touched them. His fingertips dragged across the sensitive skin and suddenly the press of lips wasn't enough. His mouth moved on mine, hungry, hard, and heavy. Lips bruised, teeth gnashed, and moans mingled. One of his hands fell to my hip, slipped under the waistband of my pants, and dug into the soft skin that lived there. My body took no time to follow his subtle direction and soon I was moving across his throbbing cock in earnest. There were layers of clothing separating us, but I could feel him twitch and kick against my center. I shifted, wanting more, needing the contact to hit the spot that none of my previous lovers had seemed interested in taking advantage of.

I panted against his mouth, which was wet from my ravenous lips, and rested my forehead against his as I continued to move on him, desperately searching, urgently seeking. I cried out as his fingers circled one begging nipple and applied pressure. The pinch made me jerk on top of him and move even more frantically. My hands were pulling at his flesh and my mouth was pleading with him to do something, anything, to help me get where he had been taking me all along.

The fingers on my hip dug in and his voice rasped across my parted lips as he said my name. When I didn't stop my hectic and uncoordinated grind, he kissed me hard and tugged on my aching nipple with enough force that I pulled back and let out a startled yelp.

"Honey, I know what you need but you gotta let me get my hands on you. You gotta remember that I'm here too." The fingers on my hip pressed in again and I slowly started to still where I was perched on top of him.

I blinked at him slowly, trying to recall how I'd ended up on top of him, using him like he was some sort of battery-operated sex toy. I wanted to forget all the bad stuff so badly that I forgot to focus on the good stuff that was right in front of me.

"I don't know what I'm doing." My voice sounded small and shattered.

He gave me a narrow-eyed look and leaned forward so that he could place a biting kiss on my swollen lips. "You know exactly what you're doing, you're making yourself feel good because no one you were with before bothered to do it for you." His eyes burned right through me and his words sent my entire world spinning out of the orbit it had always been in. "I'm not them. When we're together, I'm going to make you feel good." His dimples flashed. "So good. You have to trust me."

We stared at each other, his hands on me, my hands on him, and I slowly nodded. I trusted him . . . it was myself I still had doubts about. "You can use your hands."

His dimples dug into his cheeks even deeper as his smile tugged at his mouth. "And my mouth."

I was going to shake my head because I wasn't sure I was ready for the double assault to my most sensitive places but I didn't get a chance to protest before his lips circled one pebbled peak that was clearly visible under the fabric of my shirt. His tongue lashed at the covered skin but I felt the lapping all the way through to my core. I tossed my head back and involuntarily moved across the still-hard erection trapped between my legs. His mouth tugged, pulled, suckled on one nipple until I had my hands in his hair and was pulling on it while muttering his name over and over again. I thought I was going to melt into a puddle on top of him when he turned his attention to the other pointed tip.

The hand he had on my hip urged me to find a rhythm I liked as I rode him furiously, all the sensation trapped between us because of our clothing. He was thick enough and big enough that he was hitting all the right spots, but I still felt a hollow, empty ache that was begging to be filled. I was close to something, right on the edge of the unknown and unfamiliar. I wanted to reach out and take it, to make whatever it was that was hovering just out of reach my own, but I didn't know how to do it, so I wailed Wheeler's name and asked him to help me find whatever it was I was looking for.

His teeth slashed in a wicked and knowing smile. I told him he could use his hands but he was waiting until I really wanted him to, until I needed his touch more than I needed my next breath. He was good, far better than any man I'd ever been with before. Not because he knew how and where to touch, but because he knew *when* to touch. He waited until there was no going back. He waited until I needed what he and only he could give me. He waited until I was ready.

Panting, practically crying with want, I pressed into his chest as his fingers left their hold on my hip and started a slow, torturous descent between my legs. They traced the bend at the top of my thigh and dipped down over smooth skin and disappeared between damp folds. I jolted in shock at being touched where I swore no man would ever have his hands again, but that quickly turned to a shudder as his clever fingertips tracked over delicate skin and sought out hidden places with the utmost care and reverence. He wasn't only using his touch to make me feel good, he was using it to soothe me, to calm me, to entrance me. He was erasing every touch that had hurt and giving me a million more that didn't.

My thighs quivered like I had run a marathon and I stopped breathing as he memorized every secret place I had.

"Move, honey." His raspy order shook me out of my stupor and I did what I was told. I moved.

I rocked back and forth. I rubbed my still-tight and aroused nipple against his bare chest. I put my mouth on his and rode his fingers and they slid inside of my underwear, his thumb circling my swollen clit over and over again, his movements hampered by the fabric that kept me covered. I moaned and he growled. I partially roared his name and he whispered mine back. I watched him with worried eyes as feeling built, huge and fast, ready to overtake me. He watched me with awe and admiration as I shattered into a million pieces of pleasure on top of him.

His fingers dragged wetness across my skin as he pulled them out of me. He used the same hand to catch my waist so that he could pull me off of him and turn me so my back was to his front. His cock was still hard, still hot and unbending behind me. I felt every inch of it as he nestled it against the curve of my ass. I wanted to push back into it, wanted to give him more, but as if he read my mind he quietly ordered, "I think that's enough playing with fire for one night. I'm not going to let us burn through each other this fast. We need to get some sleep."

He let go and turned off the lights only to roll right back and capture my waist again. We stayed silent and still for a long moment but I couldn't close my eyes and I couldn't ignore that very obvious reminder that he had given me something amazing and I hadn't given him anything but a headache and a hard-on.

"If you're going to make me feel good, shouldn't you expect the same thing from me?" I'd done my best to make the men that came before him feel good so they would give me the same consideration. It hadn't worked. I'd given Wheeler nothing and he had given me an entire world I didn't even know existed.

I felt his lips hit the back of my head and his hips shift tighter into mine. His cock seemed perfectly content where it was at.

"Poppy, you let me in your bed, you let me in your life." He gave me a squeeze and tucked the top of my head under his chin. "Trust me, you letting me in makes me feel very, very good. The rest will come when it's meant to."

As I closed my eyes and settled into his warmth and the darkness that surrounded us, I couldn't help but think that if getting lost meant he would come find me, then getting lost wasn't such a bad thing.

Chapter 10

Wheeler

I felt like I was having a panic attack.

I could feel the doctor looking at me expectantly and I knew Kallie was fidgeting nervously on the table as we both stared at the black-and-white screen that showed a weird-looking blob that definitely had identifiable human features. The nose poked up in the air as minuscule fingers waved on the end of a tiny little hand.

This was real. So real.

I was going to be a father.

That was my kid growing inside the woman that had shredded my heart and annihilated all my previous dreams of happy-ever-after.

I felt like I was suffocating. There was no air in the room, and each time the small heartbeat, strong and loud, filled the silence, I felt mine race.

The doctor cleared her throat and shifted her questioning gaze between me and my ex. The tension between the two of us was palpable and I'm sure the situation was as uncomfortable for her as it was for us.

"Well, everything looks exactly like it should at sixteen weeks. At this point in your second trimester you're going to be seeing more significant changes in your body and you'll be coming in to see me more frequently. In a few more weeks we should be able to tell if you're having a boy or a girl. That is, if you're interested in knowing the sex beforehand." She nodded at the ultrasound screen and gave a reassuring smile. "We'll get you a printout of your very active baby so you can take it with you today. Do either of you have any questions for me?"

Kallie turned her head to look at me and I immediately looked away. I was having a hard time keeping myself in the chair I was sitting in and not making a mad dash for the door. I heard her sigh as she took the offered towel to wipe off the clear gel that was smeared all over her mostly-flat stomach. I couldn't believe our baby was living inside there. I couldn't believe that in all the years we'd been together, seemingly happy and planning a future together, we hadn't had so much as a scare when it came to pregnancy. That included all the years when we were stupid teenagers fucking without much thought to safety, sex being the first thing on our minds when we were alone. It felt like some kind of ugly joke that it was when our fairy tale fell apart this new life was created. All I ever wanted was a family and a forever of my own. What I got was this clusterfuck that made my chest hurt and my head pound.

"Thanks, Dr. Ehrhardt. I think we're good. If anything comes up I won't hesitate to give you a call." I looked up at the woman that had sent my entire world spinning off its axis and flinched when I realized she was staring at me with open and obvious disappointment. She expected more from me because I had always given her everything, but this time . . . well, I wasn't sure I had anything to offer her. She swung her legs off the exam table and straightened her clothes as she got to her feet. I followed suit and paused as the doctor stopped in front of me and extended her hand for me to shake.

I gave it a quick pump expecting her to immediately let go but instead she gave my fingers a tight squeeze and offered me a soft smile. "It can be a lot to take in. Don't worry, Mr. Wheeler, you'll get used to the idea of being a father, and before you know it you'll be anxiously awaiting the moment when you can hold your baby in your arms. You're here. That's a huge step, one a lot of young men don't bother to take." She looked back at Kallie, who was now standing directly behind me. "Take care of each other. That's my best advice to both of you, regardless of your circumstances. You'll need one another going forward and your baby will need both of you." She finally let go of my hand and gave a cheerful wave as she left the room.

I gave Kallie a hard look over my shoulder as she let out a dry laugh. I lifted a questioning eyebrow at her as she stepped around me and reached for the door. "My first appointment with her, when I showed up with my mom, she told me that plenty of young women my age had babies without a partner in the picture. She told me that being a single mother was challenging but completely rewarding. I think she has a pep talk in reserve no matter what the situation might be."

I followed her down the hallway silently and paused when she stopped at the checkout desk to schedule her next appointment and to collect the grainy black-and-white image of our baby. When she handed me my own copy all I could do was stare at it numbly. That was my baby. I still couldn't wrap my head around it.

Outside, I was ready to tell Kallie good-bye so I could find the closest bar and shoot back some whiskey and hide from my problems like the mature, rational adult I was. Unfortunately, Kallie had other plans. She put a hand on my arm as I started toward the Eldorado and pulled me to a stop.

"Wheeler . . ." Her voice was strained and the look on her face was one that would have made my heart bleed before. "I hate that things are so tense between us, that other people can tell you don't want to be around me." She blinked and I realized there were big fat tears in her eyes. "You have always been my favorite person in the whole world and it hurts that you've completely shut me out of your life."

I opened my mouth to tell her I was doing the best that I could but the words wouldn't come. I was hardly trying and we both knew it.

"Listen, Kallie, you have a lot of people at your back to help you with all of this. Your mom and dad, Dixie, and even Roni, if you come clean about what she means to you." I pointed at the center of my chest where that lone wolf lived. "I'm navigating this on my own. I'm trying to figure out my new place in your life and in our baby's life with no help at all, so you need to let me work this out whatever way is easiest for me."

"That's bullshit and you know it. I'm right here, Wheeler. If anyone knows how hard this is, how complicated it is, that would be me." She crossed her arms over her chest and narrowed her eyes at me. "I get that this isn't the ideal situation for either of us but I wasn't alone when this baby was made."

I shook her hand off and moved toward my car. "I loved you then, Kallie." I saw the way my words cut into her. "I'm still trying to figure out how I feel about you now."

She sniffed a little and stepped away from me. "I love you, I always will. It's a different kind of love than we had before, but that doesn't make it any less important." A single tear slipped out of her eye before she could blink it away and it made me clench my fists at my sides. I'd spent so much of my life trying to be the guy that never hurt her and here I was making her cry. "I always knew I was going to have a family with you, Wheeler. I always dreamed about the babies we would have and how they would have your hair and those amazing dimples. This isn't the way either of us wanted it to happen but I refuse to be sorry that it's happening. Some things were meant to be. You and I might not be one of them, but you and I being a family sure seems to be. That family might not look the way you wanted it to, but it's going to be *our* family regardless."

I stared at her, letting her words sink in. She'd always been the spoiled one, the pampered one, in our relationship. I never expected her to be anything else but that. However, when circumstances changed, when she was suddenly responsible for another life, she had finally stopped being so self-indulgent and coddled. She was growing up and behaving far more maturely and reasonably than I was.

Sighing, I stepped up the curb and wrapped my arms around her in a hug that was awkward and stiff. I used to hug her and feel like I was home; now there was so much distance between us that it felt like I had my arms around a stranger. She tucked her head under my chin and wound her arms around my waist. It should feel familiar but it didn't. It felt foreign and strange.

"Give me some time, Kallie. I swear I'll get it together and be the guy you need me to be."

She gave me another squeeze and stepped back. Her cheeks were wet and her face was flushed but she was no longer looking at me like I had let her down. "You've always been the guy I needed you to be, Wheeler. I know you will be the man this baby is lucky to call daddy." She rubbed her face with the back of her hand. "You were always so patient with me. You never called me on any of my bullshit and you forgave me when I hurt you time and time again. You might not be driving this time but I promise I'm not going anywhere without you." A weak smile tugged at her mouth. "You can be the navigator. You're good at making sure no one gets lost." She nodded at the Eldorado. "The Caddy is gonna look really cute with a car seat in the back."

I choked a little and looked at my car and back at the former love of my life and current mother of my child. "Shit. I just got used to the idea of having a nursery in my house. I didn't think about my car." I rubbed a hand across the back of my neck and sighed. "I don't think I'm ever going to be the minivan type."

She laughed and rolled her eyes at me. "Who's asking you to drive a minivan? As long as you can belt a safety seat in the back you're fine, and if that doesn't work you own a garage. You can borrow a family-friendly car on the days you have the baby and keep the Caddy for the days you don't."

I felt both of my eyebrows shoot up as I considered her thoughtfully. "You've been giving this a lot of thought." I was surprised she was the one making all the sense. The screaming she-devil that had made the last year of my life a living hell was nowhere to be found. In her place was the girl I fell in love with all those years ago, but this version was even better than that one. It made my heart hurt for everything that could have been if Kallie and I were different people.

"Well, Roni won't talk to me until I get things squared away with Mom and Dad, Dixie is stupid in love and has her hands full settling into her new life in Mississippi, and up until today my best friend was ignoring me and pretending like I didn't exist." The last was a jab at me and I felt it slide right under my skin just like she intended it to. "All I've done is go over and over the best way to make all of this work and I know that asking you to change or expecting you to be anything other than the guy who I made this baby with is not the answer. You spent our entire relationship trying to be the guy you thought I wanted you to be, but the reality is you couldn't be who I wanted no matter how hard you tried. That scared the crap out of me, and instead of dealing with it, I put you through the wringer and made you jump through endless hoops. I was terrible to you, Wheeler, and I'll never be able to make up for all that wasted time."

I grunted and pulled open the door to my car. "You wasted a lot of years on me, Kallie. Don't make the same mistake with the person you really want to spend the rest of your life with."

On my way to the shop I paused at a stoplight and pulled the sonogram picture out of the back pocket of my jeans and stared at it. I let my thumb rush over the little nose and tapped my fingers on the minute-sized hand that was barely detectable. Out of nowhere, images of a little boy that looked a lot like me playing with plastic tools and banging on toy cars flooded my brain. I'd never had anyone to show me the way when I was young, never had anyone to teach me how to be a man and do the right thing. I wanted to kick myself for not realizing exactly what it was going to mean to be a father. I'd never had one and I was standing in front of an opportunity to give someone else everything I'd missed. I was an idiot for squandering any of that, for telling myself that if it didn't happen the way I wanted it to, then it wasn't good enough.

Someone honked behind me and I turned my attention back to the road. It was still early afternoon, so I should head back to work, but instead I found myself headed downtown toward the vet clinic where Poppy worked.

We'd been spending a lot of time together over the last week or so. She didn't flinch or move away when I got close to her anymore, in fact she moved closer when she could. There were stolen kisses here and there and sometimes they led to heated embraces and seductive touches that had me spending a lot of time in the shower with my fist wrapped around my cock.

Wordlessly she was asking for more, her touch getting braver, her eyes getting bolder, but she still wasn't ready for everything we could do to each other. She never complained when my clothes started coming off but she also wasn't in any kind of hurry to remove hers. I'd never seen those pert breasts or that silken, hot place between her legs. I knew the strangled sounds she made when she was close to breaking apart and I heard the way she gasped my name when I made her come in my dreams almost every single night.

She let me touch her while she crawled all over me, rubbing, arching into me, begging me for release, but she never took it further. I hadn't had a girl grind on me and ride me over my clothes since I was in high school. I also hadn't come inside my jeans from those kinds of innocent ministrations since I first figured out how good girls felt pressed against me. Everything with Poppy was some kind of perfect torture, and while my dick was more than ready to know what kind of pleasure her body held, my heart knew that if we went too far too fast, all the trust I'd meticulously cultivated would crumble. She trusted me to touch her, to take care of her needs, and I wanted her to know that I always would even if it meant I drove home with a hard-on so stiff that felt like it was going to break off. I didn't ever want her to think that my taking care of her meant I was expecting her to return the favor.

She wasn't being rewarded for her performance. It was my privilege to pleasure her, my honor to be allowed in her bed, and I never wanted her to question the fact that I appreciated her allowing me to be there after everything the men before me had put her through.

She'd yet to go into detail about what had happened after her husband pointed the gun at her sister and forced Poppy to go with him. But I'd spent the night next to her on more than one occasion and she couldn't keep the horror away and locked behind her walls when she slept. It didn't take Sherlock Holmes to figure out that he had forced her, hurt her, and terrorized her. She screamed "no," "stop," "you're hurting me," and "don't do this" over and over again. She was loud and thrashed around on the bed like she was trying to get away. I was surprised her neighbors didn't complain because it was obvious her outbursts were a common occurrence and she slept through them all.

At first, I thought I should wake her up and try and settle her down, but as soon as I touched her, she curled into me and burrowed as close as she could. I wrapped my arms around her and held on to her as she shook like a leaf for the next hour. Eventually, she went still and melted into me, but throughout the night she would let out these little whimpers like a trapped animal, and they tore my guts to shreds. She didn't need to relive what that bastard had done to her by giving me the words . . . the memories were clearly alive and well inside of her. She told the story without words and I heard every gory, awful detail of it.

When I got to the clinic, I texted her that I was outside and wanted to show her something. She shot back a message that said she was in the middle of an exam and would be out as soon as she could. I left the car running because it was cold, and while I waited for her I sent another message, this one to Zak, telling him I was in with the Hudson. I'd always wanted one and Kallie was right, no one was expecting me to be a minivan guy just because I had a baby on the way. I was the only one thinking my entire life had to change because of my new addition, and while my priorities were going to be rearranged for sure, there was no denying that getting my hands on one of my dream cars was an opportunity I would be an idiot to pass up. I got an immediate response that he was on it. He assured me again that he would score the lowest price he could, even after he told me the bottom-line price was fair. I was slightly bemused because the guy seemed more excited about the project than I did. I assumed he was stoked that the car was going to be in Denver, where he could visit it instead of shipped off to parts unknown.

I was still wondering about the guy and why I was so certain our paths must have crossed before when the passenger door swung open and Poppy slid into the seat next to me. She was shivering as the outside chill followed her into the warm interior of the car, but there was a small smile on her face and she leaned toward me with no hesitation when I crooked my finger at her. Every time her lips landed on mine it made my entire body come alive. My nerves sparked with sensation, my skin tingled from head to toe, and without fail my dick twitched and reminded me that there were other parts of my anatomy that really wanted a shot at touching her besides my hands and my mouth.

"I only have a second. There was an emergency case that

came in a couple hours ago and that pushed all the appointments behind." The tip of her tongue traced the curve of my bottom lip and her eyes gleamed gold at me. "What did you want to show me?"

I pulled the sonogram picture out of the dash and handed it over to her. Her tawny brows dipped in confusion as she looked at the odd little blob that was eventually going to be my baby. I saw her mouth turn down and watched the blood drain from her face as she silently handed the picture back to me. The gleam in her eyes went dull as she stared at me blankly.

I frowned at her and tucked the picture back into my pocket. "Kallie had a checkup this morning and I went with her. We had a come-to-Jesus meeting afterward about the baby and being a family even if we're no longer together. She said some things I didn't know that I needed to hear and it helped me get my head out of my ass." I crossed my arms on the steering wheel and rested my chin on my folded hands. "I'm all in. I guess I didn't realize I wasn't before. That's the first picture of my kid, I wanted to show it to you." She wouldn't look at me, and the longer she sat in silence, the more confused I became. A littler harsher than I meant to I snapped, "I thought you would be happy that I'm finally on board with all this baby stuff."

She curled her hands into fists and tucked her chin into her chest so she wasn't looking at anything but her lap. Vaguely, I recalled the way she almost fell over the day she showed up with the dog at the garage and I told her I couldn't take him because of the baby. There was something going on with her that I didn't understand, and if we were ever going to get to a place where we were all in with each other, then she needed to trust me with more than just her body.

"Poppy . . ." I waited until she looked up at me. It took a hell of a long time. "What's going on? What's your deal with babies? You're telling me to man up and be the best dad I can be one minute and in the next you look like me having a kid is the end of the world. I know it's not the best situation for me to be in while I'm trying to start something with you, but I can't change it, and honestly, I wouldn't want to."

She stared at me and I could see her trying to figure out what she wanted to say. I watched her weighing how many of her secrets she wanted to share with me. Finally, she uncurled her hands and rubbed her palms back and forth on her thighs. She turned her head so that she was looking out the windshield and her voice was barely audible when she spoke.

"You and I wanted similar things out of life, Wheeler. I had two parents and a roof over my head but I often wished I was anywhere else but home. I wanted a family that loved me. I wanted a home that was full of happy memories, bursting with laughter and children. I wanted the opposite of everything I had ever known . . . just like you."

I felt my shoulders stiffen as a frown fell over my face. I hated that she knew how hard it was to be the kid that was lonely and lost as soon as the school bell rang at the end of the day.

"When I went away to college I picked the one that would get me as far away from my father as possible. I had stars in my eyes and big dreams. I was so sure that without his constant disapproval, without his unrelenting judgment, I would be able to spread my wings and fly. I was convinced it was going to be just like the movies. I was going to find a guy that was the opposite of my dad, he was going to sweep me off my feet, we were going to get married, have babies, and live happily ever after." She snorted and pushed the heels of her palms into her eyes as she tossed her head back onto the vintage leather of the seat behind her. "Rowdy went to the same school on a football scholarship. He kept an eye on me and he told me over and over again that I needed to stop being so naive. He told me college boys were waiting for pretty freshman girls exactly like me." She turned to look at me and I could see some of those things that chased her in her dreams wide-awake in her tragic gaze. "He was right. The first boy I agreed to date told me everything I wanted to hear. He promised me the sun and the moon. He assured me that I was special, and that he wanted something serious and lasting. I liked him so much and I was so smitten that I let him get away with pretty much anything. Including having sex without a condom. He knew I wasn't on birth control, I told him over and over again we should be safe, but I was in love and he told me we would be together forever. I wanted it so badly, I ignored Rowdy and I ignored my own common sense."

"Poppy." I wasn't sure if I was saying her name to get her to go on or to get her to stop. It didn't matter, she kept going even though I had a pretty good idea where the story was headed.

"I was so excited when I found out I was pregnant. I was too young, barely eighteen, and I'd just started school, but it didn't matter. We were going to be a family. All my dreams were coming true." She started to cry. Silent tears that rolled down her face and dripped off her chin. I couldn't handle the space between us anymore and pulled her into my arms. She curled an arm around my neck and I felt the moisture from her cheeks on the side of my throat as she pressed her face tightly into my skin. "When I told him I was pregnant, he laughed at me and told me I was stupid. He also told me I was one of many. He had a different girl for each day of the week. He wanted me to get rid of the baby, told me he would pay for it, and I refused. He attacked me."

"Motherfucker." The word ripped out of me before I could stop it. She hugged me tighter as anger made my entire body shake under her.

"He hurt me really badly, so bad that I lost the baby and I lost myself. Rowdy found me, did his best to put me back together, but it was too late." She sobbed quietly into my skin. "I loved my baby, Wheeler. It was the only thing in my life that I ever wanted that I actually got and then it was taken away. I know I would have been a good mom. I would have loved that baby and taken care of it so much better than my mom did with me and Salem."

Feeling helpless and furious, all I could do was hold her while she grieved for a little life that had been snatched away from her.

She shuddered and pulled away from me so that we were eye to eye and nose to nose in the close confines of the car. "I'm proud of you for realizing how great the gift you've been given is, Wheeler, but every time someone close to me gets to celebrate bringing a new life into the world, it takes me back to a time when that chance was stolen from me."

I dropped my forehead down so that it was resting against hers and gently kissed the tip of her nose. "Give me the college guy's name. I'm gonna kill him."

She grinned and put her hands on either side of my face, her fingers tracing the spot where my dimples were hidden by my fierce scowl. "Rowdy already tried. That's how he lost his scholarship and ended up a drifter."

"I'm going to buy Rowdy every single drink he ever has from here until the day I die." I wasn't kidding.

She lifted her head and returned the kiss on the tip of my nose. "You're going to be a great dad, Wheeler."

"Honey." She locked her eyes on mine and I told her quietly, "You're going to be a great mom, too. That was not your only shot at having a baby."

She blinked long and slow, her breath escaping on a harsh breath. "Yeah?" She didn't sound like she fully believed me.

I chuckled a little and touched my lips to hers. "Yeah."

She climbed off my lap and scooted to the other side of the car. Her hand was on the door handle as she asked like she hadn't just ripped my heart out and handed it back to me torn to shreds, "I have to go back to work, but I'll see you later tonight, right?"

Like anything could keep me away from her after she trusted me with some of the monsters that chased her in her sleep. "Absolutely."

She smiled at me and rubbed her cheeks to clear away the evidence of her tears and I couldn't help but imagine pretty little girls with gold eyes and honey-colored hair standing right next to a little boy that looked just like me.

Chapter 11

Poppy

My sister was beautiful, inside and out, but right now her perfectly painted ruby-red lips were pulled into a scowl so fierce she looked a little bit scary. The winged edges of her meticulously drawn-on eyeliner gave her glare extra sharpness and the bright pink on her high cheekbones had nothing to do with the subtle blush that was swirled there and everything to do with the anger that was evident in every line of her curvy body. The manicured hand that was on the table in front of mine curled into a fist while her other one protectively covered the gentle swell that was visible behind her flowy off-the-shoulder top and high-waisted skirt. She still had a ways to go in her pregnancy and it was obvious she wasn't going to sacrifice style for comfort yet. She even had a pair of ridiculously high heels on her feet, the toe of one tapping in aggravation as she stared at me from across the table where our lunch was left forgotten after I told her that our mother had called me out of the blue.

"She'll get near this baby over my dead body." The words were fierce and final. "If she calls again, hang up. Do not let her get inside your head. She picked him over us our entire lives; now that she had to live with that choice without a buffer, it's her cross to bear."

Her midnight gaze was intense and hard for me to meet, but I didn't look away when I told her, "I know that, but I also know what it's like to end up in a situation that you want out of but can't find the door. No one was there to show me the way away from Oliver and I don't know that I can live with myself if I let someone else stay stuck in that kind of environment."

Salem snorted and reached for her glass of water. "She should have helped you get away from Oliver. She should have warned you that you were marrying a man just like Dad. She should have said something when he told his entire congregation that what happened was a tragedy, then had them pray for the man that abused you for years and not for you." She was unbending, but then again, she was the one that had been strong enough to walk away from all the wrongness that was our family without a backward glance. She saw the black and white of it all, but I'd lived in the gray of wanting out but staying out of fear, so I understood it.

"I don't know that she understood what marrying a man just like Dad really meant, Salem." I stuck a cold french fry in my mouth and cocked my head to the side as she narrowed her eyes even more at me. "Her parents were hardly any different. Grandpa married Grandma so he could stay in the country just like Dad married mom so he would look respectable and upstanding. Grandpa was never faithful, never kind, and his expectations of Grandma were outrageous and impossible. He ruled with an iron fist just like our dad did and there was no love lost in that home. She found a man exactly like her father, so maybe she expected her daughter to do the same thing. It's a vicious cycle, one that I've learned isn't all that uncommon." That was something that was a recurring theme in my group sessions: abuse was a vicious cycle, one that was hard to break even when you recognized the fact you were repeating dangerous patterns. "She's as much of a victim as I am."

"Survivor, Poppy. You are a survivor, not a victim." She was so adamant that I had to smile at her. She was always there to remind me to keep going, refusing to let me give up.

I chomped on another fry and lifted an eyebrow at her. "Mom could be a survivor too, if someone helped show her that there was a better way to live. I refuse to believe that anyone is beyond saving. You wouldn't let me waste away in a bad place and I'm not sure I'm the type of person that can let Mom."

She sighed and tapped her long nails on the side of her glass. "Fine, you do what you think you have to, but you promise me right now that if she doesn't want your help, if she digs her heels in and unwaveringly stands by Dad, you back off. I won't let them drag you back into their house of misery and there is no way in hell Rowdy will let either of them mess up the lives we've built here in Denver. He's protective of the present and resents the hell out of the past. I can't say I blame him."

I nodded at the waitress who stopped by and asked to take my plate, ansd then I chuckled when Salem ordered two different desserts. She rolled her eyes at me and told me she expected me to share both. She'd always had a sweet tooth; I wasn't surprised pregnancy had made her insatiable.

I wasn't fond of the past either but it held painful lessons that I had to learn in order to avoid making the same mistakes over and over again. The past brought me to my present, which was actually the reason I'd eagerly agreed to lunch with Salem when she called and told me she had a doctor's appointment, so she was only working half a day at the tattoo shop and wanted to get together. It was easier to be around her now that, sitting on Wheeler's lap, I'd unburdened myself and all my guilty envy about others that I loved being pregnant. It was so freeing to share, like a giant weight had been lifted off me. Explaining the confusing mix of joyous and envious feelings to someone that was expecting a baby had helped more than months of therapy. He wasn't mad that I both resented and reveled in his good fortune. He was heartbreakingly understanding and unendingly considerate . . . like he always was.

That understanding, and his words after I told him everything, were the reason I was beyond ready to take our relationship to the next level. I'd lost count of the number of thought-stealing, body-racking orgasms he'd given me, and while I cherished every single one, I wanted more. I wanted every line of that long, lean body on top of mine. I wanted to rub myself all across that tattooed skin. I wanted that bulge that filled out the front of his underwear and pressed insistently against me inside of my body. I wanted to ride him and feel him until I couldn't see straight. But more than any of that, I wanted to give him back a fraction of all the things he'd given me. I was ready to be an active participant. I just couldn't figure out the right way to communicate to him that I was ready for the next step. He was careful with me, so mindful, and while I appreciated it, I was ready for him to throw caution to the wind and treat me like he would any other woman that was spending a significant amount of time in his bed. I wanted this relationship to be real in all ways.

I tried telling him without words, I used my hands and my

mouth, greedy with the way I touched him and tasted him, but he always stopped. We were so close to crossing the inevitable line that would launch us from being something casual into something serious and significant. He told me we had time, that he wasn't going anywhere, but that didn't stop my insides from feeling empty and lust from making me edgy and unsatisfied no matter how skilled he was with his hands and his mouth. I wanted all of him, not just the parts that he deemed safe and harmless.

I cleared my throat and reached for my glass of water as Salem's sharp gaze shifted from the decadent-looking cheesecake and towering carrot cake that were placed in front of her. She handed me a spoon and lifted a raven-colored eyebrow at me as she waited for me to find the words that were having a hard time situating themselves on my tongue.

"About the present . . ." I could feel a fiery blush work its way up my throat and across my cheeks. "You know I've been spending a lot of time with Wheeler the last few weeks."

She nodded and scooped a spoonful of cake into her mouth. She moaned in pleasure and gave me a grin. "I couldn't be more thrilled. Rowdy gives him his stamp of approval, even with the baby mama in the picture."

The fact that Rowdy liked Wheeler was also a check mark in the plus category in my books, but the truth was, I was so far gone over the moody mechanic that even if Rowdy didn't approve I would still be trying to figure out a way inside Wheeler's cuffed and faded jeans.

"Well, things are going . . . good." I shifted uncomfortably in my seat as she set the spoon down, propped her elbow on the table, and rested her chin on her hand.

She fluttered her obnoxiously long eyelashes at me and purred, "Do tell."

I traced the condensation on the outside of the glass in front of me with a fingertip and avoided her probing gaze. "He's sweet. He's patient. He's stupidly hot." I sighed and couldn't keep the wistful, dreamy quality out of it. "I like him, way more than like him, and most importantly, I like the way he is with me, but . . ."

She tapped her fingers on the side of her face and her ruby-red lips split into a blinding smile. "But him being a nice guy in the bedroom is getting old?"

That surprised a laugh out of me and I nodded solemnly. "I never thought I would say it, but yeah. He's been giving me time to get used to him, and I adore him for that, but I feel like I'm all broken in now. I don't want him to think he's in bed with a victim. I want him to know he's with a survivor."

My sister's smile grew and she turned back to her double dessert. "So show him that's what you are. Don't wait for him to figure it out. Seduce him, show him that you're ready for the next step."

I leaned back a little and put my hand to my racing heart. "I don't want to seem desperate."

She snorted again and tossed some of her long, glossy hair over her shoulder. "Poppy, when there is a good man in your life, one you want to keep there, it isn't desperation to go out of your way to make sure he knows he matters to you." She pointed her frosting-covered spoon at me and told me with humor threaded throughout her tone, "We've all been there. *All* of us."

On the hand not holding the spoon she started ticking off examples on her fingers. "Shaw got drunk and jumped Rule on her birthday. Ayden showed up at one of Jet's shows with another guy on Valentine's Day. Cora showed up unannounced at Rome's and pounced on him when he got out of the shower and ended up knocked up. Saint promised Nash ten minutes to rock his world. I packed up my entire life and moved across the country for a boy I hadn't seen in years because I was sure he was the one, and Royal showed up at Asa's in the middle of the night wearing nothing but an overcoat." She wiggled her eyebrows up and down suggestively, which made me laugh as she kept going. "You know Sayer had ulterior motives when she offered to help Zeb paint that old house he was working on, and last but not least Avett took a header off a freaking cliff knowing good and well Quaid was going to have to jump after her crazy ass. You were there when Dixie climbed on the back of Church's bike even though she was scared to death after what happened to her dad. All the women I know that landed a good man had to give them a little push in the right direction at one point or another. Sometimes it takes a nudge to get the knight in shining armor to drop his shield."

I felt my mouth drop open in a small "oh" of surprise. Her recounting of our friends' exploits was incredibly eye-opening. They were the strongest, most well-loved women I had ever met, and if they could make a move and be none the worse for wear after, then I should be able to as well. "And honestly, those dimples. Come on, how is that even fair to anyone with a vagina? I can't believe you've behaved yourself this long with that kind of temptation close enough to lick."

We shared a laugh that had the tables next to us giving us questioning looks but Salem just smiled at the other diners and gave them an outrageous wink.

I finally picked up a spoon and dug into the still-untouched cheesecake. "What can I say, good things come to those who wait." At least I hoped they did because as of tonight I was done waiting. I was going to move him where I wanted him, the same way he always seemed to be moving me. But I was sure as hell was planning on touching him to get him where I wanted him.

When I got home, I wandered around my apartment for a solid hour trying to figure out exactly how I could plan a night of seduction when Wheeler came over after work. I cleaned the place up, dug out some really sad-looking candles I had just in case of emergencies, turned to my old standby Pinterest in search of ideas for making my bedroom something romantic and attractive rather than a place where demons chased me in the dark. All of it felt off and way too forced. Even if I set the mood in my apartment, it wasn't like I owned anything sultry and seductive that would work as a flashing, light-up sign saying DO ME NOW! All I had was my regular sleepwear that covered me from wrists to ankles and he'd had no problem keeping his basic urges in check when I curled up next to him wearing it.

It all felt like I was setting some kind of sexual trap, like I was trying to lure him into something he might not actually want, no matter how insistent he was that he was simply waiting for the right time to seal the deal.

Frustrated and feeling foolish, I decided I needed to approach this situation with the stark honesty and surprising fearlessness that only he brought out in me. I stopped by Dixie's since she was back home for a few days and asked her to watch Happy for me. She asked what was going on and when I would be back to pick up the furry handful, and when I stammered and turned neon pink, she had her answer before I got the words out. It was super awkward considering Wheeler had put a ring on her sister's finger not too long ago, but Dixie, being the bighearted, smart woman that she was, didn't seem fazed by my request or the conclusions she drew from it.

It only took a few minutes to get to LoDo and a few more for me to screw up my courage to tell him what I wanted to say. I took a minute to brace myself and wished that I had taken the time to put more effort into my appearance before showing up to proposition him like some kind of crazy woman. I was asking him to put the protective armor down but I felt like I needed a little bit of my own to get through this.

Fluffing my loose hair and slicking on a coat of the clear Chap-Stick that was in the bottom of my purse was the best I could do. It didn't make me feel invincible by any stretch of the imagination but it helped.

I climbed out of the car and made my way to the steps and the heavy metal door that led to the inside of the garage. Several of the bays were open out into the street, so I knew Wheeler still had a full crew at work for the day. The noise inside the building was almost deafening. Grinders, air hoses, engines revving, and loud music blaring over hidden speakers. The chaos was actually calming and so was the smile that lit up Wheeler's face and the light that brightened his pale eyes when he caught sight of me hovering uncertainly by the door. One of his guys put his fingers in his mouth and let out a shrill whistle that had all heads turning in my direction as he hollered out, "Boss, your lady is here!"

I'd been by the garage several times to pick up the dog and to drop food off when Wheeler had to work late, but I didn't stop to think that the guys would pick up on my presence in their boss's life. I was a little shocked that other people realized I was his when I had only recently come to that conclusion myself.

"I can see that, Derek. Take it down a notch so you don't scare her off before I can kiss her hello." He walked toward me with that easy swagger that was all Wheeler, like he knew exactly where he was headed and he had all the time in the world to get there. Nothing and no one would rush him. He was cleaning his hands off on a red rag that he tucked into his back pocket and he had a smudge of something black across the bridge of his nose. He also had on a faded black baseball hat that covered up his reddish hair and forced him to tilt his head to the side when he bent down to brush his mouth over mine. "This is a nice surprise. Is everything okay? Where's Happy?"

I should have called to tell him I was coming. He was worried, which was the opposite of how I wanted him to feel.

Taking a deep breath, I reached up and put both my hands on the center of his chest so I could feel his heart beating and breathing change when I blurted out, "Everything is fine but I wanted to ask you something and I didn't want to wait until tonight."

His hands raised and his fingers circled my wrists, his thumbs rubbing my thundering pulse. "Must be important. You have my undivided attention, honey."

I fucking loved it when he called me that. I never asked him where the endearment came from but every time he said it my insides quivered and heart skipped a few beats. I grabbed each side of his coveralls in my hands and pulled him down so that we were almost nose to nose. His eyes looked like a winter sky but there was warmth shining out of them between every single blink.

"Will you have sex with me?" The words tumbled out fast and frantic, but there was no wavering or uncertainty in them anywhere. I meant them. I was all in.

"Dammit. Why don't my customers ever say shit like that to me? And how come none of them look like her?" The mechanic that was closest to us muttered the words loud enough for us to hear as Wheeler stood there staring at me like I'd suddenly grown a second head, eyes wide and mouth hanging open.

"Shut up, Hunter. One more word and I'll fire you, which will make you cry because the Hudson is supposed to show up this week." Wheeler grabbed my hand without looking at the mouthy mechanic and pulled me toward the part of the building where his office was located. I asked him where we were going but he didn't respond. His hold on my hand tightened and he squeezed my fingers. He paused briefly to tell his receptionist that he was taking the rest of the day off and that he wouldn't be in until late tomorrow. He also ordered her to get him a room at the Crawford Hotel, which was really nice and located in Union Station. It was within walking distance of the garage, and by the woman's knowing grin and the thumbs-up sign she flashed at me as Wheeler hauled me into his office, she knew exactly why he was suddenly ditching work.

As soon as the door to his office was closed, he whipped his hat around so the bill was at the back and his hands were on my face. He backed me into the door he'd just kicked shut and tunneled his fingers through my hair. He forced my head back and attacked my mouth.

It wasn't a nice kiss.

It wasn't a soft and searching kiss.

It wasn't tender or tame.

It was a kiss that seared my soul and set my skin on fire. It was wet and messy. It was teeth and tongues clashing. It was hungry and hot. He devoured me and then pulled back and came at me from another direction so he could overwhelm me from a different angle. His thigh pressed between my legs and his chest pinned me to the door. Every jagged breath he took rubbed the rough material of his uniform against my sensitive breasts, and every time I whimpered into his mouth, he shifted his weight so that the pressure of his leg hit me high and in exactly the right spot.

He pulled back and looked at me. Eyes on fire with every dirty, sexy thing he'd been holding off on doing to me. "You know how many times you've said those words to me in my dreams, Poppy?" I opened my mouth to answer but he stopped me with a kiss. "Thousands. I hear them and I wake up with my hand on my dick and balls so tight they hurt."

I ran my hands up and down the line of his ribs and shifted against the erection that was pressed tightly into the cleft at the top of my legs. "I can make those dreams come true." I couldn't believe that I was able to say that to a man and mean it. His dreams once again weren't that far off base from mine.

He blinked at me and then lowered his eyes to my now swollen lips. He palmed my head between his hands and lowered his forehead until it was touching mine. The fabric of his hat dug into my skin but I would die before I asked him to move away.

"I have no doubt you will blow my dreams out of the water." He kissed me again and rested one of his forearms over my head so that he was caging me in. I could feel his body heat and his hardness along every nerve ending. My body drifted toward his without me being aware that I was seeking out all the things about him that made me feel so good. "But I promise you that if you let me I will give you only good things to dream about from here on out, Poppy. Once you let me in, I will chase all your monsters away."

I brushed my nose along the column on his neck and licked at the thick vein that was throbbing there. "You've been doing that since we met, Wheeler."

He made a low noise in his throat and pushed back from the door. His mahogany-colored brows lifted and those to-die-for dimples made their appearance. "The right time is today and the right place is apparently a hotel right around the corner. I'll take good care of you, honey."

I lifted my eyebrows back at him and returned his infectious grin. "Time and place doesn't matter, but the right person sure as hell does. You're my right person."

His chest rose and fell as he let out a long breath. "Let's get out of here."

My feet couldn't move fast enough as I followed his long-legged gait. I'd made him move all right. Now I just had to make sure I could keep up.

Chapter 12

Wheeler

My hands were shaking so badly that I dropped the stupid little plastic key to the hotel room twice before finally touching it to the sensor and getting the door open. It was probably a touch over-the-top to drop everything in the middle of a workday and drag her off to the closest hotel, but as soon as those sexy words left her pretty, pink lips it was all I could do to keep my inner Neanderthal caged and not drag her off to my office and have my way with her.

I'd been waiting on the words since the moment she let me put my hands and mouth on her sweet skin.

It might have seemed silly considering she was practically begging me to have at her with her body and her hands, but I needed to hear that she was ready. I needed her to take that step. I needed her permission to touch her from the get-go and I knew that if we were going to be moving on to the next, inevitable step, I was going to need permission to fuck her. I needed her to be absolutely sure, and now that she was, I wanted to make sure she never had a single reason to doubt that I was indeed the right guy, regardless of the time or the place. I wanted her to have an experience that would always be a memory that made her smile, that made her happy no matter what happened between the two of us in the future. I wanted her to know she was worth dropping everything for and that she was absolutely the kind of girl that deserved something special like a fancy hotel room in the middle of the day and for our first time together. She deserved a bed that didn't hold memories of anyone or anything else. Her nightmares couldn't find her here and there were definitely no reminders of what I thought I wanted among the sleek decorations and the dramatically plush bedding and headboard.

This was me and her, there was no space for anyone else.

The dust had cleared and Poppy and I were left standing facing each other, the dreams we used to have lying in tatters at our feet. It was time to pick the pieces up and stitch together new dreams, ones that had pieces of her and pieces of me woven in the fabric so deeply that nothing could rip them apart.

I dropped the room key again and this time Poppy was the one to retrieve it from the floor. She gave me a lopsided grin as she tossed it on the dresser next to the TV remote. I realized I was the one acting like a nervous kid on prom night. She seemed perfectly at ease as she let her purse fall from her shoulder so she could set it down. She turned to look at me with a perfectly arched caramel-colored brow and a playful smile dancing around that enticingly bare mouth. She pushed some of her long honey-colored hair away from her face as she looked at the bed and then over to me.

"I'm all dirty." I blurted out the words so fast that they made her jump. Her amber gaze drifted over me from the grease-stained hat still on my head to the worn toes of my work boots.

She took the few steps required to close the space between us and lifted a hand so that she could run her fingers over my nose. When she pulled them back and showed them to me I cringed when I realized I'd hauled her out the garage without bothering to clean up. I looked like I'd been crawling around under a car, which I had been.

"It was covering up your freckles." She rubbed her fingers together and looked over my shoulder at the open doorway to the bathroom. "I think we should clean you up."

I swallowed hard and followed her gaze. "If you go in there with me, this is going to be over before we even get started." She was the first woman I had ever waited on, and while I knew without question she was worth the time I'd spent slaying some of her furious, fiery dragons, my body was primed and well beyond ready to be rewarded for that unwavering patience. If she got naked and wet anywhere close to me and my aching cock, it was going to be game over.

She snatched the hat off my head and threw it so that it landed on top of her purse. I lowered my head so she could get her fingers into my sweaty and flattened hair. I let out a quiet moan as her fingernails scraped along the sides of my scalp and trailed along the back of my head to dig into the tense muscles at the base of my skull.

"Wheeler." My name sounded so good when she said it all breathless and needy. "You have been really great about making this all about me, and I needed that then, but now I need you and I need this to be about us." She lifted her eyebrows up and her cheeks turned a charming shade of pink that made me want to see if she blushed like that everywhere else on her body.

It wasn't like I really wanted to put up much of a fight in the first place. If she wanted to help me get clean so we could get all kinds of dirty together, I would be a fool to try and talk her out of it.

I clasped my hands around the back of her head, mirroring the way she was holding on to me. I bent my head so I could touch my lips to hers, and whispered, "Let's get wet."

She smiled against my mouth and the tip of her tongue darted out and touched the center of my bottom lip, leaving a damp spot that I immediately chased with my own tongue. Her eyes glimmered with promises and heat that made me feel like I'd had too many drinks too fast. She went to my head quick and made my body feel like it was out of my control.

"One step ahead of you." I growled at her sassy and sure words. Her newfound confidence might be more of a turn-on than her miles of silken hair and all that golden skin that only I was allowed to touch. "You need to catch up."

I growled at her again and put my hands under her backside and effortlessly lifted her up. She immediately wound her legs around my waist and her arms around my neck. I was smugly pleased with myself when I realized she no longer felt feather-light. She was still slight, lithe and easy to carry from one place to the other, but the hollows in her face had filled out and there was more than enough to fill my hands as they curled posses-sively around the soft swell of her ass.

Her nose brushed up and down the side of my neck and I shivered as her tongue darted out and flicked along the line of my pulse where it was thudding heavy and hurried as we stum-bled into the opulent bathroom. The shower was a walk-in sur-rounded by glass with multiple shower heads. It looked like it was made with all intentions of more than one person using it to get clean. I set Poppy down on the edge of the sprawling vanity and took a step back so I could kick off my boots and peel off my filthy coveralls. She watched me with avid eyes that got hotter and hotter the more clothes I lost. Soon I was standing in front of her in nothing more than aqua-blue boxer briefs.

She bit down on her lower lip and reached out a hand so that she could trail a tentative finger along the ridge of my cock that was stretching the colorful fabric to its limits. She had hesitantly put her hands on my dick when we fooled around before, but she typically pulled back like it would burn her. This time she kept up her delicate caress until she reached the waistband, where the eagerly swollen head was peeking out of the elastic. I had to lock my knees to keep them from turning to jelly when she used the tip of her finger to circle the sensitive flesh over and over again.

"You always have on underwear that's some kind of crazy color. Why no black or white?"

Of all the times she could pick to ask me about my choice of undergarments, of course she would pick the moment when I couldn't think straight because of the way her hand was sliding into those brightly colored briefs and wrapping around the rock-hard erection they were covering.

I ran my hands up the outside of her denim-covered legs until I got to her waist. I watched her carefully as I worked my palms up under the hem of her baggy sweater. I started to inch the material up her rib cage but had to stop and suck in a breath when her grasp around my dick tightened and my eyes crossed because of how good it felt. "I dunno. You can find black and white anywhere and it's kind of expected. It's boring."

I got her sweater up over her head and let out a grunt of appreciation at the sight of her in nothing but her jeans and a soft, rose-colored bra. It looked silky, so of course I ran my fingers over the outside edge and watched as the touch made her creamy skin pebble in anticipation. Her legs tightened around my hips as I trailed a lone finger directly down the center of her chest, lightly skimming her belly button and stopping to pop open the button of her jeans.

She sucked in a sharp breath, so I stopped and started to pull back, not wanting to rush her. However, I had to chuckle when she used the grip she had on the most sensitive part of my anatomy to hold me in place.

"Nothing about you is boring. All of you stands out." She lifted her hips for me, and reluctantly pulled her hand out of my underwear so that I could pull her jeans off her legs. Her underwear matched the pretty bra and did very little to hide that private place on her body that I only knew by touch and taste. She wasn't lying to stroke my ego. There was a visible damp spot right in the center of the silk that made my mouth water.

"I spent my entire childhood feeling like I was overlooked, like nobody could see me. When I was old enough to do something about it, I made sure no one would be able to ignore me." I put my hands back on her hips and pulled her to the edge of the counter so that her softness and wetness were pressed up against the straining hardness between my legs that was begging for some kind of relief. "I wanted to be seen."

She skimmed her hands over my shoulders, down over the wolf inked on my chest, and across each and every single one of the lines that were carved into my stomach. She traced the twin lines over my hips that arrowed into the elastic waistband of my underwear and brushed the backs of her fingers over the narrow shot of hair under my belly button that was practically a neon sign guiding her toward the place on my body that couldn't hide the way I was affected by her.

"I see you, Wheeler. Even when I wasn't looking, I saw you."

They were words very similar to the ones I had said to her when I was trying to convince her to give me a shot.

"I'm glad we both had our eyes open." The last of the words dropped as she hopped off the counter so all of her was pressed against all of me. She hooked a single finger in the waistband and tugged.

"Off."

Her eyes turned sultry and heavy-lidded. The insanely thick lashes dropping low as I did as she requested. It was the first time I'd been fully naked in front of her and everything inside of me quivered with the overwhelming need for her to like what she saw. I didn't need to worry, like she said, she saw me even when she wasn't looking, and now that she was looking, she couldn't tear her eyes away.

"That tattoo goes all the way down." Her voice was hushed as she traced the swirling black ink that decorated my lower abdomen all the way down to the base of my cock. The tribal flames went as low as they could without actually being on my dick. They hurt like a bitch to get but I was glad they were there as her fingers lightly drifted over them, going lower and lower. Her touch seared my skin and I knew I would feel it long after we left this bathroom.

I reached around her for the clasp on the back of her bra. She stiffened in my arms and lifted wide eyes up to mine. "I don't know that I'm ready for that just yet." She looked embarrassed to say it, which should be at odds with the way she was rubbing against my unleashed cock, but somehow it was so very Poppy.

I tucked the front of her long hair behind her ear, cupped her face in my dirty hands, and lowered my head so I could kiss her. When I pulled back, we were both breathing hard and her eyes were unfocused. I stepped back and walked over to the shower so that I could turn it on and find the right temperature. She leaned back on the vanity, her arms bent as she braced herself so that she could watch me as I stepped under the steamy water and let it sluice off all the oil and grime from work. I popped open the mini-shampoo and scrubbed my matted-down hair and rubbed my hands roughly over my face and chest, chasing any other hidden smudges and smears that might mark up her flawless skin.

"You have freckles on your shoulders." Her voice wasn't echoing across the room, so I wasn't surprised that when I peeled open my eyes to peer through the falling water, she was now standing at the opening of the shower. She still had her pretty rose-colored underwear on but the embarrassment in her gaze was gone. She looked . . . hungry.

I turned back around so I could rinse off my front and lowered my head so the hot water would hit the coiled tension in the back of my neck. The anticipation was the perfect kind of hell. I wasn't in any hurry to escape the burn. "I have them everywhere." They went hand in hand with the red hair that I must have inherited from my father, because from what I remembered of my mother, her hair was as black as midnight.

I knew it was coming but still, when her fingers hit my slippery shoulder, it made my entire body jolt. Her palm smoothed over the speckled skin and then slid all the way down my spine.

"Why doesn't the tree have any leaves?" Her lips hit the center of my back and I felt the press of her now naked breasts against my hypersensitive skin. Her nipples dug into my back and her

hands worked their way around my waist so that they were resting on the ridges of my stomach.

I put one of my hands over hers and picked it up. She didn't tug
it back or fight me in any way when I lowered it to where my cock
was standing straight up and resting against my abs. I curled her
long fingers around the shaft with my own and slowly started to
work her fist up and down. I rested my forehead against the cool
marble of the shower wall and lifted my other arm above my
head so that her entire naked length was stretched out against
my back. I felt her wiggle her hips against my ass, our joined
hands working over my throbbing cock. She was starting to get
restless but I swore I could do this all day long.

"It's what my family tree looks like, barren and empty. I got
it thinking I would add to it once Kallie and I got married and
started a family. There would be leaves and blossoms, but now . . ."
I shook my head and trailed off partly because I wasn't sure what
my family tree was going to look like anymore but mostly because
she was using her thumb to rub enticing circles around the head of
my dick. The slit was leaking slippery desire and she was catching
it before the water could wash it away.

Her teeth bit into the curve where my neck and shoulder met
and the arm she still had locked around my middle tightened in
a hug. My hips kicked involuntarily into our combined touch
and my hand tightened around hers and forced it to move faster.
My breath hitched and my eyes slammed closed as pleasure hit
hard and heavy, looping itself around all my nerves and licking
through my blood. I let go of her gliding hands and reached behind me so I could grab a handful of supple flesh. Her lips skipped
across my shoulder blade and her nails dug into my stomach as I
started rocking back and forth into her caress with no control. I

was searching for the ending, seeking the completion that only her touch could give me, and I'd been waiting for it for so long that my control snapped and the torture of waiting no longer stung, but rather dug its claws in and hurt in a way that couldn't be ignored.

"Your tree is still growing, Wheeler. It's going to bloom." Her words whispered across my skin and I felt her rest her cheek on the barren branches that stretched from shoulder to shoulder.

My balls tightened and drew up close to my body, the thick vein that ran along the bottom of my dick pulsed hard, and the entire throbbing shaft kicked insistently into her gentle ministrations. The slick tip was covered in pearly precum that she couldn't seem to keep her fingers away from. I growled her name in warning, giving her plenty of time to pull away, but she leaned in closer, tightened her fingers even more, and worked the orgasm that was impatiently waiting from my body. She kept her fingers curled around my cock as my legs shook and air whooshed in and out of my lungs loudly. I pried my eyes open just in time to watch her stick her fingers covered in my release into the stream of running water so that she could wash away the evidence of what she did to me.

I pushed off the marble and turned to catch her in my arms. I backed her against the slippery, wet wall and sealed my mouth over hers before she could protest or come up with any kind of reason to pull away. I ran my hands over her slick skin and palmed the weight of her breasts in my hands. I circled the pointed tips with my thumbs and swallowed her cry of pleasure as I continued to eat at her mouth and lick across her tongue. I used my knee to part her legs and felt the way she shuddered when I did. I lifted my head so I could get my first look at her and wished I could stop time, just for a minute, so I could appreciate my first look over and over again.

She was spectacular. Every single thing about her honey-colored and rose-tinted. Her dark eyelashes spiked dangerously in the water as she blinked at me, shyness and a hint of uncertainty creeping in. There was no room for that between us, so I kissed her again right before I got on my knees in front of her. She gasped when I was face-to-face with her most intimate of places but she was stuck between me and the wall, so there was nowhere for her to hide.

I looked up at her and couldn't stop the wolfish grin that I knew was stamped across my face. "You do turn pink everywhere else when you blush." I could see the pink tones as she flushed from her toes to the top of her head. It was a good look on her.

"Wheeler . . ." It was part question part plea.

I continued to stare up at her as I grasped her leg behind the knee and started to lift it up over one of my shoulders. She shook her head and put one of her hands on the side of my face but it was my turn to offer her a plea. "Let me in, Poppy."

There was a moment where I thought she was going to pull away. She crossed her free arm over her naked breasts and cocked her head to the side like she was considering her options, but eventually the hand on the side of my face lightly touched the dimple that dug into my cheek and she gave me the barest of nods.

I didn't waste a second after that. I moved in, using the breadth of my shoulders to make space for myself between her legs as the water continued to rain down on us. I tickled the back of her thigh as I used my other hand to trace and fondle her wet folds. I'd touched her here more times than I could count. I knew what she tasted like on my fingers and what she looked like when she came around them, but I wanted her unique flavor to burst on my tongue. I wanted to taste what her pleasure felt like. I wanted to savor it and enjoy it like the rare and sweet treat that it was.

Her hand moved to my hair and I muttered my approval as she used her hold on the slick strand to pull me closer. I let out a puff of air that made her legs shake and she said my name on a moan as I used my fingers to circle her warm center. I buried my face in the place that I'd been dreaming about for weeks and wasn't surprised at all that she felt like heaven. I used my tongue to explore every secret spot she had and my fingers worked in and out of her now undulating body in a way that I knew drove her wild. I could feel how wet she was. I could feel her inner muscles pulling at my tongue, tugging my touch deeper. Her clit was a stiff little peak against the tip of my tongue as I flicked it back and forth until she whimpered. I dragged the sharp edge of my teeth over it and sucked the entire thing into my mouth, which made her swear and then chant my name over and over again.

The velvety skin of her thighs was quivering and shaking furiously next to my face, so I surrendered her clit and pressed a sloppy-wet kiss on the skin there. I wanted to know what she tasted like everywhere.

I turned my attention back to the pretty, pink flesh that needed to be worshiped, that was begging to be adored, and told her to lean back so I could replace my plunging fingers with my questing tongue. She took the direction as I put my hands on her hips so I could hold her to my face as I proceeded to fuck her senseless with my mouth. Just the tips of her toes were touching the tile as she rolled her head from side to side as pleasure assaulted her. She stopped trying to cover up and used the hand that was on her chest to rub across the still-stiff and swollen peaks of her breasts. It was so fucking hot that my sleepy and spent dick started to wake up.

She started to pant and the hand that was tangled in my hair tightened to the point that it was almost painful. Her legs tightened around my ears and I could feel the flood of her desire coat my tongue as it thrust in and out of her. She was close, but not quite there, and I was determined to take her over the edge before I put to use the erection that was making itself known between my legs. I felt like I was a man that was on the verge of starving and she was the only thing that would assuage the hunger.

"Honey, I need you to help me make you feel good." Her wild, whiskey-hued eyes landed on mine as she continued to writhe against me. "I need you to touch yourself, just like I touch you." I ran my thumb along the crease of her leg. "It'll be so much better that way."

Her eyes widened as she stared down at me. I was asking her to be an active participant in her own orgasm, which was very different from me simply getting her off or taking her to bed. She had to be an active participant in her own pleasure and that might be pushing boundaries she wasn't ready to cross yet.

I leaned forward so I could give her a long lick, my tongue circling that tender spot that made her whole body bend toward me. "Trust me, honey."

She blinked at me a couple times and then slowly nodded. I grinned up at her before putting my mouth back between her legs, my tongue going as deep and filling up the space my cock was begging for a shot at. She skimmed her hand over her chest and down over her taut belly. I could see the way it shook but eventually it dipped between those luscious legs and found the placc between those petal-soft lips where all her pleasure was centered, tender and waiting for the dam to break.

She stroked as I swirled.

She flicked as I fucked.

She rolled as I rubbed.

We moved in perfect harmony, in sync in a way that shouldn't be possible for two people that were just starting to learn what the other liked. It was simple really: I liked her and she liked me, so whatever we did to one another worked and felt really god-damn good.

I felt her muscles start to flutter. I watched her legs go stiff and her golden skin go pink. She was about to lose control and I could feel the rush of her release all around me. She said my name, then she yelled it until it was all I could hear. It echoed off the fancy bathroom walls and bounced back to us, so that I heard it over and over again as she came apart on the tip of my tongue.

She was delicious. Her pleasure was unlike anything I had ever had before. She was something I knew I would never tire of tasting, of teasing, of testing. I thought I knew who I was sup-posed to be with for the rest of my life . . . this moment with her was a startling realization that I had been woefully wrong. Poppy was what forever was supposed to feel like. I knew it all the way down to the bottom of my soul. If my tree was going to grow, it was because she showed up when I desperately needed someone to nurture it. I'd let it wither and die. She brought it back to life.

She wilted, boneless and heavy-limbed against the wall in front of me. I got to my feet and leaned into her, my cock happily tapping against the flat plane of her stomach.

I nuzzled my nose into the hollow of her neck, licking at her thundering pulse. Her chin lifted up and she put her arms around my shoulders. My eyes locked on hers, I asked her, "Are you ready to be all in with me, Poppy?"

I hefted her up and she wrapped around me the way she had been when we entered the room. I felt a grin kick up one corner of my mouth and her lips touched the divot that indented my cheek. She left a wet spot as the tip of her tongue playfully dipped into the center of it. "I'm all in, Wheeler."

She let out a soft giggle as I carried her to the bed. I dropped her on the side and let out a string of dirty words when I realized my wallet was still in my coveralls that were in a dirty heap on the bathroom floor. I looked down at my straining dick, tempted to apologize, when Poppy saved the day by pointing at her purse and telling me to check the side pocket. When I gave her a questioning look she shrugged and told me, "I asked you to have sex with me, Wheeler. I wouldn't have done that if I wasn't ready in every sense of the word."

Always surprising me and it was always in the best way possible.

I handed her the foil packet and watched with lowered lashes as she slowly and deliberately got me dressed for the party. The way she stuck her tongue out and bit the tip while she concentrated on rolling the latex down my length, combined with the soft pressure of her fingers, had me counting backward from twenty to avoid embarrassing myself.

She stared up at me when she was done, obviously waiting for me to crawl over her and claim her. Knowing that she probably had plenty of memories, all of them bad, of men rutting into and covering her up with their dominance and control. I didn't want that for her. I wanted to give something to her, not just take.

I walked to the end of the bed and climbed into the center behind her. I crawled my way to the headboard and arranged myself so that my back was at the padded fabric with my legs stretched out in front of me and my cock sticking straight up like a beacon. I held out a hand, and after a moment where I could see her collecting herself, she took it and situated herself on my lap.

With little prompting she put her hands on my shoulders, her knees by my hips, and rose up over me so that the tip of my cock could tease her tender opening. The contact made us both gasp and her eyes slid shut. I grasped her rib cage on either side, feeling her breathe me in and exhale out anything bad that had been before me. I watched her face as she lowered herself down, slow and steady, feeling every inch of me take every part of her.

Her face was set in lines of concentration as her body adjusted to the invasion of mine. I felt her stretch and flex around me, muscles milking me as she took me farther in. When I bottomed out, when she had taken me as deep as I could go, her eyes flicked open and I watched pleasure chase away the fear that lived there. I wasn't going to hurt her. I was going to let her control how this went even if her unhurried rocking back and forth had my balls aching and my dick twitching inside of her.

I bent one of my legs at the knee, which forced her legs farther apart and lifted her up just a little bit. Every time she rocked down on me, her already sensitive clit rubbed against the base of my cock in way that made her gasp and grind on me repeatedly. I loved watching her own her pleasure, I got off on seeing her being unafraid, of finding what made her feel good and going after it with a vengeance. I was going to come from nothing more than seeing the blissed-out expression on her face . . . it felt that good.

She took hold of my hand and put it on her heaving breast. She started to moved faster and with more purpose as I tweaked her nipple between my fingers and rolled the little nub around and around. She pressed her cheek to mine, her breath choppy and uneven in my ear as she moved on me like a woman on a mission.

It was a tight squeeze but I managed to get my other hand between us so I could put the tips of my fingers on her clit. I chased her as she lifted up and fell down, her body clamped down on my dick like it never wanted to be separated from it again. I was perfectly okay with that plan because this was something more than sex. This was more than our bodies moving together and our hearts racing side by side. This was more than feeling good and chasing away bad memories. This was more than an orgasm that made us weak and turned us inside out.

This was my soul telling her soul that it had been waiting for a long time to find its other half. This was me dreaming a new dream and her making it come true just like she promised she would.

This was healing.

This was starting over.

This was reinvention.

Her palm circled the bluebird on my neck and she tilted her head so that she could lick along the outside shell of my ear. The caress had my hips lifting off the bed, which drove my cock into her harder than I intended. She whimpered in my ear and her movements got jerky and slightly frantic. She was grinding against my fingers, crashing down on my dick, desperate and needy. She wrapped her hand around my bicep and tossed her head back as she shattered into a million beautiful pieces on top of me. Her entire body bowed backward, thrusting her rosy-tipped breasts up into my mouth as I continued to lift up into her.

It didn't take long for me to succumb to the welcoming heat and snug pull of her body. The orgasm rolled through me, leaving all my limbs weak and heavy as Poppy collapsed on top of me.

I wound my arms around her back and brushed my lips across her cheek. I wasn't surprised that her skin was salty with a mixture of sweat and tears. We were going to need another shower before we left this room.

"I didn't know sex could be like that." Her voice was quiet but the words felt like she screamed them right at my heart.

I rubbed my cheek against hers and told her truthfully. "Neither did I."

It was different when you were all in. It didn't feel like drowning or treading water. It felt like being saved.

Chapter 13

Poppy

I had one hand wrapped around the back of Wheeler's head, my fingers gently scraping through the short brush of auburn hair that was surprisingly soft to the touch. The other was pressed against the tufted headboard above where his tattooed shoulders rested as I rose and fell repeatedly on the straining shaft that I was pretty sure had magical powers. I knew I was a little bit passion drunk and delicious from what felt like an endless amount of orgasms but I'd never been with someone that had the ability to make me burn from the inside out and stop time. Minutes stretched into hours and hours felt like days where I craved nothing more than the press of his cock into all my soft and sensitive places.

Sex with Wheeler wasn't about power and control, even though he kept telling me that whatever happened or didn't happen was all in my hands. He never let me forget I was the one calling the shots and setting the pace, which was why I was still stretched out on top of him, riding him like he was my favorite amusement-park attraction. I'd tried to let him cover me, tried to lie under him so

I could stare up at those winter-colored eyes and straining inked flesh as he worked over me, but as soon as his much larger frame hovered over me, panic I couldn't control and memories that had no place in any bed with a man that was as good and as kind as Wheeler barreled their way past the pleasure and anticipation. He realized I was about to melt down before I did and quickly climbed off me. What should have been an hour of mind-blowing sex and multiple orgasms turned into an hour of him holding me and softly kissing my hair as I cried and apologized over and over again for bringing the bad things that I couldn't escape with me everywhere I went.

He reassured me that when my past reared its ugly head it didn't scare him. Quietly he whispered, "Even if those scars you have from what you survived were on the outside, I'd still be right here and want you just as much. They're part of you and you are who I want to be with." That made me cry for another half hour until I realized I was sobbing all over a really hot, naked guy and the proof that he did indeed want me no matter what kind of mess I was refused to be ignored any longer. I quickly came to the conclusion that instead of being distraught over the things that I couldn't make work because of my demons, I would embrace the things that still seemed to function just fine. As long as I didn't feel trapped or imprisoned, as long as my mind understood there was room to wiggle away from him, that there was an escape if I needed it, all the fear and panic receded, allowing the desire and longing that only this man inspired to overtake everything.

There were a lot of different ways for two bodies to come together and I was loving discovering them all, but so far this one was my favorite. I loved watching the chill in his frosty gaze turn molten the closer he got to losing control. I couldn't stop rubbing against his chest, pebbled nipples digging into his colorful skin as his hands tightened on my hips each time I lowered myself on his rigid shaft. His face was flushed, there was a fine sheen of sweat on his skin, and his dimples flashed each time he made me groan or gasp with his fingers. I was controlling the pace, I liked it slow and steady, was addicted to the pull and stretch of my body as I took him in over and over again. It was the first time I'd ever felt like I was getting just as much as I gave in bed. He seemed determined to make sure that I came first, that I was satisfied and fulfilled before he let go. It was sweet but it was also unnecessary. He'd already given me more than anyone else had and I wanted to do my very best to make sure that every time we were together it was as good for him as he made it for me, so this time I was determined to send him over before he had the chance to make me combust.

I tilted my head to the side so I could trace the outside shell of his ear with the tip of my tongue. It made his big body shiver below me and I felt the press of his blunt fingers into the soft curve of my hips. I let the end of my nose brush across the intricate cluster of flowers he had tattooed behind his ear and followed the design down the side of his neck until I reached the curve where his shoulder was solid and strong. He was slick with sweat and every muscle that moved and flexed against me was straining and taut with exertion. I sighed into his skin as his hand trailed from my hip to the sensitive spot between my legs. I was already liquid and pliable from his very skilled mouth, so I thought I was going to have plenty of time to ramp him up and push him over the edge before my body was ready to go again, but all it took was the touch of those rough fingers, the knowing touch from someone that seemed to know my body better than I did, and my blood was on fire and my nerves were electrified. I felt my thighs quiver and the swollen, tender flesh surrounding his plunging and thrusting cock flutter in response. He didn't play fair but I was determined. I used to want my partner to find pleasure out of fear and self-preservation. I wanted Wheeler to feel it because I didn't know how else to show him how good he made me feel. I wanted him to feel what he made me feel.

I sank my teeth into that straining flesh where his neck and shoulder met, the bite a little bit more vicious than I intended and far more aggressive than I ever was with anyone else. I heard a growl rumble out of his chest and the soft circles he was drawing on my clit faltered as he urged me to move faster, press harder into him as I lifted up and lowered myself back down. I licked the tiny little wound and pushed off the headboard so I could run my hand over the thick muscles of his chest, petting that snarling wolf, like I could tame the lonely, wild parts of Wheeler that sometimes peeked out from behind his inherent calm and reserve. I brushed the side of my thumb over one of his flat nipples and watched wide-eyed as it puckered and lifted to my touch.

"Jesus, Poppy." His voice was jagged and just as rough as the fingers that were crawling all over my skin. His head tossed back so that it was resting against the headboard and his eyes locked on mine as a muscle in his cheek flexed. It was by far the sexiest thing I had ever seen and I was a little in awe of the fact that I was the reason for his reaction. I moved my hand to the opposite nipple and repeated the motion, which made him swear and had his reddish eyebrows lifting upward. "Can you feel what that does to me?"

I could. His abs had tightened and the thighs I was straddling were rock hard. I could feel his cock twitch inside of me and I saw the way it made his chest rise and fall with ragged breaths as he tried to keep it together. His eyes were anything but cold and there was a glint of desperation in them as I picked up my pace and repeated my soft caress. I leaned forward so that I could touch my mouth to his and wasn't at all surprised when he slipped his tongue past lips and teeth to steal a taste. Wheeler liked to kiss. He was good at it, so it was easy to get distracted by the way his tongue swirled against mine, but I was a woman on a mission and I was determined not to fail.

Breathless, I replied against his now wet mouth, "I can feel it." I wanted to feel more of it, in fact.

His eyes flared and I could tell it was taking all of his self-control not to roll me over so that he could take over and drive us both to the sweet release that was hovering just out of reach because of my steady rise and fall over him. It was torture, but not the kind that would haunt my dreams and make me wake up screaming. It was the kind that made everything inside of me feel warm and fuzzy because no matter how badly he wanted to force me to move, no matter how strong the temptation was to overpower me and take control, he held it back, kept his baser instinct in check and let me set the pace.

I lifted up higher on my knees and trailed my hand across his ribs and down those carved lines of his stomach. His eyes narrowed at me as I gently touched the back of his wrist where his fingers were still toying with my aching clit and slick folds. I brushed my fingers over his knuckles and then reached behind my rocking hips so I could scrape my fingers over the hair-roughed skin of his thighs. My destination was clear and his breath exhaled in a long sigh as he continued to watch me closely. It was bolder than

I had been but I wanted him to break so I could let go and allow my body to float away on the river of pleasure that I could feel building and threatening to overflow against his touch.

"Honey." There was warning in his gruff word but I ignored it and leaned back until I could get my fingers on those tight, sensitive, and delicate globes that rested between his spread legs. His entire body jolted at the first touch of my fingers to the soft skin. His freckles stood out starkly on his cheeks and across his nose as his features pulled taut in concentration. It was obvious he was having to make a real effort to keep his impending orgasm at bay and that knowledge made me feel more feminine and desirable than anything ever had. I'd been told I was beautiful since I was a little girl but watching Wheeler fight to keep control was the first time I really felt beautiful and wanted. I was driving him crazy and I loved it because I knew there would be no punishment, no blame or judgment, when I forced him to break before I did. It was give-and-take and I loved that it was my turn to give because as wonderful as he made taking feel, I wouldn't be okay until I knew I could give just as good as I was getting.

I fondled the paper-thin skin, used my nails carefully, and tossed my head back so that the ends of my long hair pooled like silk across his lap and my stroking hand. I closed my eyes and let him lift me up and drop me back down at a rate that was far faster than I had been moving on him before. The longer my hand stayed between his legs, the harder he thrust up into me, his narrow hips lifting clear off the mattress as he barked my name and growled dirty words of warning. I was a little dizzy and entirely lost in sensation as his hand left my hip and settled on my breast. The double stimulation of his fingers on my clit and my nipple had me gasping and moaning his name. There

was no longer a rhythm either of us was following, we were simply grinding, rocking, bouncing into one another, desperate to
fulfill the lingering promise of pleasure.

He pressed down hard on my clit and pinched my nipple between his fingers, giving the stiff peak a tug that I felt all the
way between my legs. I grasped his sac in my palm and gave the
hot, tight skin a squeeze that made his eyes slam closed and that
had his teeth sinking into the flesh of his bottom lip. It was an
image that would stay with me forever. A second later, his head
fell back and he let out a groan as his whole body shuddered and
quaked below me. I felt his cock jerk inside of me hard and hot.
His hands drifted lightly across my skin, trailing wetness and
marking his place like he might need a reminder where he left
off when he came back to his senses. He didn't need to worry
about it because as soon as he found his finish, mine chased right
after it. It hit me in a rush that had my body bowing and then collapsing on top of his like every single thing holding me together
had unraveled.

I was a boneless heap on top of him as he lifted a hand to
stroke through my hair. He was petting me much the same way
I petted him and I realized we both had jagged, pointed pieces
that could do with a little bit of soothing. I closed my eyes and
absorbed what peace of mind and security in the arms of another
person felt like. This was safety. This was the shelter I had been
looking for in the storm of my life for so long.

"I'm supposed to take care of you, honey." His voice was raspy
from satisfaction and sleepiness. It was late and we'd been at each
other since we stepped into the fancy hotel room.

I stifled a yawn and snuggled deeper into his chest. We were
covered in sweat and sex but I didn't care. I wanted to stay as

close to him as possible. "And I'm supposed to take care of you, Hudson. That's what being all in means."

His fingers twisted in my hair and his breath feathered across my forehead and he let out a chuckle. "If you took any better care of me, I would be dead."

That made me smile as pride and a sense of rightness settled around me like the warmest of blankets. His fingers moved to my spine and traced each and every bump before he yawned and told me, "I gotta get up and take care of business. We both should probably shower unless you want to be stuck together all night long."

I rubbed my nose against the snarling wolf face and made a noise of protest as he rolled out from under me and extracted himself from my clinging limbs. "I want to be stuck together all night long."

He lifted an eyebrow but didn't say anything as he turned and walked toward the bathroom. It was like watching a canvas full of the most beautiful art ever created move. The way his ink flexed and shifted with his skin was something so fascinating I couldn't look away from it and I wanted to ask him to stand still in front of me so I could examine it all and see if I could figure out what part of his story the picture told.

He thought his wolf was alone searching for its mate. I needed to tell him he was wrong; it was there to guard his soft heart and gentle soul from the ugliness of the world around him. He needed that beast to keep the bad things at bay.

The sight of him coming back to bed was even better than the one of him walking away. Of course, my gaze was drawn to the swirling ink that dipped low below his belly button and flanked either side of his mahogany-tinted happy trail. I couldn't imagine how bad that had to hurt but the pain he must have endured was so worth it. All I could think of when I looked at the black ink was tracking every single line of it with my tongue. He was so different from anything I'd ever known in all the best ways and I desperately wanted him to know that I appreciated those differences on a very visceral and primitive level.

He was watching me with a knowing glint in his eyes and a grin on his face, which made me blush. I was getting ready to tell him to stop staring at me when the shrill sound of a phone going off broke the erotic haze that we had been surrounded in since I asked him to have sex with me. I still couldn't believe I'd had the nerve to do it, but as muscles twinged with pleasant soreness, I was so glad that I had. He made me push past the fear. He wasn't simply fighting my demons for me, he was giving me the strength to do battle with them on my own. I would do my best to slay them all and proudly step over their wilting bodies if it meant walking toward him and whatever a future filled with him and not fear would look like.

His phone had fallen when he stripped in the bathroom earlier; he was looking for it there when suddenly it stopped ringing only to start up right again. When he came back he was holding it with a pained expression on his face. "It's Kallie."

I could tell he was torn between wanting to answer it and wanting to pretend like he and I were the only two people in the world. I crawled underneath the blankets so that I was covered up and told him, "You need to answer. What if it has something to do with the baby?" Reality wasn't exactly welcome but there was no getting around the fact that both of us had things in our lives that we were going to occasionally trip over. He was there to catch me when I stumbled earlier and I was determined to do the same for him.

His gaze shifted from me back to the phone, and when it started to ring for the third time he touched the screen with a sigh and sat naked on the edge of the bed as he offered up a strained, "Hey, Kallie, what's up?"

He looked over his shoulder at me and I was surprised to see a heated red move into his cheeks as he blushed, his side of the conversation giving a clear indication that Kallie wanted to know why he didn't answer the first time she called. "I was busy and it's none of your business what I was doing. What's so important that you're blowing up my phone instead of sleeping?"

His comment had me looking over at the digital clock next to the bed. I was stunned when I saw that it was past midnight. No wonder I felt like I could hardly keep my eyes open.

Wheeler cleared his throat and lifted a hand so that he could run it over his face. "If you're ready for that then I can be there. Your parents aren't my biggest fans at the moment, though, so you might want to give them a heads-up you're inviting me over." His tone was sharp and there was no missing the accusation in his tone. He sighed again after listening to whatever the voice on the other end of the phone was saying for a long couple of minutes, then told his ex, "I told you I would be there and I will be. I really think things will be easier for everyone once the air is clear. Your family loves you." He'd thought they loved him as well and it had taken something away from him when they shut him out after he canceled the wedding. Whatever he was walking into for his ex and their baby had to be a pretty big deal for him to willingly go where he knew he was no longer wanted. "All right, I'll see you this weekend." His gaze shifted to me and his lips twitched. "I have something I need to tell you too."

He went quiet as Kallie questioned him, and when he spoke it made my heart speed up. "No, it's got nothing to do with me and you, Kallie. Remember when I said I was fucking and not dating?" He winked at me as I kicked him lightly with my blanket-covered foot. "Well, I found a girl I want to do both with, and since I'm planning on keeping her around for the foreseeable future, I figured I would fill you in." There were more words I couldn't hear, which made him sigh again and roll his eyes toward the ceiling. "You don't get a vote where my dick goes, Kallie. Like I said, we can talk about this later. I'll see you Saturday."

He flipped the phone closed and tossed it on one of the nightstands next to the bed. Neither one of us reacted when it started to ring again. This time he ignored it, and threw himself back on the bed and covered his eyes with his arm.

"Do you want to tell me what that was all about?" I asked the question knowing what the answer would be as he shook his head in the negative.

"No." He lifted his arm and turned his head so he could look at me. "That's not true. I *do* want to tell you what it was about but I can't until after this weekend. The reason Kallie and I didn't work out is more complicated than the fact that she was unfaithful, but I can't lay all her business out there until she comes to terms with it herself. She was calling to tell me she's ready to start being honest with the people that love her."

I cocked my head to the side and considered him for a silent minute. "She isn't thrilled with the fact that you're seeing me?" I hated that a sliver of doubt worked its way underneath the confidence I'd slowly been building since I decided he needed a dog. If his ex, the mother of his child, didn't want me in his life, I knew that could eventually make things very difficult for us.

He barked out a bitter-sounding laugh. "Oh, she doesn't

mind that I'm seeing you now. She's upset because she knows I've been looking at you for a long time. Her ego is bruised and I think her feelings are hurt, which tends to make her act like a two-year-old."

I blinked at him in surprise. "What do you mean you've been looking at me for a long time?"

Suddenly he rolled over so that he could crawl up the mattress and settle himself next to me. He wrapped an arm around my shoulders and pulled me to his side. His lips touched my temple and then brushed across my cheek. "Do you remember the night she showed up at Dixie's right after I left her, and she saw you, or rather saw the way I looked at you. She figured out pretty quickly that she was no longer the woman that had my attention. I told you, honey, I saw you and I couldn't stop looking."

I gulped and reached out to put a hand over his heart. "I hate confrontation. She was so angry and upset. I couldn't get out of that apartment fast enough." I tapped my fingers on his tattooed skin in time to the rhythm beating under my palm. "I didn't want her to see the way I was looking at you."

His arm tightened around me and his lips hit my ear. "How were you looking at me?" His words made me shiver as I tilted my head back so I could meet his questioning gaze.

"I was looking at you the way I used to look at men before I was scared of them, the way I looked at them before I knew how dangerous they could be. I was looking at you like I found something special, and I knew if she saw it, she was going to want to take you back. She was very, very foolish to throw what she had away. I was looking at you like I would never let you go if you were mine." I let out a yelp as he pulled me, blankets and all, over the top of him. His arm locked around my waist and his cheek settled on the top of my head as he held me to him like he was the one that was never going to let go.

"I'll make sure you don't ever regret looking at me like that, honey, because I'm looking back at you the exact same way and that's what has Kallie all riled up. I watched her with blinders of youth and infatuation on. I had huge blind spots where she was concerned and we both know it. When I stare at you, my eyes are wide open and there isn't anything that makes me want to look away from you."

I yawned and snuggled down into his embrace. "Hard to watch where we're going when our eyes are on each other and not on the path we're taking."

He chuckled against my hair and wrapped his other arm around my shoulders so that I was effectively trapped in his hold. I waited for alarm to wake my sleepy senses up and for panic to make my body stiff but neither showed up. I wondered if it was possible to fuck the fear away because it was nowhere to be found as he yawned and told me confidently, "Doesn't matter what the path we're on looks like as long as we're walking it together. If I stumble you can be there to help me up, and you know I'll do my best to never let you fall."

He had a point. I'd been struggling to make my way uphill on my own for so long that the idea of having someone there to offer me a boost, to pull me up when it felt like I couldn't take another step, was so overwhelmingly comforting that if I hadn't been exhausted I probably would have burst into tears again. Wheeler could pull me up and I would help him over the rocky terrain that was waiting for him as he adjusted to being a new father. Everyone always said you should never hike alone and the wisdom in those words was very apparent.

I was woken up the next morning by insistent hands covering my breasts and warm lips tickling the back of my neck. It felt like I had only closed my eyes a couple minutes ago but I wasn't going to complain when one of those hands trailed across my tummy and his knee made room between mine so he could situate himself behind me. His teeth dug into the spot on the curve of my neck where I had left a mark on his collarbone the night before and we both let out a strangled groan as he entered me from behind. It was a long, slow press that stretched overly sensitized muscles and burned in a delicious and unforgettable way. Everything felt amped up, hotter, harder, and more intense. It was a sensation overload and felt like I was drowning in pleasure and satisfaction.

It wasn't until I came on a strangled scream, my body clamping down on his as I writhed and wiggled in front of him, that I realized the reason it felt so good was because there was nothing between us. He pulled out of me, my body greedily trying to keep me exactly where he was, and rolled on his back, his hand wrapped around his slick and glossy erection. His face had an almost pained expression stamped all over it. I watched entranced for a long minute until I realized he was going to finish without me and that was simply unacceptable. That erection was mine. I owned that impending orgasm and I fully intended to take it.

I twisted so that I was lying horizontally across the bed and reached out to replace his fist with my own. His eyes drifted shut and his fingers found my hair as I brushed my nose across those stark black tattoos that marked his lower abdomen. His happy trail tickled my nose as I dipped my tongue into the shallow indent of his belly button.

"Poppy . . . I'm close. That's a lot." His voice was shaking, letting me know exactly what was going to happen if I got my face any closer to that throbbing hard flesh that was pulsing excitedly in my hand. He was always looking out for me even when it went directly against what he really wanted from me.

I looked up at him from under my lashes and gave him a grin. "Don't worry about me, I'm good."

And I was. There was none of the tingling terror from yesterday under my skin. The only thing I could feel was the desire to know what his coming undone tasted like. I had a feeling it was going to be flavored with victory and triumph. Putting the tip of my tongue on the slit that was already leaking pearly fluid, and circling it around, I found that he tasted like man and musk with a tiny bit of me thrown in just to keep things interesting. He said my name as his hips lifted off the bed, his hand fisting my hair at the back of my head.

"I need you to suck it, honey." If he was asking I knew it meant he *really* needed me to do it, so I opened my mouth and took him in. The thick vein that ran underneath the shaft throbbed against my tongue as I took the swollen length in as deep as I could.

He swore, long and loud, as he wrapped his heavy hand around my much smaller one and squeezed it tighter than I would have dared. He showed me what he needed and told me that he wasn't going to blink as long as I had his dick in my mouth. He shifted restlessly beneath me and I heard my name barked in warning a split second before his release hit my tongue in a salty, furious rush.

When I lifted my head, his eyes were locked on mine. His dimples flashed and he reached out to rub his thumb across my bottom lip. I chased the touch with my tongue and blinked at him when he asked me quietly, "Are you ever going to stop surprising me?"

I sure as hell hoped not because every time I surprised him it was me figuring out the person I was supposed to be, the woman I was always meant to be. It was my heart speaking for itself after far too long.

Chapter 14

Wheeler

The last time I had felt this nervous and uncertain walking up to the Carmichaels' front door was when I picked Kallie up for our first date. We'd already been seeing each other pretty regularly on the down low, but she wasn't sure how my drastic appearance and orphan status was going to go over with her fairly conservative parents. She was also the baby, the pampered princess, and she didn't want the fact that she had fallen for an outcast and a wild card to take the shine off how everyone in her family treated her. The Carmichaels were good people but I knew it was one thing to feel sorry for the kid without a family, but it was another thing to welcome him into yours when all the evidence pointed to the fact he was doing his best to get into your teenage daughter's pants.

The reality of the situation was that I'd been the one to hold Kallie off until we were officially official, which included me being able to take her on dates. She was more than willing to go the distance as soon as I kissed her, but I wanted more than teenage infatuation and unleashed lust. I was more than willing to suffer through the grilling that I knew was going to come from her father because I was convinced Kallie and I were going to be a forever thing. I arrogantly believed my loyalty and devotion to their daughter would win them over even if my appearance and lack of a loving home gave them pause. Little did I know the battle to win them over was won before I even knocked on the door.

I knew Kallie's dad was in a wheelchair and had been ever since he was involved in a bad motorcycle accident when Kallie was much younger, leaving him paralyzed from the waist down. She never once mentioned that he was rocking just as much, if not more, ink than I had, or the fact that he had a seriously badass mustache that framed his mouth, or that he was going to answer the door in a leather cut and leather gloves as he looked at me like he could eviscerate me with little to no effort. The guy oozed biker cool and didn't blink an eye at my tattoos or dirty hands. He didn't give a second look to my torn jeans and faded T-shirt and my battered boots didn't seem to bother him at all. He stared at me until I gave in and looked away, his tone deadly serious as he told me, "Kallie is a handful and I respect anyone that takes that on, but if you hurt her, if you let her down or disappoint her, it won't matter how much of a pain in the ass she is, I will end you. Do you understand me, son?"

I was so startled to hear the word "son" that I'd blurted out without thinking, "I'm going to marry her one day, sir."

His expression shifted from stone to sunshine. "Thank Jesus someone is going to take that girl off my hands." He chuckled and rolled away from the door so I could walk inside. From that second on he and his wife went out of their way to make sure I knew I was welcome in their home. As long as their daughter was happy, they were happy to have me as one of their own. It was the first time in my life I thought I knew what family felt like and I couldn't get enough of it. I thought it would last forever because Kallie and I were going to be together until the end of time. It still hurt to know that when she left she took that sense of finally belonging somewhere with her.

Now, as I dragged myself up to that same door, I again felt like that kid that had been ousted from home after home. I was never good enough and it was always far too easy for everyone that was supposed to love me to tell me good-bye. It made my heart twist and left a bitter taste across my tongue. I knew Kallie's parents didn't have the whole picture as to why I'd had to call the wedding off, but I thought I'd more than proven that I would do right by their youngest daughter regardless of what the circumstances were. I foolishly believed I'd earned a spot in the family; it sucked when I figured out I was only a temporary guest.

As soon as my now new and expensive boots hit the top step, I wanted to turn around and go back to the Caddy. I was lifting my hand to knock on the door I used to be able to walk through without any hesitation when my phone rang. I couldn't stop the smile that played around my mouth when the picture I snapped, without either of them realizing, of Poppy and Happy playing flashed across my screen. She was smiling that soft smile that only came out of hiding on rare occasions and the puppy had his tongue hanging out in a ridiculously excited expression. It was a good reminder that while I might have lost something important and special, I had also been lucky enough to find something that was more than everything, something that you had to look really hard to find because it was buried so deep underneath bad memories and wounds that would never fully heal.

"What's up, honey?" I knew now that she didn't just look like the sweet treat from head to toe, she also tasted rich and honeyed wherever my lips happened to land on her pretty, golden skin.

"I know you have plans with Kallie and her family today and I'm sorry to interrupt, but I'm concerned about something and I can't ask Salem about it because it will upset her." She sounded even more anxious than she normally did. "I would have called Sayer and asked her opinion but she's already held my hand through more than one crisis and she has her own family to worry about now."

Her words eerily fit with the disjointed feeling I was having standing in front of the Carmichaels' door. "If you need me you've got me, Poppy." I couldn't promise that she would always come first, not with a baby on the way, but I could promise that I would always find a way to be there for her when she needed me.

"It's silly, really." She sighed and I could hear her moving around the puppy making noise in the background.

"If it matters to you, then it matters to me. Tell me what's got you tied in knots." I heard movement on the other side of the door I was standing in front of and saw the curtains twitch. I was expected but I wasn't welcome.

She sighed again and I could picture her tugging on the ends of her hair and chewing on her bottom lip as clearly as if she was standing in front of me. "I told you that my mom called a few weeks ago and asked about Salem and the baby. I haven't heard from her since, and honestly I'm a little worried. My father is not a nice man. If he found out she contacted me, if he knows she's interested in her children and their lives after he pretty much disowned us, it won't be good for her."

I let out a grunt and lifted my head as the door in front of me opened to reveal my scowling ex-girlfriend. She looked pointedly at the phone in my hand and gave a little growl when I held up a finger indicating that I would be a minute. "Why worry about her if she was so willing to throw you to the wolves your whole life?" I knew the answer to my question before she replied. The men before me in her life had tried to shred that soft heart of hers, but they failed. It took blow after blow, and each time it healed. That heart was stronger and more resilient than anyone gave it credit for.

"I know what it's like to live with a man that will do his best to destroy you before you've had a cup of coffee in the morning. I just want to check on her, make sure she's okay, but I can't call the house. I can't risk my father answering the phone." Her voice shook with bone-deep fear as she told me, "I can't allow him to break all the things I've worked so hard to fix."

I wouldn't allow him to undo everything she had worked so hard to put back in place. "Text me her name and her number and I'll call their house when I'm done here. I can check on her for you." Kallie was tapping her toe in front of me and had her arms crossed over her chest. I rolled my eyes at her obvious impatience and told Poppy, "I'm not scared of your father, honey. I'll take him on for you."

Her relief was practically palpable as she thanked me and told me she would send the info over. She wished me luck with my upcoming powwow and told me she would be around if I needed to talk, or anything else when it was all said and done. Just like that, the balance between the two of us evened out some of the unsteadiness I was feeling about having to face the Carmichaels. I would do what I could for her and she would be there for me. I'd always wanted something solid, something sure and steady . . . who knew my stability would come in the form of a girl that seemed so fragile and breakable? She didn't seem like she should be able to withstand the weight of anything pressing down on her, but somehow she managed to hold not only herself up but me as well when I needed her to.

"You call her *honey*?" Kallie slid to the side as I stepped through the doorway. Her eyes had a hint of hurt in them that I chose to ignore.

"I do. Everything about her looks like honey—her hair, her eyes, her skin—plus she's sweet."

Kallie flinched. "You never gave me a cute little nickname."

I understood how hard it was to watch someone you had given so much of your life to move on. That being said, I had no time or place in the new way Kallie and I were together for any kind of misplaced jealousy. "No, but I gave you nearly a decade of my life and I bought you a house, in case you forgot. Not to mention the fact we made a baby together." I looked meaningfully at her slightly rounded waistline.

She huffed out a breath and led me toward the living room. It felt a lot like the walks I used to take when the social worker would show up at whatever temporary home I'd been placed in only to tell me it was time to move again. I was dreading every second of this family get-together, but even after she tore my dreams apart, I couldn't abandon Kallie, and not just because she was the mother of my child. We'd grown up together. We'd had a life together. We'd been each other's safety net for a long time and there was no way I could let her jump off this cliff alone.

"I want to meet her." Kallie's tone dropped so that only I could hear her as we got closer to the living room, where her parents were undoubtedly waiting to pounce. I felt a little like a lamb being led to slaughter, which wasn't fair since this was all Kallie's show and I was just here for moral support. "If she's going to be in your life then she's going to be in our baby's life. I want the chance to get to know her."

I bit back a groan and gave Kallie a narrow-eyed look. "She's been through a lot in her life, Kallie. She isn't just some girl off the street or some chick I picked up in a bar. She's a woman that's been through the kind of hell neither of us can imagine and I'm not going to let you put her through the wringer just because you're suddenly jealous I'm moving on. She doesn't deserve that." I wasn't going to let Kallie punish Poppy for wanting me in all the ways she didn't.

She shook her blond head and reached out to put a hand on my forearm. "It's not like that, Wheeler. I mean I *am* a little jealous . . . it was you and me for so long that I'm not really sure how to deal with you and her, but I know that's my problem. I'll work through it. I want to thank her."

I blinked at her in surprise and suspicion. "Thank her for what?"

"I know how hard it was for you to get on board with this baby and I know you were nowhere near forgiving me for the things I did and the way I treated you. This girl showed up and all of a sudden you're back to being the thoughtful, reasonable man I loved for most of my life. I pushed you into being a person I didn't recognize; she brought you back. I mean maybe you would have found your way without her, but since I'm impatient and scared shitless about becoming a mom, I'm super grateful that she sped the process up. Plus, I could see how scared of me she was that night I showed up at Dixie's apartment. I want her to know I'm not normally a shrieking she-beast."

I snorted out a laugh and took the hand that was on my arm and curled my fingers around it. "Oh, you can be a she-beast on thc regular, but like I said, she's survived far worse. I'll ask her how she feels about meeting up with you and if she's comfortable with it we'll set something up."

Kallie's fingers squeezed mine and she whispered, "Another relationship where you're letting your lady call all the shots? I thought you would be sick of that after me."

"It's not about calling the shots, it's about me doing what's best for her because in the long run, what's best for her is what's best for me." And the reverse was true. She wanted whatever it was that was going to make me happy because that was what made her happy. I was pretty sure that was what the definition of true love broke down to.

"I hope she deserves you, Wheeler." We rounded the corner and I fought not to stumble as her father's eyes immediately went to where our hands were locked together and her mother's eyes sharpened and her mouth tightened in a frown I could read from all the way across the room.

"She more than earned me, Kallie. Now it's up to me to prove to her that I'm the one who deserves her." I squeezed her hand one last time and let it drop so I could make my way over to her dad. I stuck my hand out, fully expecting him to ignore it, and was stunned when he clasped it with his far more callused one and gave it a firm shake. "Long time no see, Russ."

He gave a somber nod. "That it has been, son."

I looked at Kallie's mom and decided it was in my best interest not to try and make nice. I tilted my chin down and muttered, "Nice to see you, Deb."

She let out a huff and took a seat on the couch next to her husband's wheelchair. Russ reached for her hand and held it on his lap as Kallie and I took our seats on the opposite love seat. I could feel the way she was shaking, so I put a hand on her knee. I watched her close her eyes and compose herself as her mother snapped, "If you asked to meet with us to tell us that you're getting back together, I have to tell you that your father and I do not support that decision. We're too old to keep moving you in and out of places, Kallie, and we'll never recoup the money we lost in deposits on that damned wedding."

Kallie made a strangled noise in her throat. I sighed and looked Deb right in the eye as I told her, "Tell me how much it cost and I'll pay you back. I'm the one who canceled it, I don't mind being the one out the money."

"Son." Russ's tone was warning. "The money isn't the issue and you know it." I did know it. I also knew they still thought I had simply left their youngest high and dry even after everything I'd done to prove that I would never let her or them down.

"We aren't getting back together, not now, not ever." Kallie's voice had a tremor in it but she spoke clearly and with obvious determination. "But even though we aren't going to be in a relationship, we are going to raise this baby together and continue to be in each other's lives. You two should know that Wheeler would never have canceled the wedding without a good reason. He would never hurt me, or you, on purpose."

"Princess." Russ's warning tone was now aimed at his daughter. "All we know is you called us crying, asking us to move you out of the house we had just moved you into. You told us the wedding was off, that Wheeler pulled the plug, and then you announced you were pregnant. All of that combined paints a pretty clear picture that your boy did indeed go out of his way to fuck things up royally."

I stiffened in my seat and bit my tongue to avoid snapping out an angry defense of myself. If they wanted to believe I could be that callous and cruel, so be it. I was done trying to prove my worth to people that didn't want me.

Kallie's head shook violently from side to side. "No, Dad, you and Mom only have the picture I painted for you. I left out lots of details because I was scared of how you would react when you knew the truth."

"What truth?" Deb sounded impatient but she was no longer glaring at me like she wanted to throat-punch me and kick me in the balls. "What's going on, Kallie?"

She looked at me and I nodded encouragingly. I flipped my hand over and laced our fingers back together. She blinked a couple of times and took a deep breath before blurting out in a rush, "Wheeler canceled the wedding because I cheated on him. I didn't give him much of a choice."

"Oh, Kallie." Her mom lifted her fingers to her mouth and shook her head much like her daughter had done. "How could you do that to him?"

Russ looked at me and looked back to his daughter. His mustache was pulled down as a scowl crossed his stern face. "You sure the baby is yours, son?"

Kallie balked in horror next to me as I stiffened in response. It seemed like I wasn't the only one in the room that they were going to automatically assume the worst about. "The baby is mine, Russ. I'm not going anywhere."

He gave a jerky nod as Kallie continued to bare her soul. "The reason he's so sure the baby is his is because the person I was having an affair with isn't a man, Dad. She's a wonderful woman named Roni and we've been involved for a little over a year."

Silence greeted that bombshell and out of the corner of my

eye I saw tears start to fall over Kallie's dark lashes. I let go of her hand and wrapped my arm around her shoulder so I could pull her into a side hug like I had done a million times in the past. She shuddered against me and I felt her tears soak into my T-shirt.

"Are you telling us that you're involved in a relationship with a woman, Kallie? That she's the reason you and Wheeler are no longer together?" Kallie's mom asked the question softly, obviously seeing how close to the edge her daughter was.

Kallie nodded and sniffed loudly. "I am, and I can honestly say, I've never been happier, minus the lying and sneaking around so no one would find out."

Kallie's mother cocked her head to the side and considered both of us thoughtfully for a long moment. "Are you sure this is a real thing, Kallie, and not just some kind of experiment? You two got very serious at a young age and it makes sense that both of you would be curious as to what else was waiting for you in the world."

Kallie violently shook her head in the negative and looked at me instead of them when she spoke. "I know I can be selfish and shortsighted but I would never willfully throw away the amazing life I had for a fluke or a phase. I never intended to hurt Wheeler and I never wanted to lie to my family, but I couldn't stop myself. I love Wheeler and I know that there is no better man out there. I'm so proud that I'm having his baby but our relationship wasn't working." She lifted a hand to my face and cupped my cheek in a gesture that was far more tender than any she'd given me all the years we were together. "I know you tried, that you nearly killed yourself trying to make us work, and I know I rewarded your effort by being nasty and horrible. I felt so guilty. I knew I was hurting everyone I cared about but I couldn't stop. You deserved better." She turned to look at her parents and told them softly, "From all of us."

I circled her wrist with my fingers and moved her hand so I could kiss the center of her palm. As heartfelt apologies went, it was a pretty good one and it went a long way toward smoothing some of those jagged edges she'd left when she ripped apart my heart.

"I . . . well . . . we . . . um . . . your father and I need some time to process all of this." Deb reached out and put a hand on Russ's leg. "I'm so sorry you thought you had to keep this to yourself, Kallie. We're your family. We want to be there for you no matter what you're going through."

Kallie smiled and it was easy to remember why I'd loved her the way I had. "That's what Dixie told me you would say."

Deb huffed, "You told your sister before you told us?"

Kallie laughed and muttered, "Of course I did. I *knew* Dixie wouldn't judge me. After the way you guys wrote Wheeler off without a second thought when you thought he wronged me, I wasn't so sure you would understand how hard all of this was."

Russ made a strangled sound in his throat and shifted his gaze to mine. I saw remorse and regret heavy between each blink but that didn't undo what had already been done.

"You're our baby, sweetheart. How else are we supposed to act when you come to us heartbroken, alone, and pregnant?" Deb sounded defiant but Russ had the good grace to look down at the ground.

"I appreciate the shelter you offered me, but putting Wheeler out in the cold wasn't the right move, especially since he's always going to be family. He's this baby's daddy, which means he's always going to have a place in our lives." She made it clear there was absolutely no room for argument.

"We thought we were doing right by our daughter, son. Surely, you have to understand that. You've always been welcome in this house, we considered you one of our own. It wasn't an easy decision to put Kallie first when things fell apart between the two of you." Now, that was an apology that could use some work. I knew deep down Russ was just a man that was trying to protect his child but it didn't lessen the sting of being cast as the villain when all of this went down.

"It might not have been an easy decision but it's one you made anyways, Russ. I spent most of my teenage years and a solid portion of my twenties making sure I never gave you a single reason to regret letting me date your daughter, and it took you no time at all to turn on me even knowing Kallie liked to stir the pot and burn bridges. Neither one of you gave me the benefit of the doubt." I looked between the two of them and had to clear my throat before I could finish what I wanted to say. "You were the first people that showed me everything a family could be, you made me feel like I belonged, and then you shut the door in my face. I've had to stare at that closed door a lot in my lifetime, Russ. I never planned on you being on the other side of it."

Deb made a whimpering sound and Kallie's father cleared his throat. Before he could speak, I held up a hand and went on. "Kallie and I are both moving on but we're also moving forward together. I want my kid to have as much love as possible, as many people to call family as we can find. I'm not holding a grudge but I'm also not letting myself fall back into thinking you're going to be the people I can rely on when I need to. I don't want to fall and end up on my ass. I'm happy you guys didn't let Kallie twist in the wind, not that I thought you would, but she's been terrified about how you'd react and all that stress is bad for the baby. Now, after I've had the chance to meet Roni and Kallie gets the opportunity to spend some time with the woman I'm seeing, we can work toward getting all of us together and figuring out how this is all going to work." I gave Kallie a final squeeze and got to my feet. "Everyone in this room wants what's best for the baby and for Kallie, so we're gonna make sure that is our only priority."

I gave Kallie a wink and started toward the front door only to be brought up short when Russ called my name. I looked at him over my shoulder and told myself not to be taken in by the stark distress that was caught in his gaze. "Believe it or not, we all want what's best for you too, Hudson. We've just done a piss-poor job showing you that lately."

They really had done a terrible job but that wasn't my problem; tracking down Poppy's mother so I could put Poppy's mind at ease, that was my problem.

"I'll see you around, Russ."

As soon as I was back in the Caddy, I had my phone to my ear and was making the long-distance call to Texas. It rang for so long that I figured no one was going to answer, but just as I was about to hang up a slightly accented male voice barked a less than friendly hello into my ear. Knowing what I did about Poppy's parents, I knew there was no way I could outright ask the man to put his wife on the phone. He would never allow her to speak to some strange man and would more than likely get mad and take it out on her if he thought she was interacting with someone without his permission.

"Hi, my name's Hudson Wheeler and I'm looking for Paola

Cruz. She has a '64 Barracuda listed for sale and I'm interested in purchasing it."

There was absolute silence on the other end of the phone until the man snapped, "You have the wrong number. My wife doesn't own a car. If she needs to be somewhere I take her."

"Are you sure this is the wrong number? I'm looking at the listing on the Internet right now. Can I speak with her just to verify I have the wrong information? The car is a real beauty and I'd do just about anything to get my hands on it." I was laying it on thick but I couldn't think of another way to get Poppy's mother on the phone to find out if she was indeed all right.

"My wife does not converse with strange men; that is unseemly and inappropriate. I assure you she does not have a car for sale. Do not call here again."

The line went dead and I swore loudly as I put the phone back in my pocket. It was easy to see why Poppy didn't want that asshole anywhere near her and I wanted to give Salem a hug for doing whatever she did to keep him away from my girl. I had an uneasy feeling in the pit of my stomach as I pulled away from the Carmichaels' home.

Poppy didn't owe her mother a goddamn thing but something told me she wasn't done trying to save her and that would mean she had to walk right back into the fire she worked so hard to put out. Good thing the only time I was going to let her burn was when she was in bed with me.

Chapter 15

Poppy

I stared at the beautiful blonde woman seated across from me with a mixture of fear and admiration. I was waiting for her to rage at me, to yell and make a scene the way she had done when she showed up at her sister's apartment to confront Wheeler after he called their engagement off. She looked like a supermodel but I knew she had the temper of a reality-TV housewife. Along with being nervous that she was going to snap on me, I was in awe of how friendly and welcoming she seemed to be. She's been asking Wheeler for weeks to set something up so that she could meet me and I'd finally given in, more so he could get some peace and quiet than out of any real interest in meeting the woman who was pregnant with his child. That being said, my reserve was met with nothing but warmth. Kallie even brought me a fancy jar of artisanal honey as a cheeky gift, though Christmas was several weeks past.

I'd spent the holidays with my sister and Rowdy, as well as with Sayer and Zeb and their son. Salem whined about the fact she would just be starting to really show when she was supposed to be a bridesmaid in her friend Cora's upcoming wedding, and Sayer bought out an entire Toys "R" Us for Hyde's first Christmas with his dad. All in all, it was the perfect mix of family and friends even though I missed Wheeler. He'd agreed to spend Christmas day with Kallie and her family. I understood why, but I knew we both would have preferred that he got to spend the day with me. It was good practice for the choices we were going to have to make when the baby came, and while it wasn't easy for either of us, knowing we were doing the right thing for the baby took some of the sting out of it. My willingness to let him go when Kallie needed something from him was one of the reasons she'd been so desperate to meet me. The first thing she did when I walked into the coffee shop was throw her arms around me, tell me I was a saint, and then burst into tears as she apologized for all the havoc she caused in my relationship with Wheeler.

It was a lot to take in, which is why I was waiting for her to swing the other way emotionally. Wheeler warned that she was a naturally dramatic person and that her now raging hormones had made her even more so. He'd gotten really good at picking and choosing which of her whims he was going to cater to over the last month or so, making himself available only when she really, truly needed him. He told me he'd been taking care of her for so long that she still hadn't quite figured out how to be okay on her own.

I wrapped my fingers around the warm, white-and-green cardboard cup in front of me and listened patiently as Kallie rambled on about how they were going to find out the sex of the baby at her next appointment. They'd gone right before the holidays started but the little thing had been uncooperative and refused to get in position for the ultrasound. They were still in the dark about what they were having, much to Wheeler's dismay. I obviously already knew they were anxiously awaiting a determination because even if he wouldn't tell her, Wheeler had told me on numerous occasions he was hoping for a little boy. Her excitement was nearly palpable, and after a few minutes of endless one-sided conversation, I realized that her nervousness was too. She was just as anxious as I was about this little get-together.

"This is going to be weird. No matter how hard we try and not make it weird, we both love the same man." I lifted an eyebrow and let a tiny grin tug at my mouth. "We both know what he looks like naked and that he snores when he sleeps on his back."

She blinked wide blue eyes at me and cut off her flow of words with a grateful nod. "I didn't want it to be weird. I know you know why Wheeler and I split and why we're not getting back together. I thought knowing that there wasn't a chance in hell that he'd ever come back to me, or that I would ever try and take him from you, would make it easier." She returned my grin. "It didn't. I'm sitting over here thinking about how stupid you have to think I am. You know exactly how good I had it and I threw it all away."

I shrugged and traced the logo on my cup with my thumb. "I don't think you're stupid at all. I think it would have been far more foolish to stay in a relationship that didn't make you happy."

She looked down at the table. "I probably would have stayed if my secret hadn't gotten out." She lifted her eyes back up to mine and there was shame and embarrassment threaded throughout. "I didn't know anything else, how to love someone else, and I was terrified to live a different life. Wheeler always made everything so easy; he took care of everything and I knew no one else would do that."

I tilted my head to the side and considered her thoughtfully before telling her truthfully, "That's why a lot of women stay in failing relationships, even ones that are dangerous and unhealthy. It's all they know and they don't know how to walk away. They're scared to be alone, scared no one will understand what they've been through, and won't try to understand why they couldn't leave. They feel like damaged goods, like they've somehow brought everything bad that's happening to them upon themselves. The lucky ones eventually find their way out and find their way to something better." I cleared my throat and reached up to push my hair out of my face. "But far too many stay."

She wrapped her hands around her own drink, a hot chocolate, and copied my pose as she looked back at me with serious eyes. "Would you have stayed? If things hadn't happened with your husband the way they did, if he hadn't kidnapped you and hurt you, if he hadn't shot himself, would you have gone back to him?"

This wasn't the kind of conversation I planned on having with her. I thought we were going to make small talk about the weather and chat about the baby. I thought she was going to ask me if I was serious about Wheeler and serious about staying a part of his life after the baby came. I wanted her to like me because that would make things easier for all of us but I had no plans on letting her into all those dark corners where the scary parts of my past lived.

I shifted uncomfortably in my chair and shrugged again. "I don't know. I'd like to say that I would have left for good; he broke my arm and beat the crap out of me, which was what sent me running to my sister in the first place. There was no more hiding or covering up the abuse and I was ashamed, but when the bones were set and the bruises faded, he was still going to be my husband, the man I promised to spend the rest of my life with, and I didn't take that lightly." I bit down on my lower lip and felt my brows knit together over the bridge of my nose. "He wanted to have kids, that's what we were fighting about the night I left. He wanted to know why I wasn't getting pregnant. He called me terrible names, told me God left me barren and empty because I'd had sex before marriage. He told me I didn't deserve a baby because of my loose ways and claimed that's why I'd miscarried my first pregnancy when I was a teenager." Kallie gave an audible gasp from across the table and lifted her hands to her horrified face.

"I could take what he threw at me. Like I said, I think part of me believed that I hadn't been the best daughter, sister, girlfriend, wife I could be, so I deserved it. But I knew there was no way on earth I could subject a child to that kind of life." I shook my head a tiny bit and swallowed back the bitter taste in my mouth that talking about Oliver always left. "So I can't honestly say that I would have left for me, but I know without a doubt I would have left to keep him from hurting anyone else."

"That's so scary, Poppy. He would have killed you."

I nodded in agreement. "Yes, he would have, which is why I do my best to make sure anyone in a similar situation knows that there are options, knows that there is someone out there that has been where they are and can show them that it gets better once they get out. The person I am today never would have given Oliver the time of day, let alone married him. The woman that survived all of that knows life is a precious thing, that time is limited, and none of it should be wasted on people that want to cause you pain."

Kallie sat back in her chair and put a palm over her belly. She was a month further along than Salem, so she was just now starting to show. The burgeoning bump was adorable and I couldn't stop the pang of envy that worked under my skin as she caressed it.

"This baby is going to be so lucky to have you in its life, Poppy." The sincerity of her tone warmed me up more than my latte had. She was actually very sweet and I could see why Wheeler had been so into her from the start.

"Well, I feel pretty lucky that both you and Wheeler are allowing me to have a place in your baby's life. That's not a responsibility I take lightly. It means the world to me." It really did. Thinking about babies and everything that I'd lost used to paralyze me, the pain of that loss crippling me and stealing my motivation to move on from the past, but now the idea of cuddling a newborn, of touching that baby-soft skin and smelling their innocent, sweet smell, brought nothing but joy. I was going to be the best auntie in the world and I was going to soak up every minute I got with Wheeler and Kallie's baby. Watching the man I was undoubtedly falling in love with figuring out fatherhood was a fantastic motivation to keep putting one foot in front of the other every day. Slowly but surely, I was leaving what was behind me and moving solidly into what could be.

"Well it's obvious that you mean the world to Wheeler. He's different with you, I mean he's still great, still pretty much the most perfect guy anyone could ask for, but he seems . . . happier." She made a face at me. "That was a hard pill to swallow at first. I thought I made him happy but seeing him with you . . . I wasn't even close." She leaned forward in her chair and her ocean-colored eyes doubled in size. "Did he tell you today is the day we were supposed to get married? I tried to call him and check on him but he didn't answer."

It was my turn to fall back in my chair with a horrified expression stamped across my face. "No, he didn't mention it. I told him I was coming to meet you for coffee and he said he was going to take Happy for a walk." He hadn't seemed upset or withdrawn but I was learning that he was really good at locking down anything that might lash out and touch anyone else. I wanted to tell him that nothing he let escape could be anywhere as bad as the monsters my father and former husband had set free, but in order to do that I needed him to know I wasn't scared of his brand of dark and dangerous. I'd spent a lot of time in hell, so I was intimately acquainted with all variety of demons and devils. Wheeler didn't have it in him to be evil and purposefully malicious. The boy should have a halo tattooed around his head.

I pulled my phone out and fired off a text asking where he was. He'd been putting a lot of hours into the Hudson lately, so I was hoping he was going to reply that he was at work. What I got back instead was:

Had things to do at home. I'll touch base tomorrow.

It was more dismissive than he ever was with me and the absence of his usual "honey" made my jaw lock and had my eyes narrowing on the short response. I lifted my gaze back up to Kallie and saw that she was watching me intently, clearly waiting to see what I was going to do.

I slipped my phone back in my purse and picked up my drink as I rose to my feet. "I'm sorry to cut this short but I need to make sure he's okay."

A grin tugged at her mouth and she nodded in understanding. "I didn't really expect anything less. I knew today was going to be hard on him because I woke up sad and felt like shit. I knew that I was the last person he was going to want to see. I'm glad he found you, Poppy."

"I'm glad he found me too. I might have stayed lost forever without him."

I turned to go when her next words stopped me short. "For the record, I had no idea that he snores. I'm not much of a cuddler, so we always slept with our backs to each other on opposite sides of the bed. He never made a sound in all the years we shared a bed."

My mouth shaped itself into an oh of surprise and I could feel heat work its way into my face. When we fell asleep, we typically did it wrapped around one another and he seemed to prefer me and the weight and warmth of my naked body to any of the blankets I kept in the house. I woke up every single morning with his arm wrapped around my waist and his chin on the top of my head. I didn't mind the rattling air moving in and out of his lips at night any more than he seemed to mind my midnight screams of terror. I was disgustingly relieved that there was a part of him I had that she hadn't.

I offered softly, "We can do this again and again until it gets less weird." She stood up and gave me hug that I had no trouble returning. I'd gone from avoiding strangers and interaction with others at all cost to hugging my boyfriend's baby mama in the middle of a busy coffee shop. Instead of walls to keep everyone out, ones that were heavy and exhausting to lug around everywhere, I now had doors, and it was up to me who I decided could come in and out of them. That was far easier and a lot less lonely. Everyone liked company now and again.

I decided not to let Wheeler know I was coming over. I knew

he would do his best to wrestle his emotions until they were under control and I didn't want that. I wanted him to be able to let
his wild out with me, I wanted him to know that I could handle his chaos the same way he handled my catastrophe. I wasn't
afraid of the Big Bad Wolf, not the one on his chest or the one that
lived inside of him.

It took longer than normal to get across town because sometime during my coffee date with Kallie it started snowing. The
roads were starting to get slick and the last thing I wanted to
do was slide into a ditch and have to call Wheeler to rescue me
when I was on my way to save him.

I parked behind the Caddy and noticed that along with his
boot prints and paw prints in the snow there was also a set of tire
tracks that looked much bigger and wider, and led all the way
to the front door. I picked my way carefully through the snow
and made my way up to the door. It opened before I could knock
and I fell back a step when I was confronted with a scowling,
shirtless Wheeler. His auburn hair was standing up in a million
directions like he'd been pulling at it and he had an open bottle of some kind of liquor in his hand. I heard Happy bark from
somewhere inside the house behind him and narrowed my eyes
at him when he didn't immediately open the door and let me in
from the cold.

"Are you going to let me come inside?" I lifted my fingers to
my mouth and blew on them to warm them up and to make a
point.

He lifted the bottle to his lips and took a healthy swig. "I don't
think that's a good idea, Poppy. It's not a good day. I'm not feeling
very nice at the moment."

Annoyed at his attitude and the fact that he thought I would only take him when he was sunshine and roses, I pulled open the glass storm door and wiggled my way around him into the warmth of the house. I took my coat off and went to throw it on the back of the couch when I suddenly realized the living room was completely empty except for the flat-screen TV that was sitting woefully alone on the floor in the corner. Every stick of furniture was gone. The walls were bare. The floors were barren and the windows naked. It looked like a home that had yet to have anyone live in it.

I spun around to face Wheeler, who was propped up against the wall still sucking back booze and glowering at me through narrowed eyes. "Where is everything?"

He lifted a tattooed shoulder and let it fall. His eyes looked like ice and his demeanor felt about as warm. "I finally hired some people to take it to storage. Kallie's going to take it all when she gets her own place."

"You got rid of everything without having anything to replace it?" I cocked my head to the side and asked, "Why would you do that?"

He swore and lifted a hand to shove through his disheveled hair. "Kallie told you what today was supposed to be, didn't she? That's why you're here."

I dropped my coat and my purse on the floor and crossed my arms over my chest. "She told me but that's not why I'm here. I'm here because I was worried about you and I couldn't stand the idea of you hurting and dealing with it all by yourself."

He lowered his head and rubbed his mouth with the back of his hand. "You've had enough hurt in your life, Poppy. You don't need to take any of mine."

I gritted my teeth and pointed a finger at him. "That's bullshit and you know it. 'All in' means we're in it together through the good and the bad, Wheeler. It means we tackle the ups and enjoy the downs *together*. I'm not going to fall apart because you're surly and don't feel like playing nice. I'm not going to run away from you because the wolf is off the leash and looking to sink its teeth into anyone that might be close by." I took a few tentative steps toward him, and when he didn't move I reached out and snagged the bottle of booze from his limp hand. "I gotta tell ya, Hudson, a bad day with you is still better than the best day without you."

His chin dropped until it almost touched his chest and I watched his shoulders lift and fall as he battled emotion that threatened to overwhelm him.

"I have you, so I didn't think today was going to hurt so bad." His voice was raspy and raw.

I set the bottle on the floor and moved into him so that I could wrap my arms around his waist. I tucked my head under his chin and kissed his chest where his heart was thundering erratic and wild under my cheek. "Of course it hurts, you wouldn't be the man you are if it didn't."

I felt him sigh against my hair and slowly his arms lifted so that he was holding me the same way I was holding on to him.

"Did you really get rid of everything?" I couldn't keep the disbelief out of my voice.

He nodded, his chin bumping into the crown of my head. "I did. Happy's in my room playing with all the clothes I threw out of the dresser before they hauled it off. I don't even have a bed to sleep on tonight. I didn't want any part of Kallie in this house. It was always supposed to be ours and it's about time I made it mine."

I tightened my hold on him and tilted my head back so that I was looking into his frigid gaze. "When you first started coming around, when you made it known that all my issues and hang-ups didn't scare you, I noticed that all the bad things I couldn't forget were slowly being replaced by all the good things you forced me to focus on. We need to do that here, replace the memories of you and her and create memories that are just yours so you don't have to try as hard to forget."

All he was wearing was a pair of thin, nylon track pants, so when I pressed my hips into his I felt the immediate response. His body tightened and his dick twitched where I was rubbing against him.

He cupped the back of my head and I felt his lips touch my forehead. "I told you I'm not feeling very nice today and I've been drinking. That's not a good combo, honey. I don't want to scare you, ever. Right now, I'm scaring myself."

I appreciated the warning. A lesser man would never give one, he would simply take my offer to kiss it and make it better, damn the consequences. Not Wheeler. He was always protecting me even from himself.

"Do you know why I'm here, Wheeler, why I had the courage to show up at your garage and ask you to take me to bed in front of all your guys and anyone else that might happen by?"

He slowly shook his head in the negative and moved his hands so that he was cupping my jaw in his rough palm. "Why are you here, honey?"

I let out my breath slowly and flattened my hands on his chest. "Because when I couldn't trust myself, when I didn't know anything or believe in myself, I believed in you. I knew that you wouldn't hurt me, that you would be careful with me, so I didn't have to trust myself and my choices because you were never going to be anything but a good man." I slid my hands up around his neck and lifted myself up on my tiptoes so I could press my mouth to his. "I knew it then and I know it now. You are not a guest in this house, Wheeler. This is your home. You belong here and the only thing you should let through that door is happiness."

He chuckled low and deep and shifted so that I was the one with my back to the wall and he was pressed all along my front. My nipples immediately contracted into tight points and my legs found their way around his narrow hips without me having to think about it.

"I didn't have to let happiness in. She forced her way in while I was being a jackass." This close, his words smelled like bourbon and he tasted smoky and rich when his tongue found its way to mine. "This house isn't the only place I belong, is it, honey?"

He urged me to lift my arms above my head so he could work my sweater up my torso and off my body. He popped the clasp of my bra with one hand, wiggled his eyebrows at me when I made a face at him, and ran the tip of his nose along my now naked collarbone. "I don't want to be a guest in your life, Poppy. I'm not interested in visiting your heart. I want to move in, stake my claim, and plant roots so deep nothing will ever be able to move me out. I don't want you to ever have to replace the memories you have of me with something better."

"There isn't anyone better than you, Wheeler. You are the only person I made room for in my heart, so if you want to live there it's all yours." I looked into his eyes as he struggled to get my pants unfastened without putting me down. "You need to get some furniture if you plan on staying, though."

He rolled his eyes at me and begrudgingly dropped me to my feet so I could wiggle denim and lace down my legs after I kicked my maroon Free Bird boots off. Naked, caught between him and the wall, I'd never felt more safe and secure in my entire life. He wasn't the only one that knew how to slay demons and exorcise ghosts.

His lips landed on mine, his hips rocking seductively against mine as his hands found their way to my backside so he could lift me back up all while he pressed between my legs. I wound my arms around his shoulders and let my head loll to the side against the wall behind me. He licked a long line up the side of my neck and nibbled delicately on the curve of my jaw. It made me whimper and had my thighs tightening where they were wrapped around him.

His teeth grazed my earlobe and one of his hands moved between us so that he could free himself from the confines of the slippery material of his pants. I loved him in his torn jeans and his dirty coveralls but I liked the ease of access those running pants offered a whole hell of a lot. It took no time at all for his hardness to meet my wetness and we both groaned at the contact. After that morning in the hotel room, I'd gone on birth control. Knowing how good he felt, how good we felt without anything between us, made the decision easy. He shifted his hips, lifted me up higher so that just the tip of his erection dragged through my damp and quivering folds. The friction made my breath shudder and had my fingernails digging into the solid muscle of his shoulder, and when the tip knocked stiffly into my swollen clit, I felt like I was going to come out of my skin. He repeated the motion over and over again while he dropped biting, wet kisses all along the side of my neck and across the top of my chest. I was going to look like I'd been eaten alive tomorrow and I wasn't even the slightest bit sorry about it. He was definitely handling me rougher than he normally did when we had sex, but I loved everything about it.

His chest pressed into my sensitive breasts as his hips kicked forward. My body moved against him, opened for him, and welcomed him. Usually he took his time, prepped me, played with me, and worked me up so much that I was beyond ready for him to be inside. This time there had been no foreplay, no warm-up, so I felt every single inch of him as he slid inside. My body had to adjust, had to soften and relax in order for him to move. He groaned as the slight resistance forced him to slow down, but he did it because he was perfect and I was right to trust him. He was never going to hurt me and I was never going to be afraid of him.

He lifted a hand to my breast and started to swirl his thumb around my puckered nipple. The other was holding me up and keeping me braced against the wall, so his eyes blazed with heated demand when he ordered me to touch myself. "Touch your clit the way I touch it. Get yourself off the way I usually do."

I sucked in a breath as my hand skimmed over my chest and across my stomach. The winter in his eyes thawed by several degrees as I did what he asked. I started circling slowly with my fingertips, exactly the way he did. The backs of my fingers brushed against his cock as it pounded in and out of me. Every time he pulled out and sank back in, my body went more liquid and took more of him in. It only took a sweep of my thumb across the stiff little nub for everything inside of me to go molten. His hips ground into me and my fingers rasped against that happy trail that led to heaven.

"I told you, I'm not feeling very nice today and I told you to touch yourself the same way I would. If I had a free hand, I would be showing that pretty little clit how nasty I can be."

His words made me whimper and my fingers reflexively closed tighter on the sensitive bundle of nerves. It stung in a delicious way but I knew it would feel even better if it was his callused, rough hands doing it. I tossed my head from side to side as he did his best to fuck me through the drywall, then on a strangled scream I demanded that he touch me. I needed more, wanted all the not nice he was promising me.

Wheeler swore, and before I could blink or protest I was yanked from my position pinned against the wall and laid out like some kind of sacrifice across his barren living room floor. It was just as hard as the wall, so no more or less uncomfortable, but in this position we ended up with him stretched out over the top of me, his weight braced on an arm above my head as his eager lips found my breast and his talented fingers found their way between my legs. There was the scrape of teeth and the graze of rough fingertips. It all felt so good that I didn't have any room for the uneasiness that usually overtook me when he was above me. I didn't feel trapped or threatened in any way. No, all I felt was pleasure, burning hot and bright everywhere we touched, and his desperation as his body pounded relentlessly into mine.

I wrapped my fingers in his hair and lifted myself up to meet his frantic thrusts. I shoved my eager nipples deeper into his mouth and writhed across his fingers and he continued to torture me with his touch. I was going to have bruises and a sore ass tomorrow. He was going to have claw marks among his tattoos and there was a good chance he was going to be sporting a bald spot by the time I got my hands out of his hair. He was relentless with my clit, unrelenting against my nipples. His cock wasn't taking any prisoners as he wrung first one then another orgasm out of me, all while his much bigger, heavier body hovered over mine.

His fingers dug into my hips and his forehead found mine as he eventually reached his own release. His eyes drifted closed and his breath huffed out in a long sigh as he lowered his body to mine. He wrapped his arms around me and slowly rolled us over so that he was the one lying on the hard and unforgiving floor.

"You okay, honey?" He was asking if I was freaking out after the fact about the position he put me in.

"I'm fine, but I think the first thing you need to buy yourself is a new bed." I ran my hand down the inked length of his side and tilted my head so I could kiss the underside of his jaw. "You aren't the only one making new memories in this house, Wheeler."

"Floor sex is fun but hell on the knees." He chuckled into my hair and gave me a squeeze. "I'm glad I didn't scare you."

I snorted and told him, "Your not-so-nice is still pretty damn nice, Hudson. That's who you are." And it was also why I loved him.

Having him on top of me, looking up at him while he took me to places I'd never been before, was the opposite of feeling imprisoned . . . it made me feel free. Now there really was nothing and nobody between us.

Chapter 16

Wheeler

I'll take this one."

I looked at the salesman over the top of Poppy's head, which at the moment was buried in the center of my chest. Her face was hot with embarrassment after I pulled her down on top of me and stretched out the full length of the couch I was contemplating buying. Obviously, I wasn't spending money on anything we both didn't fit on. There was no way anything was going in my living room unless I knew it was comfortable to sit on and to fuck on. Plus, I was annoyed at the way the guy's gaze kept drifting to Poppy's ass every time he thought I wasn't paying attention. I made it a point to flatten my palm against that perfectly rounded part of her body as I held her to me.

The couch was fire-engine red and the legs were some kind of shiny metal that looked like chrome. It was the hot rod of couches and it was surprisingly comfortable. I didn't even look at the price tag that had made Poppy wince when she flipped it over. I wasn't going to worry about the cost. I liked it, and Poppy didn't cringe because it was gaudy and tacky, so I bought it. It was the first time I was actively making myself a home instead of waiting for someone else to invite me into theirs. I was going all out. I deferred to Poppy's choices when it came to the softer stuff that I needed, like the rugs and the curtains. I let her pick out the bedding for both my new California king and the new crib that was going in the smaller guest room. I figured she was going to be spending as much time between those sheets and underneath the comforter as I was, so it might as well be something she really liked. Because she was awesome and the perfect girl for me, she picked out a black-and-red chevron pattern that was both stylish and sexy. She got me. She had me.

I swung my legs over the edge of the couch and sat up with Poppy in my lap. She was laughing silently against the side of my throat and the guy that had been eyeing her for over an hour finally had the sense to look away.

"Great. We'll get everything on the truck and scheduled for delivery as soon as possible. If you follow me up to the computer, we'll get you all squared away . . . uh . . . congratulations on the purchase of your new home." He stuck a finger in the collar of his shirt and waited while I set Poppy on her feet so I could climb to mine. I didn't correct his assumption that we were furnishing a new house together and neither did Poppy.

I put my arm around her shoulders and lowered my head so I could growl into her ear, "I think I liked it better when you were hiding from the world. I didn't feel like throat-punching every guy that looked at you back then."

It wasn't that she'd done anything really drastic with her appearance or her mannerisms, but the subtle changes were enough that most couldn't help but do a double take when she walked by. She was still thin, built delicately and dainty, but now that she was eating more regularly she looked less like a broken bird. She was curved in all the right places and her flawless, golden skin glowed instead of being chalky and stretched too tightly across her bones. Her amazing eyes still flashed with the occasional spark of fear and uncertainty but more often than not they gleamed with amber heat and quiet contentment. More than any of that, though, she wasn't jumping out of the path of strangers anymore. She didn't automatically look away and she no longer seemed to shrink inside herself when out in public. She still wasn't overly touchy-feely. The people she put her hands on willingly were me and her family, but she didn't quake and crumble when it was time to shake hands like she used to and she didn't cower away from the suggestive looks from strangers even though I wished she would.

She wound her arm around my waist and rested her head on my shoulder. "No throat-punching. It doesn't matter who might look at me or might look at you because we've only had our eyes on each other since the beginning."

It was true. I couldn't see anyone but her, and I had to say: the view was spectacular. "You mind letting me crash at your place for a couple of days until I get all this new stuff situated?"

She shook her head no and her arm tightened around my waist. "No, it will give me the chance to ask you for a favor I've been putting off since Christmas."

She looked up at me from under the inky veil of her long lashes and I knew there was no way I would ever deny her anything. "Since Christmas? That was weeks ago, why didn't you bring it up before now?"

She sighed and waited while I handed over my credit card to the jackass with the roving eyes. Filling out the paperwork took longer than I would have liked and the sales guy's eyes lingered on the fit of Poppy's sweater way longer than was appropriate. Once I scrawled my signature on the last form, I handed the guy his pen and leaned in close so that our noses were practically touching. I narrowed my eyes at him and poked him right in the center of his ugly, cheap tie. "A word of advice, friend." I bit the word out through gritted teeth and an angry snarl. "The way you leer at women suggestively the entire time they are trying to go about their business, and not showing any signs of interest in what you're laying down, makes them uncomfortable. They are not here for you. They're here for furniture."

His Adam's apple bobbed up and down and a fine sheen of sweat broke out across his forehead. "I think you got the wrong impression, sir. I was just trying to be attentive. We work on commission."

I growled at him, which made him take a step back. "Right, you work on commission, so you creep on women, make them so uncomfortable they'll buy anything just to get away from you. Not cool, and it's really not cool when you try it with a woman that happens to be with her overly possessive and extremely protective boyfriend. That also makes them even more uncomfortable and it pisses the boyfriend right the fuck off. You got me?"

The guy blinked rapidly and I felt Poppy place a calming hand on my arm. The muscle twitched against her touch. I stepped away from the guy and pointed at the stack of papers that equaled a hefty commission for him. "You can keep your cut of the sale but you bet your ass I'll be getting in touch with whoever your manager is and letting them know your sales tactics leave a lot to be desired."

I grabbed Poppy's hand and pulled her around in front of me

so that we could walk out of the store with me at her back. Guys like that rarely acted on the ugly intent that shined out of their eyes, but with my girl, I wasn't taking any chances and I never would. We got to the massive 1973 Dodge Power Wagon that I drove when the roads were too bad for the Caddy to navigate and I helped boost her into the seat. The truck was a behemoth, lifted to the sky and painted black with silver flakes. The thing looked like it would survive the end of the world and drive over anything that tried to stop it. It got crap gas mileage, was a bitch to park in the city, but when the weather got cold and the snow piled up, it was my favorite toy to play with.

When I climbed up behind the steering wheel, I expected her to gently scold me for taking the lecherous salesman to task but instead she turned to look out the window and told me quietly, "I asked my sister to try and get in touch with our mom over Christmas. She told me no, but I asked again, and again, until she finally gave in and reached out. Mom knows Salem is pregnant, and when she called me the first time, she mentioned how she couldn't imagine not knowing her grandchild, so I thought for sure if she knew Salem was reaching out she would respond. My dad answered, called Salem a whore, and hung up. She called back and there was no answer. She asked Rowdy to call, and again, nothing. I don't know what's going on in that house but I do know it can't be anything good. I'm worried about my mom, not because she's my mother, but because I know firsthand how bad it can get living with someone that sees you as a thing. I don't want my father to kill my mother, Wheeler. I have to do something." She craned her head in my direction and blinked wide, innocent eyes at me. "I didn't say anything before now because I wasn't sure I could actually do it."

I frowned and shifted my attention from the road over to her for a split second. "Do what?"

She sucked in an audible breath and let it out slowly. "Go back home. I wasn't sure I could face my father and deal with whatever it is he's done to my mother and I realized I couldn't, at least not alone. I need you to come with me, Wheeler." She reached out and put her hand on my thigh as I steered the massive truck through the snow. "Salem said she would go and Rowdy lost his mind. He offered to take me after he forbade her from getting on a plane, and Sayer and Zeb also offered to go, but the only way I can do it is if I know I'll be safe and the only time I feel safe is when I'm with you."

I hated it.

The last place on earth I wanted her was anywhere near the man that had given her over to her tormentor without a backward glance, and as far as I was concerned, her mother was just as bad. She should have taken those girls and run as far and as fast as she could away from the man that did nothing but try and destroy them. But I knew Poppy needed this. To her, it wasn't about rescuing her mother, it was about saving another abuse victim. No one should have to live like that even if the person was the one behind her horrible upbringing.

I wanted to pull a Rowdy and flatly forbid her from going but she needed this and I needed to be there to keep her safe when all the skeletons came falling out of the closet. They could bury her. "Give me some dates and I'll get things squared away at work so I can be gone for a few days."

She made a noise and leaned across the seat so that she could plant a kiss on my cheek. I turned my head at the last minute so that our lips brushed and she sighed at the contact. I put my

hand over hers where it was still sitting on my leg and gave it a
squeeze.

"If I'm going to do this for you, I want you to do something for
me." I lifted an eyebrow at her and turned the truck toward downtown instead of Capitol Hill, where her apartment was located. I'd
been waiting for a way to work this into a conversation and was
grateful she'd unknowingly given me the perfect opening.

"I'd do anything for you, Hudson."

She smiled at me sweetly and I had to fight the urge to move
our joined hands up a few inches higher to where my jeans were
getting tight because my cock really liked hearing those words.

"Right . . . well, that's good to know because something tells
me you're going to freak out."

Her mouth fell open and her shoulders tensed at my words.
"Why am I going to freak out?"

"Because I'm going to give you something that's bigger than
a bread box." It had been a knock-down, drag-out fight to get her
to take the pretty, delicate poppy earring and necklace set that I
bought her for Christmas. She told me it was too much, that she
didn't want our relationship to be about the material things we
could give to each other. I knew she was trying to protect me from
falling into the trap I'd just escaped of giving the woman I loved
literally everything. However, I knew she wasn't greedy and ma-
terialistic like Kallie had been and I wanted to be able to give her
things that reminded me of her, things that made me smile when
I saw how much she liked them.

She stiffened next to me as I used my phone to unlock the gate
to my garage and pushed in the code that made it roll open.

"What are we doing here?" Her fingers spasmed in mine and
her voice was higher and thinner than normal.

Without answering, I turned her hands over and kissed the back of one of them. I slid off the bench seat and walked around to her side of the truck so I could help her down. The snow she was standing in went all the way up to her ankles and the stuff falling from the sky caught in her honey-colored hair. I bent so I could kiss the tip of her nose and asked her, "You trust me, right?"

She stared at me silently before slowly nodding. "I trust you."

With that, I tugged her hand until she followed me up the steps and into the vast, chilly darkness of the garage. I took a minute to hit the lights and to crank up the heat. I guided her through the different bays until we reached the back of the garage, where the Hudson was sitting on a lowered rack. The car had just come back from painting, so it was now a perfect pale blue, the convertible top a rich cream color that matched the pinstriping that swirled over the curves of the hood and along the rounded fenders. It was hands down one of the prettiest and most memorable cars I had ever worked on. It was a true classic and I knew in my gut that the closer I got to finishing the restoration, the harder it was going to be for me to let it go.

"The paint is the same color as your eyes." She trailed the tips of her fingers over the rise in the hood and looked at me with a wide smile. "It turned out beautiful." I'd been unable to keep my excitement about this car to myself. She now knew more about struts and shocks, torque and transmissions, than she probably ever wanted to know.

"I'm glad you like it . . . because it's yours. At least it will be as soon as I get the rest of the motor reworked. So by the time the snow melts, it will be yours." I crossed my arms over my chest as she whirled around and gaped at me with wide eyes.

She snatched her hand away from the cool metal of the hood and jumped away from the car like it had suddenly shocked her.

"No. I can't take this car, Wheeler. Thank you for offering, but no." She shook her head and her words were firm.

I sighed because I knew that was what she was going to say and I really wanted to get to the part where I bent her over the hood and sank into her sweet heat from behind without having an argument first.

"Poppy, that Camry is a fine car but it isn't you. It's boring and basic. You should be driving something that is unforgettable and special, just like you are." I walked over to her, put my hands on her shoulders, and waited until she tilted her back to look at me. "I bought the car and started building it knowing I wasn't going to let it go. I built it for you. I want to give you unforgettable and special."

She lifted her hands and curled her fingers around my wrists. "You gave me unforgettable and special the first time you kissed me."

I blew out a breath and moved in so I could lower my forehead until it touched hers. "Poppy, this is my dream car, my one in a million. It was the one I would do anything to get my hands on, the one I would spare no expense to repair and return to its rightful glory. This car has every single piece of me in it—my heart, my soul, my greatest passion, every iota of skill and knowledge I've learned over the years. This car *is* me, do you understand?"

Her mouth opened and closed repeatedly, making her look like an adorable fish. Her eyes blinked a couple of times and finally she drew in a shuddering breath. "You're giving me you."

I nodded slowly and shifted my hands so that I was cupping her jaw. "I love you, honey, but more than that I love the way you love me. I've never had that, never understood what it truly means to be cared for, so I'm giving you me because I know you will take care of me, treasure me, and that you will never, ever let me fall apart. Both Hudsons need someone like that to keep them running." I touched my lips to hers and whispered against her lips, "Give me a good home, honey, please."

She wavered for half a second before quietly acquiescing. She smiled against my mouth and her hands ran up the outside of my arms so that she could wind them around my neck. "It's the nicest thing anyone has ever given me, Wheeler." I knew she didn't mean the car. "I'll make sure you are both well loved and properly cared for until my last breath." She kissed me long and slow, her tongue twisting with mine until it was hard to breathe and even harder to think straight since there was no longer any blood circulating in my brain. All of it had rushed below my belt and was making my cock dig painfully into the teeth of my zipper. "I love you too, Hudson. Real love, the kind that feels right, the kind that is healthy and strong, the kind that is scary in a good way."

Hearing her tell me that she loved me had that lonely wolf that was always feasting on my insides finally howling in victory that it had found its mate. There would be no more loneliness, no more sense of being unwanted and invisible. Everyone else had thrown me away; she picked me up and promised to always have a place for me. It had every animalistic, primal instinct inside of me roaring to life with the need to mate, claim, mark. She was mine for the taking from here until forever and that's what I wanted to do . . . take and take and take some more.

I walked her backward into the front end of the car. She gasped when her backside hit the metal and I took full advantage of her open mouth. I dipped my tongue into the wet heat and slicked it across her teeth. I stroked it against her tongue and used the tip to trace the perfect bow that shaped her top lip. I used my teeth on her bottom lip and swallowed every breathy sigh she let escape. She yelped when I lifted her up by her waist and set her on the hood. Typically, I would have an aneurysm if anyone got that close to a new paint job with rough denim, snaps, and zippers, but I knew she wasn't going to be dressed for very long and her skin was velvety smooth.

I worked my hands to the front of her tight-fitted flannel shirt and started popping annoying little buttons through the holes. She watched me with patient eyes as she reached out and ran her finger over the candle that inked across my throat. "It's a light so you can always find your way home, isn't it?"

I started on her jeans, cautioning her not to slide across the paint as she lifted herself up with her hands on my shoulders so I could work the denim off her hips and down her legs. I liked her naked. I liked her naked and spread out on the hood of the car that I'd built just for her even more. It was like every dirty dream I'd had about those girls in hot-rod magazines when I was younger come to life.

"It worked. Took longer than I would have liked and there were some wrong turns that were a real fucking headache, but I found home and it is definitely where my heart is." I put my hand flat on the center of her chest and gave her a gentle push backward so that she would lie down on the blue metal. Her hair spread out all around her head like spilled honey and her eyes went liquid and warm like spiced cider. I smoothed my hand along her breastbone, down over her stomach, and stopped to tickle her belly button. She let out a giggle that sounded so carefree and unburdened that I knew if I screwed up everything else in my life, I would always have that giggle as something I got really, really right. I slipped my thumb along the top of her pussy, feeling her quiver and watching as her legs stiffened. I put a hand on her knee and roughly ordered, "Put your foot up on the bumper." It was chrome and I was going to have to buff the shit out of it before the guys showed up for work tomorrow, but again I didn't care.

She obeyed and I had to suck in a breath as all that pretty pink flesh was exposed. She was already slick and soft, her body telling me that it was good with whatever I had planned for it and for her. I skimmed my fingers up the inside of her thigh and lightly tapped her clit with the tip of one. It made her shoulders lift off the hood of the car and had her giving me a pointed look through narrowed eyes. I smiled at her and leaned over her so I could kiss her pursed mouth. She kissed me back but there was a bite to it as I dipped my fingers into her wetness and scissored them open. She groaned and I growled as I started to move my digits in and out of her while circling her clit with my thumb. She went from wet to soaked in seconds and I had to lean my chest against hers to keep her from writhing wildly across the surface of the car.

I pulled one of her pointed nipples into my mouth and sucked, hard, cheeks hollowing out and my tongue lapping at it unrelentingly. She curled her fingers around my biceps and begged me to stop and to keep going all in the same breath. I could feel her body quickening, her heart thundering, and it made my cock twitch. I was still fully dressed and that was the only thing that kept me from ramming myself into her like a rutting bull, but I'd had visions of her bent over the hood, her golden hair cascading over her back and tangled in my hands, her incredible heart-shaped ass bouncing and pushing back into me as I pounded into her from behind for months. She was good at making my dreams come true, even when they were dirty and erotic.

I lifted my head, leaving her nipples far closer to red than rosy from all the blood that rushed into them. She had dark finger-prints on her curved hips from rolling across the floor with me and I'd left marks on the side of her neck and the upper swells of her breasts with my mouth. I should feel bad that I'd been so rough with her, but I didn't. The marks made me hot, made me want to add even more where only she and I could see them. I'd sucked at the foreplay yesterday, so I was determined to make it up to her this go-around.

I ran my nose down the middle of her body, taking the same path my hand had traveled earlier. I tasted her along the way, stopping when I reached her wet center. I let out a sigh of satis-faction that fluttered across her distended clit and she groaned in response. Keeping my fingers moving in and out of her pulsing, pulling channel, I put my mouth over that sensitive point and circled it with my tongue. The scrape of my teeth across that oh-so-responsive bundle of pleasure had her back arching off the car and her hands clutching at the side of my head. I heard her say my name but I was drowning in the taste and feel of her, my mouth full of her flower and honey flavor, so I didn't reply.

I licked her faster, thrust my fingers deeper and harder, pushed her legs open wider so that there was no way I could miss any of the delicious and enjoyable reactions she had to what I was doing to her. She glistened from her pleasure and from my mouth. Her eyes were staring somewhere up at the ceiling of the garage but her mouth was open as soft pants puffed out of her lips. One of her hands had left its death grip on my ear and was now moving across her chest. Her elegant, tapered fingers plucked at first one nipple and then the other, moving slowly and deliberately as I continued to feast on her.

I bent lower, lifted one of her legs, and tossed it over my shoulder. I had to put a hand on the hood of the car to brace myself and I shivered as the chill from the metal hit my overheated skin. It was a lot of sensation and it was no wonder she felt like she was about to go off like a rocket. I dragged my tongue the entire length of her, catching every shiver along the way. When I reached her ready opening, she jerked against my face with unrestrained desire as I thrust my tongue inside. She moved against me, wanton and wild, her thigh tightening next to my head and her hand moving into my hair.

"It's too much, Wheeler."

The words sounded strangled and breathless. She was going to come on my face and all across my tongue while she was plastered across the hood of a rare, vintage car. It was going to be stunning and it was going to be far from the last time it happened. In fact, I was going to start working it in as a standard part of all my test drives. "It's not nearly enough, honey." I hummed the words against her, nibbled on her clit with more force than I typically did, and swallowed her up as she came apart for me. I was never going to get enough of her.

I let her leg drop as I dragged my wet mouth across the soft skin of her tummy, trailing sex and satisfaction as I went. I kissed her belly button and put my hands on either side of her hips so I could push off the car. Her chest was rising and falling rapidly as she tried to catch her breath. I took one of her limp hands and placed it on the buckle of my belt. I lifted an eyebrow at her and flashed a smile. She pulled herself up into a sitting position with some obvious effort and worked the leather through the fastening until it was free. She carefully pulled my zipper down, my eager cock practically falling into her hands as she did. She smothered her thumb over the already damp slit, circling the head of my dick until I could no longer see straight.

I slid her closer to me until our pelvises touched. My cock was really happy that she was already so wet and warm between her legs, and tried to find its way inside of her like a heat-seeking missile. I swore as the tip worked its way inside of those soft and silky folds. I could die a happy man with nothing more than that, but she was making a fantasy come true for me and I was determined to see it through to the end.

I kissed her pliant mouth and used my hold on her hips to turn her around so that she was facing the car. She gave me a questioning look over her shoulder that was accompanied by lifted eyebrows. I put one hand on the center of her back so I could guide her where I wanted her, facedown, that round ass up and pointed right at me. It made my mouth water and my blood burn. I wrapped her long hair around my hand and gave it a tug so that her head bowed back. I leaned forward to kiss her but got lost in a groan as my cock found its way between the valley of her ass cheeks. I rubbed up and down, lost in how good it felt, wondering if she trusted me enough to take her there when the time was right. That was a whole different fantasy, her bent over one of my builds, letting me take her ass. If I wasn't careful the thought was going to have this over before it began. There was time for me to savor all of her. We had forever.

"You trust me, remember." I brushed my hand down her spine and stopped to caress those lush globes where my hard flesh was currently nestled.

"I do trust you but it's not every day I find myself bent over a '53 Hudson."

She grinned at me and my fingers dug into her hips as she lifted up on her tiptoes so I could slide into her. She was already pliable and supple, so I hit bottom quick. "No, but you are used to being bent over *this* Hudson and all *he* wants to do is take care of you."

She jolted as I pulled out and thrust back in, moving her across the hood. Her palms flattened on the metal and she turned back around so that she could drop her forehead to the pale blue paint. "He is taking care of me and it feels amazing."

I grunted in response as I picked up my pace. She was snug around me in this position and watching her ass move as she met me thrust for thrust was making me sex stupid and drunk on lust. I couldn't think anymore, all I could do was feel.

I felt the way her inner walls fluttered around my straining cock.

I felt the way she went slick and slippery the harder I moved on her.

I felt the way her spine stiffened under my hand as I kept her plastered to the hood of the car.

I felt the way her hair slipped and slid through my fingers as I used it like a rope to pull her head back when I wanted a kiss.

Then there was the way my balls tightened and my knees started to shake. There was the way my vision blurred and how my breath got stuck in my lungs. There was the way my dick felt like it was going to explode and the coiled ball of pleasure that pulsed insistently at the base of my spine.

All of it was too much to take and I was emptying into her without making sure that bending over the hood of the car had been worth it for her. I groaned as she milked my body dry and wiggled her hips back into mine. I dropped my forehead to the center of her back, curved my hands around her rib cage, and pleaded, "Please tell me that was as good for you as it was for me."

She turned her head so that her cheek was resting on the now warmed metal. "It's always good for me, Wheeler, because it's with you."

When I stepped back so I could let her up and pull her into my arms, I realized there were going to be more than footprints and fingerprints I was going to have to buff off before the morning. I looked good smeared all over her and I didn't give a crap how messy it might be.

I held her naked body against mine and whispered into her ear, "Wanna see what I can do in the backseat next?"

She laughed against my throat and wound her arms around my neck. Because she was perfect and the best thing that ever happened to me so far in this life, she whispered back, "Of course I do."

Chapter 17

Poppy

I liked the way he tasted and felt in my mouth.

I liked the way his hands held the sides of my head, holding me as I moved on him and over him but not demanding.

I liked the way his abs tightened and flexed as I pulled him in deeper and swirled my tongue around the tip over and over again.

I liked the way his entire body stiffened and went on alert when I slipped a hand between his legs and palmed his extra-sensitive skin.

I liked the way his legs shifted restlessly on either side of me, indicating that he was rapidly losing the fight to hold back and enjoy what I was doing to him for as long as possible.

I liked the earthy, salty flavor of him when he finally let go on a long groan that came from somewhere deep in his chest.

I liked it that he shivered when I tickled my fingers over the heavy sac between his now pliant legs.

When he used his hold on my head to pull me closer so that we were almost nose to nose, blue eyes blazing with the kinds of things I'd been looking for my entire life, and gruffly told me, "I really fucking love you, Poppy" . . . well, I loved that. It was the best part.

"I love you back, Wheeler." I settled myself on his stretched-out legs and reached out a finger so I could run it over the adorable divot in his cheek. I loved those dimples and I was thankful every minute of every day that I was seeing more and more of them the longer we were together. "Thank you for taking time off work to go with me tomorrow."

It was the weekend after furniture shopping and unforget-table sex in his garage. He'd had some clients already scheduled for the week that he couldn't cancel so our trip to Texas had been postponed until he could get away. Salem was still pissed I was going at all, but the fact that Wheeler had agreed to go with me and hold my hand had endeared her to him for eternity. Rowdy again offered to come with since he was well aware of what we could be walking into, but I knew if I stood any chance of getting my mother away from my father, I had to make my approach as nonthreatening as possible. She was going to need a friend, not a confrontation, and there was no way Rowdy could be the guy that did that, not with as much animosity as he had toward both my parents for what they had done to me and Salem growing up.

His hands moved so they were resting where my legs met my hips. That seemed to be their favorite resting place and I didn't mind it one bit.

"I would never let you walk into a possibly dangerous situation alone, with or without a spectacular blow job." He lifted his eyebrows up and smirked at me. "Not that it wasn't appreciated."

I smacked him lightly on the chest and moved the heavy fall of my hair over one shoulder. His eyes narrowed a fraction as the tip of my breasts peeked through the caramel-colored veil. We'd been at each other for hours because there was no way I could sleep knowing I was going back to everything I'd nearly died trying to get away from. If I couldn't sleep, then neither could he, which led to lots and lots of sex. He had to be tired—I knew I was—but my brain wouldn't shut off and my body didn't seem to mind that it was sore and tender in several places. "I know you wouldn't let me go alone. The blow job was for the car." Really it was just because I liked having the power over him. I adored being the one in control of making him feel good and getting him off.

He snorted out a startled laugh and gave my hips a squeeze. "If that's what I get when I give you a car, then be prepared for a new ride every Christmas, and maybe even on your birthday."

I fell forward and snuggled myself into his chest. His arms immediately wrapped around me and his lips found the top of my head. "I already gotta find a place to keep the Hudson. The Camry is fine parked on the street but there is no way that beauty is staying out in the cold unprotected."

I gave a little squeak as his arms tightened around me to the point that it was difficult to breathe. His words ruffled my hair when he told me, "I have a perfectly good garage behind my house. You are welcome to park it there."

I blinked and lifted my head so I could look at him. "Why isn't the Caddy parked in it? You always leave it in the driveway." Except for now, when it was parked in his shop to wait out the winter.

He sighed and ran his thumb along my jawline. "I always let Kallie park in the garage. I didn't want her to have to scrape her windows in the morning. If you don't want to leave the Hudson at my place, you can always leave it at the shop."

I nodded slowly and moved my hands over his chest. "That's

probably best for now. I'll think about moving it to your place when I'm ready to come with it."

His eyes flared and those dimples dug into his cheeks. "You want to move in with me?"

It had taken a lot for me to get out of the safety of Sayer's house. I still wasn't one hundred percent comfortable on my own but I was getting there. "Eventually. After you have time to settle in with your baby and you and Kallie have some time to figure out what coparenting is going to look like, I want it to be an option. I want to make the decision knowing that I want to live with you because I can't live without you, not because you make me feel safe and I know nothing bad will happen to me under your roof. I know what the right reasons are, but I'm not in a place to make choices based on them yet."

He gave me a jerky nod and pulled me back to his chest. "My door is always open for you, honey. You can walk through it anytime and stay for as long as you like." He chuckled and it rumbled under my cheek. "Does that mean I'm going to have to buy all new furniture again?"

I huffed out a breath and closed my eyes as his body heat started to soak into me. My limbs felt languid and all the fears and what-ifs spinning around my mind started to slow their frantic twirling. His hand smoothed over my hair and stopped to rest right above my ass as he slowly lowered us both to a supine position. "I don't care what your furniture looks like. As long as it's comfortable, durable enough to survive a puppy and a baby, and can be easily cleaned after you have your wicked way with me, it stays. I need you, not a designer couch and custom cabinets."

I let out a yawn that was so loud my jaw popped. My eyes started to drift closed as he continued to pet and lightly play with my hair.

"Go to sleep. I've got you." And because he did indeed have me and because we were all in, no matter what tomorrow might bring, I finally fell asleep.

"Seriously?" Wheeler huffed the question at the poor car-rental guy with so much venom that I was surprised the kid didn't bolt for the back room. "All you have available is a Camry?"

I tried to stifle a laugh but a snicker escaped anyways. Wheeler glared at me in a way that if it wasn't him, I would have found the closest place to hide and cower from him. I patted his arm reassuringly and reminded him that Loveless was a very small town and that we were lucky to get any kind of rental on such short notice. With any luck we would be in and out today, so he wouldn't have to suffer the embarrassment of driving the economy car for very long.

In a much quieter tone I warned him, "This is South Texas, Wheeler. There aren't very many folks around here that look like you, so you stick out like a sore thumb. We're trying to be unobtrusive, and if you scare everyone we run into, eventually someone is going to call the sheriff and my dad will know I'm in town and that I'm not alone." My breath caught and I had to work words around the lump of emotion that lodged there. "He's already keeping my mom isolated. If he knows someone might be here to help her, he'll put her somewhere we can't find her and punish her for making him expend the effort."

My words tempered most of his aggravation. I knew he was riled up and on edge because he didn't know how going back home was going to affect me. He was worried that I was going to fall apart, that I was going to end up back behind the walls I'd been hiding behind when he first found me. I wanted to reassure him that I would be okay, that everything would be fine when it was all said and done, but I couldn't lie to him. I already felt like I was unraveling and all my loose threads were getting tugged and pulled, which was making me jumpy and uneasy.

"The Camry is fine." His words were begrudging at best as he took the keys from the clerk and signed off on all the rental waivers. He took my hand and led me to the minuscule car lot that had a whopping five cars to choose from. All of them were basic, four-door sedans. He wouldn't have liked any of them.

He pulled the passenger door open for me and we drove to the one and only motel in town to check into the room that I'd reserved online. The girl at the reception desk recognized me from high school and immediately launched into trying to catch up on every aspect of my life that had happened since I ran away from Loveless. She offered her condolences about Oliver and I nearly threw up all over the polished wood desk. Wheeler took over the small talk and guided me to our room with a hand on the small of my back, whispering over and over again that everything would be okay, and because he said it, I believed him. He wouldn't lie to me either.

It took twenty minutes of him holding me and talking me down off the ledge in the dingy motel room before I could catch my breath and stop shaking.

"How do you want to play this, Poppy?" He was rubbing my back and brushing circles on the inside of my wrist with his thumb. "You can give me the address and I can go to the house. I'll wait awhile to make sure your old man isn't around and find a way inside to check things out."

He was sweet to offer to take this burden on, but it was my show and I had to see it through to the end.

"You have a baby on the way. The last thing you need is to get locked up in the middle of nowhere for breaking and entering." I exhaled a long breath and shoved my hands through my hair. "It's Monday night, Dad will be at the church. He does marriage counseling for new couples on Monday nights, if you can believe that garbage. It consists of him telling young women to obey the men in their lives or God will punish them." I tugged on my hair hard enough that it hurt and looked at Wheeler out of the corner of my eye. "I still have a key to the house unless they changed the locks. Once he's gone, we should be able to walk right in."

"What if they did change the locks?"

It was a good question, one I luckily had an answer for. "Salem used to sneak in and out of the house all the time. Dad tried to put her on a leash but she always slipped out of it. The lock on the window in our bedroom is jammed. She took a screwdriver to it so that it wouldn't stay shut. Dad used to put a bar between the top of the window and the frame when he found out she was gone at night. I always removed it and put it back even though it meant I would spend months grounded and that my dad would be extra horrible to me when we weren't in public." I rested my head on his shoulder and laced my fingers through his. "He is not a good man."

"No, he's not, which makes it even more of a miracle that you turned out as wonderful as you did. It seems that *what* we've overcome is what ultimately molded us into the people that we are instead of *where* we've come from." He gave me a grin that didn't quite reach his eyes and cocked his head to the side. "So, what do you want to do to kill time while we wait for your old man to leave the house?" He wiggled his eyebrows at me. "I have some suggestions."

I felt a twinge between my thighs, but while my body might be on board with his type of distraction, my mind was a million miles away and not interested in being vulnerable and bare even to him. "I think we'll put a pin in that for later when I don't feel like I might throw up and pass out at any minute."

He nodded and rose to his feet. "Well, we're in Texas, so how about you take me for some barbecue."

I put a hand over my roiling stomach. "I don't think I can eat right now."

He reached out his hands and waited patiently until I placed my palms over his. He pulled me to my feet with a gentle tug. "That's fine; you can watch me eat and laugh at me when I get barbecue sauce all over my face. I'm not going to let you sit in the room and wind yourself up so tight that you snap."

I followed him out of the room and let him load me into the car. On autopilot, I tonelessly gave him direction to the place that used to be my favorite barbecue joint when I lived in town. I hadn't eaten there in years and years. Oliver thought it was too messy, so he forbade me having it in our home. The one time I snuck away and grabbed some with a friend from church, I of course got it on the outfit I was wearing. When he found the garment buried deep in the laundry, he wrapped the fabric around my throat and pulled on it until I blacked out. When I came to, I was covered in bruises and missing all of my clothes. I should have left long before it got to that point, but today, I was simply glad I was around to know better and to tell others that they deserved more than that. Life shouldn't be about merely surviving and enduring; it's about living and savoring every single day we had.

The hostess took us to a secluded table near the back of the restaurant. I realized as she was walking away that she had purposefully picked a place to seat us that was all the way across the room so that she could eye-fuck Wheeler for as long as possible. He seemed oblivious but I quickly learned he wasn't the only one fighting the urge to throat-punch someone when they wouldn't keep their eyes to themselves. I would never actually hurt anyone in any way, not when I knew what kind of lasting damage flying fists could do, but that didn't stop me from envisioning the girl with her hair on fire when she coquettishly looked over her shoulder at him on her way back to the hostess stand.

Luckily, our server was a guy who didn't seem to care about either one of us very much. Wheeler ordered a platter of meat that was big enough to feed a small army and a beer. I stuck to water and told him I would pick at the corn bread that came with his meal. We made small talk, mostly about the baby and how anxious he was to find out if he was having a boy or a girl when we got back. I didn't bother to remind him that the baby still might not cooperate, they could be flying blind about knowing the sex right up until the little bundle made an appearance. I kind of hoped the baby would keep being difficult. It was fun to watch Wheeler try and wrap his head around being responsible for a little girl. In his mind, a boy would be easier and I didn't have the heart to tell him how wrong he was. All girls were daddy's girls at heart. I asked if he and Kallie had started talking about names for either eventuality and he made a pained face. Apparently, Kallie was all for names that he considered boring and basic. He wanted something strong and memorable. He tossed out a couple that sounded like all the guys at his shop had voted on and deemed badass but I could see why Kallie wasn't a fan. He was asking if I had any suggestions when a shadow suddenly fell over the table. Thinking it was the server with Wheeler's food, I didn't look up until a throat was cleared.

Standing at my elbow was a man dressed in a sheriff's uniform. I didn't recognize him right away but when he spoke his voice was familiar. Case Lawton. He'd been a deputy when I lived in Loveless with Oliver. He was at the sheriff's office the night my husband had broken my arm and cracked several of my ribs. He was there when his father, the acting sheriff at the time, asked me if I really wanted to press charges. It was a small town and people would talk. My father had done a lot for the community and he would hate to drag my entire family into a domestic situation. He told Case to take me to the doctor, ordered him to get me checked out, and then mentioned he should go talk to Oliver about the proper way to keep his wife in line. I'd bolted before any of those things could happen. When the people that were supposed to help you were just as bad as the people that hurt you, all you could do was take care of yourself until you found someone that really cared.

"Poppy Cruz. I thought that was you. I followed your story on the news a while back." He ran a hand over the lower half of his face and took off the wide-brimmed hat that was covering his dark hair. He looked older than I remembered, tired and jaded, but still very handsome in a rough and rugged kind of way. "I told my old man that your husband was a loose cannon. I knew something terrible was going to happen if we didn't lock him up for assault. That bastard never listened to me."

I looked at the sheriff's star on his chest and over to Wheeler, who was watching the other man through narrowed eyes. "He should have listened. Oliver would be in jail, instead of dead, and I might not have spent the last year of my life jumping at shadows and waking up in the middle of the night screaming. He put a bullet in his head right in front of me. I had bits of his skull and his brain stuck in my hair." I sucked in a breath through my teeth and lowered my lashes as my hands curled into fists on the top of the table in front of me. "All of that came after two days of rape and torture. I'm lucky to be alive, but more than that, I'm lucky to still have my sanity and belief that not all men are made like my father and my deceased husband."

The cop rocked back on his heels and looked like he might be sick. His face went pale and his mouth pulled into a furious frown. He put his hat back on his head and dipped his chin. "We're supposed to protect and serve, ma'am, but not all cops are created equal either. My father was cut from the same fabric as yours, which is why he no longer has the big office. This town is small and word gets around when the people that are supposed to be paying attention are purposely looking the other way. I'm glad you made it out, and if you need help with whatever brought you back, know that I will answer the call personally. I knew I let you down that night, failed to protect you, and it's been a sore spot I've carried with me for years."

I gave a stiff nod. "I'll keep that in mind, Officer."

His lips quirked in a lopsided grin as he motioned toward Wheeler. "Your boyfriend is pretty hard to forget, so try not to do anything in the view of witnesses. They'll be able to pick him out of a lineup with no problem."

Wheeler let out a grunt in response as the cop moved out of the way so the server could put his tray down next to our table. The sheriff muttered a subdued good-bye, and before he started shoving food in his face, Wheeler asked me if I was okay.

I shrugged and reached out to snag a piece of bread off his

plate. "A lot of people in this town let me down before I left the first time. I should have known better than to come back but I did, and I was let down even worse the second time. That's how I know no one is going to help my mom. If they don't see it or speak of it, it's not really happening in their mind. But it is happening to way too many people, women and children, and even men."

"So, we'll do what we can to help because we know it's happening and we refuse to look the other way."

I gave him a sad smile and told him, "I really fucking love you, Hudson."

He replied by shoving a big bite of brisket in his mouth and chomping away happily. We killed the rest of the afternoon driving around town so I could show him my old haunts. Through now wide-open eyes, I could see that there wasn't anything particularly special about my home town, which made being back slightly less scary. After I talked to my mom, saw for myself that she was alive and well, I knew I would never be back. There was nothing here for me and I wasn't leaving anything that mattered behind.

We parked around the corner from my childhood home and had to wait for an hour until my father's sleek, black Mercedes SUV pulled out of the driveway. Men of the cloth were supposed to be humble and modest . . . my dad was neither of those things. He liked to flaunt his power and position in everything that he did.

"He looks like a dick." Wheeler's softly muttered words made me giggle when all I wanted to do was cry.

"He is." I turned my face to his and leaned in for a kiss when my dad drove around the corner so that there wasn't even the slightest chance he would see my face. Wheeler kissed me back, slipping in some tongue and leaving my bottom lip wet. When he pulled back we were both breathing hard and it wasn't from fear. He slipped out of the car and I followed with the key to the house that had never really been a home, clutched in my shaking fingers.

I stopped being able to breathe when I touched the doorknob. It turned easily under my hand and swung open with a barely noticeable creak. The interior of the house was dark and silent. There were no lights on, no TV going, no sounds of voices or life anywhere. It was like walking into a tastefully decorated tomb.

I looked over my shoulder as Wheeler pressed into my back, shutting the door behind him. "Their room is at the back of the house. The floor creaks, so tread lightly."

He jerked his chin in understanding as we started to creep through the dreary hallways that had no pictures or art on the walls. Everything was so sterile, made to look like a picture in a magazine. I clearly remembered my mother scrubbing and cleaning every surface until her fingers bled to keep my father happy. Without fail, he would come home after a service or a fund-raiser and find some microscopic piece of lint or dust she missed. His barely controlled fury would follow and that inevitably led to not just my mother bursting into tears.

I trailed my fingers along the wall like I used to do when I was little, walking back in time as memories assaulted me from all sides. I remembered the heavy weight of repression and judgment that seemed to hang in the air in this house. I remembered the absence of warmth, how everything felt cold even though it was never below seventy degrees outside. I remembered sleepless nights worried about my sister and hating how perfect I had to be to make up for her perceived failings in my father's eyes. I remembered the suffocating feeling as every ounce of joy and light was sucked out of me.

I liked the memories I was making now much better.

We hit the closed door to my parents' bedroom. I put a palm on the wood and took a second to brace myself for whatever might lie beyond. I was expecting the worst since my dad wouldn't let anyone speak to her, but I had to hope for the best. I felt Wheeler put a hand between my shoulder blades, letting me know that he was there regardless of what we were about to face.

I turned the knob and pushed the door open, my eyes immediately meeting my mother's. She was sitting in a chair by the window of the room, in the darkness, doing nothing but staring. She looked older than she did the last time I saw her. There was more silver in her dark hair and her bronze complexion had deep lines carved into it around her eyes and next to her mouth. She had also lost a ton of weight. Her arms looked like twigs where they stuck out of the bulky sweater she was wearing even though the house was warm enough to make me sweat.

"Mom?" The word escaped as a question because she looked like a stranger. She looked like a woman that had been beaten down and forgotten.

Her eyes, the same unusual light and golden brown as mine, blinked at me sluggishly. "Poppy?" She lifted a hand to her throat and started to rock back and forth in her seat. "Am I dreaming? I have to be dreaming."

Wheeler stepped around me into the room and hit the lights. We all blinked in reaction, and the full extent of how badly my mom was wasting away hit me. Her cheeks were sunken in. Her collarbone was sharp, prominent points and her hands looked like they belonged on a skeleton. She looked like a corpse that hadn't been put in the ground yet.

"You're not dreaming, Mom. I'm here to help you. I want you to come with me to Denver. I want you to leave Dad and let me help you. I've been worried."

Her eyes blinked again and it took them an unnaturally long time to open back up. "You're here, but you can't be here. It's going to make your father angry."

"He's always angry because something is fundamentally wrong with him. When was the last time you ate something?" I walked over to her and crouched down in front of her, putting my hands on her knees.

"Your father told me I was letting myself go. He thinks I'm getting old and fat. I've been dieting."

She was starving herself for the jackass. "You don't look well, Mom. Let me help you. I'll take you somewhere safe where they can make you better."

Her head fell back in the chair and I noticed her hair was thinning to the point I could see parts of her scalp through the wispy strands. She lifted a hand like it weighed a thousand pounds and let it flutter uselessly between us. "I'm a good wife. I do what I'm told. God will reward me. Women of faith do not walk away from a marriage when it becomes difficult."

That was my father's poisoned rhetoric coming from her mouth. "This isn't a difficult marriage, Mom, it's a deadly one. You're going to die if you stay with him."

"He loves me. He needs me." Her voice was thready and weak but I could hear that she believed this, really, honestly believed it.

"Mom . . . the only person that man loves is himself. When

you love someone, you take care of them, you treasure them, and you put their happiness before your own. The only person Dad has ever taken care of is himself. If he loved you, he would be here right now forcing you to eat something. You look like a skeleton. He knows you're wasting away and he isn't doing a damn thing to stop it. Just like he knew what Oliver was doing to me and never stepped in to protect me."

Her droopy gaze shifted to Wheeler and widened slightly. "You can't be here. My husband would not approve of you being in our home. Marking your skin is a sin. You do not alter the vessel you were given by the Lord."

"Is she for real?" He sounded flabbergasted and slightly disgusted.

I sighed. "Unfortunately, she is very real. Mom, if you come with me and work on getting better, you can be a grandma. Salem will let you see the baby and we can have the right kind of family." I seriously doubted Salem would let this woman anywhere near her child, ever, but I was getting desperate and time was running out. "You deserve better than this. I want more for you for the rest of your life than for you to be Dad's doormat and emotional punching bag."

"I'm a good woman, a godly woman. The Lord will provide for me."

I shook my head and rose to my feet. "The only thing he's going to provide is a place in hell, next to Dad, which is where he's going to end up for letting you kill yourself over him."

One of Wheeler's hands fell heavily on my shoulder and gave it a squeeze. "You're talking in circles and she's not listening. We've got to cut our losses here and go, honey."

I vehemently shook my head in the negative and leaned down

to put my hands on my mother's frail and bony shoulders. "I can't leave you here. I can't leave you with him."

Her eyes drifted closed again and she turned her face back toward the window. "This is where I belong."

Wheeler pulled me back and wrapped an arm around my heaving chest. "She has options and she knows that now. She can call you if she changes her mind and wants out. We can drop by and visit with that sheriff and let him know what's going on here. He seemed like he realized he royally fucked up with you and might be willing to stick his neck out to make it right." His lips touched my ear and I shuddered as tears started to slide down my cheeks. "You can't save someone that doesn't want to be saved, Poppy. There are some things that can't be salvaged because there's been too much time and decay. You let her know she's not alone and that's all you can do."

Unable to see out of the sheen of moisture that was now obscuring my gaze, I whispered a broken, "Bye, mom," and let him pull me out of the grim and gloomy room.

We were in the hallway when I heard her softly call out, "I would love a picture of my grandbaby when it gets here. You're a good girl, Poppy, you always were."

I was a good girl but that wasn't enough to get her to go with me. Sadly, I realized nothing would make her leave, but that didn't stop me from offering one last time. "If you need me, Mom, find a way to let me know."

Just because she was ready to give up and accept this as her horrible reality didn't mean that I had to.

Chapter 18

Wheeler

I was stretched out on my back underneath a seriously leaky Ford pickup truck. The guy that brought it in told me that black goo had suddenly started dripping from the rear axle. What he failed to mention was that he'd obviously been trying to tow something the wrong way and had bent and torqued the damn thing into something that looked like a modern art sculpture. I would never understand why a customer thought minimizing their part in what they fucked up would also minimize the cost of what it would take to fix. This was going to require a whole new back end and it wasn't going to be cheap.

Swearing under my breath, I rolled out from under the truck. It was going to have to go up on a lift so I could assess the full damage and it was well into February, so the cement floor of the garage never quite warmed up and lying across it even for just a few minutes made all the bones in my back hurt. I was giving instructions to a couple of my guys to move the truck when I caught sight of a familiar head of salt-and-pepper hair. I hadn't heard from Zak since I confirmed with him I had the Hudson in my possession and was getting ready to start work on it. I assumed he'd gone back to California and our paths wouldn't cross again, so needless to say, I was a little surprised to see him standing in my garage looking at the now painted Hudson like it was a rare and priceless piece of art.

I cleaned my hands off on the rag that was hanging out of my back pocket and made my way over to where the older man was standing. He had his hands shoved deep in the pockets of his canvas coat and his expression was set in serious lines. The previous two times he'd been to the garage he'd had on reflective sunglasses; now he didn't. When he turned to look at me as I approached, I faltered a step and came to a complete and total stop. Staring back at me were eyes that were the same identical, unusual pale blue as my own. Suddenly he didn't just look familiar . . . he looked like family.

I felt my hands curl into fists at my sides as we stared at each other until he broke the silence. "Wanted to make my way back before the holidays so we could talk, but my wife isn't in the best of health, so I couldn't leave her alone." He took his hand out of one of his pockets and rubbed the back of his neck. "You did some spectacular work with this car, kid. Looks better than some of the ones I've worked on."

"Fuck the car. Who the hell are you and why are you in my garage?" I crossed my arms over my chest and narrowed my eyes at him. "Keep in mind if I don't like your answers this isn't going to go well for you." I felt like there was a hive of angry bees buzzing under my skin. I could hear each beat of my heart between my ears and every breath I took and exhaled sounded super loud and ragged in the space between us.

The older man sighed and dropped his head so that he was

looking at the toes of his boots. "I had a kid with a woman when I was very young, just out of high school and torn between joining the army and trying to figure out my own way in the world. She was supposed to be a one-night stand, a way to sow some oats before I committed to one path or the other. She was a redhead, I always had a weakness for long legs and red hair. Things didn't work out the way I thought they would. She got knocked up, asked me for money for an abortion, and disappeared as soon as I handed the cash over. Didn't know her, didn't really want to, but that was a mistake."

He looked up to see if I was still following him. I was . . . and I didn't like where any of this was going. "You trying to tell me that I'm that baby?" I knew my mom was shady as hell and that sounded exactly like something she would do.

He let out a bitter-sounding chuckle and lifted an eyebrow at me. "I know I look young, kid, but not that young. I'm trying to tell you that baby was your mother." He sighed and rocked back on his heels. "I didn't know the woman I hooked up with took the money but kept the baby. I was clueless to the fact that I even had a child until my little one showed up on my doorstep at sixteen, hungry, homeless, and pissed off at the world. Her mother hadn't done right by her and neither had I. She was already deep into addiction, something I think she turned to in order to cope with the lifestyle her mother forced on her." He cringed. "And I think she was self-medicating. Been around a lot of women in my day and I know when one is off. My baby girl . . . there was something not right with her."

I held up a hand and closed my eyes briefly so I could pull my thoughts together. "You're telling me that you're my grandfather?" He didn't look a day over forty-five, even with the silver in his hair. I was having a hard time processing that, but there was no denying that the reason I could swear I had seen him somewhere before was because we had the same face and the exact same eyes. It was like looking into the future. He was what was waiting for me as I began to age.

He nodded and started to pace in front of me. "I took your mother in, put her in a program, got her some professional help, and prayed I could undo all the damage that was done at the hands of her mother." He gave me a look full of remorse and failure. "It didn't work. She'd get clean and go right back to using. She'd go to her sessions with the doc and then disappear for two or three days. She was erratic, violent, and unpredictable on her best days. She was bringing dangerous people around and refused to see that the drugs weren't helping; nothing really seemed to make a dent. I was married by the time she showed up, had an okay life and not much to complain about. My wife left because of the chaos your mother caused and I didn't care. She was my child, my daughter, it was my job to set her straight."

I let out a snort and gritted my back teeth. "She was never straight. When I was a baby, she would forget about me when she was high and when she wasn't she was annoyed I was there. When I was older, she would take me with her to score and leave me with whoever happened to be around. She still hung around dangerous people, so I was lucky that she gave me up when she did because who knows what kind of horrible shit I would have had to face when she was blitzed out. I needed someone to save me from her."

He made a strangled sound in his throat and lifted a hand so that he could drag it roughly over his face. "I know she never got better. After my wife left, your mother and I had it out. I told her it was rehab and living clean or she was out." He tossed his head back so that he was looking up at the ceiling. "I woke up the next day and she was gone. She took my '52 Hudson with her." His face contorted at the memory, and when he looked back at me it was tortured. "She pawned the car for a couple of thousand dollars and vanished. I never heard from her again."

I laughed but there was no humor in it and I felt like the center of my chest was going to cave in on itself. "Well, she did the same thing to me but I was four, so I assure you it sucked way worse for me than it did for you."

He turned to face me with a somber expression. His body was stiff and I could tell he was trying to keep his emotions in check. "I tried to find her. I hired private investigators, pulled in favors from clients, asked some guys I knew from back in the day who had connections that weren't exactly legal. No one could find her, maybe because she was living on the streets, hanging with people that didn't want to be found. I got close once when she got locked up on a solicitation charge in New Orleans." He looked down at the ground and then back up to me. "Her pimp bailed her out before I could get down there and she disappeared again. She must have changed her name after that; maybe she stole someone's identity because she was a ghost. I looked for her for years and years, waiting for the day I was going to get a phone call telling me they found her body in a ditch somewhere." His entire frame shuddered and I saw his eyes go shiny with unshed tears. "That call came in the middle of September. She overdosed in a women's shelter in Dallas. She was sick, kid, really sick, and there was no way to heal her."

Fuck me but that hurt. I put a hand to the ache that was kicking hard at my ribs and closed my eyes. I always thought she was terrible not just to me, but an actual terrible person. I knew she didn't end up the way that she did without some help and now knowing she might not have had any control over her sickness made me feel guilty for downright hating her all these years. There wasn't a shot in hell that she was ever going to be a good mom and do right by me, so the kindest thing she could do was let me go. I'd never really had her, but knowing she was gone in such an ugly, lonely way burned bright and fierce in my blood.

"The only reason I found out about her passing was because she kept a box of personal belongings on her. Inside they found one of my business cards, so they called and asked me to ID her. I flew to Dallas so I could put my baby in the ground, and when I got back to California I went through the stuff she kept close even through all her running and using." He took a couple of steps closer to me so that we were eye to eye. Both of us fighting back hot emotion and struggling with the loss of a woman that had torn both of our lives apart. "In the box was a birth certificate. My baby had a baby and I didn't even know about it." A tight smile pulled at his mouth and his chest expanded as he blew out a long breath. "She named you after my favorite car but I have no clue where 'Wheeler' came from. Maybe it was your dad's real last name, or maybe she made it up. I have no clue but it explains why I never knew you were out there. I hired the same guys I hired to find her to find you, only this time it took them half a day. Your garage is all over the Internet. People that know cars know your name. I saw your picture and nearly passed out. You looked just like me when I was in my twenties and you had my knack for fixing things most people have forgotten about. I remarried and she's a good woman. Stood by my side while I spent thousands upon thousands of dollars trying to find someone that didn't want to be found. She held me when I cried over my daughter's grave and she gave me her blessing not only when I told her I was going to meet my grandson but when I told her I was giving him that same car your mother took off in all those years ago. She's a good woman with a failing heart. She doesn't have much time left, so trying to figure out a way to finesse this, to ease my way into your life, went out the window. She wants to meet you before it's too late and I promised her I would make that happen."

I fell back a step and shifted my eyes to the car that I knew was special even before I saw it. "You were the guy I bought the Hudson from? You were the one that cut the price down to nothing?"

"The guy that bought it from the pawnshop had no idea what he had. He ran the car into the ground, trashed it like it was any regular ol' daily driver. He refused to sell it back to me, no matter what I offered. He claimed it paid for itself in pussy and considering he was a fat slob with a comb-over, I don't doubt he needed the car to get laid. He ran into some money trouble a while back and called me up offering to sell it. His price was outrageous but I bought it anyways. Little shit didn't bother to tell me he'd parted the thing out for some quick cash before sending it my way. I was holding on to it, telling myself I would rebuild it when the time was right. I walked onto your lot that first day, saw your Caddy, and knew the car wasn't mine, it was yours." He gave me a sheepish grin. "Part of the reason I drove my Hornet across country was because I was hoping you would recognize it, that there would be something there."

I tossed my head back and let out a laugh. "It's actually my girlfriend's. I gave it to her a couple of weeks ago." I knew the car meant something.

His dark eyebrows scrunched together and the corners of his

mouth pulled down. "The pregnant one? My wife nearly lost her mind when I mentioned there was a great-grandbaby on the way."

"No, my girlfriend isn't pregnant. My ex-girlfriend is." It sounded like a Jerry Springer episode when I had to explain it to someone else.

"Oh . . . well . . . that is complicated, isn't it?" He gave me a grin that revealed a dimple in his weathered cheek in the exact same place as mine. "Do you know if you're having a boy or a girl? My wife will be all over great-grandma duty if you wouldn't mind. It would be much appreciated if you let her be a part of your life for whatever time she has left, Hudson."

I placed my hands on my hips and rocked my head from side to side. "Don't know. We've done several ultrasounds but the baby seems fond of mooning us and not much else. Kallie, the baby's mom, decided she wants it to be a surprise, so I'm rolling with it. Poppy, my girlfriend, decorated the nursery in my house yellow and gray, so those are the colors we're sticking with."

I'd been so happy when she asked if she could tackle the project of turning my spare room into an actual room for the baby. She'd been pensive and quiet lately, the events in Texas weighing heavily on her mind. Every time her cell rang she rushed to see if it was her mother calling for help and her face fell when it wasn't.

I'd taken her as my date to Cora and Rome's wedding on Valentine's Day hoping that being surrounded by nothing but family and friends celebrating the love of two wonderful people would shake her out of it . . . and it had, slightly. She turned her attention away from the woman she couldn't help and instead focused on the ones she could. She was spending more and more time with her victims' advocacy group but now she was going in as a counselor and an advocate as well as a survivor. She was serious about helping other women who had been where she was and I was proud of her, but I was also worried that for every one woman she saved there would be another one, like her mother, that she couldn't. I knew that would weigh on her soul. There was a balance there that she was going to have to figure out and I had no problem holding on to her until she found it.

"Yellow and gray it is, then."

He looked at me expectantly and all I could do was shrug. "I've been on my own a long time. Never had a family that I could call my own. Made a baby with a girl that promised me hers but that didn't work out because promises are easy to break. I found the girl that was meant to be mine all along. She's more than family to me. She's the first person that has ever made me feel like I really, truly belong somewhere. I belong with her." I lifted an eyebrow at the older man who had my face and my eyes and gave him a slow grin. "Because I know what it feels like to be alone and unwanted, I would never want that for my kid. I want my baby to be loved by as many people in this life as possible. My baby is going to have family through blood but also through choice. I don't see why you and your wife can't be both."

He exhaled a long, relieved sigh and briefly closed his eyes. "You made this a lot easier than I thought you were going to, kid."

"Mom made shit hard for both of us. I'm not into a repeat of that, lived with enough struggle and sacrifice already. I choose to believe you when you say you tried to help her and I choose to believe that if you had known about me you would have done your best to help me as well."

He swore under his breath and nodded. "Kills me that you were in the system . . . fucking kills. I would have given you a home. I could have been the one to teach you about cars, not some underqualified shop teacher. That's like a knife right in the center of my chest."

"Can't focus on what was, only on what is." I reached out a hand and clapped him on his shoulder. I was going to be one good-looking motherfucker when I was an old man. "I'm sorry about your wife."

"Don't be. We had a lot of good years and she isn't gone yet. She took care of me when all that stuff with your mom was going down. Now it's my turn to be strong and take care of her."

"That's what love should look like." I was certain of it.

"That *is* what love looks like, kid. You want to pop the hood on this beauty and show me what you've done so far? Everything looks original. I'm impressed."

I couldn't help but feel proud. I'd never had anyone to tell me what I did was impressive before, at least never anyone whose approval mattered. "Thanks. I told you I had a guy that could find anything." My phone started to go off in my back pocket. I recognized Poppy's ring tone right away, so I held up a finger. "Give me a sec to take this. My girl doesn't usually call when she knows I'm working."

I tapped the screen, and before I could get out any kind of greeting, all I heard was a blood-curdling scream and the sound of Happy losing his little puppy mind. "Poppy?" I couldn't keep the panic out of my voice as I immediately turned away from the man who wanted to be my family and started toward the front of the garage.

The phone clicked and scratched, making me think she dropped it. I could still hear the dog barking and Poppy screaming but now it all sounded muffled, kind of like it was underwater and far away.

"Poppy!" I screamed her name so loudly every single head in the shop turned to look at me as I bolted out one of the open bays and jumped down to the snowy ground below. My boots hit the asphalt with a thud as I ran toward my truck. "Honey, where are you?" I knew she couldn't answer me because I could hear her struggling and choking on the other end of the phone.

"Give me your keys, kid. You don't look like you have it to-gether enough to get behind the wheel in this weather." I didn't think, just tossed the keys to Zak and kept calling Poppy's name into the phone. I could hear Happy growling and getting more agitated by the minute.

"D-ad . . . st-o-pppp." Her wail was cut off and I could hear her trying desperately to suck air in. I screamed her name again and jumped into the truck. Knowing I couldn't listen to her die over the phone without doing something to try and save her. I hung up and called 911. The dispatcher had to ask me to repeat myself three times because I was talking so fast and barking out orders to her and to my grandfather at the same time.

"My girlfriend is being attacked by her father. You need to send help." I was breathing hard and I felt light-headed. I couldn't see straight.

"Where is the attack taking place sir? I need an address to give the responders."

I was blindly guiding Zak toward her apartment assuming she was home after work but the reality was she could be anywhere and I wouldn't be able to get to her in time. Nobody would. I narrowed it down to the veterinary clinic where she worked, her apartment, and my house because those were the only places she typically brought Happy with her.

I rattled off her address and also told the dispatcher to send someone to the vet clinic in case her crazy father had jumped her when she was leaving work for the afternoon. I pleaded with her to also send someone over to my place. The woman stayed calm and assured me she would get units to all the locations but I didn't know if they would arrive in time. Poppy had sounded like she was slipping away as she begged her father for her life. I couldn't believe she had come all this way, done everything in her power to escape, only to end up back in his breaking hands.

"We'll find her, Hudson." The stranger sitting next to me suddenly became my only grounding point in a world that was spinning too fast and totally off center.

I knew we would find her. It was the condition she was going to be in when I got to her that I was worried about.

Chapter 19

Poppy

I was distracted, and like always . . .
   I should have known better.

Distracted was dangerous.

Distracted could be deadly.

When I left work, Happy had found something dead and decaying buried in the snow in the parking lot and he already had it in his mouth and was chewing on it by the time I realized it wasn't just a stick or rock. Of course, his adventure led to him getting sick all over the backseat of my car, which was gross enough as it was, but the silly dog had to go and turn the disaster into even more of a horror show by trying to lick up his vomit. I couldn't get to my apartment fast enough, and when I pulled up to the curb out front, instead of checking my surroundings and making sure I had a clear path from my car to the front door, I was preoccupied getting the dog out of the backseat while trying not to get puke all over my coat.

   I was bent over at the waist, clipping the dog's leash on his monogrammed and studded collar, his Christmas gift from

Wheeler, when the first blow landed on the back of my head. Immediately I went to my knees, the puppy blurring into a brown blob as red started rolling over my face and staining the snow scarlet in front of me. I went to lift a hand to the burning, bleeding ache at the back of my skull when my wrist was grasped in a grip so tight and painful it made me cry out. Another hand fisted in my swinging ponytail and jerked my head backward.

Even though my vision was fuzzy there was no mistaking the man that was dragging me backward so that he could sit on my chest while he repeatedly banged the back of my head into the icy, unforgiving sidewalk in front of my apartment.

My father had found me and he wasn't going to leave until I was dead. I should have known this was coming and I should have been prepared for it. Wheeler made me feel safe, made me feel bulletproof and invincible. I forgot I was nothing more than thin skin and breakable bone.

"Dad!" I screamed the word like it would have some effect on the madman that slapped me across the face and furiously ground his knees into my shoulders so I couldn't hit him back. My heels were kicking uselessly into the ground and I could feel the puddle of blood underneath my head spreading, soaking into my hair and running warm down the back of my neck.

"I've been waiting outside of every single veterinary clinic in Denver until I found the one you worked at." His hands flexed around my throat and I started to choke. I felt my eyes bug in my face as my oxygen supply dwindled down to nothing. I couldn't get my hands free to push at him or to pry at his fingers, but I could get them into the pocket of my coat where my cell phone was. They were starting to tingle and go numb and he continued to put pressure on my airway but I managed to tap the screen and find the home button so I could redial the last number I called. Of course, it was Wheeler. "You stupid bitch. You and your whore sister were never worth anything. You think I'm stupid, that I don't know it was you calling the house, that it was you who had that nosy sheriff showing up on my doorstep day after day, demanding to see your mother? You were dead to me, Poppy, dead." His hands tightened more and more as he spoke and vaguely I heard Happy whining and his nails nervously tapping on the sidewalk as he danced around my struggling body.

I heard Wheeler scream my name from the phone in the pocket, and since I could hear it, so could my father, which had him letting go of my throat just long enough for me to sputter out a raspy "D-ad . . . st-o-pppp." It was a plea that went unanswered.

When he leaned over to pull my phone out of my pocket, he lifted up just enough that I managed to flip myself over, my hands hitting the cement hard, palms sliding and skidding as the skin tore. Out of the corner of my eye, I saw a bloody rock the size of a man's fist that had bits of my hair still clinging to it. He'd tried to cave my skull in, and from the amount of blood that was splashed across the snow I scrambled across, he had done a pretty good job of it.

Happy tried to jump in my face, which slowed me down as I tried to crawl away. Tears stung my eyes as my hair was yanked once again, pulling me back so that I landed on my ass with a loud cry. My father's arm clamped around my throat, the curve of his elbow completely blocking any air from making it past his choke hold. I clawed ineffectively at his arm, the stiff fabric of his wool coat keeping his skin protected from the only weapon I had at my disposal. He growled poison at me and spit venom in my ear as he continued to hold me down while I struggled to breathe and escape.

"That bleeding-heart lawman took one look at your mother and told me if she didn't get help he was calling adult protective services. Your mother has always had a roof over her head, food in her belly, and a man of God in her bed. She has nothing to complain about and that's what she told that policeman, but he still came around." The arm around my throat tightened even more and Happy jumped up and started pawing at my dad's legs. I was worried the little guy was going to get hurt. When Oliver showed up to do the exact same thing to me that my father was doing now, he'd kicked Salem's puppy so hard that the poor thing limped for weeks, but my dad seemed to have a single-minded focus and that was to make me pay. He didn't even seem to notice the dog. "The last time he showed up at the house with some of the women from my church. They said they were worried about her, that they were concerned for her well-being. Seems your sister reached out to some people she thought might take an interest in your mother's health, meddling like she always does. They convinced your mother that she needed to leave, both the house and me. It was humiliating. First, I have to suffer the embarrassment of daughters bathed in sin and immorality and then I have to explain to my congregation why the police are questioning me and why your mother is no longer in her rightful place. You ruined everything, you and your sister. I'm going to show you both what happens when you disobey and go against God." Not only was he mean and violent, but apparently he'd crossed the line into delusion as well. "I never, not once, raised a hand to any of you, even when you so rightly deserved it. Do you see what you've driven me to,

Poppy? Do you understand that this is the only way you will ever learn?"

God, I loved my sister. She didn't give two shits about Mom or what was going on in our childhood home. She left it all behind and never looked back. But she loved me and she knew I was worried, knew it was under my skin that I couldn't do anything to help our mom without going toe-to-toe with dad. She did what she always did and intervened. She got involved, pulled strings, played on sympathies, manipulated and coerced until she got me what I wanted . . . my mother away from my father. She was the best sister ever and she was going to lose her ever-loving mind if my dad managed to do any more damage to me than he already had. If he didn't end up in jail for killing me, he was going to end up in a shallow grave when she was done with him.

My entire body bent back as he cranked his arm even tighter around my throat. I gasped and blinked rapidly as starbursts started to shoot off behind my eyelids. Everything around me was fading into a narrow pinpoint, blackening out around the edges, and I could hear the rush of my blood through my head as my brain scrambled for the oxygen it so desperately needed. The chill that was soaking into my knees and shins had more to do with my limbs going numb than it did with the cold. My father's breath was warm on my cheek and lashed across my skin like a razor blade when he snarled, "That baby was lucky it didn't make it into this world. You saved it from having someone like you as a mother, you stupid, useless girl. Your mother should have given me sons—strong, loyal, obedient sons. She's just as worthless as you and your sister."

I couldn't see anymore. I could hardly hear, but I could feel that my entire face was wet with blood. I could smell the coppery scent of it and taste the salty wash of it on my lips, which were open, trying to suck in any kind of air and failing.

"Hey! What are you doing to that woman?" I vaguely heard Happy let out a yip and the creak of the front door to my apartment building.

My dad loosened his hold just enough that I managed to inhale a massive gasp of air. More afraid of dying and leaving Wheeler all alone again than I was of the man that had done his best to destroy me, I threw back an elbow with as much force as I could muster and heard a satisfying grunt of pain when it connected with my father's soft belly. The arm dropped from around my neck as hurried footsteps pounded toward us and multiple voices demanded that my dad move away from me.

"Get away from her!"

"Take your hands off her!"

"I'm calling the cops!"

All of it was a blur and a swirl of things that made no sense as I pitched forward, no longer able to keep myself upright. I was expecting a faceful of concrete . . . what I got was gentle hands that wrapped around my upper arms to keep me from falling. I blinked and tried to bring the face in front of mine into focus. It looked vaguely familiar, but considering I was bleeding profusely, probably had a concussion, and had been choked out, I couldn't place it right away.

I heard sirens wailing off in the distance and closed my eyes as tears of relief started to burn in my eyes and leak out over my lashes. Considering the blood all over my face, I was sure I looked like something out of a horror movie.

"She's my child, my daughter, you have no right to interfere! I'm a man of God!" My father was wailing at the top of his lungs.

"Let me go!" I looked over at him and saw that two other men that also looked slightly familiar were holding on to each of his arms as he strained and struggled to get free.

"Not a chance in hell, Pops. We're staying right here until the cops show up so we can tell them you were trying to kill her right out in the open." I wanted to hug the guy that was keeping me propped up but I was covered in all manner of gross things and there was a good chance I might puke on him. I felt my stomach rolling hard.

"She needs to be punished. She never learns her lesson, never." My dad sounded crazy, just as crazy as Oliver did the entire time he held me captive.

The sound of an angry and powerful motor and big tires coming to a sudden stop had everyone's attention turning to the big truck that came to a screeching halt in the middle of the road. The passenger door flew open and Wheeler hit the ground running before the vehicle fully stopped.

"Poppy!" My name ripped from him, terror and fury making the word vibrate with enough force that my rescuer wisely let me go so my man could get to me.

He was on his knees in front of me with his arms wrapped around me in the next heartbeat and finally I let myself collapse, knowing nothing and no one else was going to be able to get to me unless it went through him first.

My forehead hit his throat and my arms shook as they wrapped around his neck. He was panting harsh breaths into the side of my neck and I could feel his lips against the angry, swollen skin at my throat. I tried to tell him that I was okay, that I would be all right, but nothing but a scratchy squeak came out. He shook against me and I felt his hands ball into fists at my back. His head lifted and looked over to where my father was still struggling in the hold of the other two young men that had unquestioningly saved my life.

"The sirens are getting closer. You got two minutes max if you want to get a shot in, kid." I didn't recognize the voice, but when I looked up at the man that quietly gave Wheeler the warning, I gasped and did a double take. He looked just like Wheeler, only older, with salt-and-pepper hair and darker skin that was sun-weathered and set with attractive lines around his eyes.

"Two minutes is plenty." Wheeler's lips hit mine even though they were cracked and marked with spots of drying blood. "Honey, I'm gonna let Zak hold on to you for a minute, okay?"

He was asking but I could see the way rage was making his eyes electric and his freckles pop on his cheeks. I knew he wouldn't let me go if I asked him not to, but the wild inside of him was wound up and needed a place to go. The wolf that prowled around inside of him wanted to protect its mate and I needed to let it.

"He's not worth it, Wheeler." I let the older man help me to my feet and promptly fell into his arms as my legs gave out. The words were nothing more than a puff of air that sounded like sandpaper and smoke. My throat felt like it was on fire.

"No, but you are." Wheeler's words were barked out as he took striding, stalking steps toward where my father had gone still, watching his approach with trepidation clear on his face. Wheeler jerked his chin at the other men holding on to the man that brought me into this world and had done his best to take me out of it. "Let him go."

They complied immediately and took a few steps to the side so that there was no way they would get caught in the torrent of pure, unadulterated fury that was pouring off Wheeler in waves.

A massive hand lifted a red shop rag that seemed to magically appear to the back of my head, and applied soft, steady pressure. "He got you good, didn't he, sweetheart?" The stranger with Wheeler's eyes gave me a little squeeze and I closed my eyes as I heard Wheeler tell my father this was the last time he was going to get anywhere near the woman in his life. Suddenly a warm wiggly body was in my arms and puppy kisses were licking across my face as the stranger who felt like I had known him forever cuddled both me and my dog. I needed the comfort as the sound of flesh hitting flesh suddenly filled the air around me.

I wanted to tell Wheeler that my dad hadn't gotten me good enough because I was still here, still standing and willing to fight. He had never been good enough to take me all the way out. I always managed to fight my way back. The words rattled around my head but they couldn't find their way out of my battered throat.

I heard a scream.

I heard bones crunch.

I heard my father beg for the mercy he had refused to show me, or my sister . . . or my mother.

I heard clapping and wolf whistles as the witnesses to this entire ordeal happily encouraged Wheeler to take my father apart piece by piece. Something he was accomplishing with ease if the horrific sounds that were hitting my ears were any indication.

"Boy is good with his hands. It's good you gave this moment to him." The older man gave me a squeeze and Happy barked up happily at him as he reached out to rub the puppy's head between his ears. "It's gonna eat at him that he wasn't here when your old man blindsided you. Letting him do something, anything, to prove he can take care of you, he needs that. We like to think we'll be able to take on anything, tackle anyone that threatens what we love. The truth is we can't always be there, but we will always protect what we love." He swore as blood started to seep through the towel he was holding in a crimson rush. "Your pops is gonna go away for a long time, sweetheart. This is the only shot Hudson is gonna get to show him why you don't put your hands on women, why you don't put your hands on anyone that doesn't want them there. He had to take his shot."

He was right. I didn't think there was any way to end violence with more violence, didn't believe blood for blood was going to make my dad any kinder or more tolerant. But Wheeler obviously had a point to make and he made it by breaking every single bone in my father's hands. In those two minutes, the man that I never wanted to see again also earned himself a broken jaw, knocked-out teeth, twin black eyes, split and broken lips, a dislocated shoulder, a sprained ankle from where he fell when he tried to run away, and a plethora of other bruises and scrapes he collected while trying to get away from my furious and vengeful boyfriend.

The sirens were suddenly upon us and I was enveloped in a swarm of police and paramedic uniforms. Someone shouted and pulled Wheeler off my dad and I cried out when Happy was pulled from my arms as I was hustled toward the back of a waiting ambulance. The older man that called himself Zak took hold of the puppy and promised me that he would take of my little guy. Out of the corner of my eye, I saw Wheeler arguing with a police officer and I was all set to push away from the EMT that was messing with the gash on the back of my head and shining a light into my eyes. I wanted to keep Wheeler from getting arrested. Luckily, the three guys that had rushed to my rescue stepped in and explained the situation, so Wheeler avoided handcuffs.

It took a few minutes for him to get cleared and answer the police's questions, but as soon as he was free, he jogged over to where they had loaded me into the ambulance. He climbed up into the back without waiting for an invitation and found one of my hands. His were torn, the knuckles raw and bleeding, but I wrapped my fingers around them anyway and held them to my cheek. I couldn't talk—my voice was gone, my windpipe seriously bruised and swollen—but I think he understood I was saying thank you for standing up for me, for the physical fight I would never win. I could hold my own when it came to the battle for my soul and my heart, but I was always going to be out-matched when it came to swinging fists and powerful punches.

"Shoulda known if we pushed he was going to push back. Shouldn't have left you alone." His thumb ran along the curve of my cheek and I closed my eyes only to have the paramedic that was hovering near the top of my head prod me and tell me I couldn't rest until I had a doctor check me out. He was guessing it was a concussion, as well I gathered.

I wanted to tell Wheeler it was about time I pushed. Pushed my father. Pushed my mother. Pushed against everything that had landed me in an abusive marriage and feeling like that was what I deserved. I pushed and pushed until it was no longer a part of me, and if that meant having to face off with another man that wanted nothing more than compliance and obedience, then I would do it again and again. For myself and for anyone else stuck in a bad situation.

Obviously, Wheeler couldn't be by my side 24/7 but I couldn't

tell him that until my voice started working. It was sweet that
he wanted to be a living barrier between me and the rest of the
world, but I was done hiding. I'd been slowly working my way
out of the protective shell I'd surrounded myself in after Oliver's
attack and I realized today that no matter how careful I'd been,
or how deliberate I'd been in the people I let into my life, danger
was always lurking close to home. It was never strangers that did
the most damage: it was the men that were supposed to love me
the most.

I'd had some really bad people in my life, ones that had left
their mark and taken bits and pieces of me that I didn't want to
give. But I'd been fortunate enough to have some really amazing,
special people in my life as well. Instead of taking, they gave me
what I needed to heal and to make myself whole. They also left
marks, but theirs were ones that I didn't want to hide in the dark.
They made me smile. They made me brave. They made me bold.
I wasn't living my life where the scars and wounds were—no, I
was living it where the love and light found me every single day.
What happened with my father wasn't going to drag me backward. It was going to propel me forward, knowing he had made
his own bed, stuffed with consequences and penance. I would
rest easy at night knowing he would never be able to hurt me, my
mother, or Salem again with either his words or his fists.

This was his end and my beginning.

"You're gonna be okay, honey . . . we're gonna be okay." Wheeler
sounded so sure of the fact that all I could do was believe him. I
trusted him and he never lied to me. His wild was still riled up
and needed soothing, but there wasn't anything I could do about
it while I was strapped down to a gurney with an IV in my arm.
That wolf was going to have to howl just a little bit longer.

ONCE I GOT into the ER, it was a flurry of activity. I was separated from Wheeler, much to his aggravation and very vocal
displeasure. Salem and Rowdy showed up to keep him in check
and run interference as he snapped at every person that tried to
get between me and him even though they were just trying to
help. I needed X-rays of my head and throat, plus I'd lost a lot of
blood and needed a transfusion. Luckily, Saint Ford, a friend of
my sister's who happened to be married to the guy that painted
Wheeler's garage, was the attending nurse. I managed to avoid
having a panic attack when she started fluttering around me
and cutting my bloody clothes off. She handled getting me visu-
ally checked out and into a hospital gown efficiently and professionally, so I didn't really have time to freak out. I didn't know
her well but she was super nice, very patient, and treated me like
I might break. She didn't touch me any more than was necessary
and she let Wheeler into my little cubicle that was divided from
the one next to it by a curtain as quickly as she could. My sister
and Rowdy fussed over me for as long as I could tolerate without being able to respond to anything they were asking. Sensing
my growing agitation, Wheeler gently convinced them to come
back in the morning when I wasn't holding on to my composure
by the very tips of my fingernails.

He was sitting on the edge of the bed, one of my hands held
in his as his other hand traced over the features of my face like
he was trying to memorize each and every one when the curtain
swished back and another familiar face made an appearance. I
knew I was going to have to talk to the police eventually but
I didn't think I was going to get lucky enough to land in Royal
Hastings's lap. She was also a friend of my sister's and someone
that I knew in passing. She'd been instrumental in starting the

manhunt for me as quickly as possible when Oliver snatched me from Salem's apartment. All the stars were aligning to make this horrific attack as easy on me as possible—the stars and some well-meaning women. Saint let it slip that she saw my name on the intake board and bounced her coworker to another room so she could take care of me. As she gently and lightly laid me back on the hospital bed so I didn't jostle the stitches and bandage that was now wrapped around my head like a mummy, she told me how she saw too many women come through the doors of her ER battered and bruised at the hands of someone they loved. She frowned as she told me how much it bothered her when they left with the person that put them there in the first place. She was ecstatic to hear that I would be leaving with Wheeler.

Royal watched me with knowing, cop eyes as she told us both, "I heard the call and recognized the name. I told my sergeant you'd been through enough with these men in your life and would prob-ably be more receptive to a familiar face taking your statement than some strange man. Plus, I doubted Slugger here was feeling like letting anyone with a dick anywhere near you. I even told my partner to sit this one out." She pointed a finger at Wheeler and wagged it back and forth. "Lucky you had witnesses to back up your story that you attacked Pastor Cruz in self-defense, Speedy. You'd be looking at a night in lockup if not." I wondered at the nickname and made a mental note to ask him about it later.

Wheeler grunted and ran his thumb over the curve of my bottom lip. "She can't talk. Her trachea is all fucked up and she has a severe concussion. The doc is keeping her for a few days and doesn't know when she'll be able to talk." He sounded so frustrated and overly protective over it all, so I reached up and patted his shoulder reassuringly.

Royal rocked back on her heels and clicked her tongue. She was kind of a goof, and stunningly gorgeous . . . it was an odd combination for a police officer but it seemed to work for her. She was good at her job and obviously gave a damn about the people she was supposed to protect and serve.

"That's okay. We'll talk when you're better, Poppy. I just thought you might want to know that the D.A. is looking at charging your old man with attempted murder. We found the rock he hit you with and it was obvious he stalked you until he found an opportunity to attack. That's not a crime of passion, that's a plan, one that thankfully, backfired. You're lucky those college kids that live in the building were headed out for happy hour when they did."

I made a noise in my injured throat and blinked. That's when I recognized where the guys that stepped in came from. They were the rowdy group of guys that I'd done my best to avoid and had almost flipped out over the first night I invited Wheeler up to my apartment. I had spent so much time scared of people and things for no reason. The entire world wasn't out to get me; in fact, there were lots and lots of people that seemed interested in protecting me, and I was so very thankful for that.

"Anyways, I'll let you rest up and check in on you in a few days. Wheeler, I need you and your grandfather to swing by the station and give formal witness statements as well. Pastor Cruz is going away for a long, long time. I'm thrilled we get to do that for you, Poppy. I hated that we couldn't get to you before your husband hurt you." She shook her head, dark brown eyes going soft and sad. "That's the worst part of the job, wanting to help and not being able to." She pointed at Wheeler again and told him, "Take care of your girl."

Royal left the room in a whirl of police blues and fiery hair, leaving me and Wheeler alone again. If I had a voice I would have asked about the grandfather revelation Royal had just dropped. I knew the older guy looked *just* like my guy, but my guy was a lone wolf . . . at least he had been until he met me. There was a story there I needed to hear, but it wasn't the one he wanted to tell me.

"Never been so scared of anything in my entire life." His breath whooshed out and he lowered his forehead so that it was barely resting against mine. "Not when my mom drove away from that fire station. Not when I got bounced from my first foster home or my fifth. Not when I met Kallie's parents the first time or when she cheated on me the first time and I realized there was no way she could love me the way I needed to be loved. Not when I bought a house knowing the woman I was buying it for didn't want me. Not when I found out I was going to be a dad. Not when we went to bed and I realized you were it for me, you were the one I'd been waiting for, and it was never going to be me and only me again. Nothing has ever ripped open my heart and made time stop the way it did when I got that call." He lifted his head and his eyes met mine. They glistened like blue glass under the crystal veil of unshed tears. "I could have killed him and not felt a single ounce of regret over it."

He said that but I knew it wasn't true and so did he. He was lying with his words but his eyes always told the truth. The reason I loved him and had let him in when all I wanted to do was keep everyone out was because he was a man that wanted to take pain away, not cause it. I loved him because the last thing he wanted to do was hurt anyone, unless of course they were a direct threat to someone he loved. He was a lover not a fighter, but that didn't mean he wouldn't protect what was his until his last breath.

He used his heart, not his fists, to win wars.

I couldn't respond with words, so I reached up and cupped his cheek. I tapped the spot where his dimple was missing until he took the hint and lowered his lips to touch mine. I didn't want to waste a second worrying about what had hurt either of us in the past. Those things weren't changing and there would always be reminders to keep us humble and keep us kind. It was the things that made up happy, the things that restored us, that I wanted to focus on from this point on.

We deserved happy.

We fought for it and we won.

He was my victory and I was his triumph.

I couldn't tell him that I loved him, that I loved that he took better care of me than anyone else ever had, myself included in that. I couldn't tell him that I didn't know what a life worth living looked like before he came into mine. I couldn't promise him my future and forever—whatever that looked like—even though I knew it would be absolutely beautiful because it had me and him right in the center of it. I couldn't whisper that he was the best I'd ever had, that no one compared in or out of bed to him, and I couldn't scream from the top of my lungs that the best thing that ever happened to me was him deciding he could rebuild me.

I couldn't say any of those things because I had no voice, but I knew they were all shining out of my eyes, that he could see them, because he always saw. When I was hiding, when I was afraid, when I was worried, when I was lost and looking behind me instead of where I was going, he still found a way to keep his eyes on me. It didn't matter that I built walls to keep him out . . . he walked right through them.

He was looking at me the same way I was looking at him and I knew that no matter what we faced from here on out, we would always, only, have eyes for each other.

EPILOGUE

I like the name Royce." I whispered the words into Wheeler's hair as he rested his head on my shoulder and closed his eyes.

It was three o'clock in the morning, Kallie's water had broken a little over an hour ago, and all three of them—Kallie, Wheeler, and the baby—had just survived an emergency C-section that brought a perfectly healthy, seven-pound-five-ounce, furiously wailing little boy into the world. Royce Hudson Wheeler had ended up breech and no matter what kind of yoga, chiropractic, holistic healing methods, or old wives' tales Kallie tried, the baby was stubbornly staying put. He refused to flip just like he refused to reveal his sex so that his parents could plan accordingly. It was actually Zak who suggested the name Royce. One of the first classics he rebuilt and sold was a 1944 Rolls-Royce Silver Phantom. Wheeler brought the name up to Kallie after one of his grandfather's visits, stating that Royce could work for either a boy or a girl, and surprisingly she agreed.

I was happy to play messenger for both of them while they worked to bring their son into the world.

Kallie's mom and dad had shown up shortly after we did and were now in her birthing suite meeting their grandson. Dixie and Church would be on the first flight out of Tupelo tomorrow and Zak and his wife, Shannon, were coming in from California sometime in the afternoon. Zak had gotten choked up when I called. He was a really nice man, one with a heart nearly as big and as pure as his grandson's. He was overwhelmed with relief that his wife was still well enough to travel and that she was going to be around long enough to meet Zak's great-grandson. They were good people and I hated that Wheeler's mother's selfish and unthinking actions had kept him from the family he was so desperately seeking his whole life. It reminded me too much of the way my father had isolated me from the kind of life I knew was out there for all of us, and forced me to live under his tyranny.

I called Roni and let her know Kallie was in labor even though the two of them had recently split. They'd done their best to make a real relationship work, but it turned out that while Roni wanted Kallie, she didn't want everything that Kallie came with. She wasn't ready to be a mom, wasn't ready to have not only Wheeler but me as well in her life. She claimed it was all too complicated, too messy. They stayed friends and Roni assured me she would stop by to see the baby when she had a minute.

Kallie was heartbroken when Roni pulled the plug and had reacted in a way that scared everyone. She shut down, quit eating right, quit going to her birthing classes, and started skipping doctor's appointments. Wheeler tried to talk to her, tried to reason with her, but she was despondent. She didn't want to hear anything. All she wanted to do was wallow in pain and feel sorry for herself. She told Wheeler that she finally understood what it was like to have the love of your life stomp all over your heart.

Watching the way her behavior was stressing Wheeler out, I finally decided to intervene. Kallie wouldn't listen to anyone that was close to her but I had a feeling she would listen to someone that knew firsthand what could happen if she didn't get her act together. We met for coffee one morning and I told her what it was like to lose a child. I told her how I felt like I had a hole in my heart that would never be filled, that every time I saw her protruding belly, jealousy ate at me, sharp and pointed. I told her how I still grieved every single day and that I still woke up in the middle of the night crying for that lost life. I explained that it was a hurt that never healed, that eventually it just turned into an ache you learned to live with, and sometimes, like when a baby started crying in a restaurant, or when you went to a baby shower, the ache turned into a burn that felt like it would turn your heart to ash. I softly admonished her for not taking care of herself, for worrying Wheeler, and for putting her baby at risk. I promised her that a heart that had been broken by a lover would heal with time, but one that was ripped out of your chest when something happened to your child was one you could never get back.

My words must have sunk in because she snapped out of her stupor and found her footing. We also went from being uneasy allies to being friends. She didn't have many, and with Dixie being down in Mississippi setting up house with Church, she needed someone, and for whatever reason that person was me. I was the one she called to go baby shopping with. I was the one she called with updates and questions. I was the one she called when she butted heads with Wheeler over the name. She wanted to hyphenate the last name so that it was Carmichael-Wheeler or Wheeler-Carmichael, Wheeler was adamant that no kid should be saddled with having to write that monster out for their entire school career and they should just use Wheeler. It was an ongoing argument that I frequently heard both sides of, but I'd had to inform Kallie that I was always going to side with Wheeler. It was my job to take his back even though she mattered to me and I cared about her opinion.

It was a weird situation, one that had to look impossible and unbearable from the outside. But to those of us on the inside . . . we were doing what we could to make it all work and make it all as normal as possible. It was our life, so all we could do was live the best we could. It wasn't anyone's idea of a traditional family unit, but it was *our* family and we would do whatever it took to fight for it and defend it.

I also called my sister, who immediately offered to pull her very pregnant self out of bed and come wait with me since she instinctively knew it would be difficult for me to sit and wait while surrounded by so many reminders of what I had lost. Of course, I told her to stay in bed, that I would be fine, but I wasn't surprised when not twenty minutes later her man came walking through the door looking bleary-eyed and rumpled. Rowdy collapsed in a seat next to me, took my hand and squeezed it, then silently waited with me, offering steady, unwavering comfort until Wheeler came through the doors marked LABOR AND DELIVERY wild-eyed and still dressed in the green paper gown the nursing staff had given him to wear over his regular clothes. As soon as Wheeler found his way over to my side, Rowdy lumbered to his booted feet, offered a handshake and a heartfelt congratulations, and promptly muttered that he was going back to his pregnant girlfriend and his warm bed.

Wheeler laced his fingers through mine and I could feel the tremor in them. "I'm a dad." The words whispered out in awe.

I kissed his temple and brushed his ear with my nose. "You are."

His fingers flexed in mine and he pushed himself up in the chair so that he could turn and look at me. He reached out a finger and pushed some of my hair behind my ear. "Thank you for being here."

My lips twitched. "Anytime."

He grinned and those killer dimples did what they always did, made my heart skip a beat and my skin shiver. I hoped against hope his little boy was going to be blessed with those twin dots of adorable. All his kids needed to have them.

"It's you and me from here on out for everything. We're all in." I returned his smile and was leaning forward to give him a kiss when we were interrupted by a throat clearing.

We both turned to look at Kallie's mom and dad where they were standing behind us. I liked the Carmichaels. They were nice, and as accepting as they could be of the role I was going to play in their grandchild's life. They treated me with consideration and kindness once Wheeler explained everything that I had been through, and they did their best to include me in family things that involved the baby, like Kallie's baby shower.

"Kallie asked us to send you back." Wheeler went to rise to his feet but Kallie's dad, Russ, shook his head. "No, she wants to see Poppy."

I blinked in surprise and looked questioningly at Wheeler. He shrugged in confusion and helped me to my feet. "You okay sticking your head in the room?" He was asking because he knew I was still hesitant to be around the baby, that it would hurt watching Kallie hold and cuddle that precious little life.

It would hurt, but it would ultimately be far worse if I didn't figure out a way to play through the pain. I couldn't avoid the things that wounded me, couldn't lock myself away so they wouldn't touch me. I had to confront them and fight them head-on. I patted Wheeler reassuringly on the chest and gave him a wobbly smile. "I'll be fine." I'm sure it seemed off to Kallie's folks, him asking if I was okay when Kallie was the one that had just been cut open and sewn back together, but he was always taking care of me. It wasn't something that needed any explanation.

I put a hand on the door and made my way inside. The lights were down low but there was a glow from the heart monitor and other medical machines Kallie was hooked up to. She had the hospital bed elevated and she was partially sitting up with a tiny, blanket-wrapped bundle in her arms. When she caught sight of me she smiled and tilted her chin so that I would come closer. She looked tired and a little ragged but there was definitely a glow about her that made her look absolutely beautiful. Her hair was in a tangled mess on top of her head and she had shadows under her eyes, but her smile lit up the room and had me smiling back even though my heart was in my throat.

"How you feeling?" I took slow steps toward the bed, faltering when the baby started to fuss as he searched for comfort and food.

"Like I was sawed in half and superglued back together." She lifted an eyebrow at me and her smile grew even bigger. "So never better." She lifted a hand and motioned me closer. "Come meet Royce." She brushed a finger over his cheek. "He looks just like Wheeler. I hope he gets his dimples."

I let out a startled laugh that her thoughts mirrored my own. Those dimples were in high demand, it seemed.

It took me longer than it should have to get to the edge of the bed, and when I did I felt my heart fall right out of my chest and land at that little boy's feet. His face was scrunched and irritated, red and splotchy, his eyes squeezed shut, and his miniature hands curled into fists where they rested against Kallie's

chest. He had a tuft of fuzzy hair on his head that was clearly the
same reddish brown as his father's. It was way too early to actually tell but my heart agreed with Kallie that he looked just like
Wheeler. I felt like a fool for ever questioning whether or not I
could handle loving someone that was so much a part of the man
that lived inside of my heart. This little boy was created by the
best man I had ever known, so there should have been no doubt
that he would own me the second I laid eyes on him.

Tentatively, I reached out so I could rub my knuckle over his
velvety soft cheek. "He's beautiful. I'm so proud of both of you,
Kallie."

She blinked her eyes and I noticed they had tears in them.
"I'm proud of you too, Poppy. I wasn't sure you were going to
come in."

My smile was lopsided and my breath caught as Royce's eyes
flickered open and looked up at me. They were muddy, newborn
blue, but I would bet good money they turned to pretty, pale
blue as he got older. He was going to be a little mini-Wheeler
and I was going to have a heartbreaker on my hands. "I thought
it was going to hurt, that all I was going to feel was loss, but I
don't. All I feel is grateful you're both okay, that he's healthy and
here. I'm lucky to have all of you in my life, lucky that you trust
me to be in his. There is so much happiness and celebration happening inside of me right now that there is no room for that ache
and the hurt." It might come later when I was alone, when it was
quiet and I had a chance to process everything, but for now all I
felt was full of goodness and love for that little boy.

"You want to hold him? You should see him when Wheeler
holds him. He looks like a little doll." She snickered and lifted
the baby up in my direction. "You might as well get used to it. I

have a feeling you'll be giving him plenty of brothers and sisters to play with in the not-so-distant future. Wheeler was born to be a family man and I'm so glad he found someone that can make all his dreams come true."

I stared at the baby for a long minute trying to decide if I could actually take him from her. It felt like such a big step, one I knew I was going to have to take eventually, but that didn't mean I felt prepared for it at all. As if sensing my hesitation, the baby started to wiggle, arms waving and body moving. Kallie made a startled noise and I reached out and grabbed him to make sure he was secure before I could think about what I was doing.

As soon as my hands wrapped around the precious bundle and his sweet, baby scent hit my nose, I knew it would all be okay. I pulled Royce to my chest, buried my nose in the curve of his neck, and blinked away the tears that flooded my eyes. He moved into my heart right next to his dad and I wasn't at all surprised he took up nearly as much room.

The last of my demons were dead, crushed under the weight of my very full and overflowing heart.

I brushed a fingertip over one of the baby's feather-soft eyebrows and told him in all seriousness, "I'm all in with you too, little man." I couldn't get any deeper in if I tried. I was drowning in love and it was the one time in my life I wasn't wishing to be saved.

MY EYES SNAPPED open when the baby monitor next to the bed emitted a soft cry. Sometimes I thought I was dreaming when Royce started fussing in the middle of the night. I thought I was hearing another baby cry, one I would never get the chance to hold, to cuddle and care for. Those painful thoughts always quickly dissipated because there was an adorable baby boy that looked just like his daddy across the hallway that needed me to be present, not caught up in the web of what might have been.

Wheeler let out a groan from somewhere behind me and tightened the arm he had locked around my middle. His long legs shifted behind mine and I felt him roll over onto his back with a sigh. "I got him." His voice was raspy with sleep but alert. I don't think either one of us slept soundly when it was his week with Royce. The baby had just crossed the six-month mark, so Wheeler's time with him had exponentially increased from when he was a newborn and had to spend the majority of his time with Kallie.

I pushed up from the warm cocoon of the covers and brushed my hair off my face. I swung my legs over the edge of the bed and climbed to my feet. Wheeler looked up at me, pale blue eyes practically glowing up at me in the dark. I bent to find the T-shirt he had peeled off me hours earlier and slipped it on over my head, which made him groan again. I had to have a mini tug-of-war with Happy, who was curled up on the garment, in order to get it back. He was no longer a little dog, but his goofy disposition hadn't changed one bit. He rolled on his back, legs in the air, kicking as I tried to get my shirt free. That sent all my naked parts jiggling and moving in ways that made Wheeler groan once more. This one sounded like he was actually suffering some kind of torture. It made me grin, so I put a hand on the bed and leaned over so I could touch my mouth lightly to his. "I got him. You have to work in the morning and I'm off. Go back to sleep."

His eyes blinked at me, slow and sleepy. His mouth kicked into a grin, and even with the lack of light in the room, those dimples did me in. The monitor made another noise but now Royce was really awake and obviously agitated, so I heard him cry out from the other room. "You sure?"

He always asked me. He always made sure that I knew I was here for him, he didn't have me in his bed and in his life because he was looking for me to play mommy to his little boy. He had me there because that was where he wanted me, where I belonged, and no one else would ever be able to fit in that space besides me. For the first few months it had been a delicate balancing act, letting Wheeler figure out just how much he could take on with the baby without me offering to help. Everything inside of me wanted to scream that I was there, that he could take advantage of my two capable hands, and that I was dying to help, but the fact was I had to let him bury himself before I could dig him out.

"More than sure." The baby wailed again and I pushed off the bed and hustled across the room before he got really agitated and worked himself into a fit that would be impossible to quiet down without hours of cuddling and rocking in his favorite chair.

Those unforgettable eyes slid shut and that broad, tattooed chest heaved a grateful sigh that made my heart thud heavily and happily. "I'm here if you need me." The words were sleep-slurred and sloppy but I knew he meant them with every single fiber of his being.

"You always are."

He'd been there through every step of my father's arraignment and subsequent trial. He'd been there through the media circus that surrounded it all when the local press put together that the victim (me) was the same woman that had been abducted and raped by her husband. The fact that Dad was so heavily involved in the church made for a story too juicy to resist. He was there when my father was convicted and sentenced, showing zero apology or remorse for the things he did as he was led away. Wheeler was the one that kept me together when I got the call from Case Lawton that my mom had been skipping church and her weekly meetings with the counselor that her friends forced her to go see after my father no longer had control over every single aspect of her life. I knew even before he told me that it wasn't good. Her skipping mandatory therapy was one thing; her skipping church was something she would only do if something was seriously wrong with her.

She was dead.

Sheriff Lawton told me he found her in the chair by the window and an empty bottle of pills on the floor by her feet. She left a note but all it said was:

I can't live without him.

My father killed her just like I knew he would. Even if it wasn't by his own hand, he was the reason she was no longer alive.

It was hard. Dealing with the funeral arrangements, fielding questions from the nosy people that hadn't bothered to step in before it was too late, and trying not to let the guilt Salem felt for shutting her out and letting her go overwhelm me. It was hard but I managed because I had Wheeler to lean on. Every time I stumbled he was there with a hand on my elbow to keep me upright. Every time I felt lost, all I had to do was look for that bright spot of color, that boy who was impossible to miss, and find my way back to where I was supposed to be. He was absolutely there when I needed him, which is why I had no problem slipping out of the room and into the nursery just as Royce's clenched little fists lifted to his tiny, furious face. I could see he was gearing up to scream his displeasure to the world, so I rushed to the side of the crib and picked him up before he could really get going. I shushed him, rubbed his back, and rubbed my cheek against the velvety softness of his. I made a face when I got a whiff of what was obviously making him so uncomfortable and irritated.

I held the baby out in front of me and wrinkled up my nose at him as he grabbed for fistfuls of my hair. He cooed at me and blinked eyes that were the exact same icy blue as Wheeler's. His face scrunched up into a baby grin and my heart felt like it was going to burst because it was so full when the single dimple Royce had in his left cheek appeared. He was going to appreciate inheriting that from his daddy when he was old enough to understand the effect it had on the opposite sex.

"Let's get you cleaned up, little man. I'll make it all better." And like he understood that I would always be there, I would always do what I could to make things the best they could be for him. He quieted right down and switched from fussing to giggling as he grabbed at my hair, trying to shove handfuls of it into his mouth.

I laid him down on the changing table and went to work getting a new diaper on him and getting him all cleaned up. He'd had a blowout, so he needed a new set of pajamas. I put him in ones that had little elephants all over them, courtesy of Zak and his lovely wife. Royce had more baby stuff than I'd ever seen. His nursery was filled to capacity with gifts and gadgets that were constantly arriving from California. Shannon's health had steadily declined the last few months and Zak hadn't been able to visit as often as he wanted to. Wheeler and I were planning a trip to California around my birthday so we could take the baby to see his great-grandfather since his great-grandfather couldn't come to him. It was all about family. It was the way I had always wanted it to be.

"All better." I put Royce to my shoulder and settled us into the rocking chair Wheeler had bought when he realized how soothing the baby found the gentle back-and-forth motion.

The first time I held Royce, and I looked into those eyes, Wheeler's eyes, I felt like the biggest idiot in the world. He was so much a part of Wheeler, so innocent and pure, so sweet and helpless, all I wanted to do was protect him and make sure he knew he was loved, that he would always have a place to call home.

I was all in and I never wanted out.

I muttered into Royce's neck. Telling him stories about his dad and his mom, telling him that Wheeler had already bought him his first car, that it was sitting at the shop under a tarp waiting until he was old enough to use a socket wrench. I told him all about my niece, Glory, who had made her way into the world a couple of months after he did. She was the perfect mixture of both Rowdy and my sister, with a cap of fuzzy blond hair and endlessly dark eyes and perfectly glorious, golden skin. At some point while I was talking, the baby fell asleep on my shoulder, his whispery breaths in my ear the sweetest sound I'd ever heard. The dog had also made his way into the room and made himself comfortable next to my feet. It was every dream I'd ever had come true.

"You look good holding my baby, honey." Wheeler's words had my gaze lifting to where he was propped up in the doorway, one arm lifted above his head, the other lazily scratching across his chest. He always made my breath catch and blood run hot, but his words had a new kind of longing unfurling and working its way through my entire body.

"I love holding your baby, Hudson."

I smiled at him as he put his hand over his heart and smiled at me like I had given him the greatest gift in the entire world. "Good to know, honey, good to know."

It was good to know.

It was good to know I could do this. I could be a mom, a lover, a sister, a friend, a survivor, and I could be someone that someone else might need in order for them to understand that there were options and something better out there. I could be all the things I always wanted to be. I could be all the things I'd never been allowed to be before.

"Come back to bed, Poppy." His eyes really were glowing now in a way that was intimately familiar and impossible to resist. They promised wonderful, decadent, delicious things. They promised sweaty sex and sore muscles in the morning. They promised thundering hearts and pounding pulses. They promised multiple orgasms, even though I'd already had one that I could still feel, and they promised dirty words that were going to make me blush. But the thing that had me laying the baby in the crib with a kiss on his forehead and a sweep of my fingers through his reddish-brown hair and tiptoeing out of the room was that those eyes always, whenever they were directed at me, promised me they would take care of me however I needed to be cared for. He would always give me whatever it was I needed, which was nice, because all I really needed was him.

BONUS (BECAUSE MY READERS ARE RAD) EPILOGUE

Sometime down the road . . .

"Two minutes is plenty of time." My voice was rough in Poppy's ear as I flipped the skirt of her frilly bridesmaid's dress over her ass and tugged at the barely-there thong she was wearing under it. Her eyes met mine in the mirror over the sink and her hands braced on the vanity I had her bent over. She shook her head no but her hips pressed back into mine, rubbing against my cock where it was hard and tenting the front of my tuxedo pants. Her teeth bit into her bottom lip and her eyes glowed with golden heat.

I'd gotten good at doing a lot of things in two minutes and under, you had to when you had a growing kid underfoot. There were diapers that needed to be quickly changed, messes that needed to be cleaned up, a dog that needed its fur rescued from strong, grabby hands, feedings that had to happen at the drop of a hat, and tantrums that needed soothing regardless of what the adults in the house might be doing. I was quick; often Poppy was quicker when Royce needed something, but we still always tried to take our time with each other. I would always give her more than two minutes, but today we didn't have that luxury.

Sayer and Zeb had gotten married an hour earlier and we

were both supposed to be down at the reception before the bride and groom arrived since we were in the wedding party. Zeb had asked me to be his best man and I couldn't have been prouder to stand up there with my oldest friend as he tied himself to his perfect girl. He also had Rowdy and his brother-in-law stand with him while his son, Hyde, acted as the ring bearer. Sayer asked Poppy to be her maid of honor, so I got to walk her down the aisle in a lilac dress shirt that matched the fluffy underlay of the bride's cream-and-ivory dress. No boring white for Sayer, not anymore. She'd also asked Salem, and Zeb's sister, Beryl, to stand up with her, so the entire wedding had been a family affair.

The reception was held at the Crawford, so of course I had gotten us a room. Royce was with Kallie for the weekend and I had no plans on letting Poppy out of bed after all the pleasantries of the wedding and reception were said and done. That gave me plenty of time to have my way with her, but I couldn't wait. I was always hungry for her, starving for a taste of her unique honey and spice flavor.

"You're going to take longer than two minutes." Of course I was. With her, I felt like I could last for hours and even days if my body was capable. There was humor in her tone but she obediently opened her legs when I nudged my knee between them. Her shoulders stiffened and her head dropped forward on a sigh as my lips hit the back of her neck and the sound of my lowering zipper filled the room.

I grunted in response and ran a questing finger along the lush line of her ass before dipping it inside and tickling my way down to the sweet spot between her legs. She was already wet, already quivering and unsteady on the tall heels her feet were still encased in.

"No one will even notice that we're not there." That wasn't true, but I was sliding my cock along her cleft and coating myself in her slick moisture, so I was willing to say anything to get her to stay exactly where she was.

She gasped as I pushed in, spreading her open and sinking in. It never got old, the feeling of taking her and of being taken in by her. I groaned into the curve of her neck and moved my palm over the curve of her ass.

"If we take too long Royal will come looking for me and you know it." She was breathless and I barely heard her warning. If Royal did come looking, she was going to get an eyeful because there was nothing on this planet that would pull me away from this woman, not when she was whispering my name in pleasure and lifting up on her toes so that she could push back against me.

After Poppy's dad put her in the ER, she'd gotten close with both Royal and Saint. Saint made it a point to stop by and check on her every day she was in the hospital and even asked if Poppy would consider working with the victim outreach program through the hospital. Royal stood by her side through all the court proceedings and even went to court on the day Pastor Cruz was sentenced to twenty-five years in jail for the attempted murder of his daughter. Royal was surprisingly protective of my girl so she would come looking for her, but luckily Asa was good at keeping her distracted. Knowing the Kentucky charmer, I would put good money on him having coerced his wife into finding their own dark corner to race against the clock in. They were still acting like newlyweds even though they'd been together for years and married for several months now.

Asa had given Royal her dream wedding, a low-key ceremony on the beach in Hawaii that we'd all flown out for a couple of months after Salem and Rowdy's little girl, Glory, was born. It was the perfect winter getaway and Royal made a beautiful bride. It was no surprise to anyone when Shaw announced shortly after the trip that she was expecting baby number two. Rule was over the moon about it, telling anyone that would listen that he was going to have a little girl with his mom's pretty green eyes. There was something about the balmy beach air that made everyone seem particularly amorous. Rowdy was already planning on another baby even though his first wasn't yet at the age where she slept through the night. He and Poppy's sister were in no hurry to get married, claiming they'd been born to be together and a ring wouldn't change that. Salem was his last and he was hers.

Nash and Saint had been forced to skip the wedding because Nash got an offer to do several guest spots in some world-renowned tattoo shops all across Europe this summer. Since Saint didn't have school she took a leave of absence from work and went with him. The girls were taking bets on whether the pretty, redheaded nurse was going to come back in the fall knocked up, because, apparently, vacation sex was extra potent. Saint insisted she wanted to wait, and Nash insisted that all he needed was ten minutes to change her mind. I knew if Saint had been around at the wedding today, she would definitely notice my girl was missing, so I was glad that was an interruption I didn't have to worry about.

"The only person I'm worried about coming is you, honey. Lift your knee up on the counter." I was breathing hard and there was a light sheen of sweat dotting my forehead. "I've got you, so don't worry about those shoes."

She lifted her eyebrows at me in the mirror and then did what I asked her to, her mouth dropping open as I sank even deeper and hit her spot even harder. I rubbed my thumb up the part of her spine that was exposed and let my head fall back on my neck. Her heat and the snug pull of her body were my favorite sensations in the world. Every time I buried my cock inside her I knew it was the only place I wanted to be and the one place that was all mine. It was where I belonged.

I slid a finger between the perfectly heart-shaped cheeks of her bouncing ass. Her eyebrows shot up even higher, to the point where they were almost lost in her caramel-colored hair. She liked it when I touched her there, liked it even more when I took her there, but we really didn't have time for that at the moment.

I could hear my phone ringing in the other room and I knew by the ring tone that it was Rome. Typically, I dropped everything when the big man called. He was a primary investor in my business and had just recently come to me with an expansion proposal. He wanted to know if I would be interested in spearheading a custom motorcycle shop that focused on commissioned builds and restoration projects. I didn't know all there was to know about motorcycles; I mean, I could make one run with no problem, but beyond that I was pretty clueless. As it turned out, all Rome wanted was for me to keep an eye on the shop and the guys working out of it. He had a bunch of bikers that liked to come in and out of his bar, and since he rode himself he thought it would be a good opportunity. I had a lot on my plate already with Royce and getting Poppy to the point where she was ready to move in with me; as soon as she said yes, I was putting a ring on her finger and a baby in her belly. Royce was almost a year old and I couldn't love him more if I tried. It wasn't always easy juggling his childhood between two homes and I always felt his absence when he was with Kallie, but we made it work and I was more than ready to make it work with Poppy. She was amazing with my son. I knew she would be.

The truth was I couldn't tell the big man "no" to much of anything, so now I was running two garages and everything badass in Denver on two wheels or four came through me and my guys. I found myself with more family and more opportunity than I ever expected.

As soon as Rule started on and on about Shaw's pregnancy, everyone assumed that Rome was going to step it up and put a third baby in his wife, Cora. As it turned out, the little, blond firecracker was done with the baby making, claiming their daughter, Remy, was like having five kids. She had her hands full with the precocious little girl, the one that had made a big production of kissing Hyde right after Zeb kissed Sayer. They also had a little boy who was the sweetest thing ever and both claimed one of each was perfect.

I ignored the call. I ignored everything except the way Poppy's body tightened around mine and the way she whimpered as I plowed into her over and over again. I let out a low moan as her wetness spread across my cock in a hot rush. Her eyes were closed, her cheeks were flushed, and her hands had curled into fists on the edge of the vanity. Her chest was rising and falling rapidly and her thighs shook against mine. I dug my fingers into her hips, let my cock dive into her over and over again until my spine stiffened as a ball of pure pleasure wrapped around the base of it. I told her she was everything and promised her anything as I emptied myself inside her.

It wasn't two minutes but it was close. We went off hard and fast, pleasure spiraling and spinning through us like a storm.

I pulled out with a groan and watched as the evidence of time well spent marked her thighs. I always liked the way I looked smeared all across her tawny skin. It was hands down one of my favorite sights to see.

I reached around her for a towel and cranked on the sink as she lowered her leg back to the ground, keeping her dress up around her waist so that she wouldn't get anything on it. The caveman part of me wanted her to stay just like that but I knew time was running out and we had to put in an appearance.

I cleaned her up, made sure there were no telltale signs of what we'd been doing on the front of my black pants, and took her hand so I could lead her back to the ballroom. Luckily, Zeb and Sayer hadn't arrived yet, but everyone else was already milling around the room and I could tell by the knowing smirks and twitching eyebrows that everyone knew what we had been up to.

Ayden gave me a wink when I walked past her and muttered under her breath, "Jet likes a quickie in the bathroom too. It's always worth the embarrassment of walking in late."

The stunning brunette and her husband were still based out of Austin and no one got to see them as much as they would have liked. Jet was still on the road but he'd picked up a young band out of Denton, Texas, that was on the verge of blowing up huge. They had the potential to be superstars, and if they did that, attached to Jet's record label, it would enable him to stay home more, which was what both he and Ayden wanted. Being married to a rock star was far less glamorous than anyone wanted to believe. At the beginning of the year Ayden had suffered a miscarriage when Jet was on the road; their loss rippled through our extended friends and family like a wave of sorrow. Poppy being Poppy had stepped in as the only person who could understand exactly what Ayden was going through. She offered an ear and a shoulder, and as a result the two had forged a bond that only that kind of loss could solidify. They spoke on the phone regularly and I was no longer surprised to find my girl crying over the absence of a baby that wasn't hers. She cared so much that sometimes I wondered where she put it all.

I tilted my chin in Dixie's direction when she caught my eye and gave me a leer. I still missed her, but watching her cuddle into the massive man by her side, I knew she had also found the place where she belonged. She loved Church and she loved the place he called home. She'd even picked up a slight southern twang in the short time she'd been in Mississippi. They were the next couple up at the altar, a small wedding that was going to take place in the backyard garden of the woman that had helped to raise Church. She was well into her eighties and couldn't travel, so we were all going south to watch Dixie say "I do." Kallie got really emotional every time we talked about it because it meant her sister was really never coming back to Denver and that was a hard pill for her to swallow.

I was leading Poppy to the front part of the ballroom where Rowdy was smirking at me knowingly as Salem shook her head at her sister. Zeb's sister seemed oblivious to what they were laughing at and didn't bother to ask as she cuddled into her husband. Hyde was doing his best to avoid a very persistent Remy Archer, a plan that included trying to hide behind his cousin Joss. Joss sold him out to the adorable demon in pigtails because it was an unwritten rule that Remy got what Remy wanted. That's what happened when you were the first kid.

A quiet murmur went through the room as Sayer and Zeb arrived at the back. They didn't want to do a formal announcement, they just wanted to present themselves to all of their friends and family as husband and wife, so that's what they did. The gigantic, bearded badass and his elegant, polished bride. They didn't look like they belonged on the top of the same wedding cake, but there was no doubt when he put his hand on her lower back and she leaned into him that they belonged together. Hyde escaped Remy long enough to run to his dad and a collective sigh went up when the big man bent and picked the smaller version of himself up in one arm. They were a united front, and they always would be.

"She looks good in lilac." I glanced over at the table closest to the one where Poppy and I were sitting and silently agreed with Quaid Jackson. He had his arm draped over the back of his girlfriend's chair as they both watched the bride and groom make their way through the room. Quaid had tried to start something with Sayer a million years ago, and though it went nowhere because she loved the massive mountain of man on her arm now, the two of them had remained friends. They were both in the legal field and often referred clients to one another. Quaid's girlfriend nodded her head in agreement, the lights from overhead catching in her smoky, silver-tinted hair. There was a significant age gap between the two of them, one that was obvious when you looked at them together, but there was also an understanding and acceptance there that no one questioned. Quaid had loosened up significantly since Avett moved into his million-dollar loft in LoDo and the free-spirited, wild child had settled down and really worked toward making something of herself. She was rocking an engagement ring that had a diamond the width of a quarter in the center of it, and if you asked her, she was getting married in Vegas by an Elvis impersonator, so she didn't have to plan a wedding. It was probably a good idea considering how different her style and Quaid's were. The two of them trying to combine their styles in order to say "I do" could be disastrous.

"I think my hair would look awesome that color, don't you?" Avett whispered the question under her breath and Quaid just nodded and kissed her temple.

"Do it. It'll look great." The response came from Orlando Frederick, who was sandwiched between her and his boyfriend, Dominic Voss. I liked Lando a lot and not just because he was a fellow freckled ginger. He was gentle and kind in the same way Poppy was and there was a familiar shadow of loss that sometimes crossed his gaze that let me knew he was intimately familiar with how precious and precarious life could be. Fortunately, he had a boyfriend that came armed and dangerous. Dom worked as a police academy trainer and looked like he could stop all the crime in Denver single-handedly. They'd been together for a while, and though I knew through the grapevine that their respective families were pushing for them to make it legal, neither man was in any hurry to take that step. They were committed to one another, had a life together, and between the two of them had a plethora of younger siblings they were busy keeping in line and out of jail. Eventually, they wanted to have a family, so they made a pact that when the time was right for them to expand their brood, then and only then would they tie the knot.

I put my arm around Poppy's shoulders and pulled her into my side. Her hand found its way under the lapel of my jacket and her cheek rested on my shoulder. "You ready to move the Hudson to my house yet?"

She gave a little laugh that made her shoulders shake and had her amber eyes shining up at me. "Maybe tomorrow."

It was a conversation we had a least once a day. I wanted her under my roof so she was always there with me and Royce and Happy, but she insisted she wasn't ready for reasons I understood but still hated. I assured her that having unfettered access to my cock was a good enough reason, but she would just shake her head and laugh at me. She insisted that she had to prove to herself that she could take care of herself because she never had before. She also told me time and time again that I needed this time with my son and I inevitably replied that he was much happier when she was there as well because he took after his old man. It was true. My kid loved her just as much as I did and I swore the nights she didn't make it over, he cried extra hard and acted more fussy than normal. I admired her independence and strength, but the nights we spent away from one another were the worst, and I hardly slept.

"Tomorrow it is, then."

She smiled at me and my heart tried to beat its way out of my chest so that it could put itself in her hands. "Tomorrow it is."

One step at a time we moved toward each other and toward the next thing that waited for us. Tomorrow, I would wake up and make sure I took better care of her than I had the day before and she would do the same for me.

That's what love looked like.

SALVAGED PLAYLIST

"Wind Up Bird": Heartless Bastards
"You're a Wolf": Sea Wolf
"My Favorite Part": Mac Miller and Ariana Grande
"Dog Days Are Over": Florence + the Machine
"Warrior": Demi Lovato
"Gentle on My Mind": Billy Bragg and Joe Henry
"You Are My Sunshine": Morgane and Chris Stapleton
"Girl on Fire": Alicia Keys
"Wonderwall": Oasis
"Best We've Ever Been": Sean McConnell
"Shine a Different Way": Patty Griffin
"Survivor": Destiny's Child
"Wreck You": Lori McKenna
"Feel Like Making Love": Bad Company
"To Love Somebody": Lydia Loveless
"The Arrow Killed the Beast": Heartless Bastards
"I Will Survive": Gloria Gaynor
"Move Me": Sara Watkins
"Things That I Lean On": Wynonna Judd and Jason Isbell
"Nothing to Fix": Jack Ingram

AUTHOR'S NOTE

I took some liberties with the real-life pit bull regulations in Denver to fit the context of this story. There is no way Dixie would actually be allowed to keep Dolly, and for Wheeler and Poppy to keep Happy in the city limits they would need a special license even if they owned their own property. If you are interested in the actual ban you can read about it here:

https://www.animallaw.info/local/co-denver-breed-sec-8-
-55-pit-bulls-prohibited

I know I'm going to get questions about timeline and continuity because of the babies and both Kallie and Salem being pregnant, so I'm going to do my best to clear some of that up. Keeping in mind that all of the Saints of Denver books take place in the time frame between the end of *Asa* and up until . . . and beyond Rome and Cora's wedding.

In *Asa*, at Rome and Cora's wedding, Salem had just announced she was pregnant to everyone, so for me that put her at right around four months or so in February, since Rome and Cora got married on Valentine's Day. That would mean she told Sayer and Poppy about the baby in *Built* around late November or in early December. I was locked into that time frame because it was already written in stone since the books had long since been published. It might not be EXACT but it's as close as I can figure it out without my mind exploding. I do words . . . not numbers.

I knew I wanted Wheeler to face what his idea of family was, so I had planned all along on his ex having a baby . . . but I didn't figure out how that would affect the timeline I'd already laid out. It forced me to get creative and do a lot of counting on my fingers.

Kallie had to be further along in her pregnancy for things to fit all the events that happened in both *Charged* and *Riveted* and for her to be at the point where she was able to try to find out the baby's sex during winter. So my best guess how all of this would work is Kallie got knocked up in early September or maybe even late August and was right around four months in December. In my mind, she was already pregnant when she was throwing a fit in *Charged*. I think she was scared out of her mind about what she was facing . . . that's why she acted so crazy . . . on top of her being a drama queen to begin with.

I hope that helps some . . . I know it might not be spot on, but for those who are sticklers for continuity and consistency it does offer a little bit of perspective as to my reasoning and rationale.

The other thing I want to throw out there is that if you or someone you know is in a bad situation, I hope this book and these characters remind you that you are not alone. There is always a light at the end of the tunnel. It never burns out. There is always hope and everyone deserves a shot at something better.

You are valuable.

You are necessary.

You are important.

You are appreciated.

You are treasured.

You are loved.

I don't know much but I do know that no one, and I mean no one, deserves to suffer any kind of abuse at the hands of someone who claims to love them.

All forms of abuse are horrific and terrible, but patience, love, and understanding go a long way toward helping a survivor heal. I'm not an expert or an advocate, but I am someone who cares a lot about people . . . all people. So I'll leave these numbers here, and if you know someone who could use them or if you can use them yourself, please do:

National Child Abuse Hotline: 1-800-422-4453

National Domestic Violence Hotline: 1-800-799-7233

National Sexual Assault Hotline: 1-800-656-HOPE (4673)

If you are looking for a place to start to help yourself or some-one else, go here: thehotline.org.

Also, I know you are going to ask about the next generation after this book . . . there are a lot of little kiddlets running around now, aren't there? They're all so cute! I'll be honest and say I have some ideas, have been playing around with the possibility of a spin-off series based on the kiddos in the future very loosely, but I'm not there yet and I'm not sure when and if I ever will be. The idea of trying to write with no cultural references because we don't know what that far in the future will look like is intimi-dating and slightly daunting. I want to do it right if I do it and I know I don't have the time or the patience to tackle that kind of project anytime soon. I don't have anything solid or concrete planned (at this exact moment in time). I've been in this world for eleven books over the course of five years, and as much as I loved every minute of it, I need a break. I love Denver, it's my backyard, it's my happy place, but there is a big, beautiful world out there that I want to explore through words, so I'm gonna do that first and foremost. If anything changes, my readers will be the first to know. In fact, you should sign up for my newsletter right now so you don't miss a thing! It's full of everything I'm currently working on and everything I have planned for the immediate future.

http://www.jaycrownover.com/subscribe

You can also appease your inner stalker in all of these places:

https://www.facebook.com/groups/crownover-scrowd . . . My fan group on Facebook. I'm very active in there and it's often the best place to find out about all the happenings and participate in giveaways!

www.jaycrownover.com . . . there is a link on the site to reach me through e-mail.

https://www.facebook.com/jay.crownover

https://www.facebook.com/AuthorJayCrownover

Follow me @jaycrownover on Twitter

Follow me @jay.crownover on Instagram

https://www.goodreads.com/Crownover

http://www.donaghyliterary.com/jay-crownover.html

http://avonromance.com/book-author/jay-crownover/

ACKNOWLEDGMENTS

I'm going to keep this one simple.

If you have purchased, read, reviewed, promoted, pimped, blogged about, sold, talked about, preached about, or whined about any of my books . . . thank you.

If you have helped me make this dream of mine a reality . . . thank you.

If you have helped make my words better and helped me share them with the world . . . thank you.

If you have held my hand and helped me through the tough times when it feels like everyone and everything is against me . . . thank you.

If you help make the work part of writing the best job ever . . . thank you.

If you tolerate me being a horrible human and awful adult when I'm working . . . thank you.

I never thought I would have one book published and in reader's hands; the fact I've written and published so many more than one blows my mind every single day. I never imagined this could be my life and I'm grateful every day that it is.

I also want to give my editor, Tessa Woodward, a shout-out . . . this was our first book together and she really understood how important it was to get this story right for Poppy and everyone who's been rooting for her for so long. This wasn't the easiest book to start with but we finished strong.

RULE

A Marked Men Novel

Sometimes opposites don't just attract: they catch fire and burn the city down.

Shaw Landon loved Rule Archer from the moment she laid eyes on him. Rule is everything a straight-A premed student like Shaw shouldn't want—and the only person she's never tried to please. She isn't afraid of his scary piercings and tattoos or his wild attitude. Though she knows that Rule is wrong for her, her heart just won't listen.

To a rebel like Rule Archer, Shaw Landon is a stuck-up, perfect princess—and his dead twin brother's girl. She lives by other people's rules; he makes his own. He doesn't have time for a good girl like Shaw—even if she's the only one who can see the person he truly is.

But a short skirt, too many birthday cocktails, and spilled secrets lead to a night neither can forget. Now Shaw and Rule have to figure out how a girl like her and a guy like him are supposed to be together without destroying their love . . . or each other.

JET

A Marked Men Novel

With his tight leather pants and a sharp edge that makes him dangerous, Jet Keller is every girl's rock-and-roll fantasy. But Ayden Cross is done walking on the wild side with bad boys. She doesn't want to give in to the heat she sees in Jet's dark, haunted eyes. She's afraid of getting burned from the sparks of their spontaneous combustion, even as his touch sets her on fire.

Jet can't resist the southern belle with mile-long legs in cowboy boots who defies his every expectation. Yet the closer he feels to Ayden, the less he seems to know her. While he's tempted to get under her skin and undo her in every way, he knows first-hand what happens to two people with very different ideas about relationships.

Will the blaze burn into an enduring love . . . or will it consume their dreams and turn them to ashes?

ROME

A Marked Men Novel

Sometimes the wrong choice can be just right . . .

Fun and fearless, Cora Lewis knows how to keep her tattooed "bad boy" friends at the Marked in line. But beneath all that flash and sass is a broken heart. Cora won't let herself get burned again. She's waiting to fall in love with the perfect man—a baggage-free, drama-free guy ready for commitment. Then she meets Rome Archer.

Rome Archer is as far from perfect as a man can be. He's stubborn, rigid, and bossy. And he's returned from his final tour of duty more than a little broken. Rome's used to filling many roles: big brother, doting son, supersoldier—but none of those fit anymore. Now he's just a man trying to figure out what to do with the rest of his life while keeping the dark demons of war and loss at bay. He would have been glad to suffer through it alone, until Cora comes sweeping into his life and becomes a blinding flash of color in a sea of gray. Perfect may not be in the cards, but perfectly imperfect could just last forever . . .

NASH

A Marked Men Novel

Saint Ford has worked hard to achieve her childhood dream of becoming a nurse. Focused on her work and devoted to her patients, she has no room for love. She doesn't need a guy making waves in her calm, serene life—especially when he's the unforgettable hottie who nearly destroyed her in high school. Dark, brooding Nash Donovan might not remember her or the terrible pain he caused. But he turned her world upside down . . . and now he's trying to do it again.

Saint has no idea that Nash isn't the cocky player he once was. Uncovering a devastating family secret has rocked his world, and now he's struggling to figure out his future. He can't be distracted by the pretty nurse he seems to meet everywhere. Still, he can't ignore the sparks that fly between them—or how she seems so desperate to get away from him. But the funny, sweet, and drop-dead gorgeous Saint is far too amazing to give up on—especially since she's the only thing in his life that seems to make sense.

When Nash discovers the truth about their past, he realizes he may have lost her heart before he could even fight for it. Now Saint has to decide: is Nash worth risking herself for all over again?

ROWDY

A Marked Men Novel

After the only girl he ever loved told him that he would never be enough, Rowdy St. James knocked the Texas dust off his boots and set out to live up to his nickname. A good ol' boy looking for good times and good friends, Rowdy refuses to take anything too seriously, especially when it comes to the opposite sex. Burned by love once, he isn't going to let himself trust a woman again. But that's before his new coworker arrives, a ghost from the past who's suddenly making him question every lesson he ever learned.

Salem Cruz grew up in a house with too many rules and too little fun—a world of unhappiness she couldn't wait to forget. But one nice thing from childhood has stayed with her: the memory of the sweet, blue-eyed boy next door who'd been head over heels in love with her little sister.

Now fate and an old friend have brought her and Rowdy together, and Salem is determined to show him that once upon a time he picked the wrong sister. A mission that is working perfectly—until the one person who ties them together appears, threatening to tear them apart for good.

ASA

A Marked Men Novel

Asa Cross struggles with being the man everyone wants him to be and the man he knows he really is. A leopard doesn't change its spots, and Asa has always been a predator. He doesn't want to hurt those who love and rely on him, especially one luscious, arresting cop who suddenly seems to be interested in him for far more than his penchant for breaking the law. But letting go of old habits is hard, and it's easy to hit bottom when it's the place you know best.

Royal Hastings is quickly learning what the bottom looks like after a tragic situation at work threatens not only her career but her partner's life. As a woman who has only ever had a few real friends, she's trying to muddle through her confusion and devastation alone. Except she can't stop thinking about the sexy southern bartender she locked up. Crushing on Asa is the last thing she needs, but his allure is too strong to resist. And she knows chasing after a guy who has no respect for the law or himself can only end in heartbreak.

A longtime criminal and a cop just seem so wrong together . . . but for Asa and Royal, being wrong together is the only right choice to make.

LEVELED

A Saints of Denver Novella

Orlando Frederick knows what it is to be leveled by pain. Instead of focusing on his own, he's made it his mission to help others: sports stars, wounded war vets, survivors of all kinds. But when Dom, a rugged, damaged, sinfully attractive cop makes his way into Lando's physical-therapy practice, he might be the biggest challenge yet. Lando loved one stubborn man before and barely survived the fallout. He's not sure if he can do it again.

Dominic Voss is a protector. The police badge he wears is not only his job, it's his identity, so when he's sidelined because of an injury, the only thing he cares about is getting back on the force. He expects Lando to mend his body, he just doesn't realize the trainer will also have him working toward a hell of a lot more. As attraction simmers and flares, Dom sees that Lando needs repair of his own . . . if only the man will let him get close enough to mend what's broken.

BUILT

A Saints of Denver Novel

Sayer Cole and Zeb Fuller couldn't be more different. She's country club and fine dining, he's cell block and sawdust. Sayer spends her days in litigation, while Zeb spends his working with his hands. But none of that has stopped Zeb from wanting the stunning blonde since the moment he laid eyes on her—even if the reserved lawyer seems determinedly oblivious to his interest.

Sayer is certain the rough, hard, hot-as-hell Zeb could never want someone as closed off and restrained as she is, which is a shame because something tells her he might be the guy to finally melt her icy exterior. When he shows up at her door needing her professional help, she's both disappointed and relieved that she won't get the chance to find out just how good he could be.

But as they team up to right a wrong and save a family, the steam created when fire and ice collide cannot be ignored.

CHARGED

A Saints of Denver Novel

Avett Walker's and Quaid Jackson's worlds have no reason to collide. Quaid is a high-power criminal attorney as slick as he is handsome. Avett is a pink-haired troublemaker with a history of picking the wrong men.

When Avett lands in a sea of hot water because of one terrible mistake, the only person who can get her out of it is the insanely sexy lawyer. The last thing on earth she wants is to rely on the no-nonsense attorney. Yet there is something about him that makes her want to convince him to loosen his tie and have a little fun . . . with her.

Quaid never takes on clients like the impulsive young woman with a Technicolor dye job. But something about her guileless hazel eyes intrigues him. Still, he's determined to keep their relationship strictly business. But doing so is becoming more impossible with each day he spends with her.

As they work side by side, they'll have to figure out a way to get along and keep their hands off each other—because the chemistry between them is beyond charged.

RIVETED

A Saints of Denver Novel

Everyone else in Dixie Carmichael's life has made falling in love look easy, and now she's ready for her own chance at some of that happily-ever-after. Which means she's done pining for the moody former soldier who works with her at the bar that's become her home away from home. Nope. No more chasing the hot-as-heck thundercloud of a man and no more waiting for Mr. Right to find her; she's going hunting for him . . . even if she knows her heart is stuck on its stupid infatuation with Dash Churchill.

Denver has always been just a pit stop for Church on his way back to rural Mississippi. His time there was supposed to be uneventful, but nothing could have prepared him for the bubbly, bouncy redhead with doe eyes and endless curves. Now he knows it's time to get out of Denver, fast. For a man used to living in the shadows, the idea of spending his days in the sun is terrifying.

When Dixie and Church get caught up in a homecoming fraught with lies and danger, Dixie realizes that while falling in love is easy, loving takes a whole lot more work . . . especially when Mr. Right thinks he's *all* wrong for you.

SALVAGED

A Saints of Denver Novel

Hudson Wheeler is a nice guy. Everyone knows it, including his fiancée, who left him with a canceled wedding and a baby on the way. He's tired of finishing last and is ready to start living in the moment with nights soaked in whiskey, fast cars, and even faster girls. He's set to start living on the edge, but when he meets Poppy Cruz, her sad eyes in the most gorgeous face he's ever seen hook him in right away. Wheeler can see Poppy's pain and all he wants to do is take care of her and make her smile, whatever it takes.

Poppy can't remember a time when she didn't see strangers as the enemy. After a lifetime of being hurt by the men who swore to protect her, Poppy's determined to keep herself safe by keeping everyone else at arm's length. Wheeler's sexy grin and rough hands from hours spent restoring classic cars shouldn't captivate her, but every time she's with him, she can't help being pulled closer to him. Though she's terrified to trust again, Poppy soon realizes it might hurt even more to shut Wheeler out—and the intense feelings pulsing through her are making it near impossible to resist him.

The only thing Poppy is sure of is that her heart is in need of some serious repair, and the more time she spends with Wheeler, the more she's convinced he's the only man with the tools to fix it.

The W6 Book Café

Who's your favourite #bookboyfriend?

Who do you wish was taking you out tonight?
Tweet us at **@W6BookCafe** using hashtag
#bookboyfriend and join the conversation.

Follow us to be the first to know about
competitions and read exclusive extracts
before the books are even in the shops!

 Find us on Facebook
W6BookCafe

 Follow us on Twitter
@W6BookCafe